Praise for

Jamie M. Saul & *Light of Day*

"Powerful. . . . This intense first achievement that combines traditional literature against the backdrop of a disturbing mystery is a page-turner that at times is difficult to put down. . . . Saul's ability to create deep and interesting characters is a strength that no doubt will surface time and again in future works." —*Indianapolis Star*

"A moving and elegant novel that lingers with the reader long after the last page is turned."
—Sena Jeter Naslund,
author of *Ahab's Wife* and *Four Spirits*

"Heartbreaking and well written." —*Winston-Salem Journal*

"This first novel rivals Jacquelyn Mitchard's *Deep End of the Ocean* as a probing exploration into the psychology of grief . . . a gorgeous literary thriller of the highest caliber." —*Booklist* (starred review)

"An intellectual thriller laced with subtle clues throughout its gracious prose."
—*Chicago Tribune*

"A heartfelt examination of one man's grief with a dark and intriguing mystery pulsating beneath the surface."
—John Searles, author of *Strange But True*
and *Boy Still Missing*

"[H]eartbreakingly realistic and completely riveting. . . . Treating all of his characters with great respect, Saul's prose is both muscular and polished, and his sense of timing is impeccable. . . . Saul shows sensitivity and a rare understanding of the human psyche in his debut novel. . . *Light of Day* is a moving, elegant novel that lingers with the reader long after the last page is turned."
—Bookreporter.com

"Saul controls his material with almost flawless skill. . . . A fine thriller, stocked with solid, effective characters and characterizations."
—*Terre Haute Tribune-Star* (Indiana)

"A powerful look at memory, family, and unexpected tragedy."
—*Library Journal*

"How does a novel become a work of classic literature? My betting is that this first novel by a new author will eventually be seen that way. . . . Anyone who wants in on the ground floor of that decision should grab the book now." —*Lincoln Journal-Star*

"*Light of Day* is a haunting, beautifully written, and heart-wrenching debut." —Harlan Coben, *New York Times* bestselling author of *Just One Look*

"A gripping, emotionally charged tale." —*Publishers Weekly*

"An emotional novel about a man whose future has been alteed by an unthinkable tragedy." —*Dener Post*

"Quietly affecting. . . . A debut with enormous depth of charcteriza-tion and sympathy." —*KirkuReviews*

"It's the mystery of what happened to Danny that will arry you through this book. . . . The ending is a reminder that were heart-breakingly vulnerable through our children." —*Arizoi Republic*

Light of Day

Light of Day

JAMIE M. SAUL

NEW YORK • LONDON • TORONTO • SYDNEY

HARPER PERENNIAL

A hardcover edition of this book was published in 2005 by William Morrow, an imprint of HarperCollins Publishers.

FIRST HARPER PERENNIAL EDITION PUBLISHED 2006.

Designed by Daniel Lagin

The Library of Congress has catalogued the hardcover edition as follows:

Saul, Jamie M.
Light of day: a novel / Jamie M. Saul.—1st ed.
p. cm.
ISBN 0-06-074752-8
1. Suicide victims—Family relationships—Fiction. 2. Loss (Psychology)—Fiction. 3. Fathers and sons—Fiction. 4. Sons—Death—Fiction. I. Title.

PS3619.A823L54 2005
813'.6—dc22 2004056676

ISBN-10: 0-06-074753-6 (pbk.)
ISBN-13: 978-0-06-074753-4 (pbk.)

06 07 08 09 10 ❖/RRD 10 9 8 7 6 5 4 3 2 1

This is Marjorie Braman's book

Part One

I

The road into Gilbert, Indiana, is U.S. 40. It's the old highway that cuts east and west through town, a few blocks north of Main Street. Nobody drives it much these days, nobody who isn't from Gilbert or nearby. Nobody who's in a hurry, and most people driving through Gilbert are in a hurry, tearing across the interstate on their way to somewhere else.

They built the interstate, and the mall that's just off the exit, about thirty years ago. The smaller stores in town would have gone out of business, the larger ones would have followed the money, and downtown would have been a ghost town if not for a few far-thinking people on the city council who came up with the plan to save downtown by turning it into an outdoor shopping mall. Now there are parking lots on the side streets and clean, expansive sidewalks with shade trees and benches so people can sit and talk; so they can spend their time strolling down the street, looking in store windows, shopping and browsing, instead of looking for places to park their cars.

And of course, the college helps keep the town alive. The students and teachers shop in all the stores, eat at the little restaurants, at Paul's just off Main Street, where they serve the tenderloin sandwiches deep-fried on a soft bun with bread-and-butter pickles, or the meat loaf and mashed potatoes with gravy that they make at the coffee shop inside the Gilbert Hotel, which isn't a hotel anymore but an office building. Not that Gilbert was ever known for its cuisine or convenient downtown shopping. It's the air that everyone notices, or did until the winds of change blew through town and the EPA helped clean things up.

But no matter which way the wind blows, the air is always tinged with sulfur, one of the by-products of coal, the leitmotif of industrialized Indiana. If not for coal, Gilbert would be just like all the other postindustrial towns—they strip-mine coal out on the east side. It's the coal-burning power plants that keep the lights throughout the state glowing in the night. Most of that coal comes from Gilbert. But it's the sulfur that does the trick.

In sunlight it turns the air sepia, like an old daguerreotype photograph or a silent movie. The rose tint and warm brown hues look so soft and welcoming, you'd like to crawl in, pull them over your head and hide from the coming millennium. You might even think the past isn't such a bad place to step back into. Then you see the old-timers, who look like they've stepped right out of that past, hobbling down Main Street wrinkled and weathered like old leather, emphysemic and broken down, like hard times, gnarled and grizzled. It makes you think your times aren't so bad after all.

Highway 40 crosses Highway 41—another old road which heads all the way from Chicago to Miami, Florida—over by Third Street, then runs past the railroad tracks by the Wabash River and across the nameless bridge that shakes and sways, like the hammock you hook to a couple of trees at the end of May and don't take down until the leaves start to turn in late September. But if you're not in too much of a hurry, when you get to where the highways intersect and you look south you'll see the ruins rising like an apparition.

The ruins stand in grand decay on the rise of a slow hill above the muddy banks of the Wabash in Fairmont Memorial Park. It's just a façade, a replica of the Parthenon never fully realized. It was going to be the new post office back in 1936, when the WPA workers came to town. They went to work on the college first, built the Fine Arts building and laid down those beautiful brick sidewalks, and gaslights, and the grassy quadrangle, designed by some long-forgotten architect in love with eighteenth-century England. Then they moved their gear to the river and started working on the ruins and the park where it stands.

Sixty years later and all the bricks are pockmarked and broken. The corroded Doric columns strain to support the majestic entrance. The four splendid windows are sealed with cinder blocks, braced against the damp river air. A bas-relief of the American eagle—about to take wing across eternal America—stares stoically past the broken patio and rotting cement steps. Anachronistic and decrepit, the ruins are a monument to a past that was, if not efficient, certainly ambitious.

People from town, students from the college, come out to the park to sit in the shade of the sycamores, and on the steps of the ruins; lie in the grass by the river with their girlfriends; lean against the solid walls and think the private thoughts people think when their lives are falling apart or coming together. When they need to resolve their worries, or piece together their plans. It's the quiet place they come to when they want to spend time doing nothing, or nothing more exciting than watching the river flow, thinking about their good luck or recent misfortune. When they need to feel the comfort of the past. Or when there's no place left to go. This is where they found the body.

II

When Jack Owens yawned, his left hand knocked the videocassette off the desk. He didn't move to pick it up, only turned to look out of his office window at the red brick sidewalk where students and faculty began appearing, like a time-lapse film, two and three, six and eight, then dozens, a hurtling mass of determination and purpose, caffeinic, amphetamine-fed, vibrant from their all-nighters. It was a nervous progress, a jangle of arms and legs, sleep-deprived voices. Soggy brains trying to keep the facts straight for just two more hours—Please God . . .

Jack raised the window and breathed the morning air. He stuck his head outside to see an edge of sun, a corner of blue sky, while he watched the current of baggy clothes, jackets and sweats flow, unvarying and constant, toward the old buildings with the time-darkened stone.

The sun moved an inch higher and the light reflected off the windows across the quad and onto Jack's desk. The office door was open and a soft breeze blew through the room. It was going to be another cool and brilliant day in May, when the gods of meteorology conspire to drive professors crazy, and Jack wanted another minute with it, which was the same thing he thought yesterday morning—or was it the day before? He'd lost track of time, entire days, holed up in the office, busting to get the final projects critiqued and graded on time. He hadn't had an actual conversation with Danny for nearly a week. They hardly talked at all while they managed a quick supper or their gulp-and-run breakfast. But that would all change a week from Tuesday. Then they were off on summer vacation. Rafting and camping in Pennsylvania. New York to catch the Yankees' home stand. Two weeks on the Cape. Two weeks in Maine. Two more weeks in Nova Scotia. He reached for the phone and called the house, but Danny didn't answer. He had apparently picked today to start being on time for the school bus. "It's me, again. Your phantom father." Jack pushed a laugh into the answering machine. "Sorry I wasn't home for breakfast this morning. I'll pick you up tomorrow night, okay? Around six. And don't forget, softball next Saturday, so oil your glove, pardner. I love you."

On Jack's desk was a photograph of Danny standing at the tiller of a sailboat tacking into the wind, his face sun-bright and excited, smiling a full vacation smile. Jack looked at Danny's face for just a moment, poured himself a cup of coffee and walked over to the sofa, just the slightest throbbing beginning behind his eyes. He turned on the VCR and sat down.

There was always a pleasant anticipation about watching Natasha Taylor's work, but the first viewing had been a disappointment, the piece was way off the mark. It started too slowly and lacked thematic focus, and now, seeing it for the second time only allowed him to home in on all the mistakes a student could make in ninety minutes. But when he started writing his critique, he made sure to keep it gentle.

The nine-thirty bells on the Union building had finished chiming when the phone rang. Jack got up slowly to answer it, not unhappy about the interruption.

"I haven't seen you all *week*. And I miss talking with you." It was Lois. He was even happier. "I just wanted to know how you're doing these days."

"Trying to tame the beast."

"You sound tired."

"Tired would be an improvement. I've been here all night and if I work through the weekend I may still come in under budget. Next fall I'm teaching *nothing* but theory. I'd rather grade term papers any day."

"You know you love your video class."

"I'll love it a lot more when my grades are in."

Lois said something else, but Jack wasn't listening. He wanted to get back to work and was about to tell her that, but she began asking about Danny. It was Danny's name that got Jack's attention. Was Danny very upset, she wanted to know, about losing the "big game"? Jack said Danny seemed to be taking it in stride.

Lois said yes, Danny seemed to take so many things in stride, her words coming slowly, deliberately—the way they had back when she was the teacher and Jack was her student, more than twenty years ago—when she wanted to make sure she had his attention.

"He doesn't seem to be taking his absentee father in stride," Jack told her. "He's treating me like a pariah. I don't think he understands."

"Danny understands. You do this to yourself every year. You'll make it up to him. Just as you did last summer and the summer before."

"This is the last summer. This is it. A couple of weeks ago he told me he wants to get a summer job next year. I asked him what the rush was. He said, and I quote: 'It's nineteen ninety-six, Dad. Get with the program.' I asked him just what that was supposed to mean, and again I quote: 'I'm fifteen. *Duh*.' What the hell is that all about?"

"You know what it's about."

"But I don't have to like it."

"You're not supposed to."

"And how are you these days?"

"Just fine. If I told you any more you'd hate me."

"You mean you've already turned in your grades and you called to gloat."

"That's not why I'm calling. Tim and I want you and Danny to come out to the house for a barbecue next Saturday. People Tim works with. You'll like them."

"That's the softball game."

"*Next* Saturday?"

"We'll come by after."

"Say hi to Danny, tell him he's a wonderful boy with a wonderful father, and give him a big hug for me." And she hung up.

It wasn't quite eleven o'clock when Jack walked down the ha
coffee carafe with water and came back to brew a fresh pot. He
try to finish Natasha's critique by late afternoon. That would lea
even dozen to go and put him in not-too-bad shape for his dinner br
tomorrow night with Danny—he's too old to be seen with his fathe
and too young not to resent the time you spend away from him, Jack
thought. This summer and that's it.

He didn't like thinking about that and rushed back to his work and managed to get about another forty-five minutes' worth done before Sally Richards stopped by, put a paper bag on the desk—"Comfort food. I know how you forget to eat"—and wanted to know, "Did Danny say anything about Mary-Sue?"

Jack said Danny was hardly saying much of anything these days.

"Hideous, aren't they? Oh, Jack, before I forget. Howard and I are putting together a poker game for tomorrow night. Think you can make it? Easy money."

"My favorite kind. But I'm afraid not."

"All work and no play . . ." She wagged a finger at him.

Coming and going, some were just starting work, most had already posted their grades and were closing up shop. All Jack wanted was to be on vacation with his kid.

When the one o'clock bells chimed they brought with them Carl Ainsley. "I have to say, Owens, you look like shit." Ainsley leaned against the doorway, feet crossed at the ankle. His black hair combed smoothly across his head, his face clean-shaven and suntanned. He wore fine linen pants, a pink cotton sweater under a beige linen sport coat. "You're wasting your time. They don't care what you think," and he stepped inside. "Just give 'em a grade, that's all that matters to them. If they don't like it, they'll bitch to your department chair or throw themselves at you. Either way it's bullshit."

"Go away."

Ainsley laughed softly. "Why do you think they let us have student assistants? Ever since Samantha started grading papers and preparing my assignments, my backhand's improved immeasurably and I've

…es off my golf game." He took a swing at an imaginary … looked at Jack and smiled pleasantly, the way he usually … way he must have smiled at his students, who, he liked to …ck loved him—a harmless smile, without a trace of malevo-…r conceit, and when he said grading, or teaching for that matter, …bullshit, it was not meant to challenge any other teacher's assess-…ent or denigrate any other teacher's methods or motives.

Jack could only smile back. "You are one lazy man."

"I think I'm rather enterprising. But really, Owens. You're knocking yourself out unnecessarily and if you don't care about what you're doing to yourself, think about what you're doing to *me*."

"To *you*?"

"Yes. *Me*. Just knowing that you're in your office working all alone into the night is making me absolutely morose. Mandy and I were out last night for cocktails and supper and how was I supposed to enjoy myself knowing you're up here working yourself blind like some poor little Dickensian clerk? It's just not fair. It's not right."

"I suppose it is rather thoughtless of me."

"Of course it is. And there's only one thing to do about it. You and I are going out tonight. For drinks. Just to put my troubled mind at ease."

"I can't."

"Don't be ridiculous, of course you can, 'Self-love is not so vile a sin as self-neglecting.' "

"Can't."

"Then at least go home and get some sleep."

"You're a real pain in the ass, Carl, but a charming pain in the ass. I'll give you that."

"I'll take that as a compliment."

"Take it any way you like, but *please* take it somewhere else. I'm trying to finish my work."

Ainsley laughed, a little louder than before, walked over to Jack and whispered playfully, "Did I tell you about the girl in my Shakespeare class? The one with the mouth . . ." He kissed the tips of his fingers. "She hasn't done a thing all semester. Barely making a D. So, last week she said, 'Is there *anything* I can do to improve my grade?' Now what's a man supposed to do?" He grinned and for a brief moment Jack wondered if that was the same way Ainsley grinned at Mandy when he came home late at night or when she caught him in a clumsy lie.

"Oh, don't look at me like that," Ainsley said. "I didn't do anything. If I did, you'd never let me get away with it."

"Why are you telling me this?"

"Why do I *always* feel compelled to confess my sins to you?" He pushed Jack's papers aside and sat on the edge of the desk. "Because Jack Owens would never do a thing like that. Because I know it pisses you off." He leaned forward. "Or maybe, it's because you think I'm completely without morals and I think you're the most moral man I know and I afford you the standard by which that morality of yours can be gauged." He patted Jack on the cheek. "We *need* each other, Owens. It keeps us honest. You in your way, me in mine." He started to stand but stopped and asked, "Has Carl Junior been staying at your house the past few nights?"

"Not that I know of. But I haven't been there much lately. Why?"

"I don't know. Mandy asked me to ask you. It seems he's in one of his *moods*. I'm hoping he'll get himself a girlfriend this summer and it will take the edge off."

Knowing Carl Junior—C.J.—as he did, Jack found that both improbable and amusing, which he told Ainsley.

"You never know," Ainsley said, "he may be a scrawny little fuckup, but he just turned fifteen and summer is all about timid little boys becoming confident young men when those surges of testosterone . . . Anyway, I can only hope." Now he stood up and walked to the door. "Please," he called out, "stop busting your ass on these kids. It's not worth it. Nothing is."

Then there were no more interruptions. No students. No one stopping by for a quick chat. There were just the sounds of academe in the hallway. The light footsteps in the office above. A telephone ringing somewhere. The sounds on the video, the flickering images on the screen. Natasha's story was taking form, an actual narrative materializing.

When the two o'clock bells chimed, Jack absently reached inside the paper bag and removed one of the sandwiches Sally Richards had made. Pimento-cheese on white bread, crusts removed.

He heard the knock on the door.

"I'm looking for room two-seventeen."

Jack turned around. "This is two-seventeen."

"Are you Jack Owens?"

Jack put down the sandwich. "That's right."

He wasn't very old, middle thirties probably, about average height and weight, thinning blond hair, gray suit, no tie, hands tucked into his pockets. He looked like someone who'd been selling insurance most of his life, or he might have been the parent of some student and taken the wrong turn in the hallway and was trying to get his bearings. He said he was Detective Hopewell, asked, "Can I come in?" closed the door behind him and moved slowly into the office, looking around at the bookshelves, the VCR, and monitor.

Jack watched silently, thinking only the worst while at the same time his mind raced desperately for some reasonable explanation for a detective to come to his office in the middle of the day. In the three seconds it took Detective Hopewell to walk inside, Jack decided that his car must have been stolen . . . or Draper, down the hall, had finally had that heart attack . . . that someone was playing a practical joke on him . . . But the look on Hopewell's face wasn't the look that went with a sick colleague or a stolen car. The look on his face wasn't a joke.

The back of Jack's neck grew cold and damp. He had the dreadful, slippery feeling that happens when the phone rings at three in the morning or when it doesn't ring by noon or when the bed is still empty at dawn. He had a taste in his mouth that started in his stomach and crawled, dark and acrid, up the back of his throat and lay sour on his tongue, atavistic and terrifying. He felt it before he knew he was feeling it. Before the detective said another word, Jack's eyes went to the picture on the desk and he breathed, "Danny."

"Danny Owens, is he your son?" That's all Hopewell said, as though that was all there was to say.

"Yes. Danny's my son." Jack's mouth had gone dry, his throat was burning.

"I'm sorry to have to tell you this." Hopewell put his hand on Jack's shoulder. He was pressing down hard, as though Jack might leap up and out of the room. "Your son is dead. He was found by the ruins in Fairmont Park. Around twelve noon. It looks like suicide."

III

The morgue smelled of death and chemicals and pre-embalmed odors. All of life's air had been sucked from this place. It stank of necrosis. Jack turned away from the steel slab with the white sheet. He stared at the empty gray wall across the room, at the floor with the black scuff marks. He turned his face to the ceiling, where lights reflected dull and cold, and when he managed to move he found himself standing in the corner shaking his head, crossing his arms around his chest and holding on to himself.

Hopewell pulled the sheet back and Jack saw the body, the blue-faced body, Danny—no, not really Danny. Only what remained of Danny.

Hopewell asked, "Is this your son?"

"Yes," Jack said, "he's my son," and pushed the dark, curly hair away from Danny's forehead, ran the palm of his hand across Danny's smooth cheekbones. He traced the contours of Danny's lips and caressed the strong jaw that covered the vulnerability. That was when he saw the narrow purple welt around Danny's neck. "What's this?"

"It's from the plastic bag."

Jack held Danny's face in his hands. "Was there . . . was there a note?"

"No note," Hopewell answered. "He might have left one at home. I need you to call me if you find one." A moment later he said, "I'm sorry."

But Jack did not hear any sorrow in Hopewell's voice, only the dispassionate tone, empty of inflection, at odds with the words he said. There wasn't even the appearance of sorrow, or sympathy, not in the voice, not in Hopewell's eyes or the expression on his face. But there was something there, not that Jack could identify it, and whatever it was, it was disturbing to see in the face of a man watching you stand over the body of your dead son, disturbing to hear in his voice. Hopewell said, "His bike was next to him." Jack felt his stomach turn. He wanted to say something. He wanted to ask questions, but he didn't know what to ask. He didn't know what to think. He wasn't taking it in. His head felt as though it had filled with helium and was floating away from his body, like when you have a fever and everything seems to be happening far away and a beat too slowly.

Hopewell asked, "Is there someone— Do you want to call your wife?"

"How did you find him?"

"A woman found him and called us."

"What woman?"

"Just a woman. Her story holds up, if you're thinking she had anything—"

"Her *name*. Who is *she*?"

"I'm afraid I can't tell you."

"We're talking about *Danny*. We're talking about my—"

"I know. But she has a right to her privacy. That's our procedure."

"I have a right to know what sort of person found my son."

"I'm sorry," was all Hopewell said.

"I want him out of here."

"I'm afraid you'll have to wait till after the autopsy."

"What do you mean autopsy?"

"It's procedure."

"He's dead."

"We have to follow procedure. I'm sorry, Dr. Owens."

"When can I have Danny?" Jack wanted to hold his boy and cradle him, feel the weight of Danny's body. He wanted to drop to the floor and cry. But he wouldn't cry. Not here.

"It depends on the medical examiner," Hopewell explained. "We share him with three other towns. It shouldn't be any later than the day after tomorrow, maybe sooner."

"I want my son's clothes."

"I have to keep them."

"They're Danny's."

"I need them for forensic evidence. Look, I know this isn't easy for you, Dr. Owens. I'll get them back to you just as soon as possible."

"Don't wrinkle his jacket." Jack stroked Danny's head. "He was very particular about that."

"Sure. Do you have anyone to drive you home?"

"I want him out of here."

Late in the afternoon, Jack drove out to the ruins. He'd gone home and picked through all the obvious places, but Danny had left no note, no explanation, and there was nowhere else to go but the ruins, to hold one of Danny's shirts against his heart, stand on top of the hill where Danny had spent the last minutes of his life and try to sense Danny's presence and the traces left in the wake of his death.

Jack stared at the cloudless sky above the sycamores that leaned lush and heavy over the riverbank. He thought of Danny sitting here alone, crouched against the wall, hidden by the growth of Queen Anne's lace, thinking his last thoughts alone. The chill in the air must have made him shiver.

Jack knew the look on Danny's face—serious and solemn, the way he looked when there was something on his mind that he had to talk about and couldn't get started. He always got around to it, though—they talked about everything. Well, Jack thought, obviously not. A plastic bag over his head? Not something a fifteen-year-old kid just comes up with in a minute. How long had he been thinking about it? And what the hell was Jack looking at all that time? He thought he could read that face within an inch of its life. So how the hell did he miss the look of suicide?

Jack tried to remember each detail freeze-framed against the past two weeks. Their fifteen minutes at breakfast, the few nights when they ate supper together. What Danny said. How Danny looked.

He looked the way he always looked. He looked like Danny. Or maybe Jack didn't know what he was seeing.

They'd had dinner together the night before last, but Jack hadn't seen it. When he reached across the table to push the hair away from Danny's eyes, Danny didn't look any different. He didn't do anything different. It embarrassed him to have Jack fuss over him, made him feel self-conscious, but Jack knew Danny liked the attention, just like he always did.

When they had breakfast just a few days ago, Danny wasn't eating, just pushing his cereal around in the bowl. He asked, "Which is more important, Dad, honesty or loyalty?"

What was in Danny's voice?

What was the expression on Danny's face?

What had Jack seen? What did he see now?

Danny was sitting at the kitchen table looking into a bowl of soggy cereal on Saturday morning, not speaking. Yawning. Looking tired.

"You wouldn't be tired from studying too hard?" Jack said to him.

No answer.

"Too tired to talk?"

"I guess."

"My working late at the office doesn't give you license to stay up all night."

"I know when to go to sleep," Danny said. "I'm fifteen, you know."

What was in the voice? What did Jack hear?

Danny sounded annoyed but he'd sounded annoyed plenty of other times.

They were eating supper at the drive-in on Route 41, Thursday night. Danny *inhaled* his cheeseburger . . . They were eating supper at the drive-in four days later, Danny left half his burger on the plate. Jack never monitored Danny's behavior, he didn't that night, either. He assumed Danny had eaten late in the day.

A week before that, they were sitting at breakfast, Danny wasn't yawning. He ate his cereal, not with great enthusiasm, breakfast for him was never an official meal. They were talking about pitching in the sectionals. Danny said he was nervous. Jack told him, "If you aren't nervous, you aren't ready." Danny offered up a smile and ran to catch the school bus.

Jack leaned against the cement pillars. He looked down at the three terraced patios and the old stone steps descending in long leaps toward the road. The ruins had always been a safe place. This was where he'd had the courage to speak to Anne for the first time. Before they lived in the loft on Crosby Street. Before they had Danny. This was the place where he'd brought Danny when the two of them moved to Gilbert after Anne left.

He wasn't aware of walking, but now Jack was standing at the side of the road atop the river's muddy bank, where sunlight weaved through the loam and wildflowers, where he and Danny played catch when Danny was five and afraid of the ball. "It won't hurt you. Don't be scared." Or when they sat in the shade of the sycamore trees and the shadows of the grand decaying façade and Jack told Danny stories, when Danny was still young enough to fit on Jack's lap.

"Old story or new?"

"Old," Danny said.

"Any requests?"

"Casey."

" 'Casey at the Bat'?"

Danny nodded his head emphatically.

"But that's such a sad story. Don't you remember? Mighty Casey strikes out. There's no joy in Mudville. You don't want a disappointing story on such a pretty day."

"It's not disappointing if you root for the other team," Danny answered.

Jack couldn't hold him tightly enough when he said that, or love him enough. He would laugh a little and feel not only pride and astonishment but wonder.

How did Danny think of that? How did he find the loophole?

This was the place where Jack had held his little boy and watched him sleep. The place where he told him stories and recited doggerel. Where Jack made the plans parents make with the fearless faith of the convert. Plans that stretch across time. This was the place where Danny chose to die.

What had he been showing that Jack hadn't seen? Jack thought: Why would Danny want to kill himself?

Danny pitched in the high school sectionals just two weeks ago. He stood on the mound, tall and broad-shouldered, staring intently at the catcher the way he'd seen major league pitchers do, looking calm. Jack remembered the ball leaving Danny's hand and the batter swinging late and weakly, the ground ball finding the hole between shortstop and third, trickling into the outfield. A soft, seeing-eye single scoring the winning run. Danny's team lost 2–1.

Danny seemed to take the loss in stride. He didn't cry, not in front of his teammates and not later riding home in the car. "It was my game to win or lose and I put the winning run on base." He said he was disappointed. He said he'd wanted to take the team all the way. But he'd made his best pitch and the kid put his bat on the ball and it took a bad bounce.

"I'd say it was the best game I ever saw you pitch," Jack told him. "I'm very proud of you."

"I wanted to pitch in the finals."

"There's always next year," Jack promised him. "And you'll be even better and, believe it or not, bigger and stronger. About my height, I bet. And another five pounds heavier, easily, maybe ten."

"I really wanted to win the championship," Danny answered.

"Making it to the sectionals isn't too shabby." But Jack knew that Danny thought big. He thought he was good enough to take the team all the way.

Danny stared out the car window for a little while before he said, "Wait till next year," with the same equanimity he'd shown during the game. Not unlike the little boy who'd found the loophole in "Casey at the Bat."

Jack thought: But maybe there wasn't a loophole to losing the game, or Danny couldn't find one. Maybe he never found the loophole when his mother left him. Maybe there was less composure than he let on.

Maybe it was all a show because that's what he thought people expected of him. What he thought Jack expected of him.

Jack wondered: Was there that much pressure on him? Was there that much sorrow inside him?

Jack wondered: Was it enough to make him want to kill himself? Danny had stopped sleeping and lost his appetite—because he lost the ballgame? It wasn't that important to him.

Jack sat in his car, rested his chin on the steering wheel and watched the blue shadows drop and lengthen along the ruins and across the mottled ground. He began to cry. He shut his eyes and raised his head. The tears ran hot against his face and his neck and made him tremble. He wanted to kick Danny's ass for killing himself. He wanted to reverse time, like rewinding a tape, and step back into the past and pull Danny back from the dead. He wanted to push past whatever secret silence had lived inside Danny, feeding on him. Push past his own failures as a father and make everything all right; to go back and see beyond Danny's talk, beyond Danny's silence.

Last Monday, they were in the kitchen. Danny hadn't said much. He nudged his toast and eggs out of the way. It was the third morning in a row that he had pushed his breakfast aside. Jack said something about it.

Danny said, "I'm eating, I'm eating." He rubbed his eyes. His face was pale, it always was when he didn't get enough sleep.

Mutt started barking. The school bus driver honked his horn. Jack said, "Stick around, I'll drive you to school."

"Can't, Dad." Danny grabbed his books and bolted. Jack was a little surprised, a little hurt that Danny didn't want to spend another half hour with him. But, as Danny pointed out only a few days before, he was "fifteen, you know."

"Too old to be seen with me?" Jack called after him.

Danny didn't answer.

Jack worked late Monday night and overslept Tuesday morning. He didn't see Danny—they didn't have supper together, either.

The following night, they shared a pizza in town. It was a rush job on Jack's part, he had two days to finish grading final projects. Afterward, he drove Danny home and went back to his office. They didn't talk much in the restaurant, and neither of them ate much. Jack had the feeling Danny was bothered by something. He'd even asked him. Danny just shook his head.

"It seems there's something—"

"Nothing's bothering me. Okay?"

"If there's—"

"You worry too much."

It was dark when he walked up the front steps to his house and stood on the porch. The reflection of the half-moon floated in the empty windows. Mutt was barking in the backyard, but Jack didn't move. He didn't walk around back and he didn't go inside, not yet. He wasn't ready for the night without Danny. He could only stand outside for another minute waiting for he-did-not-know-what to happen, before he pushed the front door open with his fingertips, gently, the way you touch a fresh bruise.

He walked over to the piano. There was the book of sheet music Danny had left out. Jack did not touch it. He started to sit down, stopped, started to walk away and stopped again. He rested his fingers on top of the keys and noticed that his hand was shaking. He leaned against the wall and felt his knees knocking together.

The thing to do now was to keep moving. Turn on the lights. Wash up. Feed Mutt. Pour a drink. Keep moving.

He walked though the foyer turning on lights, the living room, turning on lights. He walked past the wall of photographs. The "Danny wall" they called it. The framed arrangement in polished chrome and lacquer and wood. Round and square frames. Frames bought in roadside junk shops and Manhattan boutiques, and street vendors in Florence: Danny on his first two-wheeler. Danny at the Bronx Zoo. Danny at the beach. Danny and Jack at the ballgame. Danny and Jack at the Indiana State Fair. Danny's first day at school. Danny at his first piano recital, eyes wide, tie a little crooked, hands folded on his lap. And the recital last March at his high school looking handsome in his blue suit, and confident, his eyes deep in concentration . . .

Jack hurried down the hall to the kitchen like a man pursued. He was sweating. For all he knew he hadn't stopped sweating since he left the morgue. He turned on the kitchen lights, opened the back door and let Mutt in.

The red light on the answering machine blinked, his message to Danny waiting across the room, like an assassin. Their breakfast dishes, from how many days before, were still in the sink—dried cereal still in the bowl, juice still in the glass. The things Danny had touched and left behind.

Danny killed himself today. He put a plastic bag over his head—Jack broke down. He cried as he walked through the downstairs rooms. He was thinking: Danny is still alive in the house.

Sweating and crying. In his study, turning on lights. The den, turning on lights. The back porch and front, turning on lights. Climbing the stairs, turning on lights. In his bedroom, turning on lights. In the guest room. In Danny's room—he couldn't stay away from Danny's room—where clothes were scattered like refuse. Shirts and underwear and socks, jeans, pants, jackets, shoes and ties piled outside the closet, draped over the desk and computer. Notebooks, textbooks and loose papers strewn across the floor, the wreckage Jack had left behind when he came looking for the suicide note, when he'd found only silence—he didn't remember his search being this violent, he didn't remember making this mess. Now, Mutt lay in the middle of Danny's clothes, whimpering.

Jack sat on the bed and ran his palm across the bedspread. He faced the photographs on the wall. Danny's photographs, Danny's eyes and Danny's legs and Danny's body. Playing ball, riding a boogie board. His face ready to smile, his laugh ready to happen. But what else was in that face? Was there suicide hidden just below the surface, like in those old photographs with the double exposure, the second face looming like ectoplasm in the background? Is it there if you know where to look? Is it there if you're brave enough to see it? Brave enough to admit putting it there, because Jack was sure his hand was all over Danny's death. That it was the life he had made for Danny, that Danny couldn't live.

Jack pressed his face into the pillow and inhaled the smell of Danny's mornings and nights. He sobbed plaintively, until his throat ached and there was nothing left to sob.

This wasn't supposed to happen.

Mutt pawed at the clothes, as though he were looking for his lost boy. Jack couldn't stand to watch it. He yelled at him to stop, dammit. He yelled a second and third time, but Mutt went on frantically scratching.

"Stop it," Jack shouted.

He heaved himself off the bed and, sweeping up Mutt in his arms, carried him into the hallway and closed the door behind him. Mutt squirmed free and scratched to get back in. Jack grabbed him by the scruff of his neck and pulled him away. Mutt twisted free again and lay outside Danny's room.

Jack walked downstairs, thinking: Danny killed himself today. He put a plastic—

He saw the silhouette on the other side of the screen door, silent and motionless against the porch light. Jack could only stare, not saying a word—unsure of what he was seeing, what to think. Unsure if he should move or stand still and feeling the urge to scream or cry out and believe in the existence of ghosts. He took a cautious step forward and was about to speak Danny's name when he heard: "Dr. Owens?" Softly, no louder than the evening breeze. "Dr. Owens, is Danny home?"

Jack looked closer into the darkness.

"Dr. Owens?"

It was C.J., Carl Ainsley's son.

Jack opened the door and asked him to come inside. But all C.J. did was say, "I can wait out here. I just came over to see Danny."

"Danny. Danny's—you better come in," and Jack stepped out of the way.

C.J. was breathing heavily, as though he'd been running. He stared into the room with a morose expression on his face—which was the expression he usually wore. He lowered his eyes, raised them to Jack and lowered them again. "I just came over to see Danny."

"Come in."

But C.J. took a step back. "Is something wrong?"

"Come in." Jack led him into the living room. "Sit down. Please."

C.J. looked thinner than Jack remembered. There were dark rings under his eyes, as though he might have shared Danny's sleepless nights, and his clothes, his T-shirt and jeans, were in need of washing. "Danny wasn't in school today," he said flatly.

Jack hesitated before he told him, "Danny is dead." It was the first time that he'd articulated this to anyone. The back of his throat burned and his fingertips were numb. "He killed himself. Out by the ruins."

C.J. didn't sit so much as drop onto the couch. His body sagged and he started to weep. Jack sat next to him and put an arm around his shoulder. C.J. felt so slight and frail that Jack was careful not to hold him too tightly for fear of crushing him like a piece of brittle glass—Jack might have been holding on to Danny, the fragile part of Danny, which Danny had been so careful not to show.

C.J. cried and trembled and muttered softly to himself, something that sounded like "bad luck" or "fucked up." And after Jack let go of him, C.J. rocked back and forth, talking under his breath, whispering indiscernible words over and over again like an incantation.

"What is that? What are you saying?"

C.J. only rocked and cried, his arms wrapped around himself. "I'm so sorry," he moaned. "I'm so sorry, Dr. Owens," and a moment later, "I can't—Danny—I'm so sorry." He wiped his eyes and nose with the back of his arm. When he said, "I was with him last night," it sounded like a confession.

"Last night? You *talked* to Danny last night?"

"Kind of."

"Kind of? Kind of yes? Kind of no? Kind of what?"

All the color left C.J.'s face. "We just hung out for a little while, that's all."

"And he didn't say anything about—he didn't act like he was depressed or troubled by something?"

C.J. shook his head. "He said he had things he had to do, to get ready for summer, summer vacation, and I went home."

Jack walked across the room and stared out the window, at the field across the road and the sky, which had grown darker, and a small piece of the moon. He turned to C.J. "Danny must have said *something*."

"No. I don't know. I don't know why—" C.J. started crying, softly.

"Danny killed himself," Jack said, with no small amount of disbelief, and C.J. started rocking back and forth again and talking under his breath. It made Jack uncomfortable to watch him. He went back to looking out the window.

A moment later, C.J. asked, "Do Brian and Rick know?"

"I haven't told anyone. I don't want anyone else to know about it. Not yet."

A moment after that, C.J. said, "I won't tell. I can keep a secret." It was startling, how sad he sounded when he said this, and regretful. It made Jack take a long look at him.

C.J. must have startled himself, or maybe it was the expression on Jack's face, because he stood up quickly and said, "I better go now."

But Jack told him to wait. "I don't understand something. Danny committed—committed suicide this morning and all he talked about last night was getting ready for summer?"

"That's all he said, Dr. Owens. I only came over because he wasn't in school today. That's all, Dr. Owens." C.J. started to cry and rushed out of the house.

Jack stood under the shower. He was thinking that he'd have to call his father in the morning. He'd have to arrange Danny's funeral.

"Danny's funeral." And he thought about Danny all alone tonight in the morgue. Vomit bubbled up in his throat and sprayed the walls around the stall, spilled over his chin and down his legs. It congealed like a fetid pool in a sewer. The water was slow to wash it away.

IV

Jack was in his office. He didn't hear the door open, but felt it open. He felt it open a moment *before* it opened. Someone was there. It was Danny. Jack could feel his heart inflate as though a puncture had been sealed.

"Danny," he breathed. "Danny. I thought—"

"I'm here now, Dad." He was wearing his green shirt and black shorts.

Jack grabbed him and hugged him. "Don't ever do that again."

"I love you," Danny told him.

"I love you, too. Promise you'll never go away again."

"I promise."

It was a cruel dream, made more cruel by awakening, which Jack resisted, if he'd actually been asleep. He was lying naked on the couch, his head on Danny's pillow. His neck hurt and his eyes were crusty in the corners and felt raw. There was an untouched glass of whiskey on the table behind him. He sat up slowly and looked at the clock. It was four in the morning and he was alone.

He reached for his bathrobe, walked outside and stood on the back porch. He leaned against the railing and stared past the fence, across the expanse of pasture and the fields of soy and alfalfa, at the urban glow on the edge of the horizon. He thought of the semis driving the interstate and how peaceful and private the highway is at four o'clock in the morning with the darkness riding up front, the headlights leading the way home, to the place *called* home because someone is waiting for you there, someone whose face is so familiar you can't remember what she looks like until just before the moment that she gets to the door and it all comes back, the way her eyes look at you and the shape of her mouth. How her hair is sleep-crushed but so what, just so long as she's there waiting; and there's a kid upstairs in bed fighting like hell to stay awake so he can hear the front door open and the sound of your voice.

Well, Jack didn't have a wife waiting for him and there was no kid sleeping inside, but this was the place he called home. The place he came to ten years ago with a five-year-old son after things went bad with Anne. When he and Danny needed a soft landing.

The trees were silhouettes against the straight line of fence. Beyond them, on the other side of the field, a light went on in an upstairs window in the Richardses' house, and for a moment Jack's feelings of solitude were gone, knowing someone else was awake in these wee small hours. He'd always liked the privacy here, with the pastures and field, but tonight he wished there were people right next door turning in their sleep, switching on lights. He wanted to hear the sound of a curtain rustling in a house across the driveway, the plumbing gurgling.

He pulled his bathrobe tight around his chest and paced the width of the yard, once and then again. He was thinking about his boy and how much he missed him. He was thinking that Danny would never know this new day. He was thinking that Danny had been robbed of his youth, twice in his brief life. Once when his mother had left him, taking with her the childhood illusion that life is sane and painless, and again when he robbed himself of simply growing old. It would never happen. Danny would never grow to be a man. He was frozen in time, a fifteen-year-old boy, forever. After today, people would know him as the boy who killed himself in Fairmont Park. They wouldn't know Danny who pitched high school ball and didn't embarrass himself. Or Danny who played piano Wednesday afternoons at the senior center. Or . . .

From the field rose the scent of darkness and the musky smell of soil and fertilizer and damp night air; the green smell of young crops and of earth plowed and tilled and planted. It was a country smell, riding the breeze like a child's kite. The sun had yet to appear, but the deep blue rim of dawn was inching toward a morning which, Jack knew, would be like no other morning in his life. And then what? Condolences, of course. Fathers with sons thinking, Better you than me. The pitying expressions on their faces. The patronizing looks of sympathy and commiseration.

He had to talk to someone. It was too early to call Lois. He dreaded calling his father. He started pacing the yard again. The grass was cold against his bare feet. The air was starting to change, the way it does just before sunrise. A train whistle wailed in the distance and sank down the length of silent track. He sat on the porch steps and watched the yellow light in the Richardses' window dissolve like a lozenge in the light of dawn.

Mutt was still lying outside Danny's room. He raised his eyes at the sound of Jack's approach and whined listlessly when Jack called to him.

"Come on, Mutt. Give it a rest." Jack snapped his fingers and whistled. "Give it a *rest*." Mutt turned his back. Jack walked downstairs, switching off lights, pulling up shades. He went to the kitchen and brewed a pot of coffee.

When he brought a cup with him to his bedroom, Mutt followed and lay down on the bed. Jack reached for the phone.

"Hello, Grace—"

"Jackie. What a surprise."

There was more than surprise in his stepmother's voice. There was the shot of fear, the spasm of apprehension that catches in the throat like a seed. The phone rings at six in the morning and it's her husband's son, she had to know the news was not good. Her eyes were probably doing that nervous little dance they do, looking everywhere but where they really wanted to look: at the old man with the trembly hands—who was more chemistry than biology these days, half the organs in his body dependent on the right dosage at the right time to keep them pumping and ingesting and churning—sitting up in bed, or on the living room couch, in the apartment in Manhattan, where the sunlight refracted through the large windows, sparkling on the furniture and art. Where there wasn't a suggestion of the clutter of old age, only the clean and crisp smells of comfort and care, which the pleasant young Irishwoman was paid quite well to maintain five days a week.

"I hope I didn't wake you," Jack answered.

"*Wake* us. We've been up for *hours*." When there was nothing more forthcoming, she said, "I'll put Mike on."

Those chemicals better be doing their job, Jack prayed, or his father wouldn't survive the call.

"What happened?" was the first thing his father said. His voice could still come on strong.

"It's bad." And Jack let his father absorb that much.

"How bad?"

Jack told him how bad. He told him what had happened and how, where it happened and when. He told him slowly. He told him all the details, not too graphically but he didn't leave anything out. That was how his father would have done it. It was how Jack had learned to do it: he said what had to be said. He answered all the questions.

"Christ almighty, Jackie." The voice seemed to fade before the last word was said. There was a deep gasp and then, "Danny? Dead?" coming sadly, weakly, as though the news alone had sapped what remained of his energy. Jack could hear Grace's "Oh my God" as the old man asked, "How can he be dead?" the voice cracking now. "I can't comprehend it. Christ almighty."

There was more than disbelief in the voice, more than sadness, more than grief, although that was all there, but it was something else that started deep inside his throat, a mournful, guttural sound, that came with the exhalation of his breath. It was the sound of an old man feeling the death of his only grandson. "My God, Jackie, suicide . . . My God . . ." sounding pained and full of sorrow. "Maybe it was an accident."

"The detective doesn't think so." Jack held on to the phone and said nothing else. He listened to his father sobbing and gasping and sobbing again, and Grace crying and saying muffled, inaudible things. Then the old voice said, "Danny was a very complex kid. Complex and complicated for his age, hell, from the day he was born. Even before Anne walked out." He paused to clear his throat. "She made a mess of his life, leaving him the way she did."

It startled Jack to hear Anne's name. They never talked about her, at least not when they talked about Danny.

His father said, "I don't know—who knows *what* was going on inside of him. Who can say after this, but a little boy doesn't get over being abandoned like that. Your mother always said Anne damaged him irrevocably." When he breathed in it sounded like dry leaves scattering in the wind. "Danny had a tough time. Tougher than we realized." He struggled with another breath. "Oh God, Jackie, I love that boy so much." Jack cried with him.

They cried for Danny, who had found living unbearable, and they cried for each other as well: the father who had outlived his son, the grandfather who had outlived his grandson. This wasn't a conversation they ever anticipated having. It was Danny who one day would have had to be told his grandfather died, not this, which is what the old man was saying while he cried and lost his breath and started to cough and wheeze and make hacking sounds from deep inside his chest, until there was no sound at all.

"Dad?" Jack shouted into the phone.

His father didn't answer.

"Dad?"

His father coughed a few times and cleared his throat. He said, "You shouldn't be alone now, Jackie. I want you to get on a plane and fly out here. You'll stay with us. We'll take care of each other."

"I've got to stay here." Jack wiped his eyes, adjusted the pillow behind his head while Mutt nuzzled the crook of his arm.

His father said, "This is no time to be by yourself, Jackie. We belong together."

"I can't."

"Of course you can."

"I've got to stay here."

"We have to go through this together. You'll be bouncing off the walls alone in the house."

"I'd be bouncing off the walls in New York, too. I can't leave."

"Get on a plane—"

"Listen to me—"

"Listen to *me*. You'll rattle around, chewing yourself up until you're raw and out of your mind. I want you here with me. You won't have to do a thing. My travel agent will book the flight." He may not have been in the strongest voice today, but the old man could still fight, and there was no placating him; there was no patronizing. But it was also this: his father needed his son.

But Jack insisted, "I can't."

"Don't be like that, Jackie."

"I can't come to New York. Not until I get Danny out of the morgue."

"I'm an idiot," the old man answered. "Of course. Then I'll come out there."

"I need you in New York. I need you to make the arrangements for Danny's—Danny's funeral."

There was silence for a moment at the other end. Then, "I'll call Harry Weber. He took care of your mother's funeral. He'll take care of everything."

Jack rubbed his eyes with his fingertips. "Yes, Harry's fine."

After Jack hung up, he lay on the bed with Mutt leaning against his arm. He didn't close his eyes, he didn't try to go to sleep. He simply lay there looking at the whiteness of the ceiling. A minute passed. He called Lois and told her.

"Christ, Jack," she said softly. "I'm coming over."

Then there was only the silence. Jack thought, So this is what it feels like without Danny, while he lay there doing nothing; and a moment later he thought he'd better walk down the hall and see if Danny was getting ready for school, and he sat up quickly, his body alert, ready to move, all reflexes, like the frog in the biology experiment that's nothing but nervous system. In that same moment, on that same reflex, he dropped back and lay very still.

He thought: So this is what it feels like without Danny. He thought: He's still alive in this house.

Jack arranged a few rolls on a plate for when Lois came over, a platter with butter and cheese, and put it on the table with the pitcher of cream and the sugar bowl. He brewed a fresh pot of coffee. He still couldn't bring himself to wash Danny's breakfast dishes, but he rinsed his own coffee cup and put it on the drainboard.

Outside the kitchen window sunlight was breaking through the branches of the trees. Birds were making their racket deep in the field and out by the stream. The morning paper hit the front door.

It's tomorrow, Jack thought, and found the prospect terrifying. He picked up the phone and called his father again.

"I don't know why I'm calling," he said when the old man came to the phone.

"You don't have to know."

"I just want to hear you at the other end."

"You don't have to explain."

Jack picked at the dried cereal in Danny's bowl.

His father said, "I've been thinking about him. Something he and I talked about when you were here last Christmas." He took another hard breath and coughed again. "He asked me something that I thought was really extraordinary. He seemed to be trying to understand, understand life, if I had to describe it. I don't mean he was trying to make sense of it, but—wait a second, I have to—wait." When he came back: "Danny was trying to *understand it*. He asked about Anne and about you, just general things. And he asked me where I thought *ideas* came from."

"What?"

"If I thought they came from inside of us or outside. Did I believe in God and did He put ideas into people's heads to get them to do things and behave the way they did." His father stopped to catch his breath. "He asked me where my ideas came for my inventions. From inside myself or outside, or did they come from God and how could we ever know the difference. And did Anne get ideas for her paintings from inside or outside of herself. Did she get the idea to leave from—"

Jack took the phone away from his ear, stared down the hallway at the photographs on the "Danny wall," then he brought the phone to his mouth. "Danny told his friend that he had to get ready for summer vacation, then he killed himself the next morning. Where did he get *that* idea?"

"I don't know."

"He wouldn't have decided something like that on impulse. In a moment of—what? He wouldn't have done it just like that."

"No, Jackie, he wouldn't have done it just like that."

Jack listened to his father's breathing on the other end of the line. A minute later he said good-bye and waited for Lois.

V

The expression on Lois's face wasn't pitying or patronizing, just patient. The exact expression Jack wanted to see looking at him across his kitchen table. It allowed him to have his thoughts, to say nothing, and Lois must have known that. She was not a person given to inappropriate gestures.

"I'm so sorry," she said. "Oh, Jack, I am so terribly sorry."

He didn't answer, only tapped his fingers on the table, and when the sound got on his nerves, he said, "I'm a very selfish man."

"You know that isn't true."

Jack shook his head. "I'm sitting here thinking how gratifying it must be for my father to know, even though he's sick, that he can still help me, that he can still do the things fathers do for their sons, and how close to me he feels when he does them. But when I'm an old man, I won't have that experience. All I'm thinking is how lonely I'll be, when it's Danny I should be thinking of. It was Danny who was alone."

"He's your son and you miss him. That's not selfish."

"It is when he committed suicide," Jack said bitterly. "It is when I spend entire semesters worrying about other people's children and never notice that my own son is figuring out the most efficient way to die. I'm beginning to wonder if I wasn't the only one I was thinking about all along."

"Don't do this to yourself," she said softly.

"I don't know if he wanted to leave New York. I just assumed—he didn't know what was right for him, but I did, or I should have. I told myself I did. But maybe I just did what was best for me, because I couldn't stand to stay there."

Lois slowly and meticulously rolled up the sleeves of her pink blouse as though she were about to tackle a tough job. Or maybe she was giving herself time to think. She reached across the table and put her hand on Jack's. He started to slide it away but she held on to it.

"What you're saying isn't fair," Lois told him. "To you *or* Danny."

"And everything *else* that happened to him was? Man, I feel all twisted up inside."

"I know." Lois squeezed Jack's fingers, softly. "I know." This time, he didn't try to pull away.

"I thought I really understood him. I didn't have a clue. He must have been showing me and I just couldn't see it. I should have. I should have been there to save him."

"You can feel all the sadness you want, but please, try not—"

"Something made his life unbearable and I was responsible for changing that. But I didn't. How could I not be aware of his pain? How could I let him do that to himself?"

Lois pulled a corner off one of the rolls but all she did was look at it and then let it drop onto her plate. "I will not let you think that you neglected Danny."

"He killed himself. It didn't come out of nowhere."

"No one said it did." When Jack turned away she said, "Listen to me, Jack. You did what you could do."

"I thought I undid the damage."

"There was a lot of damage. But it wasn't anything *you* did."

"This has nothing to do with Anne," he shouted at her, and it felt good to shout, even if it was Lois, even if she didn't deserve it, even if it made her wince while he snatched his hand out from under hers and stood up, rattling the coffee cups and knocking over the cream. Even if it might have had everything to do with Anne, or more than he'd ever admitted. "This has nothing to do with Anne."

Lois began mopping up the spill with her napkin. "Oh, Jack, feel whatever you want and say whatever you want," while she made long, quick swipes with her hand. "I suppose I'm just trying to protect you, and I'm only being insensitive."

He walked over to the window and turned his back to her. His legs were trembling again and he didn't want her to see it.

She said, "It sounds like a bunch of psychobabble, I know," in a tone that wasn't mother love and probably wasn't meant to be, "but I just don't want you to implode."

"I want my boy back." Jack said this simply, calmly, but he had the impulse to put his fist through the window, or grab the coffeepot and smash it, just to hear the crash and watch the flying glass and the stream of black coffee streak the yellow walls. That would stop the threat of implosion. "I'm a mess."

"You're allowed to be a mess."

"I'm sorry I shouted at you." He turned around to face her.

"You're also allowed to shout."

Jack folded his arms across his chest and breathed deeply. "I don't know what I'm going to do."

"There'll be time for that."

"I trusted my instincts."

Lois nodded her head.

"I was *sure* I knew what I was doing. It was all working out. But I was just lucky for a while, that's all." His body heaved. "I let him die."

"I don't think you're in any shape to make that judgment." She walked over to him and took his hands in hers. "Listen to me," she whispered. "You brought him to the safest place you knew, and created a charmed world for him with interesting people, stimulating people. You took him to exciting places. You made him the center of your universe, and his." She waited a moment, as though she were making sure her student was paying attention. "You gave up your life for him."

Jack said he didn't want to argue the merits of her case or his sorrow. He said he was tired of talking.

Lois turned her eyes away self-consciously, or self-consciously for her, just for a moment. When she looked at him, she said, "You were a good father. That's all I'm trying to say."

"Not good enough."

They were in the living room when the phone rang. Lois asked, "Do you want me to get it?"

Jack shook his head and got up.

It was Eileen, calling because she was a good student assistant, an efficient student assistant. She'd found the office door unlocked and Jack's briefcase open and the VCR still on. She wanted to know if everything was all right.

"I've had a little trouble. I'll be in later." Jack turned to Lois and raised his eyebrows hopelessly while he told Eileen, "The senior grades have to be in today, my student list for the fall semester needs to be downloaded and brought to—"

Eileen reminded him that she knew the drill. "Are you sure you're all right?"

"I'm fine."

"Do you need anything?"

"I'm fine."

"I'll check in on you later."

"Fine. Everything's fine." Jack hung up the phone and walked to the kitchen, forgot why he'd gone there and walked out. On his way back to the living room he stopped to look at the photographs of Danny. There was the one from the day they brought Mutt home from the shelter. Danny had just turned six. "The two puppies," Jack had called them. Danny held the palm of his hand under Mutt's jaw, lifting the puppy's head. The sun reflected in their eyes, the little boy and his puppy squinted and smiled in perpetuity for the camera.

There was the photograph taken last April, when they went to St. John, when they packed the Jeep with snorkel gear, a few bottles of water, some sandwiches and cookies, and drove the dirt roads.

Danny had liked that photograph of himself and Jack had liked seeing it hanging on the wall. He'd liked knowing that on that afternoon in the Caribbean, Danny was able to, felt compelled to, look up at the camera, smile and say it was one of the best days of his life. Danny must have liked knowing that, too. Now Jack couldn't bear to look at the photograph, or any of them. He walked quickly back to the living room.

"It's so arbitrary," he said to Lois, "isn't it."

Lois looked at him over the top of her glasses. "What is?"

"Danny—what happened to Danny. Just like that"—he snapped his fingers—"life gets turned on its head." He sat on the couch across from her. "It isn't that I thought it couldn't—something, some *thing* could always go wrong. It isn't that I thought just because Anne did what she did, that from there on out Danny and I were exempt, that he'd had his share and the rest was a skate. I knew it could all fall apart again, or else what the hell was all of this about?" He waved his hand in the air. "The photographs. The videos. The vacations. Gilbert. The whole goddamned structure."

"I don't think I know what you're talking about."

"This," he said, making a circle in the air with his finger. "What you called giving up my life for Danny. It was all part of the deal."

"Deal?"

"I made this deal with myself. If I do this, then something bad won't happen, or something good *will*. Now it sounds so childish," he said derisively. "If I'm good, I'll go to heaven. But I really thought if I was a good Dr. Owens, nothing bad would happen to Danny. It's a neurotic tic, that's all. It made me think I had some control, but I didn't. All it was was a sucker bet. I thought if I put Danny ahead of everything else, then he would be all right. If I was the good father and did my best, made my little sacrifices, everything would turn out fine." He leaned back but couldn't get comfortable, rested his hip against the arm of the couch, which was a little better, and said softly, "And it seemed to be working." He ran his hand across his eyes. "I remember I got pretty pissed off at him one time because he bitched about my cooking. I was still trying to prove to myself, to him, really, that we could be a normal family without Anne. I decided to cook all our meals. I was *fanatical* about it. So, I made beef Wellington for the two of us. Ever try to make beef Wellington? Danny took one bite and spit it back on his plate. He said cooking was something only mothers could do. I was angry. I was hurt. Most of all, I was disappointed in myself, but also in him for being less than generous. I told him fathers made just as good cooks as mothers. I knew what he was really talking about. But I told him, 'I slaved all day in the kitchen, and all you can do is treat it like garbage?' I was playing Felix Unger to his Oscar Madison. Danny was all of six but it wasn't lost on him. He got it. He always got it. We both cracked up." For a moment Jack was back in the kitchen with the little boy in the green T-shirt, feet kicking back and forth against the chair, he was laughing so hard. "It did taste pretty awful. Danny made me promise to experiment only on myself. It became a joke between us. Whenever we screwed anything up, we'd say, 'Uh-oh. Beef Wellington.' The kicker is, I didn't even like beef Wellington."

"Then why did you make it?"

"Anne was a fantastic cook and I suppose I was trying to conquer her in some symbolic way, to best her. Trying to overcome her power to make Danny and me sad. Trying to take control. Not long after that, I hired an au pair for Danny and I made sure she could cook the things he liked to eat. Yeah, I thought I had it under control. But it was just beef Wellington." He propped his feet on the coffee table and closed his eyes. "The last time I saw Anne was in the loft on Crosby Street. She had a shopping bag with I-don't-know-what in it. She knelt down to give Danny a hug and tell him that Mommy, *Mummy*, would always love him." The words came out before he could consider them, as though his mind had suddenly jumped a synapse between thought and speech—he didn't allow himself to think about Anne very often. Not about the Anne who had walked out of Danny's life. That was part of the deal.

What he felt now was very unsettling, as though he were betraying Danny, which is what he told Lois. She said it was good for him to talk about Anne. She asked, "Did she say anything else to him, besides she'd always love him?"

"No. Danny asked if he could see her tomorrow, and she hugged him and pressed the top of his head against her lips and kissed him, that's all. When she left, Danny and I watched her from the window. She was wearing her orange cape. She looked so small, like the fade-out in a movie, as though she were already a memory. When I turned around, Danny was sitting on the floor playing with a button, an orange button that had come off Anne's cape. He might have pulled it off, I don't know. That night, when I tucked him in, he asked me if Anne was mad at him. Had she stopped loving him. He asked the same question for months: Why was his mother mad at him? Why didn't she love him anymore?"

"What did you tell him?"

"I told him the truth. I think at first, he fantasized about her coming back, then he seemed to place her outside of his life. For years, when he talked about the way he thought things might have been, he'd say, 'If she were still my mother.' " Jack smiled but it was not a pleasant smile. "If she were *still* his mother. He never talked about her to anyone else but me, as far as I could tell. Maybe to my father once or twice, and my mother. He never talked about her to his friends. Then about two years ago he stopped talking about her entirely."

"How did he imagine things would be?"

"Pretty much the way they were. He seemed to think she would be a female version of me, except he'd be able to con her a little more. Just like that, she was gone. It seemed so simple as to be ridiculous."

"How long did he keep the button?"

"He slept with it under his pillow until we moved here, then I never saw it again."

Jack closed his eyes, and when he opened them again it was after one-thirty. It hadn't been a restful sleep but it was dreamless, and for that he was grateful.

Lois was still in the chair across from the couch, reading a magazine. "I can make you lunch if you like," she offered.

"I can't eat." Jack picked up the phone. He called Detective Hopewell. "Can I come get my son now?"

Hopewell told him, "I'm sorry, Dr. Owens, but the medical examiner's been delayed over in Terre Haute. He can't say for sure when he'll be done. But I found something in your son's personal effects. When you're feeling up to it, I'd like you to come by and take a look at it. It might shed some light on things."

VI

The office was small. There was buzzing from dim fluorescent lights, and even with the windows open it was hot and the air smelled stale. Hopewell sat behind a gray metal desk stacked with manila folders. His jacket was off, his shirt was open at the collar and his sleeves were rolled up above his elbows. He said hello to Jack, lifted his chin toward Lois and asked if she was "Mrs. Owens."

"She's my friend. Lois Sheridan, Detective Hopewell."

Hopewell answered, "I know this isn't the kind of thing you want to be doing, Dr. Owens," speaking in the same flat tone he had yesterday. He pointed to the pair of wooden chairs next to the desk and said, "Please. Sit down." He took a piece of paper out of one of the folders. "I found something in Danny's back pocket. This is a Xerox. Some of it's missing. I don't know how much." He pointed to the shadow of the jagged corner. "It looks like a poem." He handed the paper to Jack.

"Why didn't you call me when you found it?"

"I'm sorry about that," and again Hopewell said he knew this wasn't the kind of thing Jack wanted to be doing. He wasn't any more convincing than before. "I need to make sure your son wrote this." The detective tapped his finger on the paper. "Can you confirm it's Danny's handwriting?"

"I'd be more certain if I could see the original."

"I'm afraid I can't do that. It's evidence in an ongoing investigation and I've got to keep it on file until I make a final determination. I'm sorry about that, but it's the way we have to do things around here. I've got to follow procedure."

"I can't even *see* it?"

Hopewell rubbed his eyes with the heels of his hands, took the Xerox from Jack, then reached into one of the folders and pushed the creased and torn original across the desk.

. . . crossing the line.
He cries a silent cry.
In the night he feels
alone. There is no
mother or father, no one
to tuck him in, to say good night.
No friends come to play.
It is so very co

"Can you identify it?" Hopewell asked.

"It's Danny's handwriting." Jack held on to the paper, which Danny's hand had held, like the yellow and green pot holders in the first grade that he was so proud of and which he brought home for Jack to hang in the kitchen; the ceramic ashtrays from arts and crafts class that Jack kept in his office. And this scrap of paper that Danny had placed in his back pocket—did he forget it was there? If it meant anything, he would have left it in the house for Jack to see. Surely, it was never intended for—

Hopewell leaned across the desk, crushing the folders in front of him, and tried to take the paper away from Jack. Jack pulled away.

"Dr. Owens."

Jack didn't move.

"Dr. Owens."

Jack didn't answer.

"Dr. Owens."

Jack didn't look at him. He looked only at the piece of paper in his hands.

"The poem, Dr. Owens. Please."

Jack held on to it, reading the words Danny had written, then he just stared at them, at the shapes of each letter, the curves and lines, the simple and clear penmanship.

"The poem. Please, Dr. Owens. I can let you have the copy, but I need the original."

Jack held on to the poem a moment longer, then handed it to the detective.

Hopewell pushed the copy across the desk and dropped back into his chair. "Did he write other things like this?" He opened the folder and put Danny's poem inside.

Jack answered no, Danny had never written anything like that before. Not that he knew of.

"It sounds like he was feeling depressed." He began filling out an official-looking form. "Did he suffer from depression, Dr. Owens?"

"No. What are you writing?"

"It's my report. I have to write one up for every case I'm working on."

"Case?"

"Only in the technical sense," Hopewell explained, without looking up. "So he never wrote about being depressed and you're sure he didn't suffer from depression?"

"I'd know if my son were suffering from depression."

"Was he acting out at home or in school?" The detective still hadn't stopped writing. "Did his teachers ever call your attention to anything like that? Did he ever act depressed in school?"

"Of course not."

"Was he on any special medication or suffering from any medical or psychological problems?"

"No."

Hopewell answered "Hmm" in a way that made Jack think the detective didn't believe him, as though Jack were hiding something, and when he asked, "Is there anything you might have overlooked?" he might as well have said: "Nevertheless, Dr. Owens, your son did kill himself. There has to be a reason."

But Jack had nothing more to say.

Telephones rang outside the office, there was the sound of voices and footsteps. Hopewell's phone rang, and while he spoke low, monosyllabic answers, he continued writing. When he hung up, he took a deep breath and exhaled a prolonged, labored sigh. "How old was Danny?"

"Fifteen—he turned fifteen last month."

"His date of birth?"

"April fifth, nineteen eighty-one."

"Where did he go to school?"

"John L. Lewis High School."

"Ninth grade?"

"That's right."

Hopewell then asked for Jack's full name and date of birth, and the name and date of birth of Danny's mother.

"Danny's mother and I are divorced," Jack told him.

"I still need her name. Date of birth, if possible." Hopewell had that same look on his face that Jack had found so disturbing yesterday, and the same disturbing tone of voice. Jack looked over at Lois to see if she noticed it, but she wasn't looking at Jack, she was watching Hopewell. "I know none of this is very pleasant"—the detective kept his head down, kept to his work—"but this *is* a police matter and there's a certain protocol we have to follow, that you have to follow, the same as I do."

Jack gave him what he wanted.

Hopewell asked, "How long have you been employed by the college?"

"Ten years."

"Since, what, eighty-six?"

"That's right."

"Are you on any special medication? Suffer from any medical or psychological problems?" The way Hopewell said this made Jack feel like he wasn't there, except as a source of information, part of the protocol that the detective was obliged to respect, and if Jack were to suddenly disappear, if he'd been able to produce a stand-in, Hopewell would not have cared, so long as his report was completed, the procedure followed.

"You still have my son. I want him out of there."

"The medical examiner should get here sometime tomorrow. The day after at the very latest." When Hopewell raised his eyes, it was only to glance at his watch, then he continued writing.

"I want him out of the morgue *now*." Jack made no attempt to hide his anger. But it wasn't only anger that he felt, it was also shame. Danny's shame that Hopewell had set his eyes on the scrap of paper and that Danny was now under the detective's scrutiny, that he was a *case*. He felt shame for the questions Hopewell had asked about Danny, about his presumptions.

"I can appreciate what you're going through. I'll do all I can," Hopewell said. "Until then, I think the best thing to do is for you to go home. I'll let you know when the medical examiner is finished. Come on, Dr. Owens. Ms. Sheridan." He came around the desk, put his hand on Jack's arm and gave him a slight push. "You'll get your son. Just give it time."

Three girls in school uniforms walked down Oak Street, talking and laughing. When they came to the corner, they crossed quickly against the light. Lois sat behind the wheel of her car and let them pass. She turned to Jack. "What are you going to do about Anne?"

"What *can* I do?" Which was enough of an answer, because Lois knew the story. That Anne had left no forwarding address. That Danny's birthdays had passed, and the Christmases, without a call from her, without a card. Danny's expectations the first few years, and his disappointment. Jack had even tried to track Anne down, just to tell her off. But he never did find her.

Then Jack stopped thinking about Anne, and only thought about Danny, that Hopewell had besmirched Danny's life and death, turned Danny's suicide into something to be written up and filed away, an unimportant formality. He was thinking that he'd left Danny unprotected.

The car moved away from the corner.

Jack said, "I can't go back to the house. Take me to my office."

"I don't know about that."

"I'll go crazy if I go home."

"But you'll call me when you're ready to leave so I can drive you home?"

"I'll call you."

Jack wanted to sit in his office because time was still normal there and nothing had changed. The phone would ring at any minute and it would be Danny calling. The door would open and it would be Danny standing there. It was the place where Jack had left his future. The place that time forgot. Where Eileen was waiting for instructions. Where ignorance was bliss.

"Did you get the senior grades in?"

"Just under budget," Eileen told him, borrowing one of his pet phrases, and she smiled because she was still living in the time where Danny Owens was alive with a father who taught at Gilbert College, and the past was solid and the future assured. Jack could not readily disturb that, and he waited, allowing the minute to stretch out, languidly, like the last days of the semester.

He waited a minute longer, while he walked to the photograph of Danny, where it was always a bright and hope-filled summer day. He touched the face in the frame and held his hand there. He looked out the window at the progress of students crossing the quadrangle, and at the corner of sky that reflected back at him. He walked across the room and made sure the door was firmly closed. He waited, not because he believed there still existed some remnant of the day before, but because nothing remained of that day and he wanted to allow Eileen, allow himself, a final moment with it.

Then he said, "Danny killed himself yesterday. Post a notice that all nonsenior grades have been delayed indefinitely."

Eileen looked down at the floor and said nothing. She was a twenty-one-year-old small-town girl. The only bad news she knew about were failing grades and boring dates, the teacup crises that roommates bring with them, or days when it rained too hard to go swimming, or snowed too hard to drive to the movies. The only people who died were aged relatives, finally and mercifully. She did not know what to say. She only put her hands over her face and stood motionless.

Jack put an arm around her and led her to the couch. He sat her down. She wept into his shirt. He could only let her cry. He rocked her carefully in his arms. He dried her tears with his sleeve. When the telephone rang, she moved to answer it. Jack told her to let it be. She sniffled and put her head on his shoulder and clutched his arm. She cried and cried.

Jack sat with her a little while longer before he said, "I have things to take care of. I have to tell Stan." Only he didn't get up right away. He was in no hurry to tell the story to his department chair—each telling only making Danny's death more real, more permanent—standing at the desk, facing questions that needed to be asked, and questions left unspoken: "How could you let this happen, Jack? How did you miss it?" Trying to squeeze out an explanation.

But Stan Miller was away from his desk, and Jack, gratefully, left a note, explaining only what was necessary. All he wanted now was to get out of there and be left alone.

He was hot, his mouth was dry, his shirt and the skin beneath it were damp with Eileen's tears. He needed to sit by himself and think about Danny, to feel close to him. He needed to feel his grief, unmediated and uncontested. He did not need further conversation or company or commiseration; and he did not need Carl Ainsley, poised in the hallway.

"If it isn't our very own Bob Cratchett," Ainsley sang out.

Jack didn't reply. He tried to walk around him.

"Wait a minute. I think you ought to know, I was a very naughty boy." Ainsley laughed softly. "Oh, don't worry, it wasn't with Miss Mouth. However, one of our esteemed col—"

"Not now."

"Not even a reprimand?" Ainsley grabbed Jack by the shoulder.

Jack shrugged off Ainsley's hand. "I'm having a really bad day." He tried to sidestep him a second time.

Ainsley followed him down the hall. "It's those long hours, Owens."

"Sure."

"Then what about it? What the hell. We'll go on over to Chase's—"

"Not now."

"Come on. Where's the famous Owens *joie de vivre*?"

"Not—"

"It's cocktail time, somewhere in the world." Ainsley put his hand on Jack's arm and held him back. "You can even scold me for the *roué* that you think I am. Come on. One hour, more or less, isn't going to make a hell of a lot of difference whether or not you and Danny—"

Introspection is not part of the primitive mind, and when Jack snatched Ainsley by the front of his blue cotton shirt and slammed him against the wall, it was purely primitive.

He was surprised that Ainsley didn't resist. Maybe he thought it was a joke; more than likely, though, he couldn't believe what was happening. But when Jack slammed him a second time, Ainsley grunted, "I'm only having sport with you," and pulled himself free.

Jack went at him again, but Ainsley pushed him back and held him at arm's length. Jack grabbed him by the elbows and swung him around.

"What's the matter with you?" Ainsley cried out, and shoved Jack away. "Cut it out."

Jack came at him quickly this time, catching him low and knocking him off-balance.

"Cut it *out*."

Jack slammed him against the wall a third time. Ainsley's head snapped back, his mouth clamped shut.

If nothing else in these most unfair twenty-four hours was unfair, it was the fact that Ainsley, who had the conscience of a cat burglar, would go home to his son, who was still alive, to a wife who accepted him on his own terms—chilled martini in the shaker, kiss on the mouth—and life would be as it always was. Impulsive and predatory, Ainsley had a son who didn't ride his bike to the park and tie a plastic bag around his head. Ainsley, himself a son of Nature's indifference, did not have to go to the morgue and identify the body. He did not have to wait for the medical examiner to perform an autopsy on his boy. His son wasn't lying on a slab, dead and cold in the dark. For all that, Jack slammed him again, or tried to, but Ainsley pressed a muscled arm under Jack's chin and shoved him to the opposite wall.

"What did I say?" Ainsley cried out. "What the *hell* is your *problem*?"

The problem was, Jack couldn't beat up Hopewell for being an unsympathetic, disingenuous functionary. He couldn't beat up on the medical examiner for dragging his ass in Terre Haute, but he could try to beat up on Ainsley because the unfortunate son of a bitch happened to be standing there. But Jack didn't say that. He didn't say anything. He straightened up and walked quickly down the hall. He did not dare look back. He was disgusted with himself, and afraid of what he might do next.

Eileen was standing in the doorway when Jack got back to his office. She said, "Maybe you should go home. Please, Jack. I'm worried about you."

"I'll be all right."

"Then I'll stay with you."

"There's nothing you can do here. Please. I need to be alone now. Really."

She didn't move. "You'll call me if you need anything?"

He nodded his head.

"You're sure I can't—"

"I'll be all right. Lois is coming by in a little while."

She hugged him. "I'll be around until commencement . . ."

"I'll call."

Jack sat with the picture of Danny tacking into the wind, and with the slim vestiges of a morning in late spring when his life was whole and seemed part of a wonderful continuum, when he could reach inside himself whenever he needed to and feel the place where he and Danny were together.

He walked across the quadrangle carrying his briefcase and the work he'd left undone. He walked west through the daguerreotype streets feeling the heat of the sun on the back of his neck. He felt sorry for what he had done to Ainsley. He felt sorry for Ainsley, who was probably up in his office right now, talking on the phone to his wife and friends, licking his wounds, trying to make sense of what Jack had done to him.

He walked west, past the White Brick bakery and Laine Bros. department store, the Palomino Grille, where the old-timers sat in the smoky dark and retreated into the comfortable past. He stayed clear of the courthouse lawn, the police station and the morgue, the way a kid avoids the graveyard, even in the daylight, crossed South Third Street and, a block later, the railroad tracks, and didn't stop until he came to the nameless bridge that overlooked the Wabash.

He leaned against the old corroded railing and stared at the river, to the place where it disappeared beyond the sycamores that bent over the muddy banks, to the vanishing point, where a reverse pointillism occurred: objects dissolved back into dots. He stared at the vanishing point and wondered what he was going to do now that Danny was dead. He stared at the vanishing point as though the future were waiting around the bend and if he looked hard enough and wanted it strongly enough, he could summon it. And what if the future extended its hand, natant and roseate, and carried him away? Would it matter if he knew what was waiting for him tomorrow or the next day? Would it matter if he saw the rest of his life stretched out before him? He thought he knew all of that when he woke up yesterday morning. He thought he owned a little corner of the future. The trips to Cape Cod and New York. The fishing vacations in Nova Scotia. Classes taught, lessons learned, while his son grew into a man. It was a foregone conclusion, his reservations confirmed. But inside his pocket was a poem that wasn't part of the plan. The funeral in New York was not on the original itinerary.

Jack watched the river carry the flotsam and debris on its way to meet the Ohio, taking whatever fell in its path, leaving behind whatever dropped away, endlessly unraveling, like time itself. And what was he going to do, he wondered, with all of his time?

The old girders creaked and swayed under the weight of the afternoon traffic. Jack kept staring into the distance. And even if the future is never generous enough to make itself known, Jack stared anyway, before he picked up his briefcase and walked off the bridge and along South Third Street to Fairmont Park and the ruins.

He sat against the pitted brick near the spot where Danny had died. It made him feel close to his son, like visiting a cemetery. He reached into his pocket:

. . . crossing the line.
He cries a silent cry.
In the night he feels
alone. There is no
mother or father, no one
to tuck him in, to say good night.
No friends come to play.
It is so very co

Jack pulled his legs up to this chest and rested his chin in his knees. He thought about Danny, not the boy who came here to kill himself, but Danny, eight years old, pushing his breakfast around on his plate.

"What happened to your appetite?" Jack wanted to know.

"I ate too much last night."

"Let me guess. You talked Rosalie into ordering Mexican."

"I didn't talk her into it."

"Not *José Sent Me*."

"She said it was okay."

Jack smiled and began tapping the rhythm on the kitchen table. Danny smiled back at him, recognizing what was about to happen.

Jack started if off: "The burritos are lethal and those beans are . . ."

"Mean."

"Mean beans."

"Mean beans."

"You can serve me Doritos, Cheetos . . ."

"Or Fritos. But not the beans."

Jack laughed. "Those beans are mean."

"Those beans are mean."

"They'll empty you clean . . ."

"Down to your spleen."

"Take the tacos with cheese-o . . ."

"If you please-o . . ."

"Or try the meat-o . . ."

"But not the burrito . . ."

"Those beans are mean . . ."

"They'll turn you green."

They laughed together.

Jack said, "We haven't lost a thing."

Danny rolled his eyes. "I know, and it made my stomach ache even *worse*."

"No one likes an eight-year-old wise guy." Jack clipped Danny lightly on the chin. "How'd you like to loaf a little longer and I'll drive you to school?"

"I'd like to loaf all day and not go to school."

"Dream on, pardner. You can have fifteen minutes with your dad or you can ride the bus. Take it or leave it."

"I'll take it." Danny still didn't eat, but now he had that serious and solemn expression on his face. There was something on his mind and he couldn't get started.

"What is it?" Jack said.

Danny shrugged his shoulders.

"You can tell me. Is it school?"

Danny shook his head. "I wrote something."

"Really?"

"About my friend Eric."

"I'd like to hear it."

"It's really dumb."

"It can't be dumb if you wrote it."

Danny thought this over and said, "Okay. But don't laugh."

"I promise."

Danny took a piece of lined paper out of his notebook, stood up, cleared his throat and looked around the room, as though he were waiting for late arrivals to be seated. "My friend Eric is eight and he's my friend to the end. A friend to the end means you understand things the other kids don't. A lot of the other boys make fun of Eric because he's not very good at sports. They don't let him hang out with them. But Eric is very smart and funny. Last week, Eric had a birthday. When some of the bigger kids in my class found out I was going they said I was a weenie and they would beat me up if I went. They pushed me around after school all week but they didn't really hurt me. Eric told them if they wanted to pick on anyone to pick on him because he was bigger than me. They just spitted at him and they kept calling us weenies and stuff. I was the only kid in our class who went to Eric's birthday party. But his cousins and some relatives went so it wasn't so bad. When I have a birthday I know Eric will be there."

Danny folded the paper and put it back in his book. He wouldn't look at his father.

"Come over here," Jack said.

Danny walked around the table. Jack put his arms around him and kissed him on the cheek.

"That was a very kind thing, being Eric's friend. And that's a very beautifully written story." Jack hugged him tighter. Danny hugged him back.

"Why didn't you tell me about the other kids picking on you?"

"I don't know." Danny shrugged his shoulders.

"Were you ashamed to tell me?"

"I don't know."

"You must have felt *some*thing," Jack said, keeping his voice soft, not stern or scolding.

"I guess I was afraid."

"Of?"

"You'd think I was a weenie because I didn't fight them."

Jack smiled at him. "*They're* the weenies. *They're* the cowards. It took a lot of courage to do what you did. What did I tell you about thinking for yourself?"

"Only sheep follow the herd. Smart people think for themselves and do the right thing."

"Give me a kiss," Jack said. "I'm very proud of you. But more important, you should be very proud of yourself."

Danny let Jack hold him for a moment longer before he tried to squirm free but Jack held on to him a little bit longer than that.

He asked Danny, "May I have it?"

"Why?"

"Because I like to keep the things you write. And because it's very beautiful."

Danny gave this some thought before he consented.

Later, driving to school with the top down, a tape playing, Danny, strapped securely in the front seat, tilted his head back to watch the sky skip by. "Dad, if you were going to do something that you didn't think I'd like, would you still tell me? Before you did it?"

"Of course. I don't make important decisions without first discussing them with you."

"'Cause my friend Gregory is moving to Indianapolis and we'll probably stop being friends and he's real unhappy."

"I thought he was looking forward to moving there."

"He's thinking of running away and hiding."

"I think he's shooting without a script."

Danny didn't think that was funny. "Gregory says his dad wouldn't have taken the job except his new mom wanted him to."

"It's not at all like that," Jack explained. "They would have moved whether or not his father remarried. His father got a better job in Indianapolis."

"Gregory says if his dad didn't get married they wouldn't be moving," Danny insisted. "You're not going to get married and make us move away from here, are you?"

Out of the corner of his eye, Jack saw Danny sit up straight. "Do you want me to?"

"No. But Granpa married Grace after Granma Martha died."

"That's right."

"And Gregory's dad got married again."

"That doesn't mean *I* will. Not without clearing it with you."

"Really?"

"Really."

"What if I don't like her and you still wanted to marry her?"

"I don't think I could like someone you didn't like. Doesn't Gregory like his new mother?"

"He says *she* doesn't like him *or* Chris."

"I wouldn't worry about that happening."

"Don't you want to?" Danny asked.

"Get married? I don't really give it much thought. I like the way things are."

"Me too." Danny went back to watching the sky.

Eric dropped out of Danny's life after the third grade, and Gregory moved away, but Danny made new friends: C.J. Ainsley, brooding and melancholy, the opposite of his buff and gregarious father; Rick Harrison, gangly and restless; Brian Clarke, their leader and protector. And it wasn't long before the four boys became an inseparable quartet. They all joined the Scouts at the same time, and Little League. Only ten days ago, the boys came to the house to cheer Danny up after he lost the semifinals. So how the hell could Danny have killed himself?

Was there something lacking in Danny? Jack wondered. Some flaw masked by the equanimity? Was there something there all the time that stood out and said: "Your son is different from the other boys." That said, "This is why Danny couldn't bear to live," only Jack never knew what he was seeing?

Jack sat in the shadow of the ruins and looked out across the river where the sorry little tarpaper shacks were sunk into the lush soil, where the stink of boiled cabbage and sour diapers hung in the air and carried across the river along with the stink of failure, the culture of failure, a door opened and a yellow light spread across the black ground like an apology. It was just before sunset and behind dimly lighted windows there were halting shadows, which were people and their lives. Someone spoke unrecognizable words that sounded tenderly human and so sad Jack had to get up and leave.

He walked down Chestnut Street, the clean sidewalks edging up to the evenly cut grass. Where the white-shingled houses of Gilbert's middle class sat, with their small gardens in the back with trellises and spring vines. He stopped to watch the quick shadows behind the curtained windows, listen to muffled voices, pick out a word, a sentence. He could not take himself away from this street, from the neat hedges, the comfortable chant of the lawn sprinklers, the unceasing movement. He could not take himself away from the fathers and sons.

He pressed his nose against other people's lives and envied them in a way he would have found unthinkable, unnecessary, twenty-four hours ago. Now he would be any one of them, if only for a day; if only to anticipate the sound of the screen door slamming, the footsteps on the stairs, the sounds that tell you all is well. He wished he could walk up one of the trim little paths, knock on the front door and say, "I'm Dr. Owens, let me sit with you awhile." "Let me tell you about my son." "Let me tell you who he was." He wished he could invite himself inside and be part of someone else's family, someone else's story. But all he could do was stand apart, alone in the shadows of the oak trees, and listen to the hiss of the street lamps, watch front doors open and people he did not know walk down the sidewalk, skateboard over the curb, drive cars. All he could do was want what was happening inside those houses and feel the absence of all that had been his just the day before, as though the strength of his desire, the power of his envy, might alter this irremediable night.

Then he was walking again, where the town met the edge of soy fields and alfalfa was beginning to show through the soil. Where the sun was setting and the air grew dense with carbon dioxide, and the scent of spring crops and fertile earth spiraled up from the ground, spanning the darkness like a veil. He was going home.

There were messages waiting for him. Lois, Eileen, a couple of Danny's friends asking Danny why he wasn't in school. Bob Garvin, calling from South Wellfleet: "Getting things ready for you guys." Yoshi in Maine: "Nick and the boys can't wait." Clive Ebersol, calling from Canada to talk about the fishing trip.

There was so much to undo. So much summer to cancel.

Jack made the calls to Canada and Maine, Massachusetts and Connecticut; to airlines and inns. To people he'd known for most of a lifetime, who asked for no explanations and gave their sympathy. To strangers with nothing to give but their indifference and inconvenience. By the time Jack fell asleep on the couch, there was still more summer to cancel, more summer to undo.

He awoke with the morning sun shining in his eyes and the telephone ringing on the floor. It was Detective Hopewell: "The coroner turned in his report, Dr. Owens. It was death by asphyxiation. Thanks for your patience." And Jack remembered everything.

"When can I get him out of there?"

"Anytime."

"Did they have to . . ."

"Think of it like surgery," Hopewell answered in the detached voice. "So we can be certain about the time of death and the cause. I'm sorry about the delay."

Jack hung up the phone and screamed, "Goddamnit." He sat on the edge of the couch, breathing heavily through his mouth.

For the rest of the morning, Jack listened numbly to improbable conversations studded with the words *arranged* and *arrangements.* He felt as though he were standing outside of himself when he called the morgue: "You'll have to make arrangements with a licensed funeral home, Dr. Owens . . ." When he called his father: "Harry Weber's made all the arrangements. The Collier Funeral Home in Gilbert is going to fly Danny to New York tomorrow. You don't have to do a thing. It's all been arranged . . ." When Jack called Lois to ask her to go to New York with him tonight, she told him she'd arrange everything. Stan Miller said he'd already arranged for Jack's grades to be postponed. His friends asked if they could help with any of the arrangements. And later, sitting in the living room with Mr. Collier of the eponymous funeral home, Jack was told that all arrangements had been made.

Collier was a man of hushed and muted tones, earnest and controlled, from his deep blue suit and dark maroon tie to the modulated timbre in his voice, inoffensive, restrained and solicitous. A compelling presence, inviting a painless passivity while he "arranged everything."

Surely there was some comfort to be taken, surely that's what Collier thought he was offering, what everyone thought they were offering. But what was being arranged? Danny was dead. He was lying alone and cold on a slab in the morgue and Jack had to get him out. But there was no urgency in Collier's voice, and this was so very urgent. There were only good manners, funereal decorum. It was just another procedure, like Hopewell's investigation, the coroner's autopsy. Just another job to do and be done with. But nothing was getting done.

"I want Danny out of the morgue," Jack insisted.

"It's all arranged," Collier said, his voice calm, unctuous, annoying.

"I don't think you understand."

"We understand fully."

"Not if you're sitting around making *arrangements*. I want my son—"

"Your son," Collier said gently, "has been resting in our home"—he looked at his watch—"since eleven-fifteen this morning. I'll call my office right now for a confirmation." He reached for his cell phone. "Yes," Collier told Jack, and placed the phone back in his pocket, "Danny is in our care." He made a satisfied adjustment to his tie.

In our care . . .

"Be assured, Dr. Owens, your mother's in our care."

She had been sick a long time. There'd been time to prepare. Time to explain.

"Is Granma going to die?" Danny asked.

"She died today."

"Is Granpa sad?"

"Very sad."

"Are you very sad, Daddy?"

"Yes, I'm very sad."

"I'm very sad, too. Does she hurt?"

"Not anymore."

"Cousin Philip said I'll never see Granma again."

"That's right."

"Where did she go, Daddy? In the ground?"

"Try to think that Granma's gone on a journey far away, for a long time."

"Like Mummy?" Danny asked. "Mummy's gone away for a long time."

"A different kind of going away. It's like Granma's taking a long rest. It's like sleeping in a very peaceful place. That's why people say 'rest in peace' when someone dies."

"Will I die when I go to sleep?" Danny asked.

"No. Little boys don't die in their sleep."

"Only old people, right?"

"That's right. Only old people."

At the funeral, large and splendid, relatives and friends, men who were made rich by Jack's father's inventions and who, in turn, had made Jack's father rich, stood three and four deep at the graveside and listened to the eulogies. Women whose homes and lives were made beautiful by Jack's mother's interiors, women whose committees his mother had chaired, whose societies his mother had joined, whose charities his mother had made more charitable, said their sad farewells before the coffin was lowered and the earth piled on.

Later, after the funeral, after they'd sat with relatives and friends, who talked and reminisced; after they sat with his father, who cried and reminisced, Jack and Danny sat alone in the guest room of his parents' apartment. Danny curled himself into Jack's lap and said, "It's like going away for a long time."

"That's right."

"Is there a God, Daddy?"

"Some people think there is."

"Do we?"

"What do you think?"

"I think God's in heaven, and Granma's in heaven with God. And she's having fun. Only sometimes she gets tired and has to rest." Danny looked at Jack expectantly.

"That's a very good thing to think."

"But she misses Granpa," Danny added, "and sometimes she cries."

"Dr. Owens," Collier said, with a delicate clearing of the throat, "one other thing. Is there any particular clothing you'd like Danny to wear, or shall I arrange—"

Jack sat in Danny's room, among the books and clothes. Mutt burrowed his nose into one of Danny's shirts. Jack held Danny's blue suit across his lap, cradling it as though it were the corporeal Danny, as though Danny might feel the embrace. Jack felt no need to rush. He was content to sit in the bedroom and run his hand back and forth across the jacket and pants, to touch the pair of shoes and socks, the white shirt, Danny's favorite regimental tie. It was the only comfort he could find, touching the clothes his son had worn. Jack was in no hurry to leave this room and move that much closer to Danny's burial. There was no urgency now. He would go to New York. There would be a funeral. It would happen soon enough—too soon by a lifetime. It had all been arranged.

It was the silence that was disturbing. Jack could not get used to it and he was unable to ignore it while he made a few arrangements of his own: he called the vet so Mutt could be boarded. Called Lois about the flight to New York—she would pick him up at four. While he packed his clothes, and later, while he sat on the back porch with a cup of coffee, doing nothing in the long afternoon, there was always the silence, the absence of Danny. Jack didn't know how to sit with it, how to wait with it, and when he heard the car pull up at the front of the house and the doorbell ring, he did not mind the interruption.

A man in a sport coat and tie was standing near the porch steps. He said his name was Corey Sanderson. He was a reporter for the *Gilbert Times-Chronicle*. He was writing a story about Danny's suicide.

VII

I'm very sorry about your son. I know the last thing you want to do is talk to a reporter." Sanderson looked to be in his early thirties. He stood perfectly straight, like a soldier, and cleared his throat three times before he spoke. He did it before he introduced himself, when he excused himself for being there, and again when he said, "Danny was the second boy who killed himself in the past week, and, unfortunately, that's news. At least in Gilbert it is."

"Second boy?"

"My editor—"

"Who was he? What's his name?" Jack wanted to ask where the boy lived and where he went to school. He wanted to ask if Danny had known him. But all he asked for was the name.

"I'm afraid I can't tell you. Not until the story's published. I'm sorry."

"Christ almighty," Jack breathed. "Can you tell me where it happened?"

"I can't tell you that, either." Sanderson said this apologetically, plaintively, and told Jack, "But it wasn't anywhere near the place where Danny—it was nowhere near the ruins." He shook his head and tugged awkwardly at his tie. Cleared his throat three times before he said, "I'm awfully sorry about this, Dr. Owens."

"How old was he? Danny's age?"

Sanderson shook his head again, but Jack wasn't sure if that meant the other boy wasn't Danny's age or that was another question Sanderson couldn't answer. "I know I'm being extremely insensitive." Sanderson took a step backward and leaned his hand against the porch railing. "This can't be anything you want to do, but my editor thinks it's important that I talk to you. Maybe we can . . ."

Jack wasn't listening, all he could do was think about this "other boy" and wonder if his suicide had anything to do with Danny. Which is what he said to Sanderson.

The reporter blinked his eyes a couple of times. "Well, to tell you the truth, I don't really know."

"Have you talked to the other family?"

Sanderson answered, "No," drawing out the word, adding an extra syllable. "I'm sorry if I seem coy, Dr. Owens, but I didn't know anything about this until I got to the office this morning. Not even about the other boy."

"Have you talked to Detective Hopewell?"

"A little while ago."

"Isn't that enough for your story?"

"It's enough for *me*. My editor, however, wants me to talk to everyone concerned. I was hoping to avoid some of that at least by talking to the woman who found your son. I just came from her house, as a matter of—"

"You know who she is?"

"That's right."

"He told you?"

"What?"

"Hopewell told you? Hopewell told you who she was?"

"I really can't—"

"You really *can't*— You spoke to her?"

"In a manner of speaking. I just came from there. She wouldn't talk to me until I spoke with you first. She said what happened to your son wasn't anyone's business but yours and she had nothing to tell me until I talked with you and you said it was okay if I spoke with her."

"But she was the woman who found Danny? You're sure of that?"

Sanderson said yes, she was the woman who found Danny.

Jack needed to see her. She was part of Danny's history now and she must have understood that and that was why she wouldn't talk to the reporter. At least that's what Jack wanted to believe. He needed to talk to her. There were questions he needed to ask her. She'd been standing in the wings waiting for him to find her. Maybe she understood that, too.

Sanderson was saying, "Look, I'm going to tell my editor that I came here, you didn't want to talk, and that's all there was to it. I'll say the same thing when I write my story. Okay?"

"Who is she, the woman who found Danny? Where does she live?"

It was not a very warm day but Sanderson was perspiring. "You're putting me in kind of a tough spot, Dr. Owens." He wiped his forehead with the back of his hand. "First of all, I don't know if she wants you to know that, and second, I still have to answer to my ed—"

"If I tell you what you want to know, enough to satisfy your editor, will you tell me who she is?"

Sanderson looked down at the porch floor, tugged uncomfortably on his tie. He cleared his throat the mandatory three times and told Jack, "This was a terrible idea. I'm really sorry." He turned and walked down the stairs, repeating, "A terrible idea, a terrible idea," all the way to his car, opened the door, started to slide onto the front seat, then he looked back at Jack and said, "Her name is Kim Connor. She lives at 517 North Seventh Street."

Three blocks from the railroad tracks on North Seventh Street the houses stood atop raised, ragged lawns, in pitiful need of care. These houses had been built in the 1880s for up-and-coming merchants, for the men who managed the coal mines and the railroad. Though never beautiful, the houses were functional two-story wood jobs with high ceilings and deep narrow rooms, wedding-cake molding along the walls, indoor plumbing, coal furnaces, ample windows and carriage houses in the back alley; a step up from the company houses that the miners lived in.

Over the years, the college had bought a few of the houses and used them for faculty residences and, later, faculty offices. A few remained in the original families that owned them, bequeathed from fathers to sons to grandsons, who, feeling the entrepreneurial urge, broke up the houses into small two- and three-room flats with some Sheetrock and linoleum, a dormer window in the attic, and rented them to students, or married couples, who worked at the department stores or supermarkets or one of the shifts at the factories. Time and the constant turnover of humanity had taken their toll. The houses now all needed fresh coats of paint and new screen doors. The lawns were neglected and bare.

The corner house, 517, was in no better shape than any of the others. The linoleum on the stairs was worn to the original wood. The hall was dark and smelled of last night's supper and this morning's burnt toast. More than a few babies cried behind the old wood doors.

Kim Connor lived behind one of the quieter doors, on the second floor. She didn't look much older than most of Jack's students. She was tall, with long auburn hair that hung straight past her shoulders, her body was strong and athletic, snugly tucked inside her jeans and blouse. She stood firmly, proprietarily, in the doorway, looked Jack over and said, "Yes?" without much enthusiasm.

"I'm Jack Owens. The father of the boy who killed himself in Fairmont Park."

It was the first time he'd identified both himself and Danny by Danny's suicide, and he could not stop the feeling of defeat, capitulation swelling within him, as though he'd made a wrong turn on a dark road and while he could not know where he was going neither could he turn back. It was a bottomless feeling, and his face must have shown the recognition of this, or the recognition of something, which was reflected in the look of sadness and sympathy on Kim Connor's face.

"I can't tell you how sorry I am," she said, "for what happened, Mr. Owens."

Jack nodded his head, he asked if he could talk with her for a little while.

She said, "Of course," and stepped back from the door.

It was a three-room apartment, the rooms built at odd, slapdash angles, with not a lot of sunlight. They had to walk through the kitchen, which was painted mint green, to get to the living room, which was a shade deeper than white. The floors were uneven and warped, thick with the paint of ages, and currently a lively carnation red. A heroic attempt had been made to breathe the comforts of home into the place, fresh flowers stood in a cut-glass vase, crisp white curtains fluttered across the living room windows. A lot of rose-colored fabric covered the thrift-shop chairs and couch, several framed photographs and art posters hung on the wall with no small amount of attention paid to symmetry. There were none of the cast-off bric-a-brac and junk-store throwaways that tend to accumulate in small spaces. The air had the sweet aroma of a potpourri.

Jack sat in one of the chairs, the cushions sagging under him. Kim Connor sat on the couch facing him. Jack thanked her for not talking to Sanderson.

"I believe a person should be allowed to keep his life private until he decides otherwise," she said, formally, the way her mother must have said it to her.

Jack had come here to ask questions, but until this moment he did not realize what those questions were, and, really, there was only one question to ask: Was Danny still alive when Kim Connor found him? If there was still breath remaining in him, had he used it to talk to her, to tell her what he had been unable to tell anyone else?

Jack spoke softly, as though he were trying to excuse himself for asking, for wanting to know. Kim Connor looked at him with the same expression she had when he'd stood outside the door. She said, "Do you know what I told the police?"

"Tell me," he answered, in that same excuse-me tone of voice.

"I usually go running in Fairmont Park in the morning with my husband," she said. "But we both worked double shifts the night before, so I didn't get out till late in the morning, and I let him sleep in. I was running in the direction of where your son was and I could see him lying there with the—you know, the bag over his head, so I ran flat out to get to him." She ground down on the words, sliding her jaw to the left and right. "By the time I got there he was already—he was lying on his side. Are you sure you want to hear this?"

Jack said he was sure.

Kim Connor waited another moment before she said, "I tore the bag off. He'd tied it really tight, so I just ripped it open. I tried to revive him with mouth-to-mouth and CPR. I'm studying to be a paramedic at ISU, over in Terre Haute, part-time, in case you're wondering if I knew what I was doing." She ground her jaw against these words as well. "I could tell that it happened only a little while before. His body was warm, his head and his hands. That's why I thought I could revive him."

Jack was thinking about Kim Connor touching Danny's skin. He wanted to know if she did it gently, or did she push his body around trying to get him in the right position? Did she hold his hands when she felt for body heat, was she careful not to hurt him, or did she just give them a rough squeeze? When she held his head did she cradle it in her hands? But that's not what he asked. He asked, "Was he still alive?"

She shook her head. "I tried to get him to breathe, for ten, fifteen minutes. Then I put his jacket over him. I didn't want to leave him alone but I had to walk over to a phone on Third Street and call 911. Then I went back and stayed with him until the police came with the paramedics."

"You didn't happen to see anything there? A note?"

"No, but I didn't do much looking around. I just sat and waited."

"You didn't do anything at all?"

"No. When the police got there, they made me sit in their car. All I could see was the back of the detective walking around your son while the paramedics tried to revive him, and the detective kind of looking through your son's pockets or whatever."

It disgusted Jack to think of Hopewell touching Danny, poking Danny's body with his fingers.

Kim Connor asked, "Are you sure you're going to be okay? Do you want a cold drink or something?"

"I'm all right. What else did the police do?"

"The detective came over to the car and asked how I happened to find him and if I knew him, and was it me who tore the bag off and how come I did it. He acted like I was lying to him and asked me a bunch of questions about did I always run in Fairmont Park and things like that.

He made me sit there until they took your son away. Then he drove me back to his office and made me tell it all over again into a tape recorder."

"I think Danny left a note behind and the detective has it."

"I couldn't see if he took anything or not. I was over in the car." Kim Connor pushed her hands through her hair, away from her face, framing the arc of her cheekbones. "I'm not the smartest person you'll ever want to meet, and I'm not very good at making sense of things, but when a thing like this happens, I don't mean what happened to your son, I mean the way people meet and their lives sort of, you know, cross paths, I believe it happens for a reason. Like God wanted me to be the one who found him. Like I'd know the right thing to do. Or else I can't see the logic to it." She looked straight at Jack, making strong eye contact with him, and smiled, not a self-satisfied smile, or a sympathetic smile, either, but a sorrowful smile, like a midwestern Madonna, then she looked at her watch. "I've got to get going. I work the afternoon shift over at the Kirby's on North Ninth. Now you know why I've gone back to school." She smiled again, but it was an entirely different smile now.

They went downstairs together and out to the sidewalk.

She said, "My heart goes out to you, Mr. Owens. I know I can't begin to imagine how sad you must feel."

Jack watched her walk to the corner—if she'd been running a little faster, if she'd left her house a few minutes earlier, she would have had time to resuscitate Danny. If she'd—it was ridiculous. It made as much sense as thinking God had sent her to Danny just to be five minutes late.

There was a moment when he would turn the corner of his street and the front porch came into view, the porch swing, the white railing, and Jack would see Danny and his friends sitting there, talking, teasing each other, joking, laughing, sometimes pushing each other around, wrestling on the floor, or throwing rocks at the crows in the field across the road. Today, only three boys appeared, like a mirage, sitting on the porch as they'd done hundreds of times before—their bikes leaning against the trees—as though at any second their friend would come bounding out of the house and they would all ride away.

They kept to the pecking order: Brian in the chair at the top of the semicircle, Rick, on one side of him, Danny's chair, empty now, on the other side, and C.J. No one was throwing rocks or pushing anyone around. There was no bantering, just some talking without much animation, until they saw the car pull up, then the boys sat silent and motionless.

They watched Jack walk up the porch steps, pull up a fifth chair and sit at the mouth of the arc.

Brian said, "We're going to miss Danny very much, Dr. Owens."

C.J. shook his head to let Jack know that he'd kept his word.

"Your parents told you," Jack said flatly.

"We're going to miss him," Rick repeated.

"He was great." Brian's eyes started to well up and he was having a difficult time holding back the tears. "We're very sad about it."

They were Danny's friends, who had sat on the porch on other afternoons like this, when the sun moved a little deeper toward the solstice, when the air wasn't quite summer but close enough. When they confessed their fears to each other, spoke their plans. But none of them could have planned on this. You can't be fifteen years old and be on the lookout for death.

Jack looked at their faces and he thought about Danny, who had been their arbitrator, their peacemaker, the swing vote, and he wondered what that told him that he didn't already know.

Brian looked at Jack but only for a moment, then he sat forward, rested his elbows on his knees and looked down at his hands. Rick looked over at Brian, then lowered his eyes and tugged at his shirtsleeves. C.J. stared at his backpack. No one moved. No one spoke.

It was disturbing to watch their sadness, their inability to make sense of Danny's death. They were waiting for an explanation. Waiting for Jack to tell them why Danny would want to kill himself. Jack could only say, "Maybe we can help each other understand it a little better."

Brian said, "That's what we've been trying to do, Dr. Owens. Believe me, we've been trying, but we don't know why."

"It's not an easy thing to understand, is it?"

Rick said no it wasn't and repeated Brian's "We've been trying but we just don't know why he did it."

"Did he ever talk about being depressed?" Jack wanted to know. "Or give any indication that something might have been bothering him?"

The boys glanced at each other.

"Nothing he told us about," Rick answered, keeping his eyes on Brian.

"Nothing," Brian said. "He was the same old Danny. He was just like he always was."

"Maybe it was something he only talked about once," Jack said.

"Not to any of us." Brian's voice was shaky. He started to say something else, stopped, looked over at Rick, then at C.J. "He didn't say anything to us."

Rick crossed and uncrossed his long legs, gave his sleeve another tug. "Like Brian's saying, he was the same old Danny."

Jack looked over at C.J. and then at the other boys. "There wasn't anything he talked to any of you about? Anything he ever hinted at? Being depressed or feeling overwhelmed by school or *any*thing?"

Brian shook his head without looking up. "He was the same old Danny."

"Was he eating?" Jack wanted to know.

"Eating?" Brian and Rick asked together.

"He wasn't eating much last week," Jack explained. "Was he eating when he was with you guys?"

"You mean lunch and like that?" Brian looked at the others. "Danny was eating, wasn't he, guys?"

"Yeah," Rick said. "We all ate together. Lunch, and the usual junk after school."

"He ate supper at my house at least once," Brian said. "Honest, Dr. Owens, if there was anything bothering Danny, we would have known about it."

"Even if he didn't say anything," Rick added, "we could tell."

"But he *didn't* say anything," Brian insisted.

Jack looked from one boy to the other. "Danny didn't seem unusually upset or worried?"

"No," Brian assured him with less certainty than Jack would have liked. Or was it sadness that he heard in Brian's voice, or confusion? "He was *Danny*."

"It might have been very subtle, something that you might not have noticed at first. Think for a minute."

Brian shook his head. "I didn't notice anything like that."

Rick echoed Brian.

"Danny would have," C.J. whispered timidly.

"Danny would have?" Brian said back to him.

"If it were one of us," C.J. answered, "he would have noticed. He would have known why."

Brian frowned at him. "Don't, C.J. Come on."

Rick frowned, too, and looked over at Brian before he volunteered, "All C.J.'s trying to say, Dr. Owens, is Danny was awesome."

They were boys acting like little men, or trying to—Jack could imagine Danny acting the same, speaking in the same somber tones—the way they'd seen adults behave. But only their awkwardness showed. Rick seemed more gawky and jangled. Brian's self-command seemed forced and false. C.J. looked fragile and morose. It was painful to witness, painful to be a part of.

"If Danny was acting strange," Rick began, "we'd have—I mean, he never acted, you know, weird or like—"

Brian broke in, "He was . . . He always made us laugh," and remembered something Danny had done just the week before. Rick remembered Danny's impersonations, and one story followed another, Rick and Brian talking about when they'd become Danny's friends, and when they had sleepovers and told scary stories, Danny was the last to admit he was scared. In the seventh grade, when everyone teased Brent Ackerman because he stuttered and didn't do well in school, Danny went out of his way to invite Brent to the movies or to play ball, even though he was uncoordinated "and was always tripping over himself."

"Danny was awesome," Rick said.

"He was the best friend we ever had," Brian whispered.

"He was the best, period," Rick added.

Jack waited a moment before he asked, "Did he ever talk about—Danny asked me which was more important, honesty or loyalty? Did he ever talk to you about that?"

Brian shook his head and looked over at Rick, who shook his head silently.

C.J. whispered something, unsnapped his backpack and pulled out a blue Hawaiian shirt. He might as well have pulled out a ghost, the way the other boys stared at it. "Danny lent this to me," he said, in a voice that made Jack shudder and the other boys sit back up in their chairs. "I guess you want it."

"Why don't you keep it," Jack answered. "I think Danny would have liked that."

C.J. held the shirt tightly, bunching it in his fist. His hands were trembling and he started to cry. Brian and Rick got very quiet for a minute or two, then Rick said, with adolescent certainty, "I know Danny's in heaven right now looking down at us and he's at peace." This did nothing to stop C.J.'s crying and the other boys stayed quiet and still for a minute longer, except for their eyes, which darted from one to the other. Brian and Rick mouthed something to C.J., C.J. cried and clutched Danny's shirt. Rick got all fidgety while Brian glanced over at him and glanced over at C.J. Then they were hitching in their chairs, sitting forward and back like they couldn't wait to get the visit over with, all the while their eyes kept on working, Rick glancing over at Brian, Brian glancing over at C.J., who returned the shirt to the backpack and looked even more frail and mournful.

Jack realized their sadness was making them restless and his was making them uncomfortable. He was sure they could see his sorrow, that they knew how much he wanted them to sit with him. That must have been why they didn't know what to say or how to act, why they looked from one to the other. Why they didn't know how to leave. Or were they waiting for Jack to dismiss them? But Jack wasn't ready to let this small piece of Danny walk off his front porch. He wanted to invite them inside and stand with them in Danny's room and breathe the air that had been Danny's air. But he didn't invite them inside. He only tried to find Danny in their faces and hear Danny in their voices. To see Danny in their eyes, in the jeans and T-shirts and the sneakers they wore. But all he saw were the faces of three boys who were not his sons, trying to figure out what to do next, waiting for Jack to let them go, but he kept them there a moment longer before he finally said, "Good-bye . . . Take care of yourselves . . . You know you're always welcome here . . ." and watched them hop on their bikes and ride down the road, further and further away from their friend and his house, leaving their childhood behind.

VIII

It wasn't Danny in the casket, it was only an empty body. All the things that made Danny Owens Danny Owens had been sucked out and emptied into the plastic grocery bag four days ago. The living Danny was gone, and if there were such things as spirits and souls, they were far removed from this graveside where Jack and his father, Grace, Lois and Aunt Adele stood with their mouths set tight, their heads bowed. The old man leaned on his cane with one hand and gripped Jack's hand with the other. He read from e. e. cummings and Dylan Thomas in a halting, quaking voice. Jack read from Shakespeare. They weren't crying. There had been nothing but tears last night and this morning, but here beside Danny's grave, tears were not sufficient.

The casket was lowered into the ground. Jack tossed a fistful of dirt into the grave, his father tossed another . . .

"Breathe . . . *breathe* . . . *again.* That's it." Jack held Anne's hand. He wiped her forehead with the towel. "Easy now," he said softly. "Keep breathing. Easy." Anne lay on the hospital bed and screamed with each contraction. She cursed God for making her a woman. She cursed Columbia-Presbyterian Hospital and the nurse for going along with this "fucking-asinine-natural-bullshit-child-bir— Oh *shit.*" She gripped Jack's hand tighter. Jack told her to breathe with him, deeply and quickly. Anne's screaming grew louder. Anne, who had turned to him in the Fine Arts building and literally took his breath away when they were students at Gilbert College, was now giving birth, giving breath, to their baby.

"Nice deep breaths," Jack told her. "Nice deep breaths and . . . *push*."

Anne screamed so loud it seemed she would tear her throat apart.

"Easy," Jack said. "Breathe nice and easy. Think about the week in Eleuthera when we sang to each other in the hammock. Think about that. Okay?"

Anne screamed, her face contorted and pained.

"Think about the soothing pink light surrounding you."

Anne only screamed.

Jack started singing, "Breathe in the good breath . . . Exhale the pain . . ."

"Oh *God*," she cried.

"Breathe in. Breathe—"

"Fuck you." Anne's body heaving. She screamed. Perspiration dripped off her face. "Fuck all of you. I want drugs."

The nurse's face got tense. She whispered something to Anne. A moment later the top of the baby's head appeared, and its neck and shoulders. Anne exhaled.

"Keep pushing."

Anne let out a loud and exhausted cry.

"Push. Push. Keep pushing and breathing. Easy . . . Easy . . ."

The nurse held up the dark-wet body, more like larva than flesh. She shook it gently into awareness. "A boy," she announced.

Later, after the nurse had wiped the baby dry and wrapped him to keep him warm, she presented him like a little trophy, and said to Anne and Jack, "I'll leave you alone for now." But they weren't alone, there was a baby with them, lying on Anne's chest. Jack sat on the edge of the bed and ran the back of his hand across Anne's cheek and curled his finger around the baby's tiny wrist. Anne whispered "Oh my God" as she cradled the baby against her neck and chest.

They stared at the tiny face, wrinkled and red, his body squirming so slightly, flexing his incredibly small hands. We have a baby, Jack thought, a living, breathing person; and he was overcome with the kind of damp panic that only an irreversible act engenders.

He was Daniel Benjamin Owens on the birth certificate. It was "To Daniel Benjamin Owens" that Jack's parents toasted and his friends and colleagues toasted. But to Anne and Jack he was: The Baby. He lay on his back gurgling contentedly at the square of blue sky Anne had painted on the ceiling. He watched with alert and deep eyes all who had come to drink to his health, to his long life. "To Daniel Benjamin Owens." But it was The Baby who Anne held in her arms. The Baby to whom Jack toasted while the three of them posed, the happy triumvirate, for the camera.

Those first weeks the loft was rarely without people eating, drinking and celebrating. Jack's parents brought a crib, toys and clothes. Aunts and uncles and cousins brought toys and clothes. Anne's staff brought toys and clothes. Jack's students and colleagues brought toys and clothes. Toys that made noises and toys that did nothing at all. Toys for next year and the year after that. Mobiles that jangled or merely sparkled in sunlight. Puppets and dolls and stuffed animals. Little red coats and blue coats and mittens for winter. Hats and pajamas and bibs and jeans. Baseball caps no wider than a teacup and football jerseys the size of a child's doll. Jack's editor brought books that squeaked and books that grew into buildings and trees. People showed up to sit and watch the baby do nothing but sleep. They stood and watched him wake and gurgle.

He was a good baby. As though he'd been in on all the discussions, as though he knew the indecisions and decisions; as though he were a visitor in his parents' home, he was determined to be the perfect little guest. He cooed when he was hungry but never cried. He slept through the night. When Jack woke in the morning, the baby slept until it was time to curl up with Anne and be fed. At night, alone, with the baby sleeping between them, Anne and Jack would marvel that anything so small could have lungs that breathed so deeply, a heart that beat so strongly, a brain that dreamed. Anne would sit in the rocking chair her father had sent from Dorset, hold the baby in her arms and feed him while Jack sat cross-legged on the floor next to them. Chopin, Brahms, played on the stereo.

Standing over the crib, Anne would run her lean finger along the baby's smooth skin. "He's so very small," she said, in a voice that had only to do with love. When she said, "Look at him, Jack. So fragile," she had tears in her eyes. "So helpless," she whispered, and lifted the baby out of the crib, held him against her heart. "He's a wonderful baby," she said. "He's a beautiful baby," and, turning her eyes away quickly and just for a moment, she said, softly, "Oh, Jack. I'm so happy." And if there were any doubt in her voice that she wasn't happy, Jack hadn't heard it.

Except for Jack's father, Aunt Adele and Lois, none of the people who fifteen years before had brought Danny gifts and drank to his long life were there to mourn him.

"May he rest in peace," Aunt Adele breathed against Jack's cheek. She pressed her face against his, she hugged him. She said, "It's so awful. It's just so awful." She said Danny was a very deep boy and would be greatly missed. "It's just such a horrible loss. Terrible." She never spoke the word *suicide.*

They walked down the gravel path to the car, Jack with his father, who took small, hesitant steps, like a child, everyone else walking ahead. They passed headstones with cherubs, headstones with bouquets and names carved on them, to loving mothers, adored husbands, cherished grandfathers. Jack thought: This is no place for a boy. How far from home I've brought him; and he felt the living Danny slipping away from him.

His father said, "He was an extraordinary boy." He held on to Jack's elbow. "I'm not saying that because he was my grandson. He was very astute—" He took several hard, forced breaths. When he spoke, his voice was painfully hoarse. "In the early days, when you and Anne used to leave him with your mother and me—he couldn't have been more than eighteen months old—we could see he had an ability, a sensitivity for figuring people out—he knew what was going on. He *understood.* You don't see that in many children, not when they're that young. You don't see it in a lot of adults either."

"I failed him," was all Jack said.

"Everyone failed him," his father answered.

"It must have been there all along, and I couldn't see it. He couldn't have just woken up on Thursday morning—"

"We didn't know," his father said with sad resignation. "We didn't know until he told us, and he told us by killing himself." His eyes were moist, from age, from grief. "You did everything you could do. I want you to remember that."

They walked further along the path, the old feet sliding against the gravel. The old body trembling. Across the way, dozens of mourners were gathered three deep by a family plot listening to the intonations of a minister.

Nine limousine drivers, obviously attached to the funeral, leaned against shiny black cars, smoking cigarettes, laughing softly with each other, while the bereaved commenced the obsequy. Jack's father watched the scene for a moment and held Jack's hand. His flesh was cold and smooth.

Jack said, "It happens to everyone, doesn't it? But it's not supposed to happen like this."

"This is a miserable day. There was no one better than Danny." His father coughed more than a few times, stopped walking and leaned one hand on his cane and the other against a stone bench. "Sit with me for a minute, Jackie," and balanced himself on Jack's arm as they sat side by side. "We were never a religious family," the old man said, "and it would be hypocritical to fall back on a God we don't believe in in good times, so you're going to have to have faith in yourself and your—" He coughed a few more times. "A terrible thing has happened, and you're going to live with it for the rest of your life."

Jack nodded his head.

"I don't mean to make it sound so intellectual and didactic. It's talk, that's all. I just want to be with you for a few minutes, alone. Just the two of us."

"Just the two of us. We're all that's left."

They started to cry, softly. Two figures sitting on a stone bench in a cemetery, where there is never a shortage of tears. The old hand with the veins like aged roots, the thick fingers, which had never been anything but gentle, shaking against Jack's arm. Words were choked back. It was only tears now, without resistance, without restraint. Danny's sad lifetime unfurled in Jack's mind like a piece of tapestry, only it hadn't seemed sad when Danny was living it. Jack once believed he'd done all that he could to distract Danny from the sadness—was that all it was, distraction? He once believed he'd filled in the places that were emptied when Anne left. And before Anne left. He once believed that he could undo the damage. Now there was nothing left to believe.

His father cleared his throat, wiped the corners of his mouth with thumb and forefinger. He asked, "What are you going to do when you go back?"

"I have some work to finish. Schoolwork."

"How much?"

"What I didn't finish last week."

"And then?"

"I don't know. I did everything else so Danny and I could spend the extra week in Maine."

"You can't sit alone in that house all summer thinking about all the— I don't think you should spend all that time alone."

"My friends invited me to stay with them. The ones Danny and I were going to visit."

The old man leaned heavily on Jack's arm and stood up. "Just remember who you are, Jackie."

IX

Jack could see the garden outside the windows of his study, where the flowers were in full bloom and the piece of field where the rows were plowed and the green of late spring covered the soil. For the third time that morning he sat at his computer with his folders, the videotape set in the VCR, trying to finish the critique, but he could not get to work. Even with the coffee brewed and his cup set on the coaster next to the phone, the script open, the storyboard spread out the way he liked it, even when everything was ready as though he weren't at home but in his office and it was May and Danny was still alive. Even if he thought of nothing but the work ahead of him, he couldn't get started, but it was more than just getting started. He couldn't concentrate. Just as he couldn't sleep at night and lay in the dark until daybreak and felt nothing; and couldn't eat, except for a quick pass at a piece of toast and a cup of coffee. He could only think of Danny.

There were images in freeze-frame on the television screen next to him, and if only he could be in freeze-frame the moment before Hopewell had walked into his office. If only Danny could be in freeze-frame the moment before he breathed his final "yes." Before his capitulation, before he put the plastic bag over his head—the moment before the moment—allowing Kim Connor those extra minutes to get to him, to stay his hand.

Jack pushed his chair away from the desk and walked out of the room. He sat outside on the back steps and heard the distant hum of interstate traffic on the far side of the field, the postman dropping the day's mail in the basket on the front porch and the fading motor as the van drove away. He wanted to hear other sounds: the scrape of the bicycle against the garage. Piano music in the living room. The sound of Danny somewhere in the house.

He watched a flock of geese flying a black V-formation against the white clouds. Mutt chased after something in the rosebushes, came out the other side with nothing to show for his effort, ran under the fence and across the freshly tilled earth. Down by the creek, the sun was shining through the branches of the sycamores, and it looked so cloistered and comforting that Jack got up and walked out to the cool, muddy bank. He remembered the times he and Danny came here, where the air was always warm, or seemed so, and heavy with the smell of damp logs. They'd take off their shoes and socks, roll up their pants and wade into the cool stream. They'd watch tadpoles wriggling inside their jelly eggs, throw stones at the trees on the opposite bank. Jack threw stones at those same trees now, until his fingers were wet and cold. He sat along the edge of the water, pushing his hands through the deep, lazy moss. But he did not take off his shoes and socks, or wade in the creek or look for tadpoles. He clutched his legs up to his chest and rested his chin on his knees, unable, unwilling, to move from this spot, although there was no purpose for being here, no reason to stay other than to avoid work, the academic industry poised inside his study.

Later that morning, Lois called, just as she might have called any morning when Jack was working, just as she'd called that Thursday morning when he was working on this same critique and they talked about Danny and barbecues and the future. She did not talk about any of those things today.

She said, "Summer vacations are starting in a few days and we all want to see you before we go away."

"We?"

"Your friends, Jack. We want to be with you."

"You mean go out somewhere?"

"If you like. But we thought we'd just stop by." When Jack didn't answer, Lois said, "Only for a little while, to say good-bye. No one's seen you since Danny died." When he still didn't answer she said, "I think it's important that we do this, Jack. We won't see each other again until the end of summer. I think we should be together . . ."

He tried to prepare for his friends, make a fresh pot of coffee, put out a plate of cookies. But he knew it didn't matter. There was no way to prepare. They would look at him with pitying faces and talk soft talk, cautious talk. They would not speak what they surely would be thinking: "How could you let this happen to your son?" They would look at him and be reminded of what can go wrong and what can be lost.

They came dressed in jackets and ties and summer dresses, bearing food—they said the last thing Jack needed to think about was cooking for himself—and sympathy.

They sat in the living room, in the deep couch and the comfortable chairs where the sunlight was the sparest, where the trees and the porch hung shadows on the walls. Their voices had competed at countless cocktail parties in this room and after dinners when the talk was loud and hard and there was never a lull. Now they could only talk soft talk.

Arthur and Celeste Harrison, Rick's parents, said, "It's as if we lost our own son."

Sally Richards told Jack, "We've been through so much together, and now it—I don't know . . ."

"We know this," Stan Miller said, "nothing is the same for you and that means nothing is the same for *us,* either." Stan was thin, not very tall, his gray hair was brushed straight back over a long skull that made Jack think of an eagle. When he spoke, his voice had a firm timbre, it was a reliable voice.

Lois sat next to Jack and held his hand. "All we're trying to say is, you're our Jack. You'll always be our Jack."

Jack said he found comfort in that.

In another few days his friends would be gone for their vacations. The migration from academe, the summer ritual they'd performed most of their professional lives. The ritual Jack was now no longer part of. They each wanted him to come visit them, stay as long as he liked. Jack wanted to say yes, he would. He wanted to tell them how much he'd miss them and that he didn't want to spend the summer alone. He wanted to tell them how lonely and miserable he was. He wanted to say that he'd never felt so empty in all his life. But he only knew how to tell them not to worry about him, he was sure he'd be all right.

Mandy Ainsley, C.J.'s mother, arrived with cake and cookies from the White Brick Bakery. She said, "Danny was C.J.'s closest friend. We're all going to miss him." She moved closer and whispered, "Carl is very upset with himself for what happened the other day. He was too ashamed to come over and tell you himself."

Hal and Vicki Clarke, Brian's parents, arrived with more food.

"We all loved Danny so much," Vicki said.

Hal sat facing Jack. "So very much," and leaned forward—it seemed everyone was sitting forward, or was Jack imagining it? Were they waiting for him to do something, waiting for him to say something? Waiting for Jack to decode the suicide? Waiting for an explanation—if Danny had died in an accident, if he'd died of a disease, there would be no need to explain—or were they waiting for another kind of explanation? Waiting for Jack to tell them where he went wrong. "How could you let his mother leave him, Jack?" "Did you really think you could undo the damage?" "A boy doesn't commit suicide just like that." "We would have seen it in our children, how could you have missed it? He was your son, after all."

But no one asked for explanations. There was only soft talk. Then there wasn't any talk at all. Only their presence, silent and sorry.

Jack thought about the other boy who'd killed himself. Who were his parents? Where did they work? Did their friends bring food and gather in the living room and lean forward expectantly? Were those parents able to provide an explanation?

When Arthur got up to smoke his pipe on the back porch, everyone followed him outside. They seemed relieved to be out of the house, away from the oppressive sorrow. They needed to breathe.

Jack sat on the steps. Arthur and Stan sat in the chairs beside him.

Arthur said, "I know it's too soon to think about now, but if you ever want counseling, I know a good man in Bloomington."

Across the yard, Celeste, Sally and Hal stood along the back fence, in the corner where the new flower beds were showing their colors. They were talking about their children. Jack imagined Danny sitting here with him, leaning back, watching the day grow another minute older. That's what he wanted, to watch the day grow a minute older with Danny.

A shadow shifted along the corner of the porch, Jack's eyes tried to grab it, his heart twitched. He thought: Danny. Because that's what it had always meant before, what he'd always seen when he looked up, when he looked over his shoulder, when there was the change in the air that had its very own feel, the footsteps on the floor that had their own sound.

He thought, This is what it will be like from now on, a shadow would shift and he'd think he was seeing Danny because he used to see him all the time. It's like the phantom limb, which your eye says is gone but your brain still feels. Your hand can't touch it, so it must not be there, but tell that to the rest of the body that loves it—the slightest change in light and he'd expect to see Danny, so he's there. And then he's not.

Over by the creek the crows were caw-cawing. Out in the field, Mutt was barking and making dark parabolas across the ground. The wind rustled the trees.

A small circle of people grew around Jack. Lois, Celeste and Arthur, Hal and Vicki, Stan, Mandy and Sally.

They stayed with him for a few minutes longer, making reassuring promises, speaking their regrets, saying their good-byes for the summer. If there was anything they could do, anything at all . . .

Jack couldn't let them leave, not without asking. He said yes, there was, in fact, something they could do.

"Did your kids say anything about Danny—about his state of mind?"

"No," they said, "nothing." And looked at Jack with such sadness and pity that his insides curdled and he wanted to disappear.

Only Lois stayed behind. She put her arm through Jack's and hugged it close to her body. "I know . . . I know . . ." was all she said.

Jack sat alone on the back steps trying to absorb this day, astonished that it had ever come, astonished by the new calibration: Time-without-Danny.

He did not get the chance to consider this. A car pulled up to the house. Someone was knocking on the front door.

The man said his name was Marty Foulk. He said he was a detective with the Gilbert police department.

"I told Hopewell everything I know," Jack said.

"That's not why I'm here." Foulk held out the torn piece of paper. "It's the poem your son wrote." Jack didn't move. "It's *yours,* Dr. Owens. The investigation's over."

Part Two

X

Jack stepped outside, took the paper from Foulk and looked slowly at Danny's handwriting.

Foulk said, "I know you're going through a bad time. I put off coming out here for the past couple of weeks, the last thing you need is another detective showing up on your front porch." He said this more sympathetically than Jack expected and made it sound more like an observation than a fact. "I wouldn't be here now, except I work in the Juvenile Division. I'm supposed to investigate juvenile crime, but since there isn't a whole hell of a lot of that around here, I spend most of my time counseling kids, single parents."

"I don't need your counseling." Jack did not raise his eyes from Danny's poem.

"I know you don't," Foulk answered. He spoke, not in a midwestern accent, but in a southern accent, or traces of a southern accent, with rounded vowels and a smooth and easy tone, and when he offered his hand, saying, "Call me Marty," he made it seem like he just happened to be passing by and this was nothing more than a friendly visit. "I'd really appreciate it if you gave me a few minutes of your time. You see, Danny was the second boy to commit suicide in the past month. *Less* than that, really."

"The reporter who Hopewell gave my name to told me. But he

wouldn't tell me who the other boy is." Jack looked up from Danny's poem. "Or if Danny might have known him."

"And you've been carrying that around with you all this time." Marty shook his head slowly. "I'm really sorry about that."

Jack folded the paper along the original creases, just as Danny had made them. "The son of a bitch sent the reporter to the woman who found Danny and he wouldn't tell me *her* name, either."

"Hopewell was out of line. He thinks getting his name in the news will get him to a big-city department."

Jack put the poem carefully in his shirt pocket.

Marty said, "The boy's name is Lamar Coggin. Did Danny know him?"

Jack said he'd never heard the name before. "Were he and Danny the same age?"

"He was ten."

"*Christ*. Was it the same—did he do it the way—"

"No. He hanged himself. Out by Otter Creek. About a week before Danny." When Marty said this, Jack heard something in the voice that was more than just down-home friendliness, something that had been missing from everyone else who had spoken to him since Danny died. It was as though Marty were speaking not from outside of Jack's experience but from within it, not as a stranger but as someone who himself had lost a son.

It took Jack by surprise and it made him feel uncomfortable, that what Marty was doing, what he was saying, was a practiced act of manipulation. And when he told Jack, "I need to know a few things that only you can tell me," Jack answered impatiently, "I already told Hopewell everything I know. Ask him."

Marty quickly said, "I'm sorry if I've offended you." Then he said, "I saw the two of you together once. Back in March. At the recital at Danny's high school."

"You heard him play?" Jack said, feeling both sorrow and pride. "You heard Danny play?"

"I'm a big brother to one of the boys in the school band. Danny was very talented."

"He was studying classical piano with Ben D'Amico at the college. Ben thought Danny had great potential."

"I saw how you and Danny talked to each other. Even in that short time, I got a pretty good idea how the two of you got along. It was pretty amazing, as a matter of fact, to see that in a father and son. That you could express that kind of love just by the way you looked at each other." He nodded his head. "When I read Hopewell's report and realized that you were the same Jack Owens . . ." He had a tight, athletic face, and what he did with it, and with his eyes, was more than an act of sympathy, it was more than empathetic, and it was a remarkable thing to see in a cop's face, in anyone's face; remarkable in the way any act of courage is remarkable. For a moment Jack thought he might have been mistaken, that there was nothing remarkable at all, that it had been something calculated, some trick of eye and mouth that the detective had picked up over the years like a salesman or con artist, nothing but more manipulation, and Jack didn't trust it any more than he trusted Marty's voice. But when a stranger comes to your house and speaks to you the way Marty spoke, and looks at you like that, you have to give him the benefit of the doubt, even if you're thinking that he shows the same expression to all the other parents he talks to, and makes the same conversation in that easy, down-home voice.

Jack tipped his chin toward the porch swing. "Have a seat."

Marty thanked him and sat down. He said, "What I'm trying to say is, if it would help to talk about Danny, maybe figure some things out, I'm interested to hear what you've got to say."

"You don't have that kind of time."

"I don't doubt *that*. But maybe I could just ask you a few things. Okay?" Marty lowered his eyes for a moment and stared at the floor, then slowly looked up at Jack. "Kids who commit suicide tend to fit certain patterns of behavior and I'm gonna assume that if Danny was acting out in any way, any real obvious way, you'd've noticed. If he'd been depressed you'd've been aware of it, right? If he was displaying mood swings or showed symptoms of being bipolar. So, thinking small, was he having *any* problems at all? Problems in school?"

"He was comfortable in a learning environment."

"Excuse me?"

"I'm sorry. I don't know what made me think of that. He was a good student. Not great. B's. Some C's. A few A's when he was interested enough." Jack shook his head. "He didn't have any problems in school."

"I don't mean only his grades. Were there any kids he was hanging out with who might have been fooling around with drugs or into violent or antisocial behavior?"

Jack turned his head away and looked down the road where Danny had learned to ride a bike, as though Danny would be riding his bike right now, coasting the last few feet to the house. That's what he wanted to see. It must have been all over his face and Marty must have seen it, because he let the silence hold, the way some people do when they're not quite comfortable with what they're thinking or what they're being shown and they don't know if it was something they'd said or how to shift the conversation back to where they'd like to take it.

Jack waited another moment before he said, "Danny's friends weren't like that."

Marty gave the swing a soft push. "Did he have a lot of friends?"

"A lot?"

"I mean, he didn't spend a lot of time alone?"

"You're not thinking he was one of those lunatic kids who heard the devil—"

Marty raised his hand. "We both know those families have a mess of problems, with a kid who's been giving off warning signs six to the dozen. I'm only asking." He smiled weakly.

"He wasn't the loner type, if that's what you want to know. He wasn't drawn to anyone who was. Look, his friends were all decent kids. That's who Danny was drawn to. That's the kind of kid he himself was."

"Then I'm safe in assuming his teachers never alerted you to any red flags?"

"Of course not. Haven't you talked to them? Haven't you talked to his *friends*?"

"I wanted to talk to you first. Did Danny have a girlfriend? You know, some boys get started before they're ready and it kind of mixes them all up inside."

"Danny didn't get some girl pregnant, if that's what—"

"I was speaking strictly on an emotional, developmental level."

"Danny was a normal kid who had a pretty clear picture about sex. He was starting to think about dating, just like the rest of his friends, but it was mostly hanging out at the mall and Saturday night parties at someone's house. I'm pretty sure he was a virgin."

"I know you're divorced. I was wondering how often Danny saw his mother?"

Jack explained things in the barest-bones version. Marty leaned back in the swing and said, "That's a real shame. Did Danny ever have any counseling for it?"

"We both did, but I don't think he ever really understood what made his mother want to leave. I don't know if that's something a child *can* understand."

"I imagine he was angry about it."

"He said he was. But when he was eight, he said he'd forgiven her but he didn't want to have anything to do with her. Would that make him suicidal? I never thought so at the time. I don't know what to think now."

"Was there a woman in your life?"

"I don't think that's germane to this conversation."

"I mean, someone you brought around to sort of fill the gap for Danny?"

"Is this about me or about Danny?"

Marty apologized. He said, "Most of what I know about these sorts of things I come by in keeping up with my reading, so you might say I'm doing this by the book, and if I don't make it come out smooth as silk, well, now you know why." He gave the swing another soft push before he said, "Now don't get riled about this, but what kind of shows did Danny watch on TV? I'm just asking is all."

"The usual junk."

"Movies? Did he like a particular kind?"

"I kept him away from Disney as much as possible. He went

through a Spielberg phase. Harpo was his favorite Marx brother. Groucho scared him, until he was about six or seven. He liked *Blade Runner.* It made him cry."

"Blade Runner?"

"Do you know the movie?"

"I saw it a bunch of years ago. About homicidal robots and Harrison Ford hunts them down? Am I close?"

"Close enough. It was one of Danny's favorite movies. He must have watched it a dozen times. He thought it was sad when the *replicants* die."

"Weren't they the bad guys?"

"You want to chew on that for a while or move on to the bonus round?"

"I don't think I'd make the cut." Marty grinned at him, but quickly his expression changed, lacking anything even resembling amusement. He shifted his eyes away from Jack, just for an instant, then he looked at him again and asked, "Can you tell me what Danny was like during the days leading up to his suicide?"

"He seemed annoyed more than anything else. Or maybe he was feeling resentful."

"Any idea what was annoying him and what he resented?"

"It was finals week and I was working long hours. I didn't get to spend very much time with him. I think that had a lot to do with it. I thought so at the time."

"Was this year worse than others?"

Jack shook his head. "It's always crunch time, but somehow this year Danny took it harder. This was the last year we were going to spend the summer doing things together, he wanted to get a job next year. I don't think he knew quite how to feel about it, or that's what I thought. All I know is, I should have found the time to be with him."

"And that was all? No eating problems or sleeping problems?"

Jack took a deep breath. "I don't think he was sleeping much, the last couple of days before . . . His friends said he was eating with them, but he didn't have much of an appetite when I was with him."

"What do you mean, not much of an appetite?"

"When we had breakfast and when we met for supper, he wasn't eating very much."

"But that was something new."

"Yeah. Danny was always a good eater."

The look Marty gave Jack was not simply one of sympathy, it was the inside look again, and this time Jack found it reassuring.

"So, apart from the usual day-to-day problems, Danny doesn't sound like the sort of boy who'd kill himself, does he?" Jack said. "And yet he did."

"And yet he did," Marty solemnly repeated. "My grandmother told me a story once that her mother told *her* about a woman who was illiterate. This was back in the 1880s, in Covington, Tennessee, where it wasn't unusual for women to be illiterate. Her name was Irene Paige. She was the most beautiful woman in the county, and the gentlest. Young men used to come to her window and serenade her with that song 'Good Night, Irene.' She eventually married a man named Theodore, a carpenter, who made a good living and should have been a very contented man. But he had a mean streak in him. Maybe it would be called something else today, but in those days he was just called mean. At night, after supper, Theodore would read to Irene. She loved Charles Dickens the best, but it didn't really matter, she liked whatever he chose to read. But when his dark mood came on, he'd go into his workshop, lock the door and not talk to his wife, sometimes for days. When he recovered and got back to reading to her, he'd pick up *not* where he left off reading to *her* but where he'd left off reading for himself, so great chunks of story would be missing, and he would never fill her in. Well, Irene went along with this for some time, and then Theodore stopped reading to her altogether. Not just for a few days but for an entire month, as a way of torturing the woman. Now, they lived out in the country and they had no children, so there was no one else around to read to her, besides, the few friends they had wouldn't have interfered in a husband and wife's affairs. Irene was just miserable. This dark mood grew more intense and Theodore refused to read to her, he took to beating her. Another month, and Theodore started feeling ill, a few more weeks and he was really sick. The doctor came out but he couldn't figure out what the trouble was. Bed rest and Irene's loving care was the best prescription, the doctor said. Irene administered to Theodore as thoroughly as a professional nurse, but Theodore got sicker and sicker, suffering agonizing stomach cramps and pains and high fevers. It took him nearly a year but he died a slow, agonizing death." Marty had been leaning in closer and closer to Jack as he told the story, and now he leaned slowly back. "What no one suspected, not in a million years, was that Irene had poisoned her husband. Years later, I mean when Irene was old and getting ready to die, she told my great-grandmother what she'd done. She had to clear her conscience, for better or worse, and asked my grandmother to pray for God's forgiveness, but she was sure she was going straight to the devil. My great-grandmother told that story to my grandmother to illustrate a point and my grandmother told it to me for the same reason: she said, 'Everybody has a dark side, like the dark side of the moon, where nothing shines.' Everybody has that one thing, that button that can set them off to doing things they'd normally never contemplate. The other boy who killed himself must have had it, and, I'm sorry to say, Danny must have, too."

"You don't have to tell me about dark sides. But your story's about an abusive relationship, and Danny was anything but abused."

"Only if you take the story literally."

"Maybe I don't want to take it at all. I don't want to think about Danny like that. Anyway, you're the expert, you tell me."

"Tell you?"

"Why Danny killed himself. Why a perfectly normal fifteen-year-old boy would want to kill himself."

Marty stared at the floor for a moment. "I don't know, Dr. Owens." He drawled the words easily. "But there's always a reason. Maybe not just *one* reason. There might have been several things." He managed to make this sound acceptable, but only for a moment.

"I'm not sure which is worse, knowing or not knowing."

"I wonder that myself all the time." Marty got up. "I've imposed on you enough for one day." He thanked Jack for his time.

Jack didn't want him to leave. He didn't want to be alone. "What about the other boy?" he asked. "What patterns of behavior did he fit?"

"I can't really say. I haven't spoken to the family yet."

"Why not?"

"They've left town for a while. They're in Illinois somewhere. At a church retreat." Marty started walking toward the steps and took a look around. "I remember when the Brennans sold this place. It's a big old house, isn't it. If it gets to feeling too big for you"—he took out his card and handed it to Jack—"and you ever feel like talking." He opened the car door and before he got in said, "I'll look forward to it."

Jack watched the car drive away, kicking up dust and pebbles. Yeah, he thought, it's a big old house . . .

It was early October of their senior year. The leaves were crimson and gold. When the wind blew there was a cold flutter—like waking from a nap in an unheated room—then the leaves floated to the ground and across the backyard and the field in effortless surrender to the season. Jack and Anne sat in the old VW. Anne with her chin resting on the handgrip above the glove box, the late-day sun reflecting off of her muscat eyes. Jack sitting low in the front seat. Across the road was the house. It was big with a deep wraparound porch. A man wearing a plaid shirt sat at the window smoking a pipe and reading a book. He raised his head when the engine stopped and looked outside, not expectantly but curiously. Then he went back to his reading.

"I like looking at that field behind the house," Jack said.

"Yes," Anne said softly. "It's the light. Indiana light."

"I like the way the house looks. I like that it's out here and seems so isolated and yet you're only ten minutes from town."

Then Anne told him that she loved him because he loved an old house like this with its strong, wide porch and the field that stretched for two hundred acres or more. Because he liked to stop here in autumn and look at the falling leaves and the field and behind the field, where the old trees were bent and gnarled, and their roots bulged out of the soft earth along the creek, and in winter the snow was shiny and slick like liquid in the cold sunlight; and because he liked coming here to look at the green sprouts in spring and smell the tilled earth in the air.

Anne leaned across the small seat, pressed her chin against Jack's chin, raised her eyes and said, "Can we always be like this? Loving each other and living our lives together?"

He answered, "I don't know why not."

She whispered, "But you know how it is sometimes, people lose the thing that makes them love each other." She said, "We're a long way from settling into a house in the Midwest, aren't we."

"Yes, we are."

"I've been thinking about us living in New Haven if you decide to take your master's there. That's at least a year."

"We don't have to live in New Haven."

"Really? Because I've been thinking we should move to Manhattan after we get back from England. It's the best place to find work in the graphic arts. Don't you think? And, well, to *play* and everything. Unless you're awfully married to your plan."

"The only thing I want to be married to is *you*," he told her. "Think you can put up with East Village squalor? That's about all we can afford in Manhattan."

She touched his cheek with her lips.

Jack knew that when they left Gilbert they would never come back, but he didn't mind. Anne was the girl who'd made him stare in dumb amazement the first time he saw her. She was the girl who fit the image he had of himself. He didn't mind if his plans for being Dr. Owens would have to be realized riding the commuter train. He didn't mind.

The man in the window turned on a light and pulled down the shade.

Anne breathed softly into Jack's ear, "You know that movie with Jane Fonda and Robert Redford when they move into that apartment in Greenwich Village?"

"Barefoot in the Park."

"It could be like that."

"I'm not quite the uptight WASP lawyer type."

"No. I mean the squalid East Village apartment."

"Unfortunately, New York always looks better in the movies."

"So what?"

He looked over at her. Her chin was back on the handgrip.

"There are the thrift shops to sort through," she said, "and Canal Street. I know it's going to work out." She sang, hoarsely and dry, " 'We'll turn Manhattan into an isle of joy,' " turned to him and laughed her Carole Lombard laugh. "You know that story by J. D. Salinger, 'For Esmé—with Love and Squalor'? We'll call ours, 'For Jack—with Love, Anne and Squalor.' " She looked at him now the way she'd looked at him last year when he saw her sitting at the bottom of the hill in Fairmont Park, where the ground was soft and the afternoon sunlight bent through the dark leaves, and the air was warm the way the air is warm in Gilbert in late April, like milk when it's been on the stove just long enough to take the chill out. The day he finally spoke to her.

She was wearing tight blue jeans and a yellow shirt with the sleeves rolled up past her elbows and which fit her like a smock. She dug her toes into the earth, giving the impression that she would float away if not anchored securely to the spot. Her back was resting against a tree, her knees drawn close to her chest, her sketch pad supported on her thighs. Her brown hair, the color of dark molasses, had flecks of dried paint in it—she wore it long in those days and tied it back tightly over her ears. Her long, slender fingers worked the pencil across the paper. Her profile was a progression of diagonal lines, her forehead to the bridge of her nose, the tip of her nose forming something close to a right angle above her upper lip, which dipped gently, parting the way a spring bud would a few days before blossoming. Her chin curved just enough to soften her face.

This wasn't the first time Jack had seen her. The first time was in the Fine Arts building—she had a studio on the top floor, he shared an editing room in the basement with another guy. She was standing in the rotunda with a group of art students, boys mostly, smoking cigarettes and talking the sort of talk art students talked at Gilbert College, the "Athens-on-the-Wabash," back in 1975.

Some of the most accomplished theorists and practitioners of the visual and performing arts in America were on the faculty, and twelve hundred aspiring actors, writers, artists and young auteurs from around the world came to Gilbert, if not to sit at the feet of these learned men and women, at least to extract as much information and knowledge as they might during their four years there. One of those aspirants was an art student named Anne Charon from Dorset, England.

She wasn't tall, five-five, but looked taller because of the way she held her back. Her face was intelligent and not pretty the way those all-American girls were pretty, or the unblemished blondes or the languid Europeans. Her face went deeper than pretty. More interesting than pretty. It was an elegant face. And she turned that face in Jack's direction and only for an instant, like a flashbulb popping in the dark. Faster. And in that brief moment something happened inside of Jack, something anatomic, visceral. All he could do was stare at her in dumb astonishment until he recovered, in no more time than it took her face to freeze him.

It stayed with him when he went outside. When he met his friends at Paul's and washed down his sandwich with an iced Dr Pepper. When he was alone in his editing room; and later that night, when he lay awake on the couch with the window open and that dangerous spring breeze filling the room with the hint of lilac and the strong ripe scent of honeysuckle. He lay there in the dark and felt the same thing he felt when Anne had looked at him that afternoon, something nameless and amorphous, a craving, except he didn't know what it was that he craved. It wasn't sexual. It didn't come from his libido but from the place where the libido is no stranger: his self-image, or the self-styled self-image a twenty-year-old film student carries around with him, along with his textbooks and notes. What a film student cannot help having, *needs* to have, if he has any chance of surviving all the petty student pretensions, the self-absorptions. Jack's image of himself, or better still, his image of the film student he thought himself to be, lacked completion, lacked the necessary component that he had been unaware of until that afternoon when he saw it wrapped in full bohemian regalia, with long brown hair, a delicious British accent, and the slightest chance that it was available to him. He couldn't give a name to what he was feeling, so he decided to call it Love. It kept him awake the rest of the night.

Anne must have seen him looking at her that first time, although later she insisted that she was too involved with her friends to notice. Jack didn't believe her. He told her she'd even smiled at him. That was the first time she did her Carole Lombard laugh, before she even knew who Carole Lombard was. When Jack saw her in Fairmont Park with her sketch pad on her knees and her long hair tied back over her ears, the sunlight squeezing through the space where her elbow rested on her thigh, the swell of her hip, full and thrilling, he didn't walk over to her. Not right away. He'd been waiting a long time, at least a couple of months—which seemed like a long time then—to find her without her friends around. He didn't want to rush the moment, more to the point, didn't want to rush *through* the moment. As long as he did nothing, she would remain his creation, sprung full-blown, not from his rib but from the reflection in his eye. From the strange alchemy of hubris and self-doubt that would create the man he wanted to be from the woman he desired—this was where Anne Charon, his mythology of Anne Charon, was born. But once Jack moved from his spot, once he walked to her and heard her speak and do any of the things born of her own personality, she would no longer be of his making but a being in and of the world, fallen to earth from the heights of his imagination, and all bets were off.

He sat against the base of the ruins looking down from the top of the small hill and watched her a while longer. He studied her posture and the lines of her body, the way she dropped her hand to her side and then rushed it up to the paper, and he did not move for another minute. But nothing is possible in the absence of action; he walked slowly down the hill, because the passive observer leaves all things to chance.

Jack held Danny's poem in the palm of his hand, he didn't look at the words but at the handwriting, the paper itself—touched by Danny, folded by Danny, and which Danny had put in his pants pocket—then walked back to his study, placed the poem carefully inside his desk drawer, keeping the original creases aligned, and went back to work.

After he watched the final video and wrote his last critique, after all the envelopes were sealed and the grades were printed, he walked out to the car, took the ten-minute ride to the post office, where he mailed the critiques to his students, just as Dr. Owens always did, drove to campus, where he dropped off his grades, and began the ten-minute ride back to the house, along the quiet tree-lined streets where life seemed to progress undisturbed. He had finished his work and all he felt was that expanse of time growing larger, further into the future. He could always pack up, leave town and stay with his friends. Pack up and drive, like Danny and he used to do. Two for the road. Endless summer. Those lazy, hazy, crazy days. Days spread out like picnic blankets and baseball diamonds and the Atlantic Ocean at sunrise.

He thought: It's still June and a lot can happen in a summer. A lot can go wrong in all that time; and he thought about the call that comes, not late at night or first thing in the morning but in the middle of the afternoon, on the cell phone when he would be anywhere but home. It would be Grace calling to say, "Your father's gone into a coma." "Your father's had a stroke." Calling to say, "Your father's dead."

So much can go wrong; and his heart started beating fast. He felt a sense of vertigo. He was having trouble breathing, as though a belt were tightening around his chest. He lost control of the car, it bounced over the curb and he hit the brakes hard. The tightness in his chest grew worse. He stared numbly out of the windshield and thought: So much can go wrong. The inside of his head pulsated. He imagined Grace calling him while he was out running errands, keeping busy, calling him if he went away, to tell him his father died. He thought of the cell phone ringing with the bad news. He thought: What next?

"The worst is over," he said while his legs shook. "The worst is over," while he felt nothing but panic, while he thought: What next?

He knew it was nonsense. "There isn't going to be a *What next?* You're just having a delayed reaction to Danny. The worst is over." While his feet trembled, his hands began to sweat. While he thought: What next?

Jack stayed home for the rest of the day. Whenever the phone rang, his stomach lurched, until he heard the voice at the other end: Bob Garvin calling from South Wellfleet to say the invitation was still open if Jack could handle the visit. Yoshi calling from Maine: "Maybe you'd like to come up for a week or so." Al Barlow calling from Santa Barbara: "We'd love for you to come stay with us."

Jack did not go to South Wellfleet. He did not go to Maine or Santa Barbara. He was scarcely able to walk out the front door—a hurried drive to the supermarket, a hurried drive back home—and when he found the red light blinking on the answering machine, he wouldn't play it back, not right away. He sat and stared at it, as though the machine were a living thing, possessed of a power, benevolent or malicious, capable of meting out good news and bad. Jack would think, *Please, no disasters,* and watch the red light blink. He would try to calculate by some internal psychic measure if this was the time his father's heart had chosen to stop beating; if one of those chemical reactions that kept the saline at the right level had failed. Jack would wait a little longer, until a resolve settled in. He'd prepare himself for the bad news. He would play the message. But it wasn't the message of disaster, it wasn't bad news at all and he would think: Not this time. Not now, with a renewed sense of foreboding; scared of the next minute, the next day. Scared of the summer lying in predatory repose.

XI

Each morning when he called his father, Jack never said what he was thinking, never talked about the fear. He didn't say, "I'm afraid if I leave the house, you'll die." He didn't say, "I won't even mow the lawn for fear I won't hear the phone ring." He didn't tell his father, "I think the most gruesome thoughts about the caprices of life."

He didn't say, "I can't seem to do anything."

But he was doing a hell of a lot of thinking. About the past. About the time he was an undergraduate at Gilbert College and he had a girlfriend named Anne Charon, who was an art student with hair the color of dark molasses, who smelled of sweet perfume and perspiration. In the spring they drove along the roads in southern Indiana and followed the Ohio River. They would stop in New Harmony and look at Paul Tillich's church. They would eat lunch in Newburgh and buy candles and fruit at the little stores along the road.

He used to think he was golden, that he had the charm. That whatever he set his sights on could be his. Anne, who was beautiful and artistic and sexy, and whom he loved very much . . . their loft on Crosby Street . . . the professorship at NYU . . . the published books . . . their friends, who discussed the future of cinema, Marcel Duchamp and the death of painting . . . parties on Saturday night . . . Sunday afternoon salons . . . dinners with his parents, who were healthy and vital and who talked about art and literature and their trips to Africa and India . . . drinks with Lana, who represented Anne's work . . . dinner with Erica, who edited Jack's books . . .

Jack once thought he was golden, that he had the charm. He'd had a wife, then he'd had a wife and a son. Then his wife left but still he had his son, whom he loved very much. He'd thought he was still golden, that he'd still had the charm, that he could turn bad luck into good. He moved with his son to Gilbert and lived in a house they both loved. When Jack's mother died, he'd held it all together, he still had the charm. But now his son was dead and he was alone. He was golden no more. He no longer had the charm.

When Anne left, a piece of Jack's life, and with it a piece of himself, had been chipped away. When his mother died, he'd lost another piece. And now Danny was dead, the living Danny, receding into the past. The living Danny consumed by the dead Danny, and another piece was gone.

It was more than intellectual, it was palpable, the sensation of Danny moving further away. Jack walked from room to room, sat in his study, lay on the couch and felt the cavity within himself growing; and just as the living Danny was receding from him, moving into the past, the Jack Owens who had been Danny's father was also receding, becoming part of the past, joining his son in memory.

There was not enough left of Jack to offer resistance to this, there was only the man worrying: What next? There was only the man who was afraid to leave the house, who stopped going to the supermarket, who did not step into his backyard, where the air was rich with summer; did not walk by the creek and sit where the trees shaded and cooled the ground. Who sat on the kitchen floor dressed in a pair of shorts and a T-shirt, a sheet of labels and a pen at hand, and carefully rewrapped the food his friends had brought him. The coffee rings, the tins of cookies, the rolls and cakes; resealing the covered dishes, neatly writing the contents on the labels, food for the refrigerator, food for the freezer, the name of the person who'd brought it, keeping a list for the thank-you notes he intended to send.

When he was done, he stood, one hand in his pocket, leaning against the door, a gesture of nonchalance that was anything but, a gesture of fatigue, the fatigue of sorrow, the fatigue of anxiety, and considered his work, decided there was nothing more to do here, at least for now, and feeling neither a sense of accomplishment nor futility, went to work on the living room, dusting the furniture, dusting the windowsills, vacuuming the floor, as though he might cleanse the room, purify it, purge it, as though there were a suicidal germ alive in there, a sentient organism triumphant in the cracks. He thought: You're putting things back together, that's all.

He continued the purification, the same ritual in the halls and staircases, until this day, this piece of time without his son, had been vaporized.

The following morning, Jack began first, and second, drafts of thank-you notes. He hadn't eaten breakfast for the third consecutive day, but no matter, it was more important to get the job done. He took special care not to hurry. He did not finish until early afternoon, in time for the mailman to collect the mail.

Then the purification ritual was renewed. He reorganized the downstairs closets, touching and holding Danny's leather jacket, Danny's winter coats and gloves. Rearranging the linen closet. Stacking and restacking sheets and blankets and pillowcases.

He had fallen into a comfortable and safe routine: feeding Mutt. Washing windows. Dusting. Sweeping. Scrubbing. Working upstairs and down. Two, three, four days, an entire week subtracted from the summer, from the awful expanse of time, and always the telephone nearby, always the fear of: What next?

Jack did not think about why he was afraid to leave the house. He did not think about the work he was doing, or why he was doing it. He only thought about putting things back together. He only thought about how he could erase an entire morning with the most menial job, annihilating entire hours by simply trying to decide what to work on next, preparing the buckets, the mops, the rags, the cleansers, the soaps and waxes. He took pride in how disciplined he was, how slowly and thoroughly he planned each assignment, the organizing, the labeling, the filing, the storing; then slowly, conscientiously carrying them out, tearing time from each day, working into the night, purging and cleansing.

He dusted all the pictures on the Danny wall, cleaned the glass in the frames, polished the wood, the metal.

He vacuumed and cleaned his own bedroom, hung his clothes according to color and season.

He scrubbed his bathroom, gouged the flecks of dirt between the tiles. Re-grouted the shower and bathtub. He arranged the bottles and jars and tubes in the medicine cabinet. He put a shine on the mirror. He thought about how he was putting things back together.

He shampooed the living room carpet and the chairs and the couch. He waxed the floor in the front hallway, digging his brush into the doorjambs, careful not to miss a stubborn bit of—what?—dried mud left behind by whose shoe? His? Danny's? The plumber's? No matter, he'd get it out.

In the kitchen, on his knees waxing the floor, sweating his way across the room. Washing the dishes, the ones for everyday, the ones for company. Polishing the silver.

When he finished washing and polishing and scrubbing, finished arranging plates and cups, forks and spoons, rearranging and arranging them again, Jack retreated to Danny's room. He breathed the air, which was less Danny's air, less Danny's mornings and nights, than it had been back in May, than it had been just an hour before. He sat among the piles of clothes and books left behind in the wake of his search the day Danny had died, Danny's spring jackets and summer shirts, his shoes and sneakers—he was already outgrowing this year's clothes—and it made Jack think about the year Danny turned nine and went away to summer camp. They had shopped for new clothes at Coleman's department store. The tailor sewed name tags into all the collars and waistbands. The other boys had mothers to do their sewing, but Danny said he liked the "bachelor life."

It was Danny's first summer away from home. He was so self-assured when he came back, so much more mature, which was to be expected. Jack could see the change even before Danny left, but something else had changed as well. It was the last time Danny asked about Anne:

"Do you think she's still mad at us?"

"She was never mad at us."

"Did she stop loving us?"

"No. It wasn't because she stopped loving us. Or because she stopped loving you. She's a very talented artist, and creative people often need to be alone to do their work."

"Do you still love her?"

"I love the things the three of us did together."

"What if we went to England sometime, for a vacation, and we accidentally bumped into her on the street, what do you think she'd say?"

"She'd say you've grown into an extraordinary and beautiful young man."

Jack stayed in Danny's room, putting shoes back in the closet, organizing ties and belts, picking up books and arranging them on the shelf. He made the bed, stripped it and made it a second time. He polished the furniture to a high sheen. He vacuumed around the doorway, under the desk and windowsills. He pulled the bed away from the wall, the better to vacuum out the cracks and molding. He thought about how he was putting things back together. That's when he found the box stuck away in the corner.

It was one of those wood boxes with the sliding lids that pastels come in, that used to inhabit the loft on Crosby Street, that Anne had kept on the shelf next to her easel and filled with crayons for Danny and scraps of cloth and wire for collages. How familiar it looked, and how alien.

Jack's first impulse was to leave it where it was. He had never been the kind of parent to look through Danny's things and he wasn't comfortable doing so now. It felt intrusive, not unlike eavesdropping on a conversation or reading Danny's mail. Just an old box. It didn't mean anything—except it meant something to Danny because he'd taken it with him when they left Manhattan and never told Jack. Important enough for Danny not to leave behind. Important enough for him to keep secret—important enough to offer a clue, an explanation, if Jack had come in here looking for clues and explanations. But he'd been doing nothing more than following his compulsions and now he was afraid that whatever was left of Danny, left of himself, was about to break apart.

It was just an old box, he thought, while he stared at the smear of colors along the edges, at the dark finger stains where the lid had been opened and closed time and again, at the name in black ink: *Dearborn Pastels. Chicago, Ill.* Just an old box. But he couldn't stop himself from picking it up and holding it in his hand, the way Danny must have held it in his hands and Anne in hers. Jack ached inside thinking about that. He ached even more after he pushed back the lid.

The colors were all faded now but not the details, they were still clear and sure on the tiny cutout animals that Anne had made for Danny when he was three. There was a color snapshot of Anne with Danny when he was a baby and a black-and-white of Jack and Anne standing outside the old warehouse the day they moved into their loft, and beneath that, a folded sheet of yellowed paper.

Jack traced his fingertips across the cutouts and spread them on Danny's bed. He touched the faces in the photographs as though he might reacquaint himself with their flesh. He unfolded the sheet of paper, a pen-and-ink drawing of Danny that Anne had done the year before she left; the creases were smooth and straight, made by an adult's hand, not the hand of a child. And there was something else in the box. Anne's orange button, staring up at him like a jaundiced, myopic eye.

It startled Jack to see it, and he hesitated, just for an instant, before he lifted it out and held it in the palm of his hand. He started to sob. A few strands of thread were still attached to the eyelet, and he brushed them against his lips. The ache he felt now was the ache born of familiarity, of memories he had not allowed himself to articulate and a past which he refrained from recollecting—is that why Danny kept the box under the bed? Jack wondered. Did he think he was protecting his father? Is that why he kept it a secret?

For ten years, Danny had squeezed a part of his childhood, mementos from his life, into a corner of his room, all that was left of Anne, all that had been left to him. And when he looked at the faces in the photographs, at the delicate cutouts Anne had made just for him, did he feel time extending all the way back to the loft on Crosby Street? Could he look out of this window and see the streets of SoHo, conjure the sounds of his mother's voice, breathe the odors of linseed oil and paint? Was this where Danny could find them, inside the old box of pastels?

Had Anne given these things to Danny, and had she, in that last moment of good-bye, ripped a small piece of her clothing and clasped Danny's hand around it? Had she been afraid that Danny might otherwise forget her? Or could a four-year-old boy think far enough ahead to fill a box with his own memorabilia and hide it inside a carton on moving day?

Jack sat with the cutouts and the snapshots and the drawing for a little while longer before he returned them to their resting place. But he did not want to put them back in the corner, he did not want to leave them alone and unattended. He did not know why he felt this. Perhaps it was a way to make Danny's secret his own, or to take Danny's secret away from him. Perhaps he was unable to admit that Danny had any secrets—kids always have their little secrets, he thought, and this was Danny's. But that was the living Danny, not the Danny who killed himself.

He carried the box into his own bedroom and placed it on top of the dresser. He wondered what other secrets Danny had been keeping. What else had he been afraid to talk about?

It was late June, the longest day of the year, and pacing was everything. Jack stretched the phone call to his father into an hour of small talk and reminiscences and went about his work with a dull single-mindedness. It distracted him from thinking about the past, when he had thought he was golden and charmed. It distracted him from believing he could keep his father alive. It restrained his fear of *What next?*

He was getting used to the long days alone. He filled the silence with the sound of his own voice. Talking to Mutt, talking to himself, talking to Danny, self-consciously and ashamed at first, but soon indiscriminately: "What were you thinking?" he'd ask. "What weren't you saying?" "Why did you do it . . ."

As he cleaned and waxed, while he alphabetized the books in his study by author—then title, then subject, then back to author—he'd yell: "I was too busy to know what was happening. I had to do my work. But I still made time for you. You could have told me." He'd say, pathetically and desperately: "You could have *talked* to me. We still had time." Then he'd look around quickly and whisper: "This isn't normal."

Some days he would think about Anne. He would see her in quick flashes, her face against the gray urban sky, sitting at her easel, her hand poised above the canvas, out of context, out of time. Sometimes he would recall the sound of her voice or a piece of conversation. He would remember the expression on her face when she spoke to him, when she said, "Sometimes people lose the thing that makes them each other," and how that had confused him, how he didn't understand it.

He would remember things he had not allowed himself to remember before and it made him feel guilty, it felt like a betrayal. Only there was the box he'd found under Danny's bed, and was that all the permission he needed? He would wonder if he'd forced Danny to hide his memories. "Would that have made a difference? Would that have . . ."

At night he'd lie awake thinking about Danny, thinking about Anne. Or fall into a shallow sleep knowing that he was losing more than the illusion of control over a capricious universe, he was losing control of himself. He'd whisper "This isn't normal" into the dark, and assure himself that tomorrow he'd walk out to the creek, take off his shoes and wade in the water. He'd eat more than the few crackers, the cups of coffee. He'd make himself a full meal . . . Tomorrow . . . The next day, definitely . . . Or maybe the day after that . . .

Jack was standing on a stepladder in the pantry, reaching into the corner to smooth the shelf paper he'd just put down. He'd been working on this particular shelf since early morning and wasn't even half done—at this pace he wouldn't be finished until sunset. The air breezed through the screen door warm and heavy with the earthy scents of pasture and field. "July. You can smell it," he said to himself. He thought of where he would have been, where he had planned to be, this July Fourth weekend: "Yankees-Detroit." He had the tickets in his bedroom. "Two days after that we'd be heading to the Cape. That was going to be fun, the Cape with Bob and the kids. Danny was looking forward to it, sailing with the boys. Tacking to the wind." He nodded his head. "Danny always looked forward to that. He was also looking forward to turning sixteen and getting a summer job. He was getting too old to be seen with you."

He wasn't sure if she'd heard him, he hadn't been aware that she was standing there until he heard her knock twice on the side of the house.

He turned too quickly and his foot slipped just like one of those old-time burlesque comics who steps on a banana peel and does airplane whirls with his arms to keep his balance. He managed to grab the shelf at the last second and hang on, leaning his body into the wall. Over his shoulder he saw Mary-Sue Richards, Sally's daughter, holding a covered dish.

"Dr. Owens?" she said, as though she'd wandered up to the wrong house, or was speaking to the wrong Dr. Owens. She looked a little frightened, maybe it was Jack's appearance, the three-day beard, the torn cutoffs, maybe it was just the look in his eyes. She took a step back and stayed on the other side of the door.

Jack smiled at her and said, "Working around the house. I'm starting to go to seed."

Mary-Sue smiled back. "Mom thought you might like to taste someone else's cooking for a change. It's cold marinated steak. She said to be sure to tell you she would have made it for you sooner but we were down to Brown County until the day before yesterday."

Jack said, "Tell her thanks. I appreciate it." He got down from the stepladder and opened the door. Mary-Sue handed him the covered dish—he would have to remember to label and freeze it.

"Mom wanted to bring it over herself, but I told her I would." Mary-Sue looked down at the floor and twisted her torso a little to the left, then the right, awkwardly, not like a teenager, but all shoulders and knees in her T-shirt and shorts, and just for that moment she wasn't a fifteen-year-old but the little girl who used to come over with her mother and run around the house with Danny and get modeling clay in her hair.

"I suppose I should have called first and asked if it was okay . . ." She raised her eyes and looked at him sadly. "I guess . . ." and twisted her torso uncomfortably, again.

"I'm glad you came over," he told her.

She stared at him silently, started to speak, stopped, lowered her eyes and just stood there.

"There's something you want to talk about, isn't there?" Jack said, in the voice he used when Danny had something to say and didn't know how to get started.

Mary-Sue nodded her head. "Danny. I'm really sorry about—about what happened."

"I know."

"I miss him a lot."

"I know you do." He asked her to come in and sit for a minute. "Please."

He went to the pantry, opened one of the tins, put a few cookies on a plate and poured her a glass of milk. It made him feel good to do this, to give cookies and milk to one of Danny's friends.

Mary-Sue sat stiffly in the chair. She looked at the glass and the plate and then down at the floor. Her blond hair was long and straight, gold-streaked by the summer sun. She gave the few stray ends a tug and twirled them around her finger, but she said nothing.

"Can you tell me what's on your mind?" Jack said to her.

"I don't know . . . I mean . . . I don't know . . ."

"There's nothing to be afraid of."

She shrugged her shoulders. "I was kind of worried about him, that's all."

Jack leaned forward, just a little bit. "What was he doing that worried you?"

She went back to twisting her hair. "I mean—I could just tell something was bothering him, about a week before . . ."

"Was he acting depressed? Something like that?"

"No. It wasn't real obvious or anything anyone else at school would have noticed, but you know, Danny and I were like brother and sis—" She started to cry. Jack reached across the table and put his hand on hers.

"It's all right," he said softly. "It's all right." He told her, "It's very sad, I know," and that she didn't have to talk about it if she didn't want to.

She picked up a paper napkin and wiped her eyes. "I could just tell," she sobbed. "I could just tell."

"I'm sure you asked him about it."

She shook her head. "No. I didn't. I should have but I just thought he was angry at me or maybe he was just in a bad mood, you know because of the baseball game. But I've been thinking about it and—I don't know." She folded the napkin and placed it next to the glass. "It's given me some bad thoughts."

Jack wanted to ask her why she'd waited so long to come over, why she'd waited so long to tell him. He wanted to know what she saw in Danny that had upset her. He wanted her to know what Danny hadn't been telling him. He felt a rush of anxiety beginning to overwhelm him, his legs started to shake and his hands, his neck felt cold and damp and he was sweating. He walked over to the window and kept his back to her so she wouldn't see him trembling, so she wouldn't be frightened.

He asked, "Didn't he say anything to you about, well, didn't he say anything at *all*?"

Mary-Sue answered, "No, but there was *some*thing—like when he thought no one was watching him. And like when I was teasing him one day on the bus about him and Jeanie Bauer."

"What about Jeanie Bauer?"

"Oh, nothing. I saw him talking to her a few days before, that's all. He got really weird about it."

"Weird?" Jack turned around and braced himself against the wall.

"He was like, 'Go bother someone who might care,' and like that. Actually, he said, 'someone who gives a shit.' And then the next day—the next day he gave me a *kitten*."

"A kitten?"

"A little orange and white kitten, with a broken leg. He came over to my house to say he was sorry about yelling at me, and he gave me a kitten. He said it was a stray that he found and he was worried about it and he couldn't take it home because Mutt would hurt it. He said I should take it to the vet and then keep it. He made me promise to keep it." She picked up one of the cookies, turned it over, looked at the underside and held it between her thumb and index finger. "He was real intense about it, about *everything*." She put the cookie on top of the napkin.

"What do you mean, intense?"

"Like the kitten was the most important thing in the world to him. It wasn't like Danny to be so, I don't know how to describe it. Like he was all locked up inside. It was more like a feeling I had about him. I could just see something was bothering him but I thought it was just—that he'd snap out of it in a day or so. I should have made him tell me—I don't know—like I should have taken it more seriously and done something about it. I shouldn't've been—I thought he'd probably talk to you about it, anyway."

"I asked Brian and the guys and they didn't see anything out of the ordinary," he told her, not as an argument.

"They wouldn't notice the rain until their boots overflowed."

That made Jack smile, and Mary-Sue smiled with him.

"In the cafeteria when they would just be talking and acting stupid," she said, "I could see Danny wasn't really into it." She picked up the cookie and examined it again. "There was this one day when Brian was giving C.J. a hard time, they'd cut school a few days before, an end-of-term thing that no one was supposed to know about, but I overheard them planning it on the bus. I guess it's okay to tell you now. A lot of kids do it, and Brian was talking to C.J. like he might have told his mom or something. Then Rick got on C.J., making him look real whipped, like he just wanted to run away. Usually Danny would take C.J.'s part, but this time he was just letting Rick get in his face. It was like Danny was in his own thoughts or something. But they just went on and didn't notice a thing. Even when I talked to him, it was like he was way off somewhere."

"Could he have been fooling around with drugs? Was that why Brian was giving C.J. such a hard time?" When she didn't answer, Jack promised, "It won't go any further than this room if they were."

"I think I would have found out—honest, Dr. Owens. I don't think any of them was doing drugs." She took a deep breath. "I feel real bad about not making Danny talk to me. I could always get him to open up and say what was bothering him. But I guess I thought he'd snap out of it and be Danny again." She looked down at the table. "You're not mad at me, are you?"

"*Mad* at you?"

"For telling you about Danny and crying in front of you."

"No, I'm not mad."

"I felt like I had to tell you."

"You did the right thing."

"I keep thinking that Danny must have talked to someone. I mean, when something's really bothering you, you have to tell *someone* about it."

"Any idea who that could be?"

"Usually me."

"Maybe Jeanie Bauer?"

"No *way*." She looked at him, Jack thought, with disappointment. Or maybe it was his own disappointment that he felt for having nothing better to offer.

Mary-Sue sat forward and rested her elbows on the table, raised her eyes and stared sorrowfully at the ceiling. She stayed like that for another minute, neither of them saying anything, then she pushed her chair back. "My mom made me promise not to make a pest of myself."

"You haven't," Jack assured her. But she stood up, anyway. He asked her to wait a moment, and that's when he told her about Lamar Coggin.

"His sister's on my soccer team."

"Did Danny know him?" Jack's voice seemed to shrink inside his throat.

"No. I don't think so."

Jack squeezed her hand and they walked outside together. "I'm glad you came by. You were a good friend to Danny."

Mary-Sue blushed. "I'm glad I came by, too," and she started down the back steps. "Oh, my mom says for you to come over on the Fourth of July. If you feel like it."

Jack stood on the porch while Mary-Sue slipped under the fence and hurried through the field, swinging her arms, her hair swaying back and forth like a mane.

"In the movies, the girl comes to the house of the grieving man and inspires him to rise above his sorrow. In reality, the girl tells the man his son had a sad, intense look on his face, that he was acting *weird* a week before he killed himself. She tells him his son wasn't laughing with the other kids, and no one noticed. But *she* did. She doesn't understand why—it is not understandable when you're fifteen—that while the other kids were busy being the other kids and Danny was busy being Danny, she, being Mary-Sue Richards, saw something no one else saw in Danny's face and thought Danny, being Danny, would snap out of it." Jack went back inside. "But you can't always rely on the constancy of personality, and even though Mary-Sue doesn't know that she knows it, this awful fact of life gives her bad thoughts. But what makes *you* go bloodless is knowing that you were too busy being Dr. Owens to see what was inside your son's sadness a week before he killed himself."

Jack had worked his way through the house. He was in the attic now, where it was hot and he was stripped naked, dripping sweat on the bare wood floor while he sorted through the old photographs: Danny's first birthday . . . Danny's first Little League game . . . Filling up boxes and labeling them, talking to himself, worried that the telephone would ring at any moment with bad news, worried about *What next?*

He had not gone to Sally Richards's for the Fourth. He had not even called her. Today was the seventh. "It's too late now."

He wasn't going to look through the photo albums, or the loose pictures in their yellow envelopes, he was only going to organize them, by month and year, and box them, but there was always that one photo that he had to stop and look at: Danny playing, Anne smiling, mugging for the camera. Jack experienced a perverse pleasure from the pain he was inflicting on himself, the sensation of pain becoming familiar and acceptable. He took an almost clinical approach to it, stepping back, stepping out of himself, watching himself.

"This is what it feels like when your son kills himself. This is what it's like to go mad." He was surprised at how calm he was, as he arranged the next package of sorrow.

He used to tell Danny that memory is what makes people moral. But memory also makes people time machines of sorts, although it never brings satisfaction. The old letters found in the shoe boxes, the photographs—these manufactured ghosts—never metamorphose into life, never do more than locate the hurt, the soft spot, like the bruise on the fruit, that starts to throb and ache before the shoe box gets unwrapped or the photograph catches the first light, before you realize what you're thinking about, the way it throbbed when Jack turned over the next picture and saw Danny's face, when he opened the next box.

He wondered what Danny would think if he saw his father sweating naked in the attic, sorting through the old photographs, talking to himself and weeping. Was this what Danny had in mind when he committed suicide? Was this what he expected?

What are the rules of behavior now? Jack wondered. What do you want me to *do*?

Did Danny expect Jack to behave the way he always behaved? Did he expect Jack to have a plan of action, a way of coping? Did he expect Jack to behave like Dr. Owens? Did he expect him to live up to the deal?

"There is no deal." Jack sat on the floor, drew his legs up to his chest. "The deal was with the living Danny."

There was no deal because there was nothing left to lose. That was why Jack could go through the week without showering or shaving, why he could walk through the house talking to himself, sit on the kitchen floor spoon-feeding Mutt while he neglected to feed himself; why he could sit naked in the attic, in the heat and the dust and the dirt.

He laid a handful of baby pictures at his feet. "What's left to lose? What's left to lose?" While the soft spot pulsed like a heart.

They were lying side by side in their bed. The gray SoHo light seemed to drip, like a slow faucet, into the loft, inching across the bare floor and along the walls. Jack was wearing the bottoms of his drawstring pajamas and drinking beer out of the bottle. Anne lifted it out of his hand and took a sip.

"I suppose I'll have to swear off this stuff," she said, not sounding at all pleased. "It's going to take some getting used to."

"Not drinking beer or having a baby?"

She didn't answer. She said, "So, what do you think?"

"I don't know. We're having a hell of a lot of fun and that's going to end."

"A *hell* of a lot of fun."

"We should be excited, don't you think?"

"I don't know what to think. I don't know what to feel. I'd like to think I'm scared to death, but I'm not sure that's what it is, either."

"We should be more enthusiastic."

"I like our life the way it is." She kissed his hand. "I'm not sure I want the honeymoon to end."

"A six-year honeymoon isn't nearly long enough." He raised the bottle to his mouth.

"No," she said, "it isn't."

"It's pretty bourgeois, having a kid. Hunting around for a neighborhood with a park. Finding a good school. Buying a *house* . . ."

"I don't know, Jack."

"Man, it's confusing."

"I never thought of us as one of those couples who needed a baby to make their lives complete."

"We're not."

"And you know it's going to change our lives dramatically. How we sleep and the way we do our work. The way— *Every*thing."

"We should have been more careful."

"Should have, but weren't," she said flatly. "I haven't called my parents yet."

"I haven't told mine. In case we—" He didn't have to finish.

"I suppose some sort of instinct will take over after a while and we'll start nesting and designing little things for it to wear. But I'm not feeling any of that right now."

"Neither am I."

"I'm not sure that I'm even looking forward to feeling it," she told Jack. "I don't know."

Jack put his arm around her shoulder and drew her closer to him. He started kissing the back of her neck and nuzzling his face in her hair. She said that's another thing they'd even have to change after the baby was born, their sex life.

"Not right away. After a year."

"Sooner," Anne told him. "They're aware of everything in six months. So, my rapacious Jack, we not only must pay the piper for our fun, we'll have to take it on the sly as well."

Later, with the tray of Italian bread and pâté next to them, Anne said, "We don't *have* to know the answer, do we? Not right this minute."

Two weeks later, sitting with his parents in their library, two glasses of whiskey on the coffee table, one for him, one for his father, a gin and tonic for his mother, Jack's father said, *"Bourgeois?"* his voice strong and resonant. "What do you think you are, Jackie, a struggling artist? You're a Ph.D. NYU professor with a published book under your belt." There was nothing scolding in his voice. If anything, he sounded as though he were simply stating Jack's credentials to the department chair, and trying hard not show any bias toward the candidate. Jack looked at his mother. She winked at him while his father went on, "And harboring the illusion of a bohemian life, *if,* by the way you ever had one, even when you were in college, is no reason not to have this baby."

His mother told him, "If either of you has any claim to the title, it's Anne. And even that's a stretch." She ran her hand along the arm of the chair, her fingers making small circles against the rose-colored fabric. Her long torso, like a Modigliani woman, like a young dancer, bent gracefully when she reached for her drink. She lifted her cigarette from the ashtray, leaving the subtle and pleasant scent of her perfume in her wake, the same perfume which insinuated itself throughout the apartment. She inhaled the smoke, almost as an afterthought, then raised her glass and said, "To your healthy new baby."

"Enjoy the miracle of life that's come to you," his father said with a catch in his throat.

Jack raised his glass and sipped his whiskey. It went down smoothly, nothing second-rate about it, or anything else in the apartment. Not the crisp arrangements of sculpture, or the way a clock defined the space on a wall. Nor the elegant line of the neoclassic couch and the way it was placed symmetrically between two chairs; the lamplight, gauged just right to show off the oil paintings. The bookcase filling the west wall: Cather and Fitzgerald first editions, some early Hemingway, Twain. Limited editions of poetry: e. e. cummings, Hart Crane, Marianne Moore, Kenneth Burke, Howard Nemerov, Wallace Stevens. The plays of George S. Kaufman—with and without Hart—Miller, Odets, Shaw, Pirandello, Noël Coward, Shakespeare, Molière; rare first editions by authors dead and forgotten, some forgotten even before they were dead; contemporary books from the bestseller list sandwiched in the corners.

Jack admired his parents' apartment the way he'd admire any work of art, more than a little in awe of it—it was his mother's creation, really, his father was the silent partner in this particular operation. "Go with your strength and know when to shut up," he would say. Interior design may be the small talk of the art world, but when it's done without apology and derivation, it can stand on its own aesthetic, or so it seemed to Jack when he sat with his parents, the evening etching a path along Park Avenue, up through the windows and across the Oriental rugs. If he knew nothing else about the people who lived here, if this were all he had to go on, he would not have doubted the substance of their hearts or the quality of their minds. If they weren't his parents, he would have envied their child.

This was not the apartment in which Jack had grown up. That apartment was on East Sixty-eighth Street, a sprawling duplex with two staircases and a long hallway, uncarpeted, he always believed, to give his parents ample time to uncouple at the sound of their son's little feet slapping the parquet floor. His bedroom was a clutter of baseballs, bats and gloves, shoulder pads and footballs, clothes and shoes. The bookcases were crammed, not with first editions, but with *Best Sports Stories* and Red Smith, Ring Lardner, *The Great Gatsby, Catcher in the Rye,* film biographies. His bedpost, gnawed and slavered on by Louie, his black Lab, who would outlive two more beds, was draped with jerseys and baseball caps. The walls were dabbed with peanut butter fingerprints, papered with movie posters. His father had set up a small projection room in what later would be the guest room, so Jack could screen the movies he made with his 16-millimeter camera. But the apartment on Park Avenue was his parents' alone, where Jack, in spite of his mother's insistence to the contrary, was a guest, which was how he thought it should be. A place of their own for which they'd waited sixteen years—when Jack went off to college—to have; and even if they never said it and surely never made Jack feel it, the wait must have seemed endless at times.

Jack wondered, after he raised his whiskey and joined in the toast, would he and Anne spend the next sixteen, seventeen, eighteen years waiting as their child calibrated their lives? Would they wait for him or her to leave home? Would they wait, always aware of waiting, to have a place of their own again?

Jack took another sip of his drink.

His father walked over to the window. His tall, broad body cast a long shadow against the floor. "You think your mother and I wanted *you*?" he said to Jack.

"Your father thinks he's funny," Jack's mother said. "You're not. You're not funny, Mike. After all these years you'd think he'd admit to himself the humor gene was lost on him." She lighted a fresh cigarette. "Please, Mike, this is no time for jokes."

"I'm not joking. I think it's time Jackie knew the truth. We never wanted you. We still don't."

"Believe me," his mother said, "we wanted you."

"It's a little late for reassurances." Jack matched his father's deadpan. "The damage is done." And they all laughed, although Jack's mother reminded them that this was "no laughing matter."

"Of course it is," his father said. "You can't take life seriously all the time."

"There are couples out there who'd give everything to have a baby," Jack's mother said, "so don't take it for granted."

"How does Anne feel about it?" his father wanted to know.

"The same way I do."

"Everyone is scared the first time."

"That's not it. Or maybe we're just not sure what it is we're scared of." He swallowed the rest of his drink. "Anne and I are happy with the way things are. We don't want a baby to spoil that. To weigh us down."

"Endless childhood?" his father asked.

"You know better than that."

"We don't *know* better than *any*thing," his mother said. "Opinions, however, are another story."

"And your opinion?"

His parents exchanged fast glances, the way they used to when Jack would ask them questions about sex.

"It goes without saying," his mother said, "that the idea of your father and me being grandparents is thrilling." There was always a hint of amusement in her voice, as though she already knew the winner of the race, the final score, but was keeping it to herself until everyone else caught up to her. It was there now. She already knew what Jack and Anne were going to decide, even as she said, "You know my stand on abortion, but if you and Anne are considering it you should have a better reason than 'too *bourgeois*' or else you're just playing Peter Pan to her Wendy and I don't think that's very healthy." She snuffed out her cigarette.

"That's *it*? That's your *opinion*?"

"Isn't that enough?" his father said.

"Trust your instincts, Jackie," his mother told him. "They'll never steer you wrong."

"By the way, where *is* Anne?" his father asked. "I'd think she'd want to be in on this."

"She's over on Seventy-first Street hanging her show. She'll be here later."

"An Upper East Side gallery." His mother smiled. "*Very* bohemian."

Jack held the tiny red sweater in his hand and the white baby shoes, then gently placed them in the carton. He looked through another set of photographs: Danny's summer in France. And another: the summer in Tuscany.

He wiped the sweat off his face and worked on the next set of pictures, slowly. There was no reason to hurry. Methodically. There was no reason not to be thorough.

He sorted through the photographs of his mother and father. There were even a few photographs of Maggie—*Not your finest hour, Jack*—and he thought for a moment about Maggie Brighton, who taught English lit in Bloomington, and played piano duets with Danny on Sunday afternoons. Then Jack quickly pulled out more pictures of Danny with Anne, Anne sitting by herself on a bench in Central Park, on vacation in Dorset.

He wondered what it would feel like to talk to Anne. He'd been thinking about talking to her ever since the funeral because she was Danny's mother—*You and Anne used to talk about everything. What would you say to her now? "We can't undo what's been done, but our son, he was ours, Anne, is dead, and you should know about it."*

Would she say: "You must have me confused with some other woman named Anne." Would she say: "I wish I could help you, Jack." Or: "It's been such a long time, I don't even know who Danny is." Would she say: "I don't even know *you*." There'd be no apology in that voice, just straight and unfiltered: "I don't know why you called me, Jack." Or would she understand why because she was Anne, and Danny's mother, and that can never change?

It disturbed him to admit that he wanted to talk to Anne, as though the past ten years had been some accident. It disturbed him to think about talking to her the way they used to talk when they were married, when they would lie on the bed and whisper in the dark; the way they used to talk before Danny was born. It disturbed him to think that some flaw in his character had weakened his resolve, that with one call he'd annihilate, demythologize, Dr. Owens, who packed his life into a truckload of boxes and took his son to the safest place he could think of. Who had the confidence—*the arrogance, Jack?*—to think he could undo the damage.

It disturbed him to think about Anne the way he was thinking about her now. It disturbed him to think that he was being disloyal to Danny even as he wanted to talk to Anne like they used to *how many lifetimes* ago, because he couldn't get through this alone, and she was the only one he wanted to talk to. The only one who would understand this kind of sorrow—"Can you help me figure it out? Can you tell me why he did it?"

It disturbed him to think about her asking: "Can we always be like this? Loving each other and living our lives together?" And he'd answered, "I don't know why not."

But he hadn't understood the question—he hadn't understood what was in her voice. Just as he hadn't understood Anne, who asked it.

He hadn't understood the meaning of the question when Anne

asked it the day they looked at the house he loved. Jack had never understood the question so he interpreted the question to his own design. Only years later, when The Baby had become Danny, did Jack understand the meaning of the question, and understand Anne, who had asked it. Only then did he know the sum total of his ignorance. Now, in the dead heat of the attic, feeling as though he were standing outside of himself, watching himself, as he wondered if he was going mad, Jack fantasized about Anne understanding, as no one else could understand, his sadness. Because he understood that Anne had never understood her own question, had never understood that asking it was asking for an answer that did not include Danny. But Jack had understood, ever since Anne said she was leaving. Only now could he tell her.

The corner of a label clung to his forearm like a lamprey. The air in the attic was hot with lint and wool dropping from the old clothes, sticking to his skin, sealing the air out of his pores; that must have been why he was having trouble breathing, but he kept looking at the pictures, aligning the corners, placing them in boxes, marking the dates and the places.

He imagined calling Danny's name, calling to him to come up for a minute: "Want to see what your first pair of shoes looked like?" Calling to him: "I want you to see a picture of you and Granma . . ." While he waded elbow-deep in photographs and baby clothes, elbow-deep in memories.

But Jack wanted to remember Danny not as a baby, or the little boy in the photographs hugging his grandmother, holding his new puppy. He didn't want to think about Danny, who was acting "weird" on the school bus, who was withdrawn and somber, or sat silently at the breakfast table while his food went untouched and asked: "Which is more important, Dad, honesty or loyalty?" Jack wanted to remember Danny who was becoming a young man, who last September asked, "What would you think if I decided to go away to college?"

"Any particular school?"

"I was thinking about Michigan or Wisconsin. Or do you want me to go to college in Indiana?"

"No. Just as long as it's a good school. I'm glad you're starting to think about it."

"What if I wanted to be a classical pianist?"

"I'd say you're talented enough to become one."

"What if I wanted to be a baseball player?"

"I'd say give it your best try. But there are better baseball and music programs than Michigan and Wisconsin." When Danny didn't answer, Jack said, "What are you really asking me?"

Danny looked away for a moment, and when he looked back his face was flushed. When he spoke, his voice was tight and strained. "What if I'm not as smart as you when I'm older?"

"You already are. And smarter, even."

"No, really."

"Really."

"But suppose I don't write books like you or become a famous pianist or composer?"

"Who says that has anything to do with being smart? Only a very smart person questions the limits of his intelligence."

Danny sat silently for a moment and Jack did not intrude on that silence.

"I'm just afraid sometimes," Danny said after a while.

"Can you tell me what you're afraid of?"

"I don't know. I don't want to talk about it anymore."

They were sitting next to each other on the back steps, it was night, after supper and homework. Jack put his arm around Danny's shoulder and pulled him close, which made Danny look embarrassed and avert his eyes.

Jack wanted to remember the feel of Danny's presence. He wanted to remember the weight of his body in the car when he sat behind the wheel just last April and Jack let him drive to the stop sign at the end of the road, the way Danny shifted gears and tapped the accelerator and smiled so broadly and proud when the car responded that Jack had to reach over and tousle his hair and tell him, "*You* are the *man*."

Danny laughed and reluctantly gave up the driver's seat. He talked about next year when he'd be old enough to get a learner's permit and how he wanted to get a job after school and start saving for a car.

When Danny was with his friends out at the mall on Saturday afternoons, when he was in school, when he stood on the pitcher's mound and looked in for the sign, was he already thinking about suicide? When he talked about college or learning to drive, was it already inside of him? Was he hiding that the way he hid the box under the bed?

"Why weren't you listening, Jack? Why weren't you paying attention?"

What was in Danny's voice back in May?

"What was he saying? What weren't you hearing?"

Jack leaned against one of the cartons. His lips were dry and his tongue felt thick in his mouth. His skin itched. When he shifted his body, his legs and arms dragged weakly beneath him and bursts of light appeared before his eyes. He felt the heat enveloping him and had trouble remembering where he was or what he was supposed to be doing. There was a humming in his ears, as though voices were in conversation downstairs, or just outside the house.

Even with the window open, the attic was airless. He listened to the beating of his heart, the pulsing of the blood in his temples. He knew he was dehydrating. If he didn't get out of this heat, he would surely die. But when he tried to stand, he fell back on the floor. He would try again in a minute.

Outside, the moon was rising over the trees and the trees beat their branches against the window.

XII

He was lying on his bedroom floor naked and sweating, the telephone pressed under his cheek. He was holding on to one of Danny's baby pictures and mumbling to himself. He could smell his sour breath, he could smell his own stale body odor. He had no idea what day it was. He could not remember coming down here, or who he'd tried to call, or when.

He put down the phone, started to get up, and his knees buckled. He leaned against the bed and when he managed to stand he saw himself in the mirror, or what was left of him. A ragged face, a gaunt body, filthy with lint and dust, a dull, abandoned look in his eye, like the survivor of a shipwreck.

The telephone rang. He felt nothing but dread. When he picked it up and said "Hello," the word broke apart in his mouth. A bitter taste of bile curdled in his throat. He waited for the voice at the other end. Grace's voice. The doctor's voice. He waited for the bad news.

The voice said it was "Marty." Jack didn't remember anyone named Marty. It said, "I saw the movie."

"Movie," Jack repeated dimly.

"Blade Runner."

"Marty, the detective?"

"I wanted to have a little more insight into Danny, so I rented it. I had no idea—that's one hell of a movie."

"I'm in the middle of something, Marty. I can't really talk right now."

"Fair enough. I just wanted to tell you it really impressed me, and I'd like to get together and talk to you about it."

"I'll call you sometime."

"I'll look forward— How are you doing? Under the circumstances. You're doing all right?"

"Sure."

"Getting out of the house, seeing people?"

Sweat ran down Jack's neck and the length of his spine. "I'm seeing people."

"Great. I was hoping you and I could have a beer or something."

"I'll call you."

"What about tonight? It's so damn hot. We can go over to the Palomino for a cold one."

"You caught me at a bad time."

"What's a good night for you?"

"There aren't any good nights." Jack felt like a drunk scrambling in the dark for his keys, scrambling to get away from this conversation. Scrambling for some part of himself. His teeth were chattering, his hands trembled. Marty wouldn't need his books to recognize the carnage. "Maybe you need him to see you like this," Jack whispered.

"What's that?"

"I'm here."

"How about seven?" Marty said, talking past him. "They put in air-conditioning."

The Palomino Grille was long past its glory days, when it was the fanciest speakeasy in town, or so the old-timers claimed. When Prohibition was repealed, it was the first speakeasy in the state to get a full liquor license—something to do with its clientele, which included the mayor, governor and both U.S. senators—and easily transformed itself into a legitimate bar and steak joint, a Grille, with beautiful stained-glass windows and a bubbling jukebox that played Fred Rose, Jimmie Rodgers, Tex Ritter and even some Woody Guthrie. It wasn't the first place Jack would have picked to have a drink, or even the second. He hadn't been here since his student days, when he and his friends came by to soak up the local color and drink the very affordable beer.

There was a relaxed, broken-in feel to the place, the oak bar, the dim lighting, the worn-out tables and soft chairs. The air-conditioning was tolerably cool and the conversations were muted, just a bunch of men, some of them old-timers, the old miners and railroad men, some simply old-timers-in-the-making, sitting around, drinking, letting the evening pass quietly and leisurely toward closing time. The Palomino was the closest thing Gilbert had to an old-fashioned tavern, not the sort of place that attracted hard drinkers or anyone looking to make trouble, where a man whose son had killed himself just two months ago might not necessarily feel too overwhelmed.

Marty was sitting by the window in the front of the barroom drinking a beer and, when he saw Jack, signaled the bartender to bring over two more bottles. Jack started sweating. The acrid taste of fear was on his tongue. He should not have left the house and the telephone unattended. It was a mistake to have come here. He tapped his foot, picked at the skin around his cuticles while Marty looked him over, not saying anything, just watching him and doing the same remarkable thing with his face that he'd done the first time they'd met, and which now made Jack sit down and keep still.

Marty said something, Jack was incapable of listening, "tough time . . ." "easy time . . ." Something about *Blade Runner* . . . Maybe they were questions, but they remained unanswered. Jack might have raised the bottle to his lips, but if he had, he was not aware of it. He was aware only of being away from his house, away from the telephone that might be off the hook, the answering machine that may have become, through some malfunction, some accident Jack had been too numb to notice—through a will of its own—inoperative. Away from all the checks and double-checks that held the next disaster at bay. His insides were tumbling over themselves, his flesh felt like it was about to crawl right off the bone and take the damp hairs with it. And Marty was talking about what? Jack pushed his chair away from the table.

"My son killed himself, Marty. My son is dead." And he rushed outside, where the air on Main Street was hot and motionless.

Marty went after him. "It's only going to get worse," he called out.

Jack walked faster.

"It's only going to get worse," Marty repeated after he caught up with him.

"What makes you so damn *pre*scient?"

"I know that look."

"We'll have to discuss it someday." Jack picked up the pace.

Marty stayed with him. "I'm no great detective, Jack, probably not even a good one, but I'm looking at you and seeing depression and damn near starvation."

"Don't worry about *me*. I'm doing all right."

"You haven't slept in days. My guess is you've got insomnia. And the way you ran out of there, I figure you're having panic attacks. You're as pale as—when was the last time you left the house?"

Jack felt as though a cold stone had been dropped in his stomach. He felt tightness gripping his chest. His fingertips had gone numb. Not because of anything Marty had said, but because something terrible had happened to his father, he could sense it, and Marty was stopping him from taking care of it.

"I'm hardly panicked or starving. And I'm not running anywhere." Jack's body strained to reach the corner.

"I can help you," Marty told him.

"I don't need your help."

"Yes, I can see that."

The empty street flashed past him, the dark storefronts, the quiet restaurants. "Everyone's gone for the summer," Jack said flatly. "Everyone but the old-timers, this lunatic cop and me."

"Nothing bad's going to happen if you don't go home," Marty said, not unkindly.

"You don't know what you're talking about." Jack wanted to believe that. Just as he wanted to believe that the man lying naked on his bedroom floor hadn't been him. But he could only think of *What next?* He could only think of getting home before the next disaster.

"I *do* know what I'm talking about," Marty said.

The heat and humidity felt oppressive and suffocating, the air was thick and hot like dog's breath, heavy with the scraps of the season: ashes from cookouts, bits of paper and gunpowder from fireworks, grease and smoke, blades of mowed lawns, and insects, all clinging to Jack's skin, choking his lungs. But he would not slow down. "I'll mourn my son as I see fit."

"I'm not telling you not to. And I'm not telling you to swallow your pain, either. I just want to talk to you."

"I don't want to talk to *you*." Jack followed his shadow as it lengthened under the streetlights. "Go help the other boy's family. They need it more than I do."

"I'm not too sure of that."

"And please don't feel sorry for me."

"I don't feel sorry for you. I admire your strength."

"Don't patronize me, either."

"Who's patronizing you? But I don't think the rules state that you have to make things worse for yourself."

"Oh, there are *rules*."

"I meant to tell you sooner."

Jack turned the corner. "This is none of your concern, so back off." He stopped at his car and opened the door.

"Talk with me for a few minutes."

Jack clenched his teeth. "I'm going to slug you if you don't get out of my way."

Marty didn't flinch. "You know, I used to be married to a woman I really loved, then my marriage fell apart and I proceeded to fall apart, too." He looked only at Jack's eyes. "I had the same symptoms as you."

"I don't have any *symp*toms."

"It's like a floating sense of foreboding."

Jack gave no answer.

"It got so I was afraid that if I didn't keep busy I'd die." Marty spoke slowly, his voice barely raised above a whisper. "I convinced myself that staying busy and my well-being were interconnected."

"I don't need to talk."

"After a month, I realized my life was out of control, that I was a slave to my obsessions. So I took a day off, drove out to Douglas Park, got in a rowboat and rowed to the middle of the lake. I made myself stay out there, doing nothing all day. By sunset there I was, still alive and none the worse for wear. I did the same thing the next day, and the day after. It took some time, but I proved to myself that my fears were groundless."

"Do you expect me to believe that?"

"Unless you think I'm a sadistic son of a bitch."

"Get out of my way."

"I just want to talk for a little while. Not about Danny. Or you. Just talk. We can talk about *Blade Runner.*"

"Some other time, okay?"

Marty ignored him. "In your book, you wrote that it raises the same questions about mortality and God that *Frankenstein* does."

"What the hell do you want from me?"

"And Danny was *eight* when he saw the movie?"

"Twelve, okay. And if you want to chew on something, chew on this: he said what made him sad was the replicants were programmed to die when they turned four. That was the same age Danny was when his mother left him. Now get out of my way."

"You wrote if we ever came face-to-face with God, the one question we would ask, the question humanity has always asked is: 'If you love me, why do you let me die?' Which is what the replicant asks his maker. You said that's what Christ was asking God on the cross."

"And hardly a question I'm prepared to ask right now. So fuck off." Jack couldn't hear what Marty said. He was thinking about Danny, who wasn't his creation, after all, and who had secrets and who killed himself. While his hands started to tremble.

". . . said he could see the movie?" Marty was saying. "Were you aware of that?"

When Jack didn't answer, Marty asked, "Did Danny ever talk about it?"

"I'm not suffering from any of the symptoms you described." Jack stumbled over the words.

"You're afraid to be here. That seems like a symptom of *some*thing."

"I'm not afraid. I just don't want to talk. I'm going home."

"Come on, Jack. You're having a tough time. What's so wrong with letting me help you?"

"I don't need your help." Jack jangled his car keys nervously. "I'm not the man standing on the ledge."

Marty looked at him and said solemnly, "You're supposed to be sad, as sad as you want, you're supposed to grieve and mourn and feel whatever the hell you want. But you can't be victim to your fears." He stepped back and sat on the curb, a Chaplinesque gesture without the comedy and the cuteness; nothing bittersweet about it, nothing baggy-pants. It was simply an act of courage. All Jack had to do now was step over him, get in the car and leave him looking like a fool. Marty must have known that, but it didn't seem to frighten him.

In the heat of summer, Jack was standing in the shadows, sweating and shaking, feeling like a scared and helpless little shit.

"All this because you saw *Blade Runner* and once heard Danny play the piano?"

Marty said, "You looking for an airtight reason? I don't know why. Maybe I'm a lunatic cop." He motioned for Jack to sit down. "Maybe it's just something I want to do. Or maybe I just like you and I'm short on people I like." He didn't look up, he only looked straight ahead, as though he expected Jack to stay there, as though he understood the meaning and strength of his own gesture; and Jack realized it was anything but calculated. For only a moment, he wanted to tell Marty about the grief and the fears. He wanted to admit that he was afraid to leave his house, that he was afraid to sleep and afraid to stay awake. He wanted to tell him about the days and nights of neglect, of sitting naked in the attic and passing out in the bedroom. His face felt damp and hot. He was finding it hard to breathe. He sat down on the hot curbstone, but he said nothing.

Marty made a fist with his right hand, stuck it in the palm of his left and pressed both hands against his chin. He kept looking straight ahead. "Did you always want to be a professor?" he asked.

Jack didn't answer.

"Was your ex-wife a professor, too?"

"Are you trying to draw me out?"

"Was she?"

"An artist," Jack said.

"You wrote that great art has the ability to transcend its genre. Did your wife transcend the genre?"

Jack said, "Yes, Anne transcended the genre." And the place inside him, the soft spot where the girl named Anne was still twenty years old with dots of yellow paint in her hair and a smile that made him stare in dumb amazement, and where Danny was still a little boy and there were no signs of trouble, the soft spot throbbed like a newborn heart.

"That's something I've always wished I could do. Be an artist. Take an abstract idea and make it something beautiful and tangible. Did you ever want to make movies?" Marty smiled. "I'm curious. Really."

"When I was in high school I wanted to be a director, a great auteur. That's why I went to Gilbert College. Because of their film department."

"And?"

"Look, Marty—I admit that I've been having a tough time—"

"Did you ever make movies?"

"I lacked a little something called talent."

"Someone once said talent is a cheap trick."

Jack's body started shaking again, and his breathing was loud and fast. He didn't care that Marty was watching him—observing him, and not accidentally; Jack was beginning to realize that there were few things that Marty did accidentally, or innocently. He leaned back on his elbows, waited while his body calmed down, and he caught his breath. "You like doing this," he said. "You like being a detective."

"There are other things I like more." Marty kicked a cigarette butt away from his shoe. "I'm not even sure I ever wanted to be a cop. But I needed a job after high school, and since I don't come from the kind of family that encouraged us to go to college, when a guy I know said he was taking the police exam, I figured I'd take it, too. I graded high and decided to join the department." He turned to Jack and grinned. "Being a cop in Gilbert is kind of like being a fisherman, it's never exactly been a hotbed of crime—even Indiana's very own John Dillinger never committed a crime here, never even *tried* to rob the banks. One of the few towns in the state he left alone. Anyway, I did a little crime scene work, mostly burglaries. I started seeing some domestic violence cases and I got into Victim Support. After a while I got it through my thick skull that people responded to my help. The department pays for half of your college tuition if you get a job-related degree, so I started taking sociology and criminology courses at ISU. I like kids, so I figured I'd do some work in the Juvenile Division where I could help them and their families."

"Which includes consoling bereaved fathers."

"What can I say?" Marty answered, in the same sympathetic tone he'd used earlier, but Jack had no impulse to punch him this time. He wanted only to go home. He felt the familiar rush of anxiety, the foreboding, unbearable and insistent. He drummed his fingertips against his knees. He tapped his foot against the pavement. He had to get away right now, even if it was too late, even if the answering machine was already blinking bad news; and he felt ashamed of himself, ashamed of his fears; and he felt something else as well, something more than shame. He felt small inside, weak and clammy because he needed to be here with Marty, he needed to be carried through the night.

"I'm in the middle of the lake," Jack said, "aren't I?"

"There are worse places to be."

"And you're trying to get me to stay out here."

"I'm not so sure about that. Maybe you're trying to get yourself to stay out here."

"I'm not so sure about that, either."

"Fair enough," Marty said, and a moment later, "I guess we're just two guys who don't really know what the hell we're doing out here," and managed again not to sound patronizing.

Half a mile away, a freight train tore a piece of silence out of the night. In a minute, the warning bells at the Third Street crossing would clang frantically and the red lights would flash like a nervous tic while the wail of the train whistle expanded and the diesel engine shined its ever-lovin' light, pulling and rolling, eating up the steel-slick tracks, in and out of town without stopping.

"You know why Dillinger never robbed the banks in Gilbert?" Marty asked. "Because the town's surrounded by railroad crossings, and there was always the chance that all his escape routes would be blocked at the same time by passing trains and he'd've been trapped here."

XIII

The red light on the answering machine had not been flashing a warning, and the cold stone lodged inside Jack's stomach had loosened its grip. Something was happening, it was not unpleasant and it was not filled with dread, if Jack didn't think too much about it, if he didn't say to himself, "Well, nothing happened tonight. Not *this* time. Not yet."

Outside the house, orange sunlight rippled just above the horizon. It wasn't so bad sitting in the backyard watching the dawn, taking off his shirt, lying back in one of the chairs, feeling the slight, excuse-me breeze rustling the trees. Maybe he'd bring a book out here and try to read, or go ahead and accept Marty's lunch invitation.

Lunch, while the rest of my world falls apart.

He watched the morning sun rise over the rim of the field. He felt all the familiar feelings of loneliness and sorrow, and something not as familiar: a sudden spasm of disloyalty to Danny for going out last night, for wanting to go out today.

What did Marty say about that? Jack couldn't remember.

He remembered, instead, that he and Danny would have been to New York and gone by now. They'd have seen their doubleheader—the rich red clay of the infield when you walk out of the dark runway and into the sunlight, which is not unlike stepping into a dream. The deep green grass and how perfectly it's cut, how perfectly it grows. He thought of the way Danny had gripped his hand the first time they went to a ballgame together, back in 1985. Danny, wearing his little blue baseball cap, red sneakers that seemed too big for his small body, looking up, asking, "Why didn't Mummy come with us?"

"Mummy's very busy today," Jack explained.

He thought about Danny lasting through five innings. He thought of all the baseball games he would never see with his son—somewhere in the basement, in a box against a wall or on a shelf, was the box score of Danny's first game.

Jack whispered, "Danny and I would've been on the Cape the day before yesterday."

He thought about the expanse of summer—wicked nights, he called them.

I went out last night, and no one died.

Jack wanted to remember what else Marty had said. He thought it might help him tolerate what he was feeling now and what he was doing, what he had done and what this summer had turned into. He wanted to remember what Marty had said because thinking about it was the only thing that wasn't filled with regret, the only thing that didn't hurt to think about, not the way remembering the day he took Danny to his first ballgame hurt, the way it hurt to think about Anne.

A June bug flung itself at the screen door, making a heavy crunching sound. A hawk rode the thermal draft bold and preeminent above the field. Jack closed his eyes. When he opened them, the sun was high above the trees and the air was the coolest it was going to be all day.

"What I'm saying is, you're supposed to grieve, you're supposed to mourn and feel all the things, *anything,* you want, but there's a healthy way to go about it. That's all." That's what Marty told him last night.

Jack got up slowly, slung his shirt over his shoulder and went into the house to shave and shower, to select the clothes he would wear; to prepare himself for the impending afternoon.

They were going to drive out to the country, to a little barbecue shack, Walter's, on the outskirts of town. Marty said it reminded him of the old chicken shacks in western Tennessee, where his grandmother used to live. He said it always cheered him up to go out there, took his mind off his troubles. Maybe it would have the same effect on Jack, if only for the few hours they were gone. "Anyway," Marty said, "it's a nice drive through the country." He said this last night, while they were sitting in Jack's car waiting for the sunrise. Marty had his eyes closed and his seat pushed back and it seemed, for a moment, that he was talking in his sleep, his voice was that soft and far away. He said, "It's a pretty remote place. I found it when I was going through that rough time of mine." Then he opened his eyes and sat up. "But I should tell you in advance, we'll probably be the only white people there. Will that bother you?"

Jack told him, "Don't be ridiculous." Which made Marty smile.

"I didn't think it would. Anyway, I think you'll like it." Marty said this as though Jack had already agreed to go, as though Jack wasn't shaking inside, certain that what remained of his world had fallen apart during the night. "But I better tell you, Walter doesn't know I'm a cop. If he did, he'd've never let me stick around. He got the idea that I haul cement over in Vigo County, and I haven't tried to change his mind. I don't have to tell you cops are not on the A-list of most African-Americans around here. In any case, a lot of his customers would be very unhappy if they knew." Marty said he didn't even bring any of the guys he worked with. "The first time I walked in, I think Walter thought I was either some crazy redneck looking for trouble or someone from the board of health looking for a bribe, but all I was looking for was some good barbecue." A moment later, he said, "It seems like a lot all at once and I know you don't really want to do it." He turned his face toward the day's first light. "But you have to start sometime."

"You're going to make me your summer project no matter what I say, so we might as well start tomorrow."

Marty put his hands behind his head. "Fair enough," he said, in a tone of calm resolve.

It wasn't a very big place, eight tables, a lunch counter with a dozen metal stools, the kind you see in a lot of diners, low backs and vinyl cushions. But it was pure country. The early afternoon breeze wove lazily off the river through the deep shade of the tall oak trees, wrapped itself around the sweet smell of pork cooking out back in the smoker, climbed through the eyebrow windows and swirled in the vortex of the ceiling fans.

There were four men seated at the counter eating their lunch, talking and joking in that way people who know each other well talk and joke. They turned around to say hello to Marty and one of the men said it was good to see him again.

Walter was short and lean and looked about sixty. He walked with a hitch, and started talking to Marty as soon as he saw him, hurrying up to him to shake his hand, shake Jack's hand and say any friend of Marty's was always welcome, asking how Marty was doing these days while at the same time pulling two chairs away from one of the tables—old Formica trimmed with stainless steel and matching chairs, only none of the chairs matched—and saying, "Sit down, sit down." He did nothing to hide his affection for Marty, the way he fussed over him and gripped his arm while he asked, "Where you been keeping yourself, young man?" in a sweet, paternal tone.

Marty said he'd been working. "Doing this and that."

One of the men at the counter said, "Just don't do too much of this and stay *completely* away from *that*." Which got a laugh from everyone, including Marty.

"That's Red," Marty told Jack, pointing to the man who got the laugh. "He's a college professor, like you. Teaches structural engineering over at Rose-Hulman."

"And the rest of us are just riffraff," the man next to Red answered.

"That's 'Big Man,'" Marty said. "And the man next to him is Doc and that's Elvin in the middle. This is my friend Jack."

They said their hellos while Walter smiled and said, "Now that we got that over with, I'll have something good for you both before too long," and walked to the grill on the other side of the counter.

There was an upright piano catty-cornered in the back of the room. The jukebox played Etta James singing: "I'll be seeing you in all the old familiar places . . ." The men at the counter were now listening to Walter as he kept on talking to Marty: he hoped Marty was managing to keep cool on these hot days, and was he planning on getting some fishing in, "the perch are biting real good."

Red asked Walter, "How would *you* know?" and made a joke about Walter's fishing skills, or lack thereof, which got the others laughing. Then Walter got off a good one about Red and they all laughed at that, too. Doc made another joke at Red's expense. Elvin and Walter showed their appreciation by clapping their hands together, just before "Big Man" got off a joke about Walter, which Red appreciated. Walter threatened to take his meat cleaver "to the lot of you." Talking and cooking.

It was something Jack might have enjoyed, had he been capable of enjoying things these days.

Marty said, "I'm really sorry." He spoke softly. "I didn't think they'd get into it like this."

Jack shrugged his shoulders. "There's nothing to apologize for."

A few minutes later, Walter came back with two bottles of cold beer, a dozen napkins and two plates of pork with that sweet smoky smell, dripping with sauce and overflowing the buns.

Marty started eating right away. Jack picked up his sandwich and put it down without taking a bite. He pushed the meat around the plate, put down his fork and took a swallow of beer. Marty looked over at him, shrugged his shoulders and said, "Don't worry about it."

Hank Ballard now played on the jukebox and Red and the others were joined by a handful of their friends, heavy-chested men with the dust of construction on their overalls and in their hair, a few wearing company uniforms, some in shorts and T-shirts. They carried trumpet cases, saxophone cases, a double bass, everyone talking and laughing. They put down their instruments, told Walter to hurry up with the food and filled the rest of the stools at the counter.

Not long after, several more cars scattered gravel in the parking lot and a small group of middle-aged women, finished with their day's work, came in, singing out greetings, telling Walter to hurry up with the food "or we'll come back there and cook it ourselves," all said with good-natured amusement.

More cars arrived and the tables started filling up, beers were dug out of the ice chest, the laughter got louder, the talk faster. Walter stayed at his grill, slathering sauce on the barbecue, filling the rolls, spooning out the coleslaw, while some of the men brought out more tables from the back and filled in the few blank spaces at the corners, leaving only a six-foot perimeter around the piano. The jukebox now played Charlie Parker and Clifford Brown.

Marty told Jack, "The place gets kind of loud when the afternoon shift gets off. Walter brings the liquor out and everyone gets loose. The guys start playing. It'll go on all night." He put his money on the table and stood up.

When they were in the car and driving down the road, Marty said, "It was getting kind of tough for you in there."

"I suppose."

"As long as you're aware of what you're up against, you're in control. Remember that."

"You're a smart man, Marty."

"I can't say I agree with you."

"I'm not looking for a consensus."

Marty grinned. "Fair enough."

The paved road turned to dirt and stone, the stones jumped and popped against the bottom of Marty's car. A few miles further, it went back to pavement. And they were getting closer to home.

It was quiet in the car now. Jack assumed Marty had had enough talk and was glad for the silence. The silence held awhile longer the way it does when your entire person gets inverted into itself. It can be a very comfortable place if you're with someone else who's got his own thoughts, which is what Jack was thinking, and that someone else happens to be a stranger, or more a stranger than not, since the only thing you two have in common is knowing each other's sorrow—if not for the summer migrations of his friends, a coincidence of season and profession, Jack wouldn't have been with Marty tonight—and Jack knew that if he thought too long, if he started poking around in the dark, he'd hit upon the question that, when asked, would make Marty a stranger no longer, that the answer would speak of deeper sorrow and do nothing to alleviate it, not even when told to a stranger, who wouldn't be a stranger after what was revealed. This was very dangerous territory to step into, asking personal questions. Marty must have known it. He stayed inside his silence, one place strangers are forbidden, riding further and further away from the cool of the country roads.

They drove through the hazy air, heavy with fumes, where the interstate cuts through the south side of town; and east, past the old houses with the tired roofs, where they kept the windows open and babies cried, where husbands and wives yelled at each other after another tough day and didn't care who heard them. Further east, Jack was still thinking about the question he wanted to ask Marty, about knowing more than a stranger should know. He was thinking: Did he stop loving his wife? But that wasn't the question.

He thought: Did *she* stop loving him? But that wasn't the question, either. That wouldn't have sent Marty into a panic.

They drove north now, where the houses are set back from the sidewalk and the lawns are mowed every week by the gardening service and when you walk down the street on summer nights like this you hear the comfortable hum of air conditioners and know that inside the house the rooms are cool, the television isn't too loud and the conversation is always civil.

Then they were on the other side of town, where there weren't quite so many houses and the lawns were replaced by cornfields and wheat fields and fields lush with alfalfa and soy. The sidewalks were narrow and melted into the road the way they do ten minutes from town. Marty pulled up in front of Jack's house.

You can't expect to spend most of the day with someone, drive into the deep country for barbecue, sit with your thoughts inside a car for an hour and a half and not say a few words before leaving, even if you have to be careful of what you say and what you ask. But Marty didn't say a few words. Maybe he knew what Jack wanted to ask. Maybe he just wanted to go home and put himself and his good deed to bed, which might have explained why he sat silently with his arms crossed over his chest and stared out the windshield. But Jack couldn't walk away. He couldn't go inside, not before saying, "Do you want to sit on the porch awhile and have something to drink?" You can't expect to spend an entire day with someone and not offer him a cold drink.

Marty said he'd like that very much.

Only after Jack made sure there were no messages on the machine, made sure nothing had gone wrong while he was away, could he attempt to play host, although all he had to offer was a pitcher of ice water and a plate of cookies that Mandy Ainsley had brought over back in June and which he had sealed and stored in the pantry.

Marty was sitting on the porch swing, his head tilted back. He said one of the things he missed since he moved out of his house on Maple Street was sitting on the porch on warm summer nights. "It's funny the things you can miss." He gave the swing a soft push. The chain creaked and groaned gently.

Jack sat on one of the chairs and propped his feet on the railing. He asked, "Did your wife get the house?" But that wasn't the question.

"I sold it. It reminded me of too many things."

"Where do you live now?" That was not the question, either.

"I bought a place over on Franklin. It's all right. But no porch."

It might have been a look of anticipation that Jack saw on Marty's face, a look of expectation, as though he knew what was coming. Or it might have been Jack wanting to see that look where none existed. Whichever it was, he paused long enough to lift the glass to his mouth and take a long swallow, then he asked, "What happened that made her want to divorce you?" That was the question.

"I left her no choice," was all Marty said, and turned his head to look down the road, at the deep rows of corn, the relentless engines of procreation. When he turned back, his face, Jack realized, did not look like the face of a cop, not a city cop, not a small-town cop. Not just tonight, not only now in the yellow glow of the porch light. It was there the first time Marty showed up, that remarkable expression. It was always there, behind all other expressions he wore, and it was also the face of a policeman with closed nerves and sealed emotions, and at the same time it was, simply, Marty's face, the way he looked, like the intonations of a voice, an accent, not the look of optimism necessarily, but of confidence: "Things may not be wonderful right now, but I got through my tough time, you'll get through yours." That was even more remarkable.

"What about you?" Marty said. "When I asked if there was a woman in your life, you said it wasn't relevant to Danny's suicide, but since we're asking questions."

"There was one, but I thought it would be too confusing for Danny. He had enough conflict." That was only part of the reason. But Jack didn't tell Marty about Maggie, who played in the softball games and liked to dance close and slow, and who, if Jack had given the chance—

"Just *one* in ten years?" Marty asked.

"The only one that I was serious about." Jack shifted uneasily in his chair. "Moving to Gilbert was not about me finding a wife, or a mother for my son. It wasn't about me at all." He stood up and walked away from Marty's assumptions. He went inside the house and refilled the pitcher. He thought about what he might tell Marty, or if he should tell him anything at all. When he came back out to the porch, he said, "I was married to the woman I wanted to be married to. We had the life that we wanted to have with each other. And then we didn't." He was silent for a moment, listening to himself breathe, listening to himself think. "I've never stopped missing that life." It wasn't a confession, merely a statement of fact. "What happened wasn't fair to Danny. What it did to him wasn't fair. I spent the rest of his life trying to make up for it."

Then Jack told Marty about the deal he'd made. It disturbed him to talk about it, not because he was embarrassed or ashamed, not because it was a secret, not for the lack of catharsis that talking about it might bring—he didn't expect a catharsis, he didn't want one; there is nothing cleansing about stating the facts you've accepted about your life—and not because any trust had been betrayed, or assumed. It disturbed him to admit the hurt Anne's abandonment left behind. It disturbed him to confess the irrevocable damage of Danny's suicide. It disturbed him, he realized, to admit that another piece of his life, his time, had been chipped away forever and dropped into the irretrievable past.

Jack didn't say this, he didn't say anything else because there was nothing more to say unless they wanted to talk about what the questions, what the answers, revealed when told to someone who was no longer a stranger. Unless they wanted to talk about what dangerous territory this was; so they sat in silence, unlike the silence in the car, which had been safe and private. There was nothing private about this silence, nothing safe. It never is after the questions, after the answers. After nightfall on the front porch when you've gone beyond the point of saying more than necessary.

There was nothing Jack could do except feel the world, and the life that had once been attached to it, lurch farther away from him. He should have expected it. After all, you can't spend an entire day with someone, drive into the deep country, sit with your thoughts inside a car for an hour and a half and not ask a few questions.

XIV

He sat under an oak tree by the creek with his notebook and a cooler with a couple of bottles of soda and two sandwiches. He was able to do that now, sit outside, write his lecture notes. He was able to run errands, to meet Marty for lunch in town, dinner, even if it was little more than a formality, really, Jack pushing salad around a bowl. He was able to go out and come back to the house that was still standing, to the benign answering machine. He was able to call his father without the cold sweat, without the dread.

Jack had never thought he'd get this far, taking short drives through town, afternoon walks along the edge of the field, alone sometimes, sometimes with Marty, who managed to find the time whenever Jack called. They'd sit out back and have a beer or drink lemonade, and it always ended up with the two of them driving somewhere or sitting in the house, talking about Danny: "Let me show this one picture . . ." "Let me . . ." Jack wasn't ashamed to tell Marty about sitting alone in Danny's room, resting on Danny's bed, putting his face in Danny's pillow, closing his eyes and talking to Danny as though he were there. He wasn't ashamed to admit that he still worried about *What next?*—but not all the time. That he didn't always listen for the ring of the telephone, or anticipate the next disaster, but it was still in his mind. He wasn't ashamed to tell Marty about the old wooden box with the cutout animals and Anne's orange button. "I can't help wondering if there were more secrets."

Marty said, "I think it was Danny's way of staying attached to Anne, to his time with her."

On this first day of August Jack was trying to think like a man with a future, however precarious that future was; built not on the solid bedrock of his own personality but balanced on Marty's shoulders, a place Jack found very uncomfortable, a place Jack preferred not to be—he had never been carried by anyone—but he'd asked Marty to help bring him back to being Dr. Owens, nevertheless, to what was left of Dr. Owens, who was going through the motions of thinking and reacting from memory; as though he'd seen another man, the other man being himself, do these same things a long time ago, on a home video, in the dark of a movie theater.

Tomorrow he would drive to the college and start screening films for the fall semester, he didn't have a choice if he wanted to keep his job, but right now it was enough to sit out by the creek with his books and prepare for the new term while Mutt lay next to him on the green, ripe ground.

From where he sat, Jack could see the field, where the crops had been harvested and come fall the earth would lie bare. The heat rippled in the sunlight. He could hear blue jays screaming in trees, the sudden scatter of wings, the plunk of a frog in the creek, and the creek rushing across the rocks and smooth stones.

"It's not so bad sitting out here today." He still talked to himself, sometimes, and to Danny when he started thinking about the past.

Later, when the sun was above the trees, he might walk over to where the water was deep and cool and wade in the creek. Right now, he would do some of the work Dr. Owens used to do.

It was noon when Jack put down his papers and books and saw the small dark shape rising in the field like a tiny ship riding the crest toward shore. After a while, the shape became Mary-Sue Richards stepping through the fence and walking toward the house.

Jack watched her knock on the screen door, shade her eyes and peek inside. She knocked on the door a second time, pushed it open and called "Dr. Owens?" a couple of times in her high, sweet voice. Jack was undecided whether to let her know he was out here until Mutt raised his ears, lifted his muzzle and barked, and Mary-Sue turned and looked in his direction and Jack called to her.

She waved to him and ran over, all in the same motion, sat on the large square rock next to Jack and said, "I came by the other day, but you were out. Mom wanted to come by today, but I told her I'd do it for her. She and Dad wanted to know how you're doing. They said to say hi."

"You can tell your folks that I'm hanging in there."

Mary-Sue had grown since Jack last saw her—he remembered how Danny ripened every summer, as though he were plugged directly into the sun, and how far removed twelve was from eleven, fifteen from fourteen. Four weeks ago, Mary-Sue had stood in the kitchen shifting ungracefully, all shoulders and knees, not yet grown into her body. Now she had come to terms with her arms and legs, no longer held in awkward disregard but carried comfortably at her side. Her hair was cut to the middle of her ears and great care had been given to styling it. She wore her shorts and T-shirt with more consideration of their shape and hers. She was conspicuously aware of herself. Jack looked at her and saw Danny grown taller, broader at the shoulders and chest, his voice a little deeper, closer to a man than a boy.

Mary-Sue looked at Jack's notebook, groaned, "*School.* Please don't *remind* me," and asked, "What are you teaching this semester?"

"Films of the sixties."

"Anything good?"

"That's the question we'll try to answer in class."

"I guess there's nothing with Brad Pitt."

"Would you settle for Dennis Hopper and Peter Fonda?"

"You really should have Brad Pitt."

"Sorry. But there'll be a cartoon between features."

She didn't seem to know that he was joking. "You really should show Brad Pitt," she said with a certainty that was enviable. She crossed her legs, rested her chin in the palm of her hand. "Did you hear what happened to C.J.? He was in a car accident, at the Ainsleys' place in Kentucky. He broke both arms, busted his right shoulder, his face was cut to shreds. He'll need an awesome amount of plastic surgery. They weren't even sure that he'd live."

"Live?"

She nodded her head. "He's doing better now, but he's really hurt."

"What about his parents?"

"That's just it. They weren't with him." Mary-Sue dug her toe into the soil, making a deep, narrow burrow. "If he'd gone along with them it wouldn't have happened. I'm beginning to think the kids around here are jinxed." Her tone of voice was earnest and heartbreaking.

"Gone along?"

"They were going to a cookout and C.J. didn't want to go. My dad says, that is, Dr. Ainsley *told* my dad, that C.J. was moping around the *entire* summer. Of course his parents couldn't understand why. I mean, *duh,* considering how he felt about Danny, if they'd bothered to notice, which they didn't. I mean, well, *all* of us have been bummed by what happened, but C.J.—he called me a few times just to talk to someone who knew—it isn't like we're that close, but his sisters were like telling him to get a life and Brian's doing Outward Bound in Maine and Rick's up at his uncle's farm in Wisconsin somewhere. Poor C.J. had no one who under*stood*. He said he couldn't stop thinking about Danny. It was *haunting* him. He was so intense it was scary. I was like, 'C.J., maybe you should get some help,' but he said he just wished he could disappear somewhere. And then the dummy gets the bright idea that he could drive his dad's old Dodge. And he *totaled* it. My dad says he lost control going around a curve. He must've been doing at least a hundred. He's in some hospital down there. Intensive care. They don't know when they can bring him home. If he'd taken the new car he might not have been banged up so bad because of the air bags, or even if he'd worn his seat belt."

"When did this happen?"

"About two weeks ago. I wanted to come over then, but my mom and dad didn't want me to bother you, but I thought—I just wanted to—I mean I know I'm interrupting your work, but I thought if I could sit here awhile with you—I don't know." She began flicking the soil with the tip of her big toe; there was still a lot of little girl left in her. "You don't like Dr. Ainsley, do you?"

"I feel sorry for Carl." Which wasn't completely untrue.

"Do you like C.J.?"

"I feel sorry for him, too." Which was the truth.

"Everyone treats him like he's such a screwup. It's all wrong."

"Yes. It makes C.J. very unsure of himself."

"Mrs. Ainsley and the twins aren't much better."

"No, they're not. You treat someone like that long enough and he begins to believe it."

"*I* don't like Dr. Ainsley. Not the way he puts C.J. down in front of his friends."

"Carl can be very thoughtless at times."

"We all did it. Even Danny. I shouldn't call him a chucklehead all the time, but—it wasn't like C.J. didn't *do* stupid things, but what Dr. Ainsley does to him is really *cruel*. Anyway, I just hope everyone'll be nicer to him now."

"They will be."

"That's why we all wished you were our dad." She said this cautiously. Her face was flushed.

"What?"

"The way you took care of Danny. Watched out for him."

"Your parents aren't exactly neglecting you."

"It's other things. The way you talked to him, to all of us. Like we're, I don't know. Like we're not *kids*. And it was *way* cool that Danny got to see all those movies with you. I mean, well, when your dad teaches linguistics and your mom teaches English lit, there's a definite lack of entertainment value."

"He didn't always like my choices." Jack smiled. "He hated subtitles."

"I wish my parents were more like you," she answered adamantly. "We all did. I mean, it's like I can tell you about C.J. and—I don't know." She hunched her shoulders and looked up at the treetops.

"Everyone wishes their parents were like someone else's parents."

"Well, if you ever get lonely for Danny, I mean I *know* you *are,* but, like watching those movies by yourself, I'll go with you. I mean, if it'll make it less lonely."

It was unsolicited honesty, like Danny's honesty, and it was more than Jack could bear. It made him want to hold his son the way he used to until their chests were pressed so close together and tight they could feel each other's heartbeat. Jack wanted to hold Mary-Sue like that, just so he could hold what he was feeling, just so he could hold a child, the way he held his child. But he couldn't go around hugging fifteen-year-old girls anytime they made him think of Danny. He couldn't tell her what he was thinking, as he watched her stare at the ground, work her toe into the soil, unaware of what she'd been able to do with what she'd said—she was still more child than not, he thought. She didn't know not to speak what she felt. Jack slipped a little further inside himself, inside the self that had been Dr. Owens, who never got ruffled by the things teenagers told him. Who always knew what to say. Who thought he might still know: "I can't offer you a movie right now, but I can give you a cold soda."

Mary-Sue looked up and smiled.

Jack didn't feel less lonely drinking a soda with Danny's friend, but he liked that she sat with him while he did his work, lying quietly in the sun, as Danny would have done. He could hear some of Danny when she talked about C.J., about Brian, and Rick. She'd shared time with Danny, and Jack could hear that in her voice, too; and he could feel her needing to sit here. Maybe she thought Jack was the only one she could be with who would understand what it was like to have one friend dead and another near death. She didn't have to explain her sadness, or anything else for that matter, and Jack wouldn't ask her any questions or try to cheer her up or do any of the obtuse things parents and adults do when children are sad and silent. Or maybe it wasn't any of those things at all. Maybe she had come here thinking that Danny's suicide had revealed to Jack the incomprehensible workings of, if not the universe, at least the slice of it located on the banks of the Wabash and he could explain to Mary-Sue what was happening inside her because she certainly didn't know and her parents were no help. Maybe Jack could explain what it was that had wrenched her and Danny, C.J., Brian and Rick away from the rest of the crowd and into a sadness children were not supposed to know. Or maybe it was the sadness itself that brought her here and all she wanted was to rest where she wouldn't be an anomaly. Maybe she needed to feel all of this and Jack needed her to feel this, needed her to be there inside the absence Danny had left behind.

Jack could not help feeling disloyal to Danny—the same disloyalty he felt making plans with Marty—for wanting Mary-Sue to stay with him, for wanting her to fill the absence, if only for an afternoon, if only for being barely more than the nothing he already had. Jack could not help feeling disloyal to Danny. Because grieving is never enough.

Mary-Sue stayed while Jack worked on his lecture notes. She took Mutt for a walk along the edge of the creek, sat in the shade of a tree as the light of the afternoon deepened and warmed. Later, after she thanked Jack for the cold soda and went home, her small body absorbed into the harvested field, Jack walked back to the house. He wondered what Marty would have to say about C.J.'s accident. Would it trouble him as Danny's suicide had? He thought this without cynicism, which is what he told Marty that night, when they met for dinner at Marlowe's.

They were sitting at a round table near the center of the room working slowly on their whiskeys. Marlowe's was a jacket-and-tie place, and Marty was dressed smartly in summer beige, blue and coral. He didn't say he was troubled by C.J.'s accident. He did say it was upsetting, and that he felt sorry that Mary-Sue thought that her friends were jinxed. "That's a terrible way for a kid to feel." He asked, "What sort of kid is C.J.?"

"A brilliant student with about enough self-esteem to fill a shot glass. He was always doing stupid kid stuff."

"So there were other occasions when he behaved irresponsibly?" Marty smiled and said, "I just turned cop on you, didn't I?"

"Just a little." Jack took a sip of whiskey. "A student in one of his father's classes paid C.J. fifty dollars to steal a copy of a final exam for her."

"That's pretty serious, don't you think. Did it bother you that he and Danny were friends?"

"No. C.J. isn't bad or malicious. It had more to do with how he feels about his father. He's pretty guileless actually, the only one he ever hurts is himself. The really sad thing is, if his father had known how desperate that student was for a good grade, he would have cut a deal of his own."

"You don't like him," Marty said flatly, and lifted his glass to his mouth.

"Let's just say I don't approve of him, which, I know, stinks of self-righteousness. But he's just so goddamned irresponsible. And he always, I don't know—"

"Gets away with it?"

"Gets away with it."

"I bet he's also one of those guys who doesn't do more than just enough to get by on the job."

"He's managed to get tenured. But he hardly distinguishes himself in his department. For him, work is an extension of the country club."

"Unlike you."

"That's not what— I'm not drawing any comparisons."

"But if you did. You've distinguished yourself wherever you taught."

"There's no professional rivalry," Jack answered, not defensively. "We're not in the same department, and he certainly isn't the only one on the faculty phoning it in. But he's the only one who goes out of his way to flaunt it. At me." He took another sip of his drink, and then another.

"So you resent this guy for getting away with it and also rubbing your nose in it. That sounds fair enough."

"And I'm sure Ainsley thinks I can be the most judgmental, pompous asshole that ever lived. And maybe he's right. But I resent that he thinks I am."

"Maybe you wish *you* could get away with something once in a while."

"I don't know what I wish."

"I'm sure as far as he's concerned, you *are* getting away with something. Your son never sold you out, not for any amount of money."

"Ainsley used to make bad jokes about my coming to Gilbert. How I was slumming. He never missed a chance to jab at me because I took my job seriously, as if there wasn't a downside to what— I gave up a lot when I moved here."

"Don't you think he knows that? Why do you think he made the jokes? He resents you just as much as you resent him, for the way you conduct yourself. I suspect what he really resents you for is for being the man that you are."

"What *I* really resent has *nothing* to do with Ainsley." Jack emptied his glass. "Maybe all I've done is make up my own rules and they were about making Danny's life whole, teaching him to have self-respect and a sense of self-worth. Ainsley, if he has any rules, breaks them all, and C.J. knows all about it. Danny killed himself. C.J. winds up in the hospital all banged up and barely alive. That's what I resent, Marty. That Ainsley and I get tossed into the same mix regardless of how we behave. Maybe what I resent is that there aren't any rules."

"I don't think that's what you resent at all," Marty said. "Everything you believed in and trusted, including your low opinion of Ainsley, has been called into question. That's what you resent."

They were about to begin the formality of ordering supper, but they didn't get the chance. Detective Hopewell stopped by the table. He was with a woman only slightly old enough not to be mistaken for his daughter and dressed more for a seaside clam bar than Marlowe's. Hopewell gave Jack a perfunctory nod as though he wasn't quite sure where they'd met before and asked Marty if they could talk for a minute.

Marty answered, "Sure," and excused himself.

The two detectives walked to the far corner, over by the pay phones and restrooms, leaving the date looking bored and unhappy. She shrugged her shoulders at Jack and said, "Tell Earl I'll be at the bar."

Marty and Hopewell talked for a few minutes, more accurately, Marty listened while Hopewell did the talking, slowly, describing something with his hands which made Marty shake his head, listen awhile longer, turn and look at Jack.

Hopewell started to walk toward the table but Marty put his hand on his shoulder and pulled him back, said something and walked away. Hopewell stared sourly at the floor, then walked to the bar.

Marty sat down, reached for his glass and finished what was left in it.

"Hopewell says the other boy didn't kill himself. He says he was murdered."

XV

Jack felt as though he were wreathed in numbness, as though his legs had vanished under him, as though he were helpless.

"Does it have anything to do with Danny?" he wanted to know.

"Hopewell needs to ask you a few questions. That's all he'd tell me."

"Then Danny—"

"They're just questions, Jack. It doesn't mean—"

"He thinks Danny was murdered." The words stuck dry inside Jack's throat.

"He didn't say that."

Jack didn't give the waiter time to come over to take their order, he dropped his napkin, put down enough money to take care of the drinks and walked out of the dining room and into the street, as though Hopewell and the murder of young boys existed only inside the restaurant, that outside, the night owned its own existence.

Marty didn't try to stop him but followed along, across Main Street, through the parking lot, past their cars and behind the post office where the alley led to the campus, where the boughs of the trees hung heavy and low and the moonlight was all but lost.

They walked through the old campus, where the sidewalks were made of red brick laid down by the WPA workers who'd come to Gilbert College to build the Fine Arts building and paint murals, to plant bushes and trees and grass for the quadrangle, where gaslights glowed along the paths and the windows throughout the campus hung empty and dark.

Marty looked at the darkness and said nothing.

"All summer," Jack told him, "I've been trying to live with the idea that something went terribly wrong for Danny. Something I did, something I *didn't* do. That he was a troubled kid with a troubled life. Now I've got to change all that and try to believe that Danny was the victim of some piece of shit who arbitrarily killed him? *Christ* almighty. I almost feel like that should be a relief, in a fucked-up sort of way. Only Danny is still dead."

"Hopewell's always looking for something big. I told you that the first day. He wants to get out of Gilbert and be a bigger fish in a bigger pond. Unfortunately, now you and the Coggins are caught in the crosshairs of his big-city dreams." They walked a little further. "Not that he's completely out of line, but he should leave you out of it."

"What do you mean?"

"The Coggins mentioned something that Hopewell doesn't think fits the profile of a suicide. He wouldn't give me many of the details. He didn't want to compromise the integrity of his investigation," Marty said derisively. "But my guess is it has *nothing* to do—"

"Guesses aren't good enough, Marty."

"I know." Marty waited a moment before he told Jack, "Lamar got into a fight with a boy in his class the morning of the day he died. The medical examiner found marks on Lamar's arm and assumed that's how they got there. Hopewell isn't convinced. He thinks they could have happened out by Otter Creek. That Lamar could have struggled with his killer. That's not at all like Danny's death. That's all he would tell me, that and he thinks there's enough to merit taking another look at the case. There must be something to it. He wouldn't have been able to do this if our captain didn't agree with him. But none of this means Danny was murdered."

"Then why does he want to ask me questions?"

"I don't know."

"Don't know or won't say?"

"You're looking for reassurances I can't give you."

"Was my son murdered?"

"It's not my case, Jack. I don't have all the facts, so I can't give you a definite answer. If you want my *opinion,* no, Danny wasn't murdered. I told you when I first came to see you, Danny's suicide has very little in common with Lamar's."

They walked the stretch of sidewalk. Jack wanted to know, "How will he go about it?" meaning Hopewell.

"He'll do a more intense search over by Otter Creek, if he hasn't already. He'll go back and talk to people who saw Lamar the day he died, at school, afterward. He'll look for anyone who saw anyone out there the day it happened, try to find anyone who might have been out that way. It's possible that someone—homeless, crazy, who knows—might have done it. And he'll see if he can match Lamar's death with the death of other boys his age around the state."

"Like a serial killing?"

"It's remote. I keep up with that sort of thing all the time. It's *more* than remote."

"There's no terra firma," Jack said. "That's what it's like to be mad, isn't it? When there's no terra firma."

They walked silently to the end of the sidewalk and crossed the street.

The silence held, reminding Jack of that evening when he and Marty sat in the car when they were still strangers. But they were strangers no more. When Jack said, "All I can think is: What next?" Marty knew what he was talking about.

Then they were walking over by the new dormitories with the deep patios and art plaza. Where the pavement was smooth and new and hadn't been laid down by the WPA. Where the postmodern sculpture sprang enormous and bold, like prehistory.

Jack said, "The first summer Anne and I went to France, she was working on her first show, and she used to talk about the blank spaces Cézanne left on his canvas. She said the blank parts suggest what's there as well as what's not there. That the absence of anything, some element, creates the presence of something else, and you have to be able to see what's missing to have any idea of what remains. Maybe it was the blank spaces that made Hopewell decide Lamar had been murdered."

"I guess you could say it was. Or maybe blank spaces don't necessarily mean that nothing's there, just that it isn't visible."

They walked along the empty sidewalk. The reflection of the moon was framed in the dormitory windows. Their footsteps echoed cold and hollow against the concrete and cement.

Jack said, "I feel like I'm sliding down an endless, bottomless sluice."

"It gets that way sometimes. But it's something you just have to cope with. Along with everything else you're coping with. I hate making it sound so cold, but that's just a fact."

"A cold fact."

"A cold fact," Marty repeated solemnly.

"I wouldn't mind a few warm ones once in a while."

"Well, for what it's worth, you seem to be handling both kinds pretty well. Under the circumstances."

"*Seem* to."

They walked a little further.

"You know what my problem is, Marty?"

"That's not the kind of question I ever try and answer," Marty said, not at all humorously.

"I was always so damn busy, *seeming* to handle every damn thing, I never let anyone see how much help I really needed. And when it was offered, I didn't accept it. Not from my friends, not from my family. I allowed them to give me pep talks, encourage me, and then I pushed them to the sidelines"—he made a sweeping gesture with his left hand—"so they could watch me seize the day. Help must have been available, but I never showed that I needed it. I came close to asking you that night in the Palomino, and it made me feel so small inside I had to back down. Call it a martyr complex, or a hero complex. When Anne left Danny and me, I was like a boxer on the ropes shaking off the punches. I packed up my son and started life all over again. Without missing a beat. We had our softball games, our vacations. I could do it all and go it alone. And if I'd showed the slightest sign of indecision, in*com*petence—"

"Go easy on yourself."

"I'd look like a failure, and I couldn't let that happen. If I know anything about myself it's this: I'm afraid to show pain or let myself look needy or, God forbid, in*com*petent." He loosened his tie and undid the top button of his shirt. "Maybe there are things a person shouldn't know about himself. Although *you'd* tell me a person can't know enough."

"I'd also tell you—"

Jack put up his hand to silence him. "The point, Marty, is this: I'm scared to death right now. I've been scared to death since Danny died. I don't know what to think, or what to feel, or what to imagine. I've been asking for your help since the day we met, or just about. As crap-headed as it sounds, I've *let* you—"

"I'd also tell you," Marty told him, not at all unkindly, "to cut yourself some slack."

"There's some slack I can't cut myself. I've got a dead son who Hopewell refuses to let rest in peace and I can't stand by and let that happen. Danny's dead and I have to protect him. I guess I also have to protect myself."

"You've been doing a good job of both since he was born."

"I'm afraid." Jack's voice sounded as though the wind had been sucked out of it. "And I need your help."

Marty nodded his head slowly.

They were past the dormitories now, and off campus, walking along Elm Street, where the stores were all closed and the sidewalk empty.

Jack said, "Since I pulled you out of Marlowe's before you had your supper, how about letting me buy you a late dinner somewhere."

Marty started to protest. Jack told him not to make a big deal about it.

"I'm treating you to supper. That's all there is to it."

"In that case," Marty said, "Let's go here." He was standing in front of Ambrosini's . . . Home of Fine Italian Food.

"You're letting me off cheaply."

It had been years since Jack was in Ambrosini's, but the place hadn't changed very much. The air inside was still thick with garlic and Parmesan cheese, the bar still stocked blended whiskies only and the wine list was still the best in the state. Jack could only hope for Marty's sake, however, that the former chef had retired.

Marty gave the menu a quick look and before the waiter came over said to Jack, "A few days ago Lamar's parents discovered a personal item missing from his things, maybe it was a piece of clothing or something. All Hopewell would tell me is it was something Lamar would have taken with him when he left the house that day. Hopewell went back out to Otter Creek to look for it, maybe he missed it the first time. You know what a mess it is out there, plus all that rain didn't help, but he couldn't find anything. But whatever he's up to, I'm positive it has nothing to do with Danny."

Jack was lying in the dark, there wasn't any breeze tonight and the air was heavy and it seemed like it was about to rain. It seemed as though all the summer's fragrances were in hiding, secreted on the other side of the field, and there was only the sweet smell of whiskey on his breath and the faint aroma of Ambrosini's dining room on his clothes and in his hair. They were not at all unfamiliar, the way a certain perfume rises in a theater, or at a party, and you remember the last time you breathed it and where you were and the person who'd worn it. Jack remembered the last time he lay in the dark and could smell the restaurant on his clothes and on his body, but that night they were mixed with the pleasant scent of a woman's perfume.

It was somebody's birthday, and they'd had a party at Ambrosini's. There were about twenty-five of them in all, Jack remembered, sitting around the large table in the big room. Lois was there with Tim. Lee and Cindy Hatfield. Jerry and Joy Parcell. And Maggie. There was a carnival set up in the parking lot across the street, the red and yellow sounds of the calliope, the smoky smell of hot dogs and greasy French fries came rolling through the open window. It was Jack who wanted to smuggle in carnival food at the risk of offending Mr. Ambrosini. But that wasn't why everyone was laughing. He couldn't remember why.

Maybe it was the wine, a good Brunello from Ambrosini's private stock, or the end-of-semester release that happened to coincide with the party. Or the toast Maggie had made.

Someone brought music. A few people started dancing, a few people sang along. The tables were pushed out of the way. More people danced.

Maggie drew up next to Jack. She was moving in time to the song, her skirt pulled tight against her hips, showing them off. "Dr. Jack Owens," she said in a husky whisper.

"Dr. Maggie Brighton."

She leaned in close, rubbing her thigh against him and resting her head against his lapel. "Are you the kind of man who leads women on and then victimizes them?" she asked in the same husky whisper.

"I'm the kind of man who saves women from themselves."

"Very noble, Dr. Owens."

"Let's not jump to hasty conclusions."

"Do you read much poetry, noble Dr. Owens?"

"Some."

"I suggest you read more." She may have had too much to drink. She may have just been acting like it.

"And why is that?"

"You have poetry within you."

She looked as though she were about to kiss him. She didn't, which Jack regretted.

"*I* taught poetry this year," she said in the deliberate way of the inebriate. "*I* taught poetry to non-English majors. Have *you* ever taught film for non-film majors?"

"I have."

"I don't mind teaching them. Do you?"

"No."

"Neither do I." She hummed softly, her cheek pressed against his chin. "Do you know what excites them in Bloomington, Indiana?"

"You?"

"Basketball. Basketball on Friday night."

"And you don't like basketball on Friday night?"

"I like *you* on Friday night." She brushed her hips against him. "Dance with me," she said.

"I thought we were," and he took her in his arms.

He liked dancing with Maggie. It wasn't just the feel of her body, firm and confident against him, or the way her fingertips rested against his neck. It was the smell of her hair, the way she followed his lead, the way she knew when to play and when to take the music seriously, but never too seriously.

"I like you, Jack. Especially tonight."

"Why especially tonight?"

"You don't hold me accountable for my behavior."

"You're behaving perfectly fine."

"That's what I mean." She held him tighter.

Sometime after eleven, they all went to the carnival. Jack won a stuffed bear for Maggie at the shooting gallery, and a gold-plated rhinestone bracelet, which she put on immediately and promised to wear until her arm turned green. They rode the Tilt-A-Whirl and threw cream pies at a clown and ate salty French fries out of paper cones. Then everyone drove down Third Street, past the trucker bars and the gas stations and the motels' neon signs, to the Little Slipper, where they listened to the jazz trio do better-than-passable work on standards. Maggie and Jack sat close to each other in the booth near the back. Lois sang "You Go to My Head," deep and hot and throaty. Jerry and Joy harmonized softly on "My Heart Stood Still."

Jack remembered that Maggie talk-sang "The Very Thought of You."

He remembered when Maggie showed up for her first softball game and he shouted across the diamond to Danny, "I want you to meet someone," and Danny came hustling over, glove tucked under his arm, cap on backwards.

"This is Maggie Brighton," Jack said. "The scouting report says she plays a decent first base. If Gary doesn't take her, I suggest you make her one of your picks."

Danny gave her a stern looking over.

"I'm not all field and no hit, either," Maggie said, "I've even got some power to the opposite field," which made Danny smile.

It was blue skies all day and the ball field over by the fairgrounds looked like candy. Maggie knew how to play softball; in the first inning, she dug out a low throw and Danny gave her a high-five coming off the field, and she knew how to dress for a ballgame as well, wearing old baseball pants that she'd fixed to fit like pedal pushers, a cast-off baseball shirt she'd found at a flea market, black Chuck Taylor high-tops and a black cap with her red hair tucked inside.

Leading off the bottom of the ninth, her team down by a run, Maggie legged out a slow roller to short. She wound up on third with two outs, danced off the bag, juking and swishing her hips, waving to Jack and shouting, "I'm running on contact. I'm comin' home." Unfortunately, she was stranded at third and never scored the tying run.

After the game, as he helped set up the picnic along the foul lines, Jack watched Maggie run over to him, propelled, it appeared, on the strength of her laughter. "Danny told me I could 'really pick it' at first base," she said. "He's wonderful, Jack. I made sure to tell him that, and that he's an excellent second baseman, too."

"He can't hear enough of it."

"And neither can you." She hugged his arm and laughed some more.

They circled the old beach chairs in the shade of the trees and the picnic was on. Sandwiches and salads, beers and sodas, smoke from the barbecue grill swirled with the aroma of burgers and hot dogs and sausages. While the adults ate and talked about their summer plans, the kids hurried through the food and chose up teams for another softball game.

That was the summer he rented the house in Maine with Nick and the boys. Danny was what, ten? No, he must have been nine. Maggie came to his tenth birthday . . .

Maggie supplied the magician and a "gypsy" fortune-teller for Danny's tenth birthday, Jack remembered. But in that softball game she was stranded at third with the tying run.

Jack thought about Maggie and felt the regret he'd felt before, it seemed to belong with all the other regrets he was feeling, and she belonged with all the other people he missed and who were gone. "Noble Dr. Owens," she'd called him, but that was just a joke, that was before what happened happened.

It started to rain. Jack got up to close the bedroom window.

He remembered that Maggie had laughed about it later, about dancing off third base. "Doing my baseball bossa nova."

There was always lots of laughter when she was around. Maggie Brighton. She made things bright.

On the Saturday nights that Danny spent at Rick's house, or Brian's, Jack would stay with Maggie in Bloomington, where she lived in one of the smart neighborhoods near campus. The first time he stayed over, it was raining, like tonight, only it was late September and cool. They sat on the floor, a tray of hors d'oeuvres in front of them, and listened to Chet Baker and Mose Allison.

"Did you always want to be a teacher?" she asked.

"Except in the eighth grade, when I wanted my own talk show."

"That's not too far removed from teaching."

"And you?"

"When I was seven, I used to force my little sisters to play school with me. I'd make them sit in and recite Dr. Seuss and A. A. Milne." She smiled. "It's goofy, I know, but I always loved the *sound* of reading poetry out loud. My family has a little cottage on Lake Wawasee and when I was in high school I used to sit on the dock by myself and read Emily Dickinson. We should go up there, Jack, in a couple of weeks, Danny, you and I. It's beautiful in the fall. I can take you both to the Olympia Candy Kitchen in Goshen, for hamburgers and malts. We'll go on foliage hikes around the lake and build a fire at night and make s'mores and tell ghost stories."

Jack still remembered how nervous—anxious, really—he felt when Maggie invited them. "I think we'll run into a few logistical problems," he said.

"Logistics?"

"Sleeping arrangements."

"I think we can manage to keep our hands off each other for a weekend," she said, and then, "Is that all?"

"No. I'm also very careful about Danny not getting too attached to women I go out with. Not that there've been that many, but—"

"He has to get to know me, I understand, and get comfortable with everything. Right?"

"That's right."

"Does he know that you stay here?"

Jack shook his head. "I think it would be very confusing for him."

"Where does he think you are?"

"Oh, he knows I'm with you," Jack said, not defensively, "he knows all about you. He just doesn't know that I sleep over."

In October, they drove up to the cabin by Lake Wawasee and did all the things Maggie said they would. Jack and Danny slept in bunk beds. Danny got the top bunk.

When they drove back to Gilbert on Sunday night, Danny said he'd had a good time. He said he liked Maggie. He told Jack, "We should invite her over to our house for supper."

Maggie came for supper. Sometimes she came for lunch on Saturday afternoons, stayed for supper and slept over, in the guest room. If she was bothered by that arrangement, she never said so. Sometimes Jack and Danny would drive to IU and meet Maggie at her office. She would listen to Danny's stories and his jokes. She'd tell him a few jokes of her own. Some nights, they all ate supper at a restaurant, some nights they ate supper at her house, where she would coax Danny into playing the piano, or she would play, and when Danny got to feeling more comfortable around her they would play duets. She used to make Danny laugh with silly rhymes and verses. "One of the perks of teaching kiddie-lit. Plenty of doggerel."

Jack thought about the afternoon just after summer vacation, when Maggie and he sat on the porch swing, Maggie barefoot, wearing shorts, her skin brown from the sun, her sleek, angular face relaxed and rested. It wasn't raining but the air felt thick and damp. The crickets and cicadas and frogs were going crazy in the deep dark of the crops and in the woods by the creek.

"I suppose you always loved movies," she said.

"Actually, I loved sitting alone in the dark, and watching movies was a very acceptable way of doing it."

"I think you're telling me more than I want to know." When she laughed her entire face laughed and her body laughed and it made Jack laugh.

It had been a long time since he'd laughed like that.

After the rain, in the early morning, the sun burned through the clouds and there was the smell of ozone in the air. The grass was still damp and nothing had changed except Jack was not alone. He sat on the back porch drinking coffee with Stan Miller, who had dropped by to say hello and to make sure Jack was ready to be Dr. Owens again, not that Stan would have been so insensitive as to ask. He wouldn't have risen to chair of the department without a large share of tact and the intelligence not to ask the obvious or state it, which is a winning combination anywhere, Jack thought, ungraciously, for he was not in a gracious mood this morning.

He didn't want Stan there. He didn't want to be reminded of who Stan thought he was talking to, who he expected, had every reason to expect, would show up the first day of fall semester. After all, Stan had a department to run and only a small cadre of teachers with which to run it, and if Jack wasn't up to the job, if he was going to turn in his application for emergency leave and avoid the carnage, or what Jack feared would be the carnage once he walked into the classroom and looked at the ten faces, sympathetic, apprehensive, wondering if Dr. Owens would give them their tuition's worth—while he wondered the same thing, himself, wondered if he would look at his students and think only about Danny, who had not lived to be their age. And would they see that in his face?

If Dr. Owens wasn't up to the job, he'd better say so now.

But Stan didn't need to ask this. They'd been colleagues for ten years, they had the same friends, their sons had played together. All Stan needed to say was, "How have you been doing, Jack?" while the birds took flight across the field, the mourning doves cooed like heartbreak, the sunlight grew and the shadows tiptoed their silent retreat.

"Trying to put things back together," Jack answered. "Slowly."

Stan could say slow was the best way. He could say, "Christine and I thought of you quite often this summer." But he couldn't know that Dr. Owens had died along with Danny and all that remained was Jack, the ghost of Dr. Owens, rattling his chains and making noises, no more substantial than ectoplasm, and Jack didn't know if he could show up come September. He didn't know if he was up to the job. Not that that's the sort of thing he'd confess to his department chair; in spite of Stan's good manners, that would not be what he wanted to hear.

Jack knew that Stan didn't have time to waste listening to equivocations, he only wanted Jack to make his job easy. He only wanted to hear the word "yes" as he moved the mug of coffee around in his hand and took another look at the scenery beyond the backyard, giving his attention to the hawks circling above the field, and not saying anything. Maybe the task of saying what was on his mind put a strain on his wealth of tact, or maybe it was the words themselves, there aren't any strict guidelines for asking a father whose son committed suicide if he's capable of teaching, for saying: "Look, I know you're feeling like shit, but I've got my own corner of self-interest to consider. I've got a job to do. So what is it, Jack, can you or can't you?" But you can't ask that question and can't say what's on your mind, at least not if you're Stan Miller.

But Jack wasn't going to let Stan sit there looking alone and uncomfortable. He told him, "You don't have to worry about being blunt with me. You don't have to measure your words."

Stan smiled and said he appreciated that. He said, "I apologize for not being very good at this, but if I have to replace you, I have to know now."

"Sure."

"I have to—" Stan stopped short when the doorbell rang. Jack got up and walked to the front of the house. It was Hopewell standing by the screen door.

"I don't mean to bother you, Dr. Owens, but I need to talk with you. Just for a couple of minutes." Something about him had changed since that day in his office. He seemed edgier, unable to come to a full stop. His right hand flayed the air when he spoke. He stepped forward and back, walked toward the swing, then pivoted on his heels, as though he'd just thought of something else to say, and came back to the door. Only he didn't say anything, but stuck his hands in his pockets and jiggled his keys and loose change. He was like a man on the run.

Jack looked over his shoulder in the direction of the back porch and closed the front door. "I've got company," and he moved Hopewell down the front steps and away from the house. They walked to the road and stood next to Hopewell's car. The engine was still running.

The detective said, "I'm afraid I have some unpleasant— I'm going to have to ask you to look through your son's e-mail." Only the detached, empty voice hadn't changed.

"Danny's *e-mail*?"

"Some sick creep's been getting into chat rooms—there's no nice way to talk about this. He's been going online with young boys—"

"Danny wouldn't get into anything like that."

"I'm sure he wouldn't." Hopewell did not sound convinced. "Just to be on the safe side—you see, guys like this, they're degenerate pederasts and predatory as hell. They can get their hooks into boys in very subtle ways."

"Can you keep your voice down." Jack looked back at the house.

"This guy's"—Hopewell lowered his voice—"been preying on young boys, mostly messing with their heads, but also trying to get them to meet him at secluded spots. He might've already been too successful at it . . . Maybe he lives in the area, maybe just close enough to drive here and far enough not to be traced." Hopewell swiped a handkerchief across his forehead. The flesh on his face was pale and drooped against the cheekbones. There were dark stains on his shirt, around the armpits and where the flesh rolled over the belt. His body stank of sweat, not the sweat of toil, but the sweat of negligence.

Jack couldn't help but feel sorry for him, having to come to people's houses and say the things he had to say, and for a moment he was able to see past the things he knew about Hopewell, the ambition, the hunger for the big time. He could see how frightened the detective was, he could even understand the fear. The look on the face might appear to be cold cogitation but it was really a look of desperation. Hopewell wasn't thinking about parents of dead children. He wasn't thinking about the dead children, either. He was thinking about his job and this case and the case waiting for him when this one was closed. He was thinking about the big-city department he craved to be a part of and the next ten years in his cramped little office on the Gilbert police force and all the things that held him back, all the things that had already passed him by. And Jack, the Coggins, even Marty, were only greasing the skids.

Hopewell rubbed his eyes with the heels of his hands. "Maybe this guy causes enough mental confusion to drive a boy to suicide, I can't rule it out. I'm sorry to have to do this to you, Dr. Owens, but I've got certain protocol I have to follow, certain procedures. I need you to take a look."

"You mean right *now*?"

"When you get the chance. Sooner rather than later." He let out a loud sigh and leaned against the car. "Even if you don't find— This guy might still try to contact your son, so I have to ask you to kind of monitor his e-mail from time to time and let me know if something turns up." He straightened himself and opened the door.

"Wait a minute. You can't just drive off like this without giving me some kind of assurance. You don't *really* think Danny was getting into chat rooms with a child molester." Jack thought about the days and nights last May when he wasn't home. What was Danny doing all that time? And he thought about how he'd taught Danny not to talk to strangers and trusted him not to—

"There's nothing I'd like better, Dr. Owens, than to tell you he wasn't involved in this." Hopewell slid behind the wheel. "All I can tell you is, check his e-mail and keep an eye on it. That's the only way either of us will be sure."

Jack watched the car pull away and drive down the road. "The son of a bitch."

Stan was contemplating the bottom of his coffee cup when Jack came around to the back porch. Mutt was rolling in a rain puddle and snapping at his tail.

"Is there a problem?" Stan asked.

"The detective investigating Danny's suicide," was all Jack said, all he had to say to Stan. "I'll be ready," he assured him.

Stan put his hand on Jack's arm. "If anything comes up in the meantime, if you need a sounding board or just someone to have a drink with and talk things over—"

"Of course," Jack said absently.

He'd told his boss that a detective had just come to the house and he was sure Stan wanted to know all about it, he might even think he had the authority to ask, even if it went against his better judgment and high principles—there's always that itch to get under the skin of someone else's life, to lift the lid, to find out, for no other reason than the reassurance that someone is worse off than you, or someone's got it better, or simply because he's concerned. Or maybe Stan was just curious enough to want to dig in the muck of the human condition. But he didn't ask.

The moment of panic came as soon as Stan's car pulled away and Jack walked inside the house and up to Danny's room, where it still felt of Danny's presence, or the presence of his absence, the blank space. Any scenario that Jack hadn't played out since the day Hopewell walked into his office played out in his head now with the same breakneck speed and calculation as when the car goes into the spin, the speed of the reflex to stop disaster from happening, the reflex to assure himself that Danny hadn't been pushed to suicide by a pederast he'd met over the Internet, to assure himself Danny would never do that. But there was this too: Jack could always trust the living Danny, the Danny who never broke the rules. But the dead Danny obeyed no rules or else there was no reason to be here and no reason to be afraid. And it was also this: there was something about Danny that Jack didn't know. The something that put the bag over Danny's head and killed him.

The world can turn in on itself just so many times and then there's nothing left to be afraid of. Jack wanted to believe that. He wanted to believe that the worst had already happened, while he sat at Danny's desk facing the computer. He hesitated, like a man facing a strong wind and needing to muster all of his strength to walk the few more steps.

XVI

He wasn't Jack. He wasn't Dr. Owens, but the creation of Danny's suicide, the creation of Hopewell's suspicions, who had searched through Danny's e-mail. He wasn't the man Danny called Dad, who had sat at the kitchen table one of the mornings during finals when he and Danny managed to have breakfast together, before they made their respective rushes to school—was Danny already planning it? Was there already something in his face that Jack hadn't seen? Could he see it now?

Danny looked tired. He pushed his food around the plate but he wasn't eating. He asked, "Which is more important, Dad, honesty or loyalty?"

"Good question," Jack answered, and Mutt started barking, the school bus driver honked the horn and Danny grabbed his books and bolted.

But that wasn't the question right now. The question now was about faith and trust because Hopewell had asked *his* questions and those questions put faith and trust in doubt. Jack had thought the worst—he could make a convincing argument that his confidence was a fragile edifice these days like the shacks out by the river, where the air stank of cabbage and diapers and the sweat of despair. He was panicked and trembling as he sat at Danny's desk and looked into Danny's e-mail—he might have been looking into his soul, for that's how it felt—and if the rules did not apply to the dead Danny, they still applied to the living Danny. The Danny who did not disappoint. If Danny had his own deal, a deal whose end Jack might never guess and might never know, it had not allowed for pederasts and predators. Jack had known that. He'd never had a reason to doubt the living Danny, never before today. The trust and faith were understood. He never made Danny live up to anything he couldn't handle. He'd been careful not to turn into one of those parents looking to catch his kid in a lie, rummaging through dresser drawers in hot pursuit of drugs or pornography or worse.

Now he stared at Danny's computer screen, scrolled through the menus, looked down the columns, cautiously, as though he were tiptoeing into the room of his sleeping child—and would he awaken something much more dangerous than a sleeping child that lived within Danny? But Jack found no correspondences from pederasts. There were no vulgar messages, nothing of insidious intent and crude suggestions. Danny still did not disappoint.

Jack thought: Those rules still apply.

The living Danny had not been subverted by the dead Danny, but Jack had been. He'd been subverted by the last act of the living Danny, which itself was a subversion by the dead Danny.

And the following morning, Jack drove to campus and went to his screening room, as though he might breathe deeply and fill his lungs with all that had been lost, as though the essence of his past were contained, preserved, in the air of this place, who he was with Danny and to Danny, who he was because of Danny, as though Danny himself were alive here and could be inhaled. As though all of Jack, who had sat here as the complete man, could be inhabited again.

The screening room was still a piece of terra firma, where Irwin McCormick waited at the foot of the projection booth stairs and said, "She's all ready for you," nodding his head with proprietary sureness, for he was attached, anchored, to this same piece of terra firma and had been since the semester Jack was tenured and had him budgeted into the film department, on call to run the projector, serve as all-around handyman and caretaker, and even carry a sleeping Danny out to the car on more than a few nights when Jack had to work late, the au pair had the day off and no babysitter was available. "You are one good little Danny," Irwin always said. "One hell of a little man."

Today, Irwin didn't mention Danny by name as he gave Jack a thorough looking-over through pale, myopic eyes. His striated face showed neither too little nor too much sympathy, ever mindful of the social amenities he'd learned, the rules of comportment, Gilbert style, which say not to overstep the bounds of someone else's personal sorrow. After all, Irwin was the son of an old-timer, who'd taught him those rules and, along the way, taught him to stay away from coal mining, another rule he obeyed, working twenty years on whatever shift they'd give him at the college's physical plant and now, thanks to Jack, supplementing his pension with a bimonthly check. All he said was, "I know how tough times has been for you, but you're where you belong now," then hitched his gray overalls over his spare hips, one of them prosthetic and apt to give him trouble, and on which he was careful to put as little weight as possible while he emitted painful grunts and carefully climbed the stairs.

Jack walked down the aisle and took his customary seat in the fifth row. He'd come to the place where there was no doubt he belonged, the place where he existed, not as a memory, not as the ghost rattling his chains. This was his little theater, with the wide screen, two dozen seats and the podium off to the side. The little theater that Irwin kept polished, waxed and shampooed. But all he could do was go through the motions, the motions of being the college professor, he could perform an impersonation of that other man, show up for the fall semester, stand in front of the ten apprehensive faces, wondering if he could give them their tuition's worth. All he could do was wonder if he could act like Dr. Owens when it counted.

But going through the motions can blur the line between the real and the facsimile, blur the line between who you are and who you are expected to be. The facsimile can never be as real as the genuine article. It will be too perfect. And the effort always shows. Although sometimes that's all there is. When there's nothing left of the genuine article, you have to settle for the sorry little man sweating the choreography, fretting the song and dance.

Jack could watch his films and be merely the Dr. Owens of memory, following the old choreography. He could look around where nothing in this room was unfamiliar and find the terrain beyond recognition. Where he was just another shadow on the screen, all flickers and light. That's what it's like when you aren't who you are.

He had come here to get lost in the dark, to watch films and make his notes and hope that it passed for normalcy, or an imitation of what passed for normalcy. But Jack was thinking about Danny, that he never should have doubted him. While Danny receded further away.

"You all settled in?" Irwin called down.

Jack said he was all settled in and the lights slowly dimmed.

When the film was over and the notes were written, when the lights came up and Irwin limped out to get himself lunch, Jack stayed in his little theater. He leaned back in the seat, closed his eyes and rested.

There were afternoons when he had imagined Danny grown up, traveling the world. "You should do some traveling," Jack used to tell him. "See what other places look like and feel like, see how other people live and what they know and how they think, before making your decisions. You'll have to make them anyway, so why not make them after you've been somewhere and had some fun." That's what Jack told Danny. "There'll be time," he promised him.

There was supposed to be time, and Jack would let nothing rush so much as one minute of Danny's life. That was part of the deal. You make the deal, you keep it and hope everything falls into place, or nothing else falls apart. For ten years the deal stuck.

Maybe Danny had his own neurotic tic. That might explain the piano lessons and the concerts and baseball . . . Why Danny's e-mail came up clean. No, Jack knew better than that, that was just Danny, that came naturally.

It was dusk when Jack walked out of the theater, into the timid glow of the gaslights. Long gray shadows stretched across the quadrangle and up the brick sidewalk. Slight indications of activity on campus were apparent, as though an organism were coming back to life, one of those ancient fish that lives on the bottom of the ocean, all nervous system and impulse, scales like coral and barnacles, asleep all day, waking at night with the sluggishness of Eternity, it sticks out its whiplash tongue and swallows some unsuspecting school of krill, which in this case was time, faculty and the student body.

Windows that had been closed all summer were raised, scattering yellow rectangles of light backward into the recesses of offices and hallways. Out of the twilight, under brick arches, faces appeared. They were to be avoided, sidestepped, dodged down the alley, through the side entrance, up the stairs to the office, where it smelled of musty paper and warm sun stains, where it smelled of summer's idleness. Where Time stood still, like in a diorama at the museum. If he turned on the light, Jack would see himself at his desk and it was early morning, the month was May, and nothing had changed.

The following afternoon, Jack was sitting at a booth in Paul's waiting for Marty and reading the morning paper. The headline read: INTERNET PEDOPHILE PREYS ON GILBERT YOUTH. It was the story about Lamar Coggin's murder. There was no mention of Danny by name, only an allusion to a suicide being "possibly related." The piece was mostly about Hopewell and how he had "determined" that Lamar Coggin's death was a homicide committed by "a perverted killer stalking young boys on the Internet." According to the paper, "Little Lamar is the only known victim so far and Detective Earl Hopewell is close on the trail of the killer." Hopewell was confident that he would soon make an arrest. The detective was quoted: "Keeping the children of Gilbert safe from these sick predators is my primary concern." The Coggin family thanked God for bringing Hopewell to them, and were grateful for the detective's efforts to avenge their son's murder. "We know that Lamar is in heaven, looking down on us and feeling grateful, too."

There was an editorial calling for stricter regulation of the Internet and admonishing parents to monitor their children's Internet activities.

Marty came in and sat down. He pushed the newspaper aside and said unhappily, "I wish you hadn't seen that."

"Is there anything to it?"

Marty started to answer, but stopped when the waiter came over. They ordered lunch, and after the waiter walked away Marty said, "It has nothing to do with Danny." He folded the newspaper and dropped it next to him on the banquette. "Believe me, Jack, Danny is so far out of this. You know that."

"I'm not sure Hopewell agrees."

The corners of Marty's mouth sagged.

Jack said, "He wanted me to look through Danny's e-mail and to keep checking it to see—well, to see if he'd been online with that pedophile." Jack shook his head slowly. "Of course he *wasn't*. I called Hopewell and told him so, but now he wants to look for himself and take the hard drive—there's *no* way I'm going to let him look through Danny's e-mail or anything else of Danny's."

"He doesn't need your permission."

"He can just come into my house and invade my son's privacy?"

"If he gets a search warrant."

"Like hell he can."

"I wouldn't worry about that happening. He has enough without having to read Danny's e-mail."

"Enough of what?"

Marty didn't answer. He only looked around uneasily and it made Jack nervous to watch him. It made him wonder what Marty wasn't saying, what he wasn't telling him, and Marty must have known it. He told Jack, "I know I'm only making you think the unthinkable by not telling you everything, but you'll just have to believe me." A look of unhappiness deepened in his face. "This is Hopewell's case and I have to respect that and how he chooses to go about it. Even if I don't agree with it." This was said so plaintively that Jack wanted to apologize for asking. He wanted to tell him: "I know that I've been leaning on you all summer. Maybe it's time I backed off and took care of all this on my own now."

But Marty spoke first. He started to say, "Look, Jack—" paused when the waiter brought over the sandwiches, and then, "I really don't want to make things any worse for you than they already are, but I have to trust—I have to have your word that you're not going to say anything about this to anyone."

"Anything about *what*?"

"Hopewell's got a suspect." Marty spoke softly across the table. "He's not ready to make an arrest. An elementary school teacher here in Gilbert. He lives with his two sisters. Really pathetic. Apparently he gets into chat rooms with young boys, gets them to talk dirty with him, in a clumsy, manipulative way, and tries to meet them. My captain sent me over to talk to the boys this guy was online with here in town. Some of these kids are pretty fragile to begin with, and once he gets started on them—it's really twisted. Hopewell's trying to get him airtight on using the Internet to talk to Lamar, then he'll work the homicide."

"And what about Danny?"

"Danny wasn't murdered. Hopewell knows that and I want you to know that." Marty looked past Jack. "Hopewell's got his hands full trying to make Lamar's case. The forensics are so iffy that without an eyewitness, a confession or finding Lamar's personal effects on the suspect, he'll have a hell of a time making the homicide stick."

"You don't sound like that's such a terrible thing."

Marty took a bite of his sandwich and chewed it slowly. He pushed a few stray crumbs around his plate before he answered. "I don't see anything pointing to this guy being a murderer, if that's what you mean." His voice was no louder than a whisper. "Not that I doubt Hopewell's ability to scare him so bad he'll admit day's night. But that's not going to catch the killer." He gave the sandwich a quizzical look, as though he didn't know how it got into his hand. "It doesn't take great police—you can pretty much profile these characters. This guy gets his kicks *talking* about sex to young boys. He's not luring them into the woods and killing them."

"Was that the only way he contacted them? Over the Internet?"

"That's all we know so far."

"Can't you stop him? Hopewell, if you think he's going to frame the guy."

"I didn't say he's going to frame anyone. But unless someone, including me, can produce the real killer, and I'm not that good, or lucky—look, Jack, the guy's still guilty of *something*. Most likely he'll get a decent enough lawyer and either take his chances in court, which I doubt, or plead out. In any case, he's going to wind up in prison and that will be the end of him."

"And Hopewell's going to make it *public* that Lamar was talking about sex over the Internet with this guy? He's going to put Lamar's parents through that?"

"Whatever it takes, I'm afraid." Marty said most detectives would have thought twice before doing this kind of damage, to everyone involved. "And by the time Hopewell's finished, he'll have done some damage. But he'll spin it so it looks like he's put a psychotic killer away and saved the lives of young boys across the entire state of Indiana. And no one's going to give a damn about anything else. It's really depressing. And the capper is, there's not one damn thing anyone can do about it."

It was the tail end of the lunch hour and the place was starting to empty out, faculty mostly. There was an ease with which they moved, vacation-paced and relaxed, carrying the scent of faded suntan oil, giving the room the feel of a new season, a new semester, even if the semester was still a week away. Jack knew them by face only, they were not the friends who had sat with him in late May and talked the soft talk, and yet these people, too, were a part of the living Danny, parents of children Danny had gone to school with, and they were seeing Jack for the first time since Danny's death—there would be no hiding naked and sweating in the attic now. They approached carefully, they spoke cautious words, they told Jack how sorry they were, in their bedside voices, their faces sympathetic and pitying. Only after Jack nodded his hello, after they saw that it was safe, did their voices loosen, their faces relax, before they returned to their routines, to the familiar environs, where the brick sidewalks led to the same offices and classrooms they had last semester, where their books were on call and waiting for a starting time, where their lives were where they'd left them, as though nothing had changed.

But something had changed. Jack had changed. Sitting with Marty was not only proof of that, it was the result of it, and the result of what had changed him. He was the father of the boy who had killed himself. The man of summer compulsions, who had passed his vacation days with good cops and bad, seen the lid lifted and knew the machinations of detectives and their plans. Who knew their setups and what kept them awake at night. He was both an outsider and an insider, still in possession of all the academic credentials but no longer insulated by that community; privy to information Gilbert faculty couldn't know, part of another community. The Community of Parents of Dead Children, where the Coggins thanked God for their avenging detective, and a sad detective's conscience had him by the throat. It was a terrible thing to concede, this change.

Jack told this to Marty, after they'd left the restaurant and were walking down Main Street.

Marty only frowned and shook his head slowly, then he started back to work. But Jack stopped him. "Hey, Marty, which is more important, honesty or loyalty?"

"What?"

"That's what Danny asked me a week before he died."

"What did you tell him?"

"I told him it was a good question."

"Did he ever say which *he'd* pick?"

"No, he didn't."

"It's a good question."

Jack went back to his screening room, where there were only more films to watch. And later, he went to his office, where the air held on to the scent of summer and sunlight. There was a message on his voice mail from Lois saying that she and Tim were back from Rome and, if Jack was in the mood, would he come out to their place for cocktails. But there were no messages from the only voice he wanted to hear and he didn't need to call the house and leave a message of his own asking Danny if he and the guys were up for a catfish fry and the batting cages over by the fairgrounds. Or maybe just the two of them could have supper . . .

When he finished his work, he drove out to see Lois and Tim. They drank cocktails on the patio while Lois told Jack how glad she was to see him and gave him a strong hug and kissed him on the cheek. She said that he'd been on her mind all summer and she couldn't get "a proper read when we spoke on the phone."

Jack said there wasn't much to read and Lois took her cue to wait until they were alone to find out what she really wanted to know.

And later still, Jack pulled up to his house that stood dark against a darker sky. There was no one inside waiting for him, he wasn't used to that yet, and he sat on the porch steps, remembering the nights when he came home to the sound of the piano, of the television, to the sound of Danny. He tried to think about the work he had to do, the films he had to screen, the notes and preparations. And only after he went inside and looked at Danny's picture on the night table, after he turned off the light, after he was in bed, unable to sleep, would he come to the discomforting realization that Danny wasn't receding further away from him, after all; he was receding from Danny.

XVII

Lois sat at her desk, stockinged feet curled under her. There was a stack of unopened mail on her desk, more than a few textbooks were still in their shrink-wrap. The sunlight bent through the window and embraced the back of her head like an aureole. Now that she and Jack were alone he told her about his summer obsessions and the compulsions. He told her about the night at the Palomino. He told her all that he dared to admit.

Lois must have had questions, but she didn't ask them. She only listened, at times looking worried, at times concerned. She said, "I can understand why you didn't tell me any of this when I called this summer. I appreciate that you're telling me now."

Jack kept on talking, impelled forward by the sheer volume of words. He told her about the day at the barbecue shack, he told her "Marty's been holding my hand all summer." He did not talk about the murder of Lamar Coggin or Hopewell's investigation. He did not talk about the despair worn on the faces of sad detectives.

He walked over to the window where he could see the back of the Fine Arts building, where Anne's studio had been. He turned toward Lois and said, "I was thinking about Maggie last week." Lois looked at him over the top of her glasses and said nothing. "It could have made a difference," he told her. "For Danny. It could have made things easier for him."

She said, "You can't think like that," in the way she might have back when she was his teacher and he thought he would make movies and would need to know something about the actor's craft. Back when Lois spoke and he listened and learned. He wasn't the young film student now but he still listened when Lois spoke, even if he didn't learn but only inferred, and she didn't instruct but only proffered, suggesting what he should and shouldn't examine about his life. She was allowed to. She knew the play and the players. She spoke with authority.

Jack didn't tell her this, although he must have years ago. What he said, as he walked to the door, was, "We still have a lot to talk about."

"Yes, we do."

"If you have time tonight, we'll go out for a drink."

"I'd like that."

He went downstairs and out to the campus, where it was another morning humming with academic industry. The sleeping organism that had stirred in the night was fully awake and beginning to feed, converting human energy to the work of hands. But when he climbed the stairs to his office, Jack was not absorbed by the organism. He was not compelled to work. He was thinking that Lois might have been wrong about Maggie. He was thinking that he might have been wrong about Maggie as well.

They were sitting on the floor of the sunroom in Maggie's house. It was her favorite room, the rattan furniture, the tan venetian blinds tinting the sun like the light in a British movie. She pulled two pillows off the couch, they rested their heads against them. They were kissing and the music was turned down low.

Jack said she looked beautiful. She said Jack looked beautiful, too, and smiled.

Jack told her, "Your hair has summer in it."

Maggie said she was glad to see summer end. "I missed you very much." She said she was happy to be alone with him.

He said he was happy to be alone with her.

He wasn't afraid to tell her that. It was what she would say next that he was afraid of, and what would happen after she said it. He'd been afraid since before the night at Ambrosini's, which meant he'd been afraid since the day they met and he went on seeing her anyway. He thought he could work around it. He never knew how afraid he really was until it finally happened.

If he'd kissed her, she wouldn't have been able to say what she said. If he talked about the class he'd taught at Stanford that summer, if he'd turned up the music or got up to make coffee. He might have tried to change the subject, tried to put off the conversation, but he did nothing. He knew what she wanted to talk about and he'd been dreading it for so long, and wanting it, wanting what she was about to offer, afraid he wouldn't turn it down, afraid that he would, and now he wanted it to be over with, and felt a calm relief when she said it.

"I don't want to do this again next summer. And when Danny gets back from camp next week and you two go away, I'd like to go with you. We can all go somewhere together."

"You know how I feel about that."

"Danny's used to me now." She said this neither defiantly nor argumentatively. She was stating a fact.

"He's accepted you as my *friend*. I have lots of friends. They don't go away with us over the summer."

"You're not thinking that I'm trying to interfere?"

Jack said no, he wasn't thinking that.

"And I'm certainly not trying to come between the two of you."

Jack said he knew that, too.

"And it's not like I'm about to propose marriage," she said lightly. "I just think that we've reached the point when it's okay to all go away together and not make a big deal about it. We've spent weekends together, so why not a week or so?"

"I won't let him get attached to someone and watch him get hurt all over again." That wasn't all there was to say, it was all Jack was willing to tell her.

"You're not talking about Danny."

"I'm talking about both of us."

"But he *is* getting attached. So are you and so am I. So why shouldn't we—"

"He might be getting *too* attached."

"What if he is? What if we *all* are? All the more reason to go away together."

Jack tried to explain it to her. "I don't want to build up his expectations for something that isn't going to happen." But that didn't explain it. "Or worry about something that *is*." But that wasn't it, either.

Maggie put her arm around his shoulder. He didn't shrug it off. "There's no reason why we have to miss each other, that's all I'm saying."

"The more time we spend together, the more time I'm going to want to spend with you."

"I should hope so," she said playfully.

"I can't do it."

"Can't?"

"When Danny's older. When he's grown, there'll be time for a serious relationship, not before."

"This already is a serious relationship."

"You know what I mean."

"I'm not sure I do. I'm not talking about playing mother to him."

He remembered thinking how calmly she said this, how her voice lacked even the slightest edge of desperation. How it made him think: The absence of anything, some element, creates the presence of something else. And how he chose not to hear the certainty of affection that was in her voice.

She said, "You know I'd never tell you how to bring him up."

"I know."

"And you know this isn't about trying to replace his mother."

"I know that, too."

"So what is it?"

"I won't set him up for more disappointment."

"I'm not going to disappoint him. Or you."

"It might not start out that way, but you never know what will happen over time."

She shook her head. "Come on, Jack. That's not what this is about."

He leaned back and took a deep breath. "I'm not going to calibrate his life. I'm not going to rush him through his childhood. And I won't do that to you, either."

"Do what to me?"

"Make you wait until Danny's an adult."

"That's something I can decide for myself, don't you think? Besides, that's not what I'm asking you to do." She stood up and straightened the blinds, keeping her back to him. "You're circling the wagons. There's something you don't want to tell me. Or is it that you don't know quite how?"

"I'm doing what I think is right for Danny."

"I never said you weren't. But does that include depriving yourself of a relationship?"

"You're exaggerating things."

"I might be *understating* them." She turned around. "I'm willing to bet this isn't the first time you've had this conversation with a woman you were seeing." When Jack said nothing, Maggie only smiled and nodded her head. "Don't think I'm trying to make a case for myself. Trying to talk you into anything. You can walk away, I can walk away, and we'll never see each other again. We'll miss each other like crazy, but we'll live." The music stopped and at the same time Maggie stopped speaking, as though she wanted the silence to hang there; as though that was the sound of the emptiness Jack was proposing and she wanted him to get a good dose of it. He didn't break the silence. He only waited for her to talk him out of it. That's what he wanted. He didn't want to leave her and he didn't know how to stay. And what if he'd said that, if he'd said, "I'm the one who's getting too attached"?

If he'd said, "You see, I've made this deal with myself. It's about self-deprivation and protecting Danny and it's the only way I know how to hold my life together and keep Danny safe, but there's got to be a way to work with it." It would have told her what she wanted to know. If he'd said, "Once I had a wife and a baby and we lived in a loft on Crosby Street and I lost that . . ." If he'd said, "You see, there's Anne . . ." they might have come up with an answer. It was something Maggie would have understood. But if he could have said that, he wouldn't have needed the deal.

Maggie let the silence hang there while she looked out the window. The sunlight lay frozen on the floor.

Jack stared at the back of her head, at the sleek cut of her hair, at the way her yellow sweater flared over her hips. He could smell her perfume.

Maggie walked back to him and sat down. She drew herself close to him and softly traced her finger along his cheek, the way she had when they danced at Ambrosini's and when they sat in the corner booth listening to jazz.

When she broke the silence, she asked, "Have you ever tried? Since your divorce, I mean."

"You know I've dated—"

"I'm talking about a relationship."

He didn't answer.

"You're afraid of something. Isn't that what this is really all about?"

He didn't answer that, either. "I've told you what it's about."

"No. You've been saying what you don't want and won't allow, but what *will* you allow?"

"I'm going to stop seeing you."

He expected her to pull away from him, but she didn't. "That's ridiculous," and she leaned into his body.

"Maybe it is, but that's the only way to resolve this."

He considered what he was doing, what he was about to do, without any pretense of rightness. It was easy to ponder the future beyond his action, to know that only a few more minutes remained and he would never see Maggie again and he would always regret this day and his decision, to consider what he was doing in the name of self-deprivation. Or was it Danny who was being deprived, and of what, exactly? A mother? A second chance at childhood? Did he really believe that he was keeping Danny safe from more disappointment and sadness? He might have wondered what he was protecting and who.

He might have wondered if all he had to do was tell Maggie, "Okay, let's give it a try." Or, "Okay, let's give it a little more time." Or he could have said, "It isn't that I don't know what I'm doing, what I'm giving up, what I'm losing. But I don't know what else to do."

All he did was wait, choking on the things he did not permit himself to say.

Maggie said, "It's not the only way," flatly, her hand touching the back of his neck where it's always soft and warm.

"And what if we keep seeing each other?" Jack answered. "We'll only have this discussion again, a week from now, a month. It will always be there."

"So? We'll eventually come to terms with it, or work through it."

"I don't think that's possible."

"So you're going to walk out on it. That's foolish."

"I have no choice."

"*No* choice? That's not a reason." She shifted a little and looked at him. He felt her breath on his face. "Tell me," she said, softly. "Tell me what you're afraid of."

He paused before he answered, "Do the math."

"But I'm not Anne."

"Everyone is Anne," he explained.

He thought: Everyone is Anne. And no one is Anne. He thought about Anne, who would curl up in the crook of his arm and breathe softly and pull his face to hers. How her skin smelled so terribly exciting. How she said, "Can we always be like this? Loving each other and living our lives together?"

He thought about how much he loved her when they were still undergraduates at Gilbert College and when he was the young professor at NYU and Anne was rushing headlong through Cultureburg.

He thought about how much he loved her when the three of them spent the summer in the country house in Loubressac. Anne was working against time, preparing to mount her second show. Jack was writing his next book. Danny was four months old and slept on the pallet Anne had made for him. She said, "He sleeps through the night and makes these little insect noises in his sleep, and when he wakes up and sees us, it's like this ecstatic recognition: 'It's *you. Yay,* it's *you.*'" She managed not to make this sound precious. She said, "He really is the best little baby," and lay with her head on Jack's chest breathing with his breathing, playing with Danny's hands, which were unimaginably small and awesome for their fragility, while Danny, tucked between his mother and father and not making those little insect noises at the moment, issued a soft purring sound.

"He has the most lovely colored eyes," Anne said. She placed her index finger on Danny's face and drew a tiny circle along his cheek. "He's quite lovely. Quite the little charm boy. Just like his father." She turned her face to Jack. "We're doing all right with him, especially now that he's emerging from his larval stage?" And she said a second time, nodding her head firmly, "We're doing all right, aren't we, Jack?"

Jack didn't hear the doubt, he didn't hear the need for reassurance, although surely it was there, that summer in Loubressac. He only answered, "We're doing all right," while Danny giggled, or made sounds that sounded like giggles.

"He does try to ingratiate himself," Anne said, "doesn't he?"

Later that month when they returned to New York, they walked through Central Park with Jack's parents. His mother said Danny was "the best little baby. So much easier than you were."

"And very cooperative," Anne said.

"Cooperative?" Jack's mother asked.

"He never makes a fuss when I'm working, or cries."

"Cooperative," Jack's mother repeated.

"He's also very alert." Jack's father lifted Danny out of the stroller. "Look at that face. I wouldn't be surprised if he's talking before he's a year."

"His first word will probably be *cinema*," Anne told them.

"Chiaroscuro," Jack said.

"Duchamp," his father said, and laughed. He lowered Danny into the stroller and pushed him along the path.

"So it's working out?" Jack's mother said in a way that made Jack tell her she sounded less than convinced.

They stopped to pose for pictures with Danny smiling atop Jack's shoulders, Jack believing it would always be like this. It was there on his face, in the photographs, but there was something else in the photographs, in the expression on Anne's face while she looked at Danny, if only for that moment, that could have been mistaken for confusion, as though something had thrown her off, and it wasn't the first time Jack had witnessed it. He'd seen that same expression when Anne sat at her easel and Danny slept in the cradle next to her. And sometimes when Danny was playing on the floor, and Anne sat on the couch sketching him or simply watching him. And sometimes when Danny wasn't even in the room.

Jack would ask, "What is it?"

Anne would shake her head and say, "It's nothing. I'm just thinking." But she didn't say what it was that she was thinking. Only, "It's not important," the inflection in her voice suggesting that it was anything but unimportant, which Jack pointed out.

"It's really nothing. Nothing at all."

And he asked her again one night, after they'd dropped off Danny at Jack's parents' apartment. They were sitting in the back of a cab, on their way to a dinner party.

Anne told him, "I'm thinking of the new paintings." And a few seconds later, "I'm thinking of naming the series 'One Foot on the Platform, One Foot on the Train.' That's how I've been feeling lately." She turned her head and looked out the window. The sparking of the street lamps, the red and green of the traffic lights, the quick flash of amber, burst against her reflection. "I don't mean about *us*. You and me. But I don't always know how to feel about Danny. About being a mother." She looked over at him. "I don't mean just in the moment when I'm with him. I'm talking about something more pervasive. I can't really give it a name, except that I want to be Danny's mother and at the same time I don't want a child at all, and all the while I don't ever doubt that I love him. It isn't about that. And it isn't about being nostalgic for when it was only the two of us."

Jack said he had a pretty good idea of what she was talking about, and that he'd sometimes felt the same way.

Anne said, "All parents do, I suppose. Once in a while." She said she really believed that, "even if half the time I don't know *what* I feel, or *how* I feel, except confused and it frightens me." She shook her head. "God, Jack. He's the best little boy."

There were mornings when the three of them would lie in bed, Danny nuzzling his cheek against Anne's neck and kicking his small feet against Jack's hips, and they would laugh and sing songs. Times when Danny would roll across Anne's lap and burrow his head in the crook of her arm. Or she would sit on the floor with him and make toys out of cardboard, old socks and yarn. There didn't seem to be any confusion then. Anne would look at Jack and smile, then look over at Danny and scoop him up and swing him around her hips and declare, "You are the best little boy."

There were times when Anne told Jack that she wanted to protect Danny from any doubts she had. She said, "I know it's only a phase I'm going through. I know it will pass." Those were the times, she said, when she had no doubts at all.

But there were those other times when that look returned, and not just when Danny was running around the loft, making noise, talking to himself, while Jack worked on his book and Anne painted—there always seemed to be a work-in-progress back then, propped on Anne's easel, stacked on Jack's desk—but when they were doing nothing at all, and Anne told Jack that she wondered if Danny could sense how she was feeling and how worried she was. But that winter, Danny did not behave like a little boy with any worries, not when he rolled around in the snow, or chased the pigeons in Washington Square. Or when he spent the weekend with his grandparents so Jack and Anne could spend the weekend alone. Jack's mother said Danny was the most contented little boy she'd ever seen, and then, with no small amount of displeasure, "I assume he's still *coop*erating."

Danny was still cooperating.

And he was still cooperating in late March, a few weeks before his second birthday. That's when Anne said, "I think all that concern was over nothing. I couldn't be happier." Maybe it had something to do with her upcoming show. Maybe she really believed, "It must have been one of those phases mothers go through." She told Jack, "I know we made the right decision."

Later that month, the gallery mounted Anne's "One Foot on the Platform . . ." show. The art critic from the *Times* said Anne's palette had grown deep and expansive over the past two years. *ARTnews* crowned her "the Queen of Postmodernism." *Art in America* praised her for the "ontological autonomy indicative of her entire body of work." It was 1983. A lot of people were throwing money at art. Some of that money came to Anne. That summer they went back to France. To the country house in Loubressac.

Anne was going to work on paintings for two private collections. They were commissioned for September. Jack was under contract to write his third book. They hired a local woman, Isabelle Pujol, to be Danny's au pair. It was very hot that June. There were no fans or air conditioners in the house, no screens on the windows, which were kept open day and night, the shutters pulled back; the shade, and whatever cooling it managed, came courtesy of the old trees in the yard. The kitchen hummed with flies. At least once a day a sparow came swooping into the big room and quickly flew out. It was never less than warm inside. The best time to work was late afternoon, break for supper with Danny, work until sunrise while Danny slept, and sleep during the hottest time of day, while Danny was off with Isabelle. Some nights their friends George and Catherine came by for drinks.

Anne worked downstairs in the big room off of Danny's bedroom. Jack worked upstairs, shirtless in cutoffs, where the clacking of the typewriter would not keep Danny awake. In the morning, they both kept Danny company while he ate his cereal or the egg Anne scrambled for him. Danny was walking and talking now, in the clutches of the "terrible twos." Fighting toilet training. Curious about everything, and defiant. His word of choice was *"No."* Anne said maybe Danny was finally acting out feelings he hadn't expressed back in New York. He needed help drinking his milk, but when Anne tried to show him how to hold his cup, he shouted "No" and splashed the milk in her face. He demanded their attention, but when they gave it to him he yelled, "Don't look at me," and threw the nearest object, a pencil, a plate, at them.

"Isabelle has a big day planned for you," Anne would say, "so finish your breakfast."

"No."

"She's taking you to her uncle's farm," Jack would tell him. "Isn't that exciting?"

"No."

"You'll see lots of animals. Horses and—"

Danny would kick his feet against his chair, shriek, "Don't *want* to go," take a handful of scrambled egg and throw it on the floor.

"Do you want to stay here with Mummy and Daddy?"

"No."

"Don't you want to go for a ride with Isabelle?"

"Hate Isabelle." Danny would pound the table and scream.

"What do you want to do?"

Danny would reach for another handful of eggs, but if Anne beat him to it and took the eggs out of his hand, Danny would start to cry.

So it went: Danny kicking and screaming, throwing his food, behaving, well, like a two-year-old.

"But you said—"

"No."

"But you *asked*—"

"No."

"But you wanted—"

"No. No. No."

Some mornings, Anne would scream back at him, and when Danny threw eggs at her she'd snatch the plate and shout, "Then, *don't* eat your breakfast," and scrape the food into the garbage. Or Jack would grab Danny's bowl of cereal just before the small hands pushed it to the floor, and leave Danny sitting in his high chair kicking and screaming at the empty room.

By the time Isabelle arrived, Jack and Anne were dripping sweat, exhausted and in no mood to coddle or charm their little boy. They warned Isabelle about Danny's present mood—they all spoke French so Danny wouldn't understand. "L'enfant terrible," Anne explained.

Isabelle smiled, lifted Danny to her ample bosom and a moment later he was sitting on her lap, eating what remained of his breakfast, drinking milk out of his cup and, after hugs and kisses to Mummy and Daddy, grinning happily and handsome from inside Isabelle's pickup truck.

"Not exactly sleep-inducing," Anne said, as they walked upstairs to their bedroom.

The evenings, after supper, were the most difficult. Danny, tired but too excited to go to bed, hurled himself through the house, distracted for a moment by a toy, then zipped through the big room, yelling, banging books together, throwing them in the air, jumping at whatever caught his attention, laughing, screaming, hopping along the furniture. Anne managed to keep her brushes on a shelf beyond his reach, or Danny surely would have scattered them on his way upstairs to Jack's room, where he banged on the typewriter, doing little damage to the work-in-progress, until he mastered the technique of turning *on* the typewriter—the law of averages notwithstanding, Danny never managed an actual word, let alone a masterpiece.

Anne told Jack, "I can't say that this is turning into the summer of my dreams," and propped her canvas on top of the table, away from their curious little boy.

"Nor mine."

"Everyone says it's supposed to only last a year."

"The question is, will *we*?"

They sat in momentary silence contemplating the odds of their survival.

Jack wondered if Anne had any of the doubts she'd talked about in New York, and when he asked her, while they sat exhausted and exasperated, she only shook her head and told him, "It's nothing like that."

The light was brightest in the big room. The air held the odors of linseed oil and paint. When Jack took a break from writing he would sit on the stairs and watch Anne work. He watched her as she drew the grid on the primed canvas, as she held the brush in her hand, her fingers supple and relaxed—the tensile connection of hand and eye—as she applied the thin line of color, the line becoming a form, the form a three-dimensional image born on the two-dimensional plane. The trick of perspective, of color and light, light and space. Anne painting over the painting, and with the sweep of her hand wiping the work clean and starting again; and starting over again the next day, and painting over that day's painting two days after that, and starting over again. The silent concentration melding afternoon to night, progress measured not by the hour but by the week.

In the early morning, while Danny slept and the sun slipped slowly across the floor, Jack and Anne talked about their work—somehow, they always found time to talk.

"I read the first two chapters," Anne said, meaning Jack's manuscript. "They're good. I like that they don't read like a sequel to your last book." She drew her bare legs up to her chin and wiped the damp strands of hair away from her face. "But I'm not sure you need to devote so much space to the Hays Office."

"I was wondering about that. But I don't know where to cut it."

"Do you have a title yet?"

Jack told her three that he'd been considering.

"You don't want to make it sound too academic," Anne warned him.

"How about 'Kissing in the Dark'?"

"The right idea but not catchy enough."

" 'Nude in Black and White'?"

"Be serious."

"May I take a look at the new painting?"

Anne turned the canvas toward him.

He told her, "The composition is excellent, of course, but the style seems more remote than your usual work."

"Remote?"

"Maybe unfinished is more accurate."

"I was going for that effect." She stepped back and considered the canvas for a moment. "Maybe I did overdo it a bit. Do you find it off-putting?"

He shook his head. "But it looks accidental and makes the work seem unsure of itself."

"You mean, it makes *me* seem unsure of myself." She yawned. "I'm sleepy. Let's go upstairs."

When they awoke, it was four in the afternoon. The sun had moved to the other side of the house. Their room was dark and cool but their bodies were warm and slick. Jack curled into the soft fullness of Anne's thighs and felt her buttocks press against him. Her hand went around to lift, then push him inside her. When she turned her head and kissed him, her breath smelled of ripe country air. They were alone in the house, and they knew it, so they made love carelessly, the way they used to when it was just the two of them in the attic apartment in Gilbert and in the loft on Crosby Street; loud and forceful, kicking the covers, twisting the sheets, their bodies draped over and inside each other under sweet, yellow sunlight. They made love like that nearly every afternoon—Jack remembered the swell of Anne's breast, her hand gripping his shoulders, her body tensed to orgasm. It never felt like stolen moments. They had woven Danny into their lives. He could still feel Anne's hair sticking damp to his skin, and sense her body, which smelled of sex and sweat and sleep.

"Do you think Isabelle knows?" Anne asked, giggling in Jack's ear.

"Isabelle is wise in the ways of love."

"But is she wise in the ways of parenthood?"

Deep in July, Anne was in a rage to finish the paintings. Sleep had become a tolerated inconvenience, there were no more morning conversations. She ate her meals at her easel. Dressed in shorts and halter top, dots of paint in her hair, she worked alone in the night solving the problems of the first canvas. Muscles sore, her face pale, soaked with the day's perspiration, she would stretch out on the floor for a few minutes, close her eyes, then get back to work. By the time Danny woke up, Anne was barely able to stay awake. She had not the slightest patience for the milk in the face and scrambled eggs on the floor, and would reach for Danny's plate just as he raised his hand, or grab the cup of milk and spill it down the sink. "Not today." While Danny kicked and screamed.

Jack was not in any better mood, and barely managed to wait out Danny and his morning tantrums until Isabelle rode to the rescue. "If he doesn't give it a break . . ."

Anne could only shake her head. "I know . . . I know . . ."

By early August, Anne was seeing some progress on the second painting and looking less desperate. She was more patient with Danny, laughing when he threw food in her hair. She and Jack even made a game out of it, and Danny seemed less contentious. This was also the beginning of a rainy spell that drenched the grass, turned the yard into a small swamp and kept Isabelle at home. "Her mother slipped on the front steps and Isabelle has to take care of her," Anne told Jack. "It will be at least a week, most likely longer, before she'll be back. She didn't seem terribly optimistic and, truthfully, neither am I."

"We'll work something out," Jack assured her.

What they worked out was a schedule: Anne slept during the day, as before, while Jack stayed up with Danny. By late afternoon, Jack slept for a few hours and Anne took care of Danny. In the evening, after Danny went to bed, Jack got his writing done.

Those first few days, Jack and Danny played inside the barn, or rather Jack watched Danny jump and roll around the deep piled hay, roust barn swallows, examine empty nests. Danny ran through labyrinths of straw, wrestled with creatures made of old burlap and his imagination. He never stopped moving, never stopped talking, while Jack laughed at the pratfalls and somersaults and dive-bombs, laughed at the nonstop patter, the narration of what had been conquered, built, destroyed. But by week's end Danny was not so easily entertained and Jack was no longer amused, the sound of Danny's voice had become just so much noise against the background of rain, his antics no longer held much surprise or delight. And the only thing Jack was aware of was feeling tired. Tired of the rain and the summer, tired of waiting for Anne. Tired of Danny.

The inside of the barn, the inside of the house, the word "inside" itself, had taken on the meaning of prison. The word "outside" took the form of invective. "Outside," Danny would insist, as the rain beat against the roof. "Outside," as they stood together at the window, watching the downpour. "Outside," while Danny sulked on the barn floor, and nothing held his interest; where the air was damp and saturated, and the gray, formless sky hung like the weight of oppression itself.

They awoke to the sound of dripping rain, fell asleep to its incessant, unchanging slop and splash. They might have been living inside a leaky faucet. The shutters swelled with humidity and wouldn't close. The sheets and blankets felt as though they'd been dipped in brine. The ground was mud soup, which clung to them in the house, caking doorjambs, ringing the sink and tub, sticking to shoes and clothes. The dense and stagnant moisture was a constant presence, like a foul odor, like a fungus.

"I'm starting to take the weather personally," Anne said, but she never stopped working, a cup of coffee at her side, hair flecked with paint, eyes red and tired.

When it was Anne's turn to watch Danny, he would rush into the big room calling out, "Play, Mummy. Play."

"We'll play later. Mummy's very busy right now and needs some quiet time to do her work."

"No," Danny screamed. *"Play,"* and he emitted nerve-splitting screeches.

"You're quite maddening today," Anne told him.

Danny answered with yelps and shouts, forcing Anne to stop work, sit on the rug and push his trucks around, cut out paper figures and animals from construction paper. When Anne went back to work, Danny demanded, *"More."*

"Come on, Danny, give Mummy a break."

"Play," Danny insisted, like a little emperor. *"Play."*

Anne would search for a toy that might occupy Danny, then hurry back to her painting, and when the toy no longer mollified Danny, she would sit at her easel, index finger raised in the air, "just one more minute . . . Mummy needs one more . . ." while Danny banged his trucks together or called out "Mummy . . . Mummy . . ." and Anne tried to squeeze in another minute's work before she stopped to roll a ball, or make up a game for them to play for another few minutes, or sing Danny's favorite song: "I went to the animal fair/the animals all were there . . ." before, "Now, let Mummy get back to work and we'll play again later."

"Play. Play, now, Mummy."

"In a minute."

"No."

"You're just going to have to *wait*."

"No."

"Yes. For God's sake. *Yes,* Danny."

Some days, Anne was able to keep Danny busy with modeling clay made from flour and water; she made him sock puppets, which he soon tired of.

At the end of the second week, Danny would do nothing but sit in his bedroom and cry, or crouch alone in the closet. He'd have sudden tantrums and throw his toys around, race through the house, knocking down lamps, climbing over the furniture, stomping up stairs and down, until Jack managed to distract him for a few brief minutes with a balloon or a stuffed animal, then Danny would call out for Anne. And all day and all night it rained, sometimes in heavy cascades streaking the window, sometimes in a slow, nagging drizzle, the air dead calm. And all the while Jack and Anne grew more intolerant and impatient, pulling Danny off the furniture, leaving him to sulk in the closet, letting him sit in his room and cry.

"I'm beginning to think of this as our summer of discontent," Anne said. "I don't know what more we can do for him."

"If he'd just let us finish, we'd be able to—"

"If he'd just let us finish."

One afternoon in the middle of the third week, Anne's painting nearly complete, she and Jack noticed a new sound: Silence. The rain had stopped. The sun was out, a dry wind cleared the sky, and everyone's spirits were lifted. Now Danny could play outside, damp grass and mud be damned. The next morning he and Jack drove to town and ate ice cream while they shopped for cheese and bread and wine and sausages. Then back to the house to play some more under the welcome warmth of the August sun. Danny was laughing again, he found amusement in everything offered to him. The simple sentence "Look, Daddy" took on the sound of poetry, a song sung loftily.

"At last," Anne told Jack, "we can all breathe again."

Those days held all the pleasures of a holiday, and Jack could not help feeling a sense of disappointment and deflation when Isabelle called to say she'd be returning to work the next day. He kept Danny outside a few hours longer, kept him up a few hours later that night, until they both fell asleep side by side in Danny's bed.

It was the sound of Anne's voice that woke Jack. "It's finished," she whispered in the dark. "Come look," and led him into the big room. She was shivering with exhaustion.

He told her the painting was magnificent. He said it was her best work ever. They opened a bottle of their best red wine. Jack drank a toast to her. They drank a toast to the summer days ahead "free of all hard work." They drank a toast to the painting, propped it against the wall, studied it in silence and raised their glasses again.

"I was considering using a smaller canvas," Anne said, "but I wasn't certain if that really suited the work." She sounded pleased with herself when she said, "In the end, I decided to stay with the large canvas."

In the end, it wouldn't matter.

It happened that morning. They'd been up all night, and were now drinking their coffee outside by the trees. The air smelled of dew, the leaves shimmered in the sunlight and the grass was tipped with crystal.

Anne asked Jack to take another look at the canvas, in daylight, when he had the chance, "and tell me what you really think of it." She took a deep breath and rubbed her eyes.

"I've already told you what I really think. Maybe you should get some sleep. Maybe you should sleep all day."

"I'm too excited. Too exhausted. Too . . . I don't know."

They stood there, feeling the morning grow warm around them. They hadn't heard Danny get up. They hadn't heard him when he was in the big room, not that he was making much noise. And if they had, would it have alerted them?

Maybe they would have looked at each other and said, "He's u-u-up," with mock dread, and laughed, waited a moment and called to him. Maybe they would have gone inside a minute before they did. But they didn't hear him, they didn't go inside a minute sooner. They saw only the destruction.

The painting lay flat on the floor and Danny was sitting next to it, an opened tube of ocher paint by his knees. His cheeks and nose were dabbed with green, his neck and arms were streaked with red and umber, his hands, the tiny hands that once looked so unimaginably small and fragile, were smearing paint across the canvas. The colors that had been crisp, the depth and perspective that extended to an infinite vanishing point, the light that appeared to radiate outward from the canvas, appeared to be manifested by the paint itself, were now a blurred mass of brown swirls, blacks and hideous violets. The imagery was unrecognizable. Destroyed. Unsalvageable.

Danny looked up and stated proudly, "I paint, Mummy."

For an instant Anne and Jack could only stare, then Anne burst into tears, which made Danny burst into tears. The two of them, Danny naked on the floor, Anne draped against the wall, wept together.

"I must be hallucinating," she sobbed. "I must be hallucinating."

Jack lifted Danny away from the painting. He put his free arm around Anne. She crumpled against his body. He could feel her jaw clench and relax and clench again. The muscles in her neck grew tight. A soft whimper pushed past her lips, "I can't believe he did this. I can't . . ." while she hung on to Jack's shoulder, and Danny buried himself in the crook of Jack's forearm, smearing Jack's shirt with paint and tears.

Jack led them out of the house, out to the corner of the yard under the shadows of the thick summer leaves. He cradled Anne against one side of his chest and Danny against the other. Anne cried. Danny cried, and there was no way to make any of it right, no way to undo the damage. There were no words, there were only tears. The only sound was crying, Anne's thick sobs, Danny's loud bursts. Then something happened behind Anne's eyes, hard and solitary—as tears dripped down her cheeks and onto her shirt—then it was gone, and she took Danny in her arms, held his body next to hers. They were both trembling, and Danny's small hands were smearing Anne's neck and shoulders with paint, smudging her face, her clothes, her hair. Whatever comfort she needed remained unattended.

What a tableau it made for Isabelle when she pulled up to the house and sang out "Bonjour," only then noticing the tears and trembling. She asked if there'd been a death in the family. Anne lifted her head but offered no answer, only turned in the direction of the big room. When she turned away, her face had an expression of utter disbelief and sadness. She pressed her cheek against Jack's face. He put his arm around her, and they stayed outside while Isabelle took Danny inside and bathed him.

"All that work," Anne breathed. "*Gone*. I can't fucking believe it."

Jack said, "It's not hopeless. We'll try to get some sleep, think things over and see what we can do about it." Because he believed that they could undo the damage.

They treated themselves to a day of rest. Jack and Anne spread their blanket in the meadow while Danny ran and tumbled, as he always did, laughing and screaming, but something had changed. He'd stop in the middle of his games, run over to Anne, hug her tightly, kiss her face and arms and run away.

"I feel so bad for him," Anne said. "He knows he's done something wrong, but he doesn't understand the severity of it, and we shouldn't expect him to." And Jack wondered what else she was feeling. He wanted to know what else she was thinking, and what she wasn't saying. But Anne only shook her head. "I don't know. I don't know what else I feel. I don't know what else I think."

When Anne got up to take a walk, Danny went with her and clutched her hand. When they came back, Danny crawled into Anne's lap and stared at her, he stroked her face with his fingers. He kissed her hands until he fell asleep. Anne rested her head on Jack's legs. She said, "I don't know what to do."

They decided to cancel their trip to Anne's parents' house in Dorset so she could work through the next few weeks. Isabelle moved in with them. Anne told her, "Danny's forays into the big room are over."

The first weekend in September, they returned to New York. Anne had finished less than half of the lost work. They hired an au pair, Madeline, to watch Danny. They made sure to keep all paints and canvases out of his reach. "I'm trying to think only good things about this summer," Anne told Jack.

They spent the week speaking French to each other and to the waiters at Café Loup, and to cabdrivers, who ignored them. They went to the Carnegie Hall Cinema and saw Alain Resnais's *Hiroshima Mon Amour* and *Last Year at Marienbad,* and tried to ignore the subtitles. They hosted a dinner party for their friends: Evan Lopez, a dancer with the New York City Ballet company; Brenda Susmann, a painter, who was represented by the same gallery as Anne; Steve Morgan, a sculptor who taught at NYU; Nan Roth, a lawyer, and her husband Barry, also a lawyer, who lived over on West Tenth Street, and whose son, Andy, played with Danny; Avril Stone, whose play *Hello and All That . . .* had been running at the Lortel for about a year and had even won a couple of Obies and was about to move to Broadway. Avril was short and thin, with curly red hair and green eyes that never stayed still, and tiny fingers that were never without a cigarette and which she jabbed in the air as she spoke. Her new play, *Shut Up, He Explained,* was about to go into rehearsal and Avril announced that she was "drinking to excess whenever possible." They talked about Loubressac, talked about the painting Danny had ruined. In time, Nan said, it would become one of those family legends that gets dragged out with the old baby pictures, told and retold with survivor's relief.

"But you must have been devastated," Avril said.

"I was in absolute shock. And panic, after I got past the neck-wringing phase."

"And Danny?" Nan asked.

"Shock and panic, too, not to mention concern about the aforementioned neck."

Nan laughed, and everyone else laughed. Everyone but Anne.

"When Erin was five, she once poured an entire can of India ink into a portfolio of my drawings," Brenda Susmann said. "I was this close to sending her to a convent. I never was satisfied with the work I replaced them with."

Avril had left the only draft of *Hello and All That . . .* in the backseat of a taxi and had to rewrite the entire piece from memory overnight.

Three of Steve Morgan's sculptures had been smashed to dust when the ceiling collapsed in his Walker Street studio five years ago.

"You just have to make the best of it."

"The only thing you can do is move on."

"Actually," Anne told them, "I think I've done a little of both. The extra time's allowed me to make the new work a bit better, so I tell myself, and my mind is teeming with new projects. I'd like to think it was a blessing in disguise."

Jack believed her when she said it. Anne must have believed it, too.

It was a clear, crisp September that year; the kind of weather that makes Manhattan look newly scrubbed, washed by sunlight, giving one faith in the restorative powers of time and distance. Anne was already thinking ahead to the next summer. "I want to go to Italy," she told Jack, "and put France behind us." She knew someone who rented out a small villa in Tuscany a few miles from Bolgheri. They would learn to speak Italian. Jack said he couldn't imagine how they'd lived *this* long without it. Anne laughed. "That's just what I was thinking."

Some days Anne spent with Danny, but most days she was at her drafting table and her easel. She was working in colored pencils and watercolors. She said she wanted to get back to media she truly loved. The gallery wasn't thrilled with this, but Anne wasn't interested in working in oils—Jack thought it might have been an accommodation Anne was making for Danny, and he wasn't sure what to feel about it.

Anne said it had nothing to do with the destroyed painting. But it had everything to do with the destroyed painting, and maybe she knew it all along, and Jack knew it all along.

They were alone in the loft, sitting at the kitchen table drinking coffee. It was a Saturday afternoon. Danny was visiting his friends on Tenth Street. Anne was telling Jack, "It's not going to end, you know." She gave her coffee a stir. "I thought what he'd done last summer was an isolated incident—" She shook her head. "That's not what I mean, I don't mean he'll destroy another painting, that's not what I'm talking about. But it's a symptom of what I'm talking about."

"He won't be two forever."

"No, Jack. I'm talking about something else." She wasn't crying but there were tears in her eyes. "It's just going to go on and on. He'll grow taller, get older, but it will always be something. He'll always need me, that's what I mean, and I find that overwhelming, and I don't think I can be a mother and still do my work. It sounds terribly selfish, I know." She reached across the table and clutched Jack's hand. "I don't mean that I can't physically sit down and work, but he'll always be Danny. He'll always be—he'll always *be* here. Even when he starts going to school, he'll be here." She rubbed the side of her face near the temple, took a deep breath. "I'm not making sense. I'm still not getting it right."

They walked over to the couch and sat next to each other. Jack put his arm around her, she leaned her head against his chin, reached for his hand and held it next to her cheek.

She said, "It's a feeling. A sensation, really. When he ruined the painting, I took care of him, made sure whatever bad feelings he had were attended to. God knows he had good reason to feel them." She laughed cheerlessly. "I wanted to take care of him, there was absolutely no doubt in my mind. He's Danny, after all. When we were standing outside and were all so close, I thought I'd get over it. I thought, it's just something little boys do. But I'm still waiting to get over it, and I'm still waiting for him to do it again, or something like it, and I'm starting to resent him, as if he's standing in my way and I have to choose between doing my art and being Danny's mother."

All Jack could feel, or think, was how could they make it right? How could they make it better? Which is what he said to Anne.

"I don't know what we can do," she answered. "But I know I'm incapable of being mother-slash-artist. There are mothers who can be both, I'm not one of them. God, Jack, everything I'm feeling is wrong." She raised her head and looked at him. "I do love him, Jack. And I love you. So, as you so clearly put it, what shall we do to make it better?" She wiped her eyes with the sleeve of her sweater, pushed her hair away from her face. "Danny doesn't deserve—he deserves a full-time mother."

"We'll think of something. We'll work it out."

Anne smiled. "I'm glad to hear you say that, because I'm feeling more than a bit incompetent at the moment. And terribly guilty and frightened."

"This has nothing to do with competence, and there's nothing to feel guilty about or be afraid of."

"I don't know. I feel so hemmed in."

"Would it help if you take a studio somewhere, so you won't be working at home? Or we'll move to a larger space. We always knew we'd need to do that sooner or later. It's just sooner, that's all."

"I've considered both, but that's not what I'm talking about. Not exactly." She looked at him and there was only sadness in her eyes. "That's not what frightens me."

Outside, a truck rumbled down Crosby Street. Much later, Anne told Jack she remembered that. She remembered the sound of the truck because she waited for it to pass before she said what she said, and she remembered it because of what would happen afterward, not immediately afterward, but what happened to them from that time forward. She would always remember the rumbling outside and the soft smell of toast from the kitchen, and Jack's breath sweet with coffee. She'd remember the line of shadows across the yellow walls, the flutter of the blue curtains over the windows and the feel of the couch under her toes. But what she remembered most was how sad she felt, how flat inside, when she said, "What frightens me is the idea of being without the both of you. Of not being *us* any longer."

"I don't think it will come to that," he answered, and Anne smiled at him.

"Let's see how you feel a month from now."

XVIII

It was six months before Danny's third birthday when Anne told Jack, "I've applied to Yaddo. If they accept me, I'll be away for two months this winter."

"Is two months enough time?"

"It will have to be for now. If I can manage one of these every year, it should keep things in balance, overall." She waited a moment. "Do you think with Madeline to help you—"

"We'll be fine."

"It may all be a bit premature, anyway. They haven't said yes yet."

That winter, Anne took her brushes and watercolors, her pencils, paper and warm clothes and left for Yaddo and the Saratoga winter. Danny was very upset to see her leave. He wanted to know why Anne couldn't paint in the loft, like she always did.

She told him, "I have to do this in this very special place."

Danny stood by the door next to Anne's valises and cried, "I want to go with you."

Anne kissed his little face and said, "We'll all go away together in the summer. Right now Mummy has work to do."

Summer was too far off for Danny to conceive. "Take me with you," he begged.

"I can't. But I promise to hurry home when I'm done and bring you a surprise."

"I don't want a surprise. I want you to stay." Danny cried harder, a fury of tears and howls, as though he knew as well as Anne her reasons for leaving.

Anne knelt down and kissed him again and hugged him. She told him, "Mummy loves you very much," then stood up, kissed Jack on the mouth, walked inside the elevator and waved good-bye, the door closing across her face.

"I'll be good," Danny said softly. "I'll be good," while he stood at the window until Anne got into the taxi. He stared at the empty sidewalk below until Jack picked him up and carried him away.

"You're not going to look out the window all day, are you?"

Danny didn't answer.

"I thought we'd take a walk to Little Italy, get some gelato and cookies. I have a feeling we might even have an adventure."

"What kind of adventure?" Danny said peevishly.

"You never know. That's what makes them adventures."

"Can I have *chocolate* gelato?"

"That's the *only* way to start an adventure."

"And cookies with jelly in the middle?"

"You want to negotiate or get going?"

When it was too cold to go out, or too raw, they'd sit on the couch, eat pizza or milk and cookies, and watch videos of old black-and-white films, broad comedies, Abbott and Costello, the Ritz Brothers, which Danny seemed to like, and lots of the Fleischer brothers' cartoons, not just *Betty Boop* but *Koko the Clown*, *Popeye* and *Superman*. They were the same cartoons Jack had watched when he was Danny's age. Sometimes Danny would sit in his little blue chair with the small table in front of him and eat his food. Jack would sit close to him on the floor. There weren't any tantrums. The days of throwing cups and plates were well past.

"New tapes, Daddy?"

"Old tapes. That's what you asked for. Remember?"

"Oh yeah."

"Granpa used to show me these cartoons when I was a little boy."

"You were a little boy?"

"That's right. And I used to watch these cartoons. And after you were born, Granpa—"

"Granpa was a *little boy*?"

"That's right."

"And you were a little boy?"

"Right."

"When Granpa was a little boy?"

"No. When I was a little boy, Granpa was grown up. He was *my* father, just like I'm *your* father. And after you were born, Granpa and I decided to transfer these cartoons to videotape. That means he saved them so you could watch them one day."

"Granpa is your daddy?"

"That's right. I tell you the same story every time we watch these."

"Oh yeah." Danny pondered this briefly and went back to watching *Popeye*. "Daddy?" he said a minute or two later.

"Yes?"

"I just wanted to say 'Daddy.'"

Anne was always around them. There were pictures of her on the walls, on the desk and on the table next to Danny's bed. Pillows she'd designed were on the couch, curtains she'd made framed the windows. They could see her clothes in the closet and her shoes, they could smell her perfume in the bathroom. There was even a video of her reading stories for Danny. She called every few nights.

"You see," Jack told Danny, "Mummy is with us, even when she's away."

On Wednesday afternoons, Madeline would drop Danny off at Jack's parents' place, Jack would meet him when classes were over, early enough for the four of them to eat supper together. They sat in the library in the Park Avenue apartment, where the stark winter light stood outside the window and the fire in the fireplace shed orange light through the room. Where Jack's mother, two years away from the cancer diagnosis, sat with the elegance of a Modigliani woman and his father, robust and strong, lifted Danny toward the high ceiling, carried him on his shoulders. Where they sipped cocktails and Danny sat on his grandmother's lap, until he got bored and played on the floor, or stared at the adults and listened to their talk.

After dinner, while Danny slept on the bed in the guest room down the hall, Jack's mother leaned back in her chair and told Jack he looked lonely. "Is everything all right between you and Anne?"

"Everything's all right."

"There something you're not telling us," she said.

"There's a lot I don't tell you. But Anne and I are fine."

"Saratoga's a long way to go just to get her work done."

"What do you really want to know?"

"I don't want to know *any*thing. I see trouble."

"There's no trouble."

"There's no trouble," she repeated flatly. "And Anne goes away for two months." She puffed on her cigarette a couple of times, looked over at Jack's father and then at Jack.

Jack said, "Lots of artists go away to get their work done."

"You two aren't having marital problems?"

"What magazines have you been reading?"

"Don't have such a smart mouth."

"Stop worrying."

"I'll worry."

"Martha," his father said, "Anne went away to get her work done, plain and simple. Leave Jackie alone. You're being intrusive."

"I'm his mother. I'm supposed to be intrusive."

One Friday night, at a dinner party at Avril Stone's apartment over on Sixty-fifth Street, it seemed everyone knew someone who'd been to Yaddo or MacDowell or some other artists' colony. No one thought it unusual that Anne had gone away.

"Remember Nadine Mauer?" Avril asked Jack. "The writer who used to live over on Leroy Street. Moved to Santa Fe about a year after you and Anne moved into your loft. She went to Yaddo. Wound up writing that incredible novel."

Evan Lopez said, "Well, not *every*one's got work on their mind when they're there."

"What are you talking about?" Avril asked.

"Lenny and Carla."

"Lenny and Carla *Russell*?"

"She met some sculptor, while she was at Yaddo. *Great* hands. They had an affair."

"Who would want to *schtup* Carla Russell?" Steve Morgan said. "Anne, I could under— You think Jack's worried about Anne fooling around up there?"

"Of course not," Evan insisted. "*No. Jack.* We're just gossiping, you don't think we're—"

"Why don't we change the subject," Avril suggested.

On the cab ride home that night, Jack wasn't worried about Anne having an affair. But he was worried, and what worried him was more complex than jealousy. He was worried because he didn't know what to expect when Anne came home, what would change and what would remain the same. When she called, he listened for any hints in her voice. But there weren't any hints. He would worry while he watched Danny playing with his friends, or running around in the park, or sitting on the floor with his toys talking to himself, a little man going about his business, going through the machinations of growing, emerging gradually, each day, into himself; and Jack would feel as though there were a bubble expanding within him, filling with love and something more than love, and he would look at Danny and feel the bubble expand until it became unbearable, until he wanted to scream and laugh and fall apart inside. And it worried him to be experiencing Danny without Anne, without translating to her what that experience was and those feelings, without having Anne's interpretation of them. It made him feel an estrangement from her that he'd never experienced before. It made him feel untethered and insecure. And he was worried because Anne was too far away from Danny.

He wanted to tell Anne all about this when she called, but he didn't. He didn't tell her that something incomprehensible was happening in their home, that a process was occurring slowly, that all the things that made and would make Danny more of himself were about to happen and had happened already, right in front of them, and must not be missed. That Danny was becoming himself, and it was enough to make him snatch Danny off the floor, or grab him as he ran past and hold him so close they could feel each other's heartbeat, hold him until he thought they would both burst, and his eyes would tear up, holding his little boy.

But Jack didn't tell Anne any of this, because she had not gone away just to be reminded of what she'd left at the loft on Crosby Street. He didn't tell her because it would only have confused her, distracted her.

He didn't tell her that it worried him to know that if there were no Danny, if he'd never been born, and it was still only the two of them, Anne would not have needed to go to Yaddo, and there wouldn't be this feeling of estrangement.

Jack didn't tell Anne that what was happening was both in their past and their future. All he did, all he could do, was wait for her to come home and see for herself.

But coming home wasn't on Anne's mind, she would tell Jack later. She would tell him about waking in the morning and doing nothing but listen to herself think, as though her entire person had been submerged in cognition and the execution of thought; and there were times when she'd reach an entirely thoughtless process, her mind empty of everything but what she was doing in the moment, when she was aware of only the pencil between her fingers, feeling the lines she drew growing out of her arm into her hand, feeling the tension of her mind and imagination. Some mornings, she would do quick sketches, or spend two or three days working on slow, elaborate studies. She drew whatever came to mind. She'd started working in oils again, expanding her palette. Where winter had turned the spare trees black against the stark white ground, she saw the full color spectrum in the crystalline flow across the frozen ground. In the bare and dark branches she saw the colors of the season and she gave face and body to them.

There were days when she would dress up in makeshift costumes and do quick self-portraits; stretches of time when she was so engrossed in her work she missed supper three nights in a row. Time itself seemed to belong only to her. She said the feeling was liberating.

She told this to Jack when she came back to the loft on Crosby Street, not immediately, not when she walked in that night. Danny was still awake and he jumped around and tugged on her arms, pulled on her sweater, burrowed his face into hers, sat in her lap and kissed her face. She clutched him and smelled his hair and his skin. She called him "my darling little boy. My angel baby." When she raised her face she was crying.

"Are you sad, Mummy?" Danny wanted to know.

"I'm very happy."

"Why are you crying?"

"Sometimes when you're happy you cry tears of joy. And tears of love."

Danny stayed up with them until midnight bouncing around and tugging on Anne; acting shy, then acting bold; watching Anne unpack her clothes while she told Jack about Yaddo, about the people she'd met, the conversations she'd had at breakfast, at cocktails in the evening with other artists and writers.

She lay in bed with Danny and told him a story about tigers and bears that danced and played musical instruments, and which ended with her giving him a tin tiger that played the cymbals and a little tin bear that banged a tiny drum. She hadn't forgotten to bring Danny his surprise.

Jack never felt closer to Anne than he did the night she came home and Danny fell asleep with his tiger and bear and later when they sat together on the floor. The loft seemed to have been another place without her, a different place, and she had restored it.

Anne said, "I missed you very much. I want to tell you everything." She pulled herself close to him. Her hair fell across her eyes when she leaned forward and rested her face against his face and whispered, "I always want to tell you everything."

She told him that it was so quiet up there at night she got lost in the silence, that in the morning the air smelled like damp cedars. She curled her feet under herself and described the way the light broke over the windowsill in early afternoon, "like a satin drape," and how each day the sunset shifted a little further to the north "and the day lasted that much longer."

They sat at the table and drank two bottles of wine that Jack bought just for Anne's homecoming, Margaux '81—Danny's year—and ate a lot of rich food.

Anne asked, "Was it much trouble, taking care of Danny without me?"

Jack said it was no trouble at all.

"Were you able to do anything?" She was talking about his writing.

He said he'd written two pieces for *American Film*. She said she was looking forward to reading them. He said he wanted to see the work she'd done.

She spread the drawings on the couch and floor. He told her they were bright and whimsical. "I like the way you've gone back to using the blank spaces."

She laughed softly. "I thought about that while I was working. An homage to our first year at Loubressac."

They made love quietly in the dark, Anne pulling Jack deep inside her.

She touched his neck with the softness of her lips. She whispered, "Your skin smells like Jack Owens." She whispered, "I love being close to you." They took comfort in the familiarity, the sureness of the way they held each other and moved together. Their intimacy excited them.

In the morning, Danny found them awake, sitting on the floor in their bathrobes. He rolled onto Anne's lap and laughed for no apparent reason. He pulled on Anne's ears. He squeezed her chin with his small fingers.

"You're happy to see Mummy, aren't you," Anne said to him.

Danny didn't answer, only buried his head in the crook of Anne's armpit.

"I think he's happy," Anne said, and caressed the top of Danny's head.

After they'd had breakfast with Danny, and Madeline had taken him uptown to visit his grandparents, Anne sat on the windowsill in the kitchen, her back against the glass pane. She told Jack, "I thought being away like that would, I don't know, ease the feelings I had, make everything seem less imminent." She shook her head. "Imminent isn't the right word. I thought I'd catch up with myself, or slow down, or get ahead. I wanted everything to change. But nothing's changed."

Jack was leaning against the wall, maybe he'd gotten up to get a cup of coffee or put something in the sink, but now he was leaning against the wall, looking at Anne framed against the gray light and the brown bricks of the warehouses across the street. She was wearing a dark green sweater and jeans, her feet were bare. It made him think of the time he'd seen her sketching by the ruins.

She said, "I still feel overwhelmed. I still feel that I have to choose between doing my art and being Danny's mother. It's more than a feeling, Jack. It's a fear."

She walked over to him and put her arms around his shoulders. "However," she said, sprightly, "I think I've found a solution. You know what we talked about before I went away? About my taking a small studio somewhere? That's what I want to do. I really think that should settle things." She pressed her head against his chest. "I was very confused, Jack, when I left. I cherish my time alone with my work, and at the same time I missed you and Danny so very much and looked forward to being with you both and talking to you about everything. I want it to be the three of us so very much. I think having my own studio will settle everything. I really do." She looked up at him and the look on his face made her ask, "What? What are you thinking?"

He didn't tell her what he was thinking, because whatever it was was not clear to him, and not just then but since she'd gone away, like an object far away at the rim of the horizon whose shape keeps changing, and color, until it seems to vanish entirely into the light.

All Jack said was, "I think it's the right thing to do."

Anne smiled at him. "Do you really?"

"Really."

She said, "I'm afraid I'm going to need a bit of reassuring," the way she'd said, "Can we always be like this, loving each other . . ." all those years ago in the voice which Jack hadn't understood and which had confused him.

That June, Anne moved into her new studio. It was a one-bedroom apartment on the top floor of a five-story walk-up on Stanton Street on the Lower East Side. It had plenty of northern light and a view of the Chrysler and Empire State Buildings. She'd found the place through a woman she'd met at Yaddo whose husband had bought the tenement and was selling apartments to artists for fairly reasonable prices. The other nine apartments were already taken when Anne bought hers.

"There are a lot of conditions to the sale," she told Jack. "Most of it has to do with capping the percent of profit if I sell, and the stipulation that I can only sell to another artist."

Danny was very upset with the move. He was used to Anne working in the loft, being there when he came home with Madeline. Now he stood in the empty space where Anne's drafting table had been and shivered and wept. Anne tried to assuage Danny's fears. She explained that the studio was only for work and she'd come home to him every night. She gave him her phone number and told Madeline, "Danny can call me whenever he wants."

When Anne took Danny to see the place, he wanted to know, "Will you live here?"

"No, it's like an office."

"It has a bed," Danny pointed out.

"That's so Mummy can rest if she gets tired."

"And a kitchen."

"Don't you worry. Mummy lives with you."

"Can I live here with you?" Danny asked.

They didn't go to Tuscany that summer. Instead, Anne worked on the new studio, doing a major renovation, transforming the rooms into an art space. She stripped decades of paint off the floors and buffed the original wood to a high sheen. She peeled and sanded the walls and molding in the living room and bedroom, lifting off a century's worth of grime, restoring the plaster to its original state. She removed layers of paint and wallpaper from the kitchen, leaving behind the strata of all the colors and textures that had been applied over the past hundred years, from the first coat of paint to the last, like rings in an old tree, the lines in sedimentary rock, gauging the passage of time, baring decades of humanity.

She worked tirelessly and alone, and came home exhausted and dirty, but she always woke up in time to eat breakfast with Danny.

She said it wasn't her original intention to get so involved, but once she got started the project took over. This was more of an apology than an explanation told to Jack a couple of times a week over the telephone, or when he stopped in to say hello and walk through the plaster dust while Anne showed him all that she'd accomplished, smiling, looking excited while she exclaimed, "I love it here. I really, truly love it here." Sounding proud of herself.

Jack said he loved it, too. "This was a great idea. I'm very happy that you bought this space. I'm very happy for you."

The other artists in the building came by to admire Anne's progress, a few were inspired to do similar excavations. By then, it was autumn. Anne was finished with the renovations. She was working in watercolors and tempera.

But the summer hadn't been all work. Anne found time in late July to take day trips to the beach with Jack and Danny. They spent a week in Maine visiting Yoshi and Nick.

In September, Anne spent long afternoons with Danny. Twice a week Madeline brought him to the studio and he would go out for lunch with Anne, just the two of them. On rainy days, they ate lunch inside. Danny napped on the narrow bed. He sat on the floor and played with his toys, talking and singing to himself, talking and singing to Anne. Some nights, Anne came home in time to give Danny his bath and tuck him in. On Sundays she and Jack took Danny to the children's theater for puppet shows, and for rides on the carousel in Central Park, to his grandparents' apartment. There seemed to be enough time now, time for work and time for Danny.

Anne told Jack, "I'm so pleased with the way this has worked out."

They had a dinner party for their friends that October. Avril Stone, Brenda Susmann, Steve Morgan, Nan and Barry Roth, Greg Moffit and Louise Crenner, two artists from the Stanton Street building.

Avril said she was very impressed with what Anne had accomplished. "You make it look too easy."

Anne was making it look easy, Jack agreed. He told her so a few nights later over dinner at a little bistro on Grove Street. It was unseasonably cool but the dining room was warm with the aroma of roasted meat and wine. Anne leaned across the small table. Her eyes flashed in the thin stream of candlelight, her cheeks were flushed. "We're doing all right, aren't we?" She sounded more than a little surprised.

"We're doing all right. You're making it look easy."

"That's only because I don't let the sweat show." She laughed the Carole Lombard laugh, the way she had before she'd ever heard of Carole Lombard; the way she had when they'd sat in the car and looked at the house with the wraparound porch.

All that month, they both made it look easy. Jack would meet Anne for supper after he was finished teaching. Or they'd stay in her studio, make love on the narrow bed and eat a late meal in Chinatown. Some nights, they would go home together, some nights Jack went home while Anne stayed behind and worked. He would feel her slide into bed just before dawn, curl up against his back and drape her leg over him. She was still getting up to have breakfast with Danny, Danny was still coming to her studio twice a week.

That January, the *Times* did a feature in its Home section about Anne's studio and used photos in a full-page spread. The article talked about how Anne was influenced by "the famous Capp Street Project of San Francisco," and how she "turned found objects into sculpture: a child's rusted tricycle, an old boot stuck in a bucket of cement, relics taken from the trash heap of the urban landscape." The writer called the space "a work of urban archaeology, a postmodern commentary on the constancy of Time and the transitory nature of Art and perception." He compared Anne to Duchamp.

Anne had the article framed and hung it on the wall by her easel.

She was also invited to exhibit three paintings at the Whitney Museum's Biennial, and was hard at work meeting the deadline. That same month, Danny got sick.

It started out as one of those colds kids pass among themselves, but then it took a turn for the worse and Danny caught pneumonia. It laid him out and for a while his high fever had everyone worried. Although Madeline was always there, Anne stopped working to stay home with him. She thought up little games to get him to take his medicine. She baked special treats for him. That's when she made the cutout animals and little puzzles to cheer him up. She'd get him giggling and laughing until she couldn't help but nuzzle her nose against his and say, "You are my darling little boy. You're my angel baby," and a minute or two later Danny would fall asleep. Anne would watch him, sometimes with a look of pity on her face, and sometimes there'd be another look. It was the same expression she showed that night in the cab when she talked about having one foot on the platform and one foot on the train. Then she'd take a deep breath, rub her eyes, and when she saw Jack standing there, grin sadly and shrug her shoulders.

Danny was always a little disappointed when Jack took care of him at night and on weekends while Anne went to her studio for a few hours' work. Danny tolerated Jack's attention but that was all. He wouldn't go to sleep until Anne called to say good night.

It was only after Danny got well that Jack realized he'd been worried that it was Loubressac all over again. Which is what he told Anne.

Anne said, "It was just the opposite of Loubressac, really. I had a difficult time staying away from him."

That February, they registered Danny for preschool.

"I suppose this is some sort of milestone in our lives," Anne said, "but I don't—it's got to be more than waiting for him to grow up, we agreed to that, and I don't want us to just count the years until we rush him off to college, use him to measure out our lives until he's gone."

"We haven't so far."

"But sometimes, I don't know—when he was sick, he needed me so much and I had that same feeling I had before Yaddo. I had all that work to do for the Whitney and here Danny was needing me like that. I began to feel—*smothered* is the only way I can describe it. I had all that work to do and this little boy to take care of and I wanted to do both, no, I *had* to do both, each had its own imperative, and I felt as if I had to choose between the two." She was sitting on the couch in her studio. They were listening to Gershwin—there was always music playing in her studio—two new paintings leaned against the wall, a work-in-progress was secure on the easel. Some of her drawings which she'd done at Yaddo and which she'd decided not to sell were framed and hung. She stood up to walk across the room, her shoes were loud against the bare wood floor. "I couldn't wait to get away. Maybe I just wanted to get away from feeling so conflicted, maybe I wanted to get away from Danny. I don't know." She took a deep breath.

"He's a little boy," Jack said. "We're his parents, for Christ sake. This is what we have to do."

Anne turned quickly and looked at him. "Don't you think I know that? That's what I'm talking about." She did not say this argumentatively. "And don't you think I'm feeling like the most self-absorbed piece of garbage when what I should be thinking about is what Danny's feeling?" She walked over to the couch and sat down. "Sometimes," she said, "I'm afraid that he feels things deep down, deeper maybe than he should. And sometimes I'm just plain afraid."

It was a damp night with rain in the air, although the predominant odors coming through the windows were exhaust fumes and garbage.

Anne said, "There are days when I'll work for hours and hours and not really crack the problem until well after dark, and I stay here all night but I'm always aware of Danny, always aware that he's waiting for me. It's like he's here telling me, 'I need you, Mummy.' Even when he's asleep he's waiting for me, and sometimes I don't know how to cope with it. Sometimes I find it just makes me feel all twisted up inside, and those times are when I resent him for needing me and resent myself for resenting him." She wrapped her hand around Jack's hand. There was green paint on her fingernails. "The other day at his school, when that pretentious Jennie Slackman was explaining how important it was to get Danny comfortable with a 'learning environment,' a '*learn*ing environment'? and all the other mothers were looking so alert, so bloody damned impressed with the place, so bloody boring, chattering on and on about their children, the bores. Chattering and chattering about how important the right preschool is for the right private school and the right goddamned— Preschool. Grade school. And—and I thought, I can't do this. This is not what I want my life to be, chattering with adoring little mums about their adorable little children. I broke out in a sweat. And at the same time, at the same time I want us to share all of that time with Danny and with each other. I want to share it and I dread it at the same time." She lowered her eyes and stared at the floor before she said, "And there are times when I listen to him, the time I spent with him when he was sick, and it was like watching him becoming more of his own person, growing into himself, like a little man, and I thought I'd burst apart with love."

That's when Jack told her about his time alone with Danny, about all the incomprehensible things that had happened in their home. That's when he told her—maybe he'd been waiting for this very moment to tell her—"I feel the same things you do. And I can only wonder what we'd be doing, how we'd be living if we'd—if Danny hadn't been born. You wouldn't need Yaddo or this studio. I wouldn't— Oh hell, Anne, you're not doing this alone and it isn't only *you*."

Anne looked at him but said nothing. She moved her lips but no words came out. Jack held her hand tightly. They slipped into each other's arms and started to cry.

"Remember," she said, "before Danny was born, when you would be writing and the typewriter would be clacking away and I'd be at my easel, and even when it was a struggle it seemed to come, the work, the ideas?"

He said of course he remembered.

"I have to say, I miss that. Sometimes. I miss being just the two of us. And our first summer in France, talking about our work, both of us so hungry for the validation."

"I wish it were like that again, just for a little while."

"We were very close back then."

"We were."

"We're closer now." She said this defiantly and it made Jack squeeze a little closer to her.

"I was more myself, or who I liked thinking I was, when I was with you."

"And I with you. But we don't need that now. You'll always be Dr. Owens and I'll always be Anne Charon, regardless. Self-images have a way of biting a person on the ass, don't they, Jack." She said this coldly, stood up and stopped the music, found her purse and started turning off the lights. "Let's not get caught in the rain," and she walked to the door.

About a month later, Danny started having nightmares and could only fall asleep after Anne came home and she let him crawl into bed between her and Jack. In the morning, he would cling to Anne's legs when she walked and she would sweep him up in her arms and kiss him and coo in his face and tell him, "You're my beautiful boy. My angel baby."

One morning he asked, "Are you and Daddy mad at me?"

"Of course not."

"Can we play today?"

"Not today. Mummy has work to do."

"*Please,* Mummy. I miss you."

"I miss you, too. We'll play on Saturday."

Anne told Jack that she was worried about Danny. "God, how I worry that I'm neglecting him, and that he's all right, that we're *all* all right, and that we're caring for him in the right way, because I know he *isn't* all right." She said, "When I'm in my studio, sometimes I suddenly stop what I'm doing and call him up, or just go numb realizing that he's, I don't know, that he's Danny, he's my son, and I'm worried about him."

Jack said nothing. He only nodded his head.

Anne said, "I love you both so much, but I love the way I feel when I'm working and who I am when I'm doing my work. I want to love being Danny's mother. Damn it, Jack. I can't make sense of anything, and all I feel right now is like a miserable, self-centered bitch and everything is slipping away." She said, "We can't do this to him. We're not doing all right any longer and I'm making such a mess of things and I'm frightened." She pushed her face against Jack's chest. He could feel the dampness of her skin under her blouse. "And I'm neglecting you, too, and I'm frightened that you'll start having affairs and we'll turn into one of those scuzzy couples, sneak—"

"Not a chance."

"We'll keep trying to make it all right again, won't we?"

They decided to take the villa in Tuscany for August. No work. No au pair. Just the three of them on vacation.

"It will get us back to being us again," Anne said. "I have to believe that."

Jack wasn't sure what he believed.

It was their last vacation together. Danny's nightmares stopped, but not his premonitions. "Are you and Daddy mad at me?" he'd ask as they drove through the countryside.

They'd sit on the terrace under the Tuscan stars while Danny slept peacefully between them, only to wake up suddenly and look at Jack, at Anne, as though he were making sure they were still both with him.

Then one night while they sat outside, Danny sleeping between them, Anne said, "Nothing's changed."

Jack answered, "I know."

"And so does he." Anne stroked the top of Danny's head with the palm of her hand. She whispered, "We can't do this to him."

"No," Jack said, "we can't."

"I think we should leave as soon as possible."

"Where are we going?" Danny asked, rubbing his eyes.

"Nowhere. Go back to sleep." Anne sighed deeply and told Jack, "I wish I had two hearts."

When they returned to New York, Anne began spending the night in her studio, not every night, but most nights. She always called Jack to let him know when she wasn't coming home. They still met for dinner, but not more than once or twice a week.

Jack told her, "I've done all I can not to put any pressure on you," late in the evening, when she came back to the loft and slipped into bed next to him, "but this is not how I want us to live. I miss you, Danny misses you. He's having nightmares again. And he can't understand why you're not here." He turned on the light and looked closely at her. "And neither can I."

"That's not pressure." She said, "It breaks my heart knowing that."

But by the end of September, Anne had stopped calling altogether. She stayed away all that weekend and into the following week. Jack would not accept sleeping without her, or lying in the dark and waiting for her, or Danny waking up every morning looking for his mother.

Jack told her, "We can't do this, drifting in and out of our lives, out of our marriage."

Anne put her arms around his shoulders and pressed her head against his chest. "At least I'm close by and I see Danny, some of the time, and I get to be with you. At least we have that. Maybe that can be enough."

Maybe she really did think that it could be enough, or thought that it could never be enough.

It is possible to love something too much, and if there had been no Danny, then it would have been their marriage that eventually came between Anne and her art. Or maybe all there was to Anne was her art? Which is what Jack told her when he went to her studio.

Anne said, "Oh, Jack. I don't want that to be true." She walked over to him and put her hand on his arm.

He pulled away from her and looked over at the paintings braced against the wall, the new canvas already primed and propped on the easel, the half dozen sketches. "Don't you think I'd like to have a place to go to and get lost in my work? Don't you think I wish that I could stay away and not have to be Danny's father, not have the responsibility, not have to see what we're doing to him? But I can't, Anne. He's our little boy, and I love him. And he needs to be taken care of. He needs to go to preschool, and elementary school, and whether or not I like being around those *chattering* little mums, I have to do it, and don't you think I want to say the hell with it and not come home? But I have to stay and take care of Danny. I *have* to be there, damn it. And *you* have to be there." It was only then that Jack was aware that Anne was standing next to him and they were holding on to each other.

In the morning, Danny and Jack were eating breakfast together, staring at Anne's empty chair. Danny asked, "Where's Mummy?"

Jack lied, "Mummy had to leave for work."

"Why does she always leave so early?"

"She's an artist.

In early October, in her studio, Anne told Jack, "I'm selling this place." Jack knew better than to think Anne was moving back to the loft on Crosby Street. He knew better than to think she'd found another space somewhere in town. He saw the look on her face. He knew.

"England?" he said, without hiding his disappointment.

"England," she repeated softly.

"That's a long way to go."

"Only for—for six months. I'm mounting a show over there and I can use a little extra time to get everything together."

Jack was sitting on the couch. Anne sat on the floor resting her head against his leg. He took a deep breath, inhaled the smell of paint and linseed oil, which were Anne's smells. He moved his body so he might smell the aroma of her hair, the light scent of her perfume, so he might breathe in all the small odors that she carried.

He thought how unextraordinary it seemed to be sitting with her, how unexceptional, but next month, next week, the day after tomorrow, next year, he'd be unable to find her, because he knew she was never coming back—and he wasn't sure that he wanted her to come back. Not if it meant going through this again. He couldn't do that to himself. He couldn't do that to Danny.

Anne reached over, took Jack's hand and pushed his fingers gently through her hair. She raised her face to him, he bent forward and kissed her. Her mouth folded into his mouth, her tongue just barely flicked against his tongue. He could not remember the last time they'd kissed like this, certainly not since they came back from Italy.

Anne slipped into his lap. He cradled her against his body. They kissed again, softly. She pushed her hand between his legs. He undid the buttons on her blouse and unsnapped her bra.

It was so very familiar and alien at the same time, the feel of her flesh against his face, the rough texture of her nipple, the scent of her sex. It was as though she were a different Anne, the Anne she would be after she'd gone to England, the Anne of some future time where there wasn't Danny and there wasn't Jack. The Anne she was becoming.

After they made love, they lay side by side silently on the floor in the dark. Five, ten minutes later, they made love again, fast and hard this time, clutching and scratching; frightened by the intensity.

Anne kept Danny out of school for the next week. They spent a day at the Bronx Zoo, they played in Central Park. They lunched on whatever Danny wanted to eat. Anne bought him toys. She stayed with him into the night, until he fell asleep in her arms. She may have thought she'd change her mind. She may have been trying to confirm what she'd already decided. She never said and Jack never had the courage to ask. She never told Jack what she and Danny talked about.

Then one afternoon that October, Anne didn't take Danny to the park, didn't take him out for lunch. She came to the apartment and explained to him that she was going away. Danny thought she meant she was going back to Yaddo. Anne said no, she'd be gone "a long, long time." Danny said he didn't understand, but it was just an act. He sat in Anne's lap and asked her again where she was going, and again Anne explained or started to, but Danny jumped to the floor and screamed. He ran to Jack and screamed. He ran through the loft and screamed. He threw his body around. He grabbed Jack. He grabbed Anne and pleaded with her to change her mind. He screamed, "Take me with you." Anne told him she couldn't do that. Sounds of grief and confusion blew out of Danny's throat like stones. He thrashed at Anne and kicked at her. He said he hated her. He punched Jack and hated him, too. He cried and pulled at both of them, they did not stop him. "I'll be good," Danny cried, and begged Anne not to go. She clutched him and rocked him. He buried his head between her breasts. Jack held Anne and Danny hard against his chest. They held each other, damp with each other's tears and sweat.

The following day, when Anne came to the loft on Crosby Street, she was wearing an orange cape and carrying a brown paper shopping bag, the contents of which Jack would never know. She knelt down to give

Danny a hug. Danny asked if she would play with him tomorrow. Anne pressed his head against her lips and kissed and hugged him.

She whispered, "Mummy will never stop loving you," hugged him for a minute longer, then walked out the door.

Jack and Danny watched from the window as Anne stood on the sidewalk four stories down, waiting for a taxi, looking small, the top of her head a dark circle of brown, the orange cape flaring in the breeze. To the people who walked past her, she was anyone and no one—how quickly that can happen. Leave your home and anonymity shrouds you in an orange cape. Extend your hand, step into a cab and you're gone.

XIX

He wasn't the Jack Owens who married Anne Charon and lived in the loft on Crosby Street. He wasn't the Dr. Owens who moved with Danny to Gilbert. As Danny had become "the boy who killed himself in Fairmont Park," Jack had become "the father of the boy who . . ." The Dr. Owens who sat alone in his office writing his lecture notes without conviction or enthusiasm. The Jack Owens who thought only about the past. Who might at any time raise his eyes and see Danny riding his bike across the quad, see Danny walking into the office on a Friday afternoon, catching his breath and already talking about what he wanted to do over the weekend. Who could hear the telephone ring and Danny say: "Hi, Dad. It's me." Who could hear the past, see the past as though it were the trailer to the feature film, or the reel for the View-Master with the three-dimensional pictures of the Grand Canyon and Neil Armstrong's moon walk and *Pinocchio,* or the wheel of fortune at the carnival with the yellow and red lights, the games of chance, which aren't games of chance at all but are rigged against you—spin the wheel and the metal arrow stops on a snapshot of your life . . . You pays your money and you takes your choice . . . Only there wasn't a choice. It was always the unalterable past, the past that was firm and fixed and predictable, which Jack could curl up with, pull over his head and slip inside.

He thought he was nothing but the past. He could feel its texture, its immediacy. He could feel its presence. Prime his ears and hear Danny's voice on the telephone. Raise his eyes and see Danny outside the window. He could see himself lying on his back in a field of grass lifting Danny in the air and holding him like a little toy. Or maybe the little boy isn't Danny. It's he who's being held. His mother is calling out, "Be careful, Mike, he's only a baby." Or he's with his mother and she's teaching him to ice-skate. She has him by the hand, she's leading him slowly, carefully across the ice, which isn't smooth like it looks in pictures, but rough with small crests and fissures, the ice creaks and whistles beneath the surface like a haunted house. His mother assures him there's nothing to be afraid of. Later, they sit on wooden chairs and drink hot chocolate and make marshmallow mustaches. His mother smooths the top of his head where his hair is electric from his blue wool cap. She kisses his face. His father holds him on his lap.

Jack wanted to curl up with that for a while. He wanted to be somebody's little boy and be held and assured, which could only happen in the past, which he could see by raising his eyes.

It was nearly one-thirty when Marty came by to pick up Jack for lunch. They decided to drive out to a diner on the south side of town, away from faculty and policemen.

Marty was looking tired and not at all happy. "Did you ever wish you didn't know half the things you knew?"

"Hopewell again?"

"And again and again. What a son of a bitch. He's going full bore at that guy I told you about last week. They've already worked out the language of his confession, Hopewell, the county prosecutor and the poor bastard. Hopewell's pissed off because the prosecutor is getting into the act and trying to push him into the background, not that he won't manage to take center stage eventually." Marty looked over at Jack and frowned. "Hell. This isn't the kind of stuff you want to be hearing about, with all you're going through."

"It's just you talking about your job. And what are friends for?"

Marty seemed to consider this as he drove a little further. Then he said, "I've done a background check on Lamar. Something I wish I'd done when they first found him. What a piece of work this kid was. Very unpopular. He was annoying, antagonizing, got on everyone's nerves. Kind of goofy-looking. No friends. The kind of kid who sits in the back of the room and doesn't get a hell of a lot out of what's going on. I'm thinking he may have had a learning disability that his teachers and parents either missed or chose to ignore, and a slight personality disorder that also seems to have flown under the school's radar. It's very sad. His older sister was the star of the family, so Lamar wasn't getting a whole lot of attention at home. He spent a lot of time alone over by Baxter Park, riding his bike, tossing a ball against the handball courts." Marty turned onto County Road 8. "He was a bully, on top of everything else. The morning of the day he was killed he'd picked on a second grader and got called to the principal's office, which put him in a foul mood, and apparently he decided not to go back to school after lunch. Most likely he was riding out to Baxter Park and decided to cut through Otter Creek. What*ever* happened to him out there—" He took a quick look at Jack. "Are you all right with this?" Jack said he was and Marty said, "We know Lamar was in contact with Hopewell's suspect, there's a bunch of e-mail between them. What they talked about is open to interpretation as far as sex is concerned, really vague stuff on this guy's part. And you can see that Lamar really craved the attention." He shook his head a couple of times. "I'm not a great crime detective, but it doesn't take a genius to see this guy wasn't luring Lamar *anywhere*. The main reason being, Lamar was too young by a couple of years. This guy liked teenagers. He had very specific taste, and Lamar was a *very* young ten. And if he *did* meet Lamar out there, I'm sure he left while Lamar was still alive. Someone else killed him. I wouldn't be surprised if Lamar knew his killer." Marty smiled slowly. "Before you get *too* impressed with me, I got a lot of this from reading Hopewell's paper. What Hopewell won't say—but if I know it, *he* knows it—is that Lamar's murder was made to *look* like a suicide." Marty turned off the county road and onto South Twenty-ninth Street. "What's frustrating and depressing is, Hopewell and the county prosecutor won't back off long enough to catch the real killer, now that Hopewell's squeezed the confession out of this guy."

"So Hopewell's sending an innocent man to jail."

"Not innocent. He didn't commit *this* crime, that's all. He was using the Internet to meet young boys and *possibly* engage in sex with some of them, which is the leverage Hopewell used for the confession and which won't be too far removed from what the prosecutor will use to build his case. When this thing goes to trial, they'll either settle for a guilty plea on second degree murder or try him on first degree murder. And with that confession, and a few other things I'm not allowed to discuss, the guy's finished."

"Can't you do something?"

"Not unless the actual killer turns up between now and when this thing comes to trial, and I don't think that's going to happen. Don't forget, the guy's a pederast, I just don't think he's a murderer. But there's nothing I can do." He told Jack, "Everyone's got their ducks lined up and they'll go down one by one." His voice sounded neither unhappy nor angry, just empty. It was a sad thing to hear and Jack felt sorry for him.

"I'm not naïve enough to think this sort of thing doesn't happen," Marty said, "but I never expected to see it happen in Gilbert. It's not even that. This is redneck bullshit. That's all it is, bullshit." A minute later he said, "It's a very isolating feeling." A minute after that: "Sometimes all it is is a job and you do it because it's what's expected of you."

"I wish there were something I could do to help *you,* for a change."

"You *are* helping. Just talking about it helps."

"Not a hell of a lot."

"Not a hell of a lot is a lot more than nothing."

They drove on, not saying anything else about Hopewell or Lamar. Not saying anything else at all; just another lunch hour spent in each other's company, and how extraordinary it would have seemed this time last year, when he would have been at Paul's with Lois and Stan and his other friends, eating and gossiping, as they always did when everyone was back from summer vacation—more had changed than Jack's being the-father-of-the-boy-who-killed-himself or being part of the Community of Parents of Dead Children. More had changed than his awareness of things that made some detectives sad and others merely ambitious. Or maybe it was just that something else had changed along with that, because, Jack realized, he had more in common with Marty than he did with any of the faculty he saw at lunch yesterday, or with Lois and Stan and the rest of his friends, and he would have found this disturbing if it were Hopewell or any other detective. But it was Marty, and that made it acceptable. That made it all right.

When he got back to his office, Jack did little more than watch the sky grow dark a minute earlier than it had the day before and autumn move a day closer. He made a pass or two at the work on his desk, which wasn't work at all but an excuse not to leave the office, not to go home to the empty house. He could always go over to the screening room, there were always more films to watch and he could set it up for himself. But he didn't want to go to the screening room, he didn't want to be alone in or out of the dark. Instead, he'd take himself over to Chase's—it was still too early in the year for the faculty to show up, and it was a good place to sit and have a cocktail.

Chase's was a dimly lighted, tweedy place, with ambience and prices forbidding to students, which made it all the more inviting to faculty, and that was Ned Chase's intention. There were two small dining rooms, separated by the bar, with big oak tables, starched cloth napkins and tablecloths, a bartender who stocked excellent scotches and whiskies, shook painfully cold martinis and did not get too carried away with the wine list. But for all its attempts not to be, the place was nothing more than an old-fashioned joint. Jack named it the "faculty dive" and for the past ten years he was Chair-without-Portfolio of the "First Friday Club": a dozen of his friends met here for cocktails and dinner on the first Friday of every month. Tonight, Jack sat by himself at a small table near the rear window, drank his whiskey and barely picked at the complementary plate of fried crayfish.

There was always some CD playing, always standards. Tonight it was the King Cole Trio, *Jumpin' at Capitol*. It seemed any minute

Hoagy Carmichael would appear at the piano, if there'd been a piano. Hoagy didn't show up, but Celeste and Arthur Harrison did.

Celeste had a deep suntan, her black hair was scooped below her ears. She wore a bright summer dress, black high-heeled sandals; the style of her hair and clothes gave her the look of an actress from the thirties, Gail Patrick or Bebe Daniels. Her lipstick was dark red and there was a perfect print where she'd kissed Arthur's right cheek. They must have been there before Jack came in, Arthur's sport coat was off and their drinks were just about finished. Celeste turned to signal the waiter, which is when she saw Jack. She waved to him and then she and Arthur came over to the table. "We've been leaving you voice mail right and left all summer," Celeste said. "I must have stopped by the office six or seven times since we got back. And your house."

Arthur laid a thick hand on Jack's shoulder.

"You were on our minds all the time," Celeste went on. "We were worried about you." She invited Jack to sit with them, please. Jack was not quick to accept the invitation. "We won't bug you with questions," Celeste promised. "We have a pretty good idea how you're doing. And if we get on your nerves, just tell us to shut up."

Jack pushed his chair out and stood up. Arthur took the plate and glass and walked them across the room. "We missed the hell out of you."

They sat for a moment, saying nothing, sipping their cocktails. Then they talked the general talk that drinks in late August require. The new semester, department politics, summer vacations.

"You were in New Hampshire," Jack said.

"Vermont," Arthur told him. "I was revising the third edition of my book while my lovely wife loafed about the lake and garden like Our Lady of the Flowers."

Celeste arched a perfectly plucked eyebrow. "Correcting endless pages of *his* text."

Arthur nibbled on the crayfish. "Don't you think it's time you revised your books?" he said to Jack. "It's quite the little racket, if you don't overplay it." He grinned. "A few additions here, update chapter twelve, delete a few pages there, throw together a new introduction, assign it for the new semester, and you have the goose whose golden eggs your students are required to purchase."

"I don't think Jack wants to hear this right now," Celeste said.

Arthur looked embarrassed. "I was only—"

Jack came to Arthur's aid. "Don't pick on him." He took a sip of whiskey. "First of all, I can't stand reading my own stuff, so revisions are out, and if I assigned my own books it would only remind the class that they don't need me. I'd finesse myself right into obsolescence."

"Let's order another round," Celeste suggested. "Okay?"

Somewhere during the second round, Celeste told Jack she was teaching an advanced film studies course.

"I thought Pruitt was teaching it this semester."

"He's on sabbatical."

"That's right." But Jack had no memory of either Pruitt's sabbatical or Celeste being assigned the course. "That's right."

"I've never taught it before and I'm on very unfamiliar turf." Celeste said she was assigning Jack's second book, *Notes After Midnight*. He thanked her in advance for the royalty and bowed toward Arthur.

Celeste said, "You can really show your thanks by doing me a big favor."

"Anything."

"Lend me your lecture notes? If it's not too much trouble."

"No trouble at all. I'll dig them out of the basement first thing."

This got Arthur talking about book revisions again and the money to be made from them, until Celeste told him, "*Enough* already," and asked Jack, "How are you holding up? Are you okay?" His answer was perfunctory and Celeste probably knew it, but before she said anything more, Jack wanted to know how Rick was doing, and had they heard what happened to C.J. and had Rick spoken to him?

Arthur and Celeste exchanged looks. "We heard, but Rick hasn't been up to calling C.J. He's had a very rough time of it," Arthur said. "Danny's— He was very upset about Danny."

Celeste said, "He can't sleep. He's lost a lot of weight. He's withdrawn into him—"

"And now," Arthur broke in, "he refuses to go back to school. He says he can't stand being here. He came home for two days and made us take him right back to my brother's farm."

Celeste took a slow sip of her martini. "Arthur managed to pull a few strings and Rick's going to spend his sophomore year in St. Louis, at Andrews Academy. We're also going to find a good therapist for him."

Jack said, "I imagine Brian's had a tough time, too."

"He's had a few bad moments."

Arthur grunted, "A few bad moments? They ran him out of Outward Bound."

Celeste frowned at Arthur. "According to Sally Richards, the Outward Bound leader thought Brian was behaving a little too aggressively."

"Too aggressive for Outward Bound." Arthur looked at Jack. "Isn't that redundant?" It wasn't clear if he was trying to be funny.

"It sounded pretty bad to me," Celeste said. "Brian was belligerent and threatening. Disruptive. It was very troubling to everyone up there."

"Brian's got that in him," Arthur said, and Jack remembered that Arthur didn't like the way Rick always followed Brian's lead. "I overheard some of the things he said to Rick when he told him he was going to Andrews. He was less than sympathetic. He can be a narcissistic little bastard when he wants to."

"It all starts with Hal and Vicki," Celeste said. "They've managed to coddle and neglect him at the same time. They treat him like he's precious cargo while putting the worst kind of pressure on him. He can't step into a room without having to be the smartest or the handsomest or the best athlete. Brian has some issues."

"Sometimes I'd like to give him a good kick in the issues," Arthur said.

Celeste glared at her husband. She asked Jack, "Is this more than you want to know?"

Jack said, "They're sensitive kids. Danny's death couldn't have been easy for them to deal with. Apparently he wasn't the only victim of his suicide." He took a sip of his drink. "I hate to think that you and Hal and Vicki blame him—"

"Nothing of the sort. Nothing like that. Not for a *second,*" and Celeste changed the subject.

It was after ten when they said their good-byes outside the restaurant.

Arthur assured Jack, "The important thing is, you got through the summer and you're staying on to teach."

"We're around whenever you need us," Celeste reminded him.

In his dreams, Jack cried, head thrown back, mouth wide open, like the faces in *Guernica*.

He cried for Anne, who said she was being pulled in two directions and followed the direction that took her back to England.

He cried for his mother, who died a slow death.

He cried for Danny.

When the crying woke him and he couldn't go back to sleep, Jack sat with Mutt on the back porch and looked out at the urban glow that interrupted the night sky.

He thought about Danny, who would have been a sophomore in high school, and how they'd always gone shopping for clothes and shoes before the start of a new term and that Danny would have wanted to do all of that with his friends this year.

He thought about Danny's friends who couldn't sleep and eat, who acted out and acted up.

He looked out at the horizon, where September would begin four days hence and the semester a day after that and where autumn progressed toward the equinox. He had dreaded the coming of summer and felt no great sadness seeing it leave. He did not look forward to the fall. He did not look forward to anything. He could only look back. He was nothing but the past, which appeared richer than anything the present possessed or the future might promise. Where Danny was still the living Danny getting ready for school, or learning to talk, or standing covered in paint in the big room in the house in Loubressac. Where Anne lived in the loft on Crosby Street.

It was something Jack could only admit to himself at three o'clock in the morning on a sleepless night and never have confessed to anyone, not to Lois or Marty. Not to his father while he listened for telltale signs in the old voice, while he said, "You're sounding good today, Dad." Even when Jack was talking to his father about the new semester, when he promised not to wait until Christmas to come out and visit, he was merely talking from within the past, where Danny was alive and where Anne loved him. That was all he had, all he was.

XX

The office door was open and there was movement inside. Robbie Stein, Jack's new student assistant, sat at the desk, phone tucked under his chin, sleeves rolled up, dutifully taking down a message with one hand and holding a container of coffee with the other. At his elbow was the list of instructions Eileen had left for him. He was hanging up the phone when he saw Jack and quickly put down the coffee, stood up, grinned meekly and gave quick, nervous tugs at his shirt collar and sleeves.

The expression on Jack's face must have shown more than simple surprise, although that's all it was, but Robbie rushed to explain, "I'm your student assistant this year, Dr. Owens. Remember?" He stepped away from the desk.

"Of course I remember," Jack answered, in no way remonstratively, "but you're a day early."

"No way."

"Page two of Eileen's notes. Right before she says that if she managed to graduate, there's hope for you, too."

Robbie tugged on his collar again. "Well, so much for impressing you with my quick and agile mind."

"You'll have plenty of chances to do that. In the meantime, I can always use your help and you can get a jump start on how to run things around here. How's that?" Jack picked the messages off his desk and stuffed them in his pocket without looking at them.

Robbie smiled and nodded his head. He started to say something, stopped and called out, "Oh dammit," at the same time looking past Jack to the open door. "Lauren Bellmore. Third time this morning."

"I'm on the verge of a nervous breakdown." Lauren shoved Robbie aside and placed herself directly in front of Jack. She was tall, buxom, with curly red hair that looked absolutely Medusan at the moment and a voice pitched several decibels louder than Jack thought physically possible. "Some *idiot* in the registrar's office screwed up and I'm not *reg*istered for your 'sixties' class. I spent two entire *hours* begging and pleading and I'm *still* not—and classes start *Mon*day." As if Jack needed to be reminded. "How can this be happening to me? I *hate* this school."

Not quite kicking and screaming, but less than willingly, Jack was pulled into the first crisis of the new semester, and into the "Kafkaesque-world-of-Gilbert-College's-preregistration-*tor*ture. And *he*"—Lauren glared at Robbie—"can't find your student list. I'm just *so* freaked."

Jack had to smile. It was Danny when his world was nearing collapse because he tore his costume on Halloween morning. Or he needed sheet music that day and Steiner's wouldn't have it for two weeks. Or Mutt had vanished. "He's gone, Daddy. I looked everywhere and he's *gone*." The tears welling up and Danny looking scared and queasy, his legs shaking, his eyes wide. "I let him out real early this morning and I went back to sleep and when I woke up he never came home. I'm scared something bad happened to him."

Even when there seemed to be no solution, a solution was found. Lois had one of her theater students fashion a costume for Danny. Jack asked Nelson Fried to give him the sheet music. Mutt wasn't lost after all, he had simply done what dogs do when front doors are locked and no one lets you in: he crawled through a basement window and, being home, fell asleep in the warm corner next to one of Jack's filing cabinets. Ever since, Danny would go down to the basement on damp and dreary afternoons, curl up in that same corner, with or without Mutt, read a book or play or daydream.

Lauren wasn't Danny and Jack wasn't her father, but this certainly had the feel of a parental moment and it wasn't at all awful playing the surrogate, even if it called for nothing more than applying an administrative Band-Aid, which was the yellow Additional Student card in the top desk drawer, which Jack signed and which he told Lauren to fill out and take to the registrar's office.

"That's *it*?"

"That's it."

"You're the best, Dr. Owens." She took a step toward the door, said, "Oh. I'm really sorry about . . ." Her eyes turned briefly toward Danny's picture and then back to Jack. Jack nodded his head once but said nothing. Lauren rushed out, leaving the door open behind her.

Robbie hissed, "I don't be*lieve* her."

"That's pretty tame stuff, wait until class starts."

"Not *that*. How she said that to you. I mean it was really cold."

"That's the way I prefer it these days," and speaking to the look on Robbie's face, Jack said, "and if you don't learn to relax around me, it's going to be a long year for both of us. Okay?"

"Okay, but Dr. Owens, I'm *really* sorry about, well, about everything, and especially for screwing up."

"I'm not sure I know how you screwed up." Jack sat down and leaned back in the chair.

"Not finding the list."

"First of all, the list isn't here, so you couldn't have found it. Second, whenever you get ambushed like that, and it's going to happen again, remember you're not responsible for fixing their world. Just tell them to come back during my office hours and I'll see what I can do. And third, my student assistant calls me Jack. Any questions?"

"I don't think so."

"Feeling better?"

Robbie nodded his head. "A lot better."

Jack was feeling better, too. He could still fill out the forms, he could still solve student problems. He still knew all the words; and even if it wasn't the smoothest beginning and breaking in a new student assistant was a more formidable proposition than it seemed back in May, he had managed to reassure Robbie that it was still Dr. Owens at work here and he was glad to see Robbie's face relax and, while he sat on the sofa, papers spread across the table, talk to Jack about the courses he was taking, his roommates and his new girlfriend. Jack said nothing, he only listened, pleased that he'd reassured Robbie, pleased that he'd done a little reassuring of himself.

He realized that among the things he'd missed these past months, being around students was one of them. It may not have ranked near the top, but he'd missed the company of a student assistant, the sudden and harmless student crises. He'd missed the small preparations for the new semester, and even if he was working from memory, wondering if this was how he used to do it, was this the way he used to sound, it was the familiarity that did not breed contempt, the familiarity that he'd needed these past ten years, that he needed this morning while he sat at his desk rereading his notes, his critiques, working from memory, wondering if this was how he'd always done it.

Carol Brink from the dean's office called to ask if he was going to address the incoming freshman class next week as planned. The slight hesitation, the soft, cautious voice. "Of course, if you aren't feeling . . ."

"I'll be there," Jack promised, hoping he hadn't betrayed himself, wondering if that was how he used to sound.

Drinking his coffee, doing his job, the reflection of the reflection, the memory of the memory, listening to the noon bells chime, talking on the phone to Stan Miller—"Do you have a minute, Jack, to come to my office so I can officially welcome you back?"—Jack could only think that he was nothing but the past.

One of Bach's violin partitas played softly on the old stereo and there was the slight aroma of Chinese tea in the air when Jack walked into the office. Stan stood up and came around to the front of his desk. "Just a little department bookkeeping," he said, nodding at the papers on the windowsill. His shirt was open at the collar, his blue seersucker suit was wrinkled and hung off his body as though on wire hangers. He straightened his jacket and tucked his shirttail into his pants, at the same time saying, "We could have taken care of all this on the phone, but I wanted to have a look at you and see how you're making out." Which is what he'd told Jack last year and the year before that and five years before that, when he was appointed department chair.

"I don't know. I don't know how I'm making out, really." Which was not what Jack had answered last year and the years before.

Stan did not appear surprised to hear this. "I appreciate what you're doing, staying on like this. I'm very proud of you." He spoke slowly and unhurriedly, with understated courtesy. "That's a very impressive class you're teaching," while he walked over to the credenza and the brass tray with the tea service. "I'm tempted to duck in to see a few of the films myself." He filled two cups, put milk in both and handed one to Jack.

"You're welcome anytime."

Stan laughed softly. "I doubt most people in the department share that sentiment." He tipped his chin toward the large unmatched chairs across the room—the sort of chairs they had in gentlemen's clubs in Edwardian England and which Stan had found at the Goodwill shop on Woodbine Street. "I'm afraid we've got to go through what amounts to nothing more than administrative junk mail," he said pleasantly, and sat in the chair next to Jack. "Susan Drake, in the registrar's office, asked if you'd stop by and go over your grades from last semester. She assures me it's just a matter of dotting some i's. Today, if at all possible, or tomorrow."

Jack said that wouldn't be a problem. "However, the registrar doesn't usually go through the department chair for something like that."

"I'm afraid some people around here are going to be taking your pulse for a while. And using me to do it."

"That can be annoying."

Stan agreed. "I'll see what I can do to minimize it."

"I mean for *you*. There's no reason for you to get in the middle of it. You don't have to run interference for me."

"There are plenty of reasons why I *should* be in the middle of it, and I wouldn't exactly call it running interference." Stan took a sip of tea, then another, and put the cup back in the saucer. "We've been friends for a long time and we've never stood on ceremony when things were going smoothly and I'm not going to stand on ceremony now.

When I have the opportunity to make your work, or your life, a little easier I intend to do it." His voice was hardly louder than a whisper. "And I'd be insulted if you expected me to turn away from helping you. If someone from the administration needs something from you and thinks she has to go through me to get it, then that's the way I'm going to handle it."

Jack said he hadn't intended to insult Stan. "I don't know what I'm talking about. Handle it any way you see fit." He said this apologetically and without contrition. "You of all people know the appropriate thing to do."

Stan leaned forward in his chair and looked at Jack straight on. "I'm not so sure of that, but I do know that I don't want the administration to sic its bureaucrats on you every time there's a blip on their computer screen." He still hadn't raised his voice. "Listen, Jack, you're coming back to work for all the right reasons. I also think it happens to be the right decision, and it takes a lot of strength. You don't need a bunch of kibitzers yapping at you and getting in your way."

Before Jack got out his "Thank you," the telephone rang. Stan's assistant cracked the door open and said Dr. Skowron was calling. Stan asked her to take a message. She bowed slightly, modestly, from the waist and closed the door.

Stan got up and took the papers off the windowsill, picked through the stack until he found what he was looking for and told Jack the Tuesday morning meeting had been pushed up to Monday afternoon, looked at the papers again and said, "I have to start thinking about next year's spring film festival. I don't mean to rush things, but I need to know if you're still going to be in charge. And your Midnight Movies. I need to sign off on your list. It's more budgetary than anything else. However, if you'd rather take it off the curriculum—"

"I'll get the list to you by the end of the day."

"Are you sure you want to schedule them?"

"To tell the truth, no. But I don't think I can cancel them, either."

Stan offered a cautious "Okay . . ."

"I'll manage it."

"I've also got you on the honors committee this year."

"I think I can manage that one, too."

"You know what? I'm going to have Celeste Harrison take over the spring film festival. With your input, of course."

Jack thought that over for a moment and said he didn't have a problem with it.

"And there's the 'Gilbert College 2000' committee, which I see no reason for you to be weighted down with." There was another phone call, which Stan did not take, and then he told Jack, "I'm afraid I'm going to sound a bit insensitive with this next bit of business. There's the President's Dinner, Friday night, to welcome everyone back. You can take a pass on it if you want. And Christine wanted me to invite you over for supper next Wednesday. If you're in the mood."

"You're not being insensitive. I'll be at the President's Dinner. And I'd like to have supper with you and Christine."

"Good. She's been quite concerned about you."

"Tell her I appreciate that." Jack pulled his phone messages out of his pocket. "Now I need your help with something. Apparently, in a moment of weakness last spring, I signed up to speak at Vigo County High School's 'College Day' in November, about the importance of a liberal arts education. Neil Weston at IU expects me to be a judge, again, for their October film competition. Carrie Mannheim's invited me to be a guest speaker at Colby, she's teaching my books this semester. And Mel Keller, at NYU, wants me to sit on a panel in March. They don't know anything about what happened, of course. But I did make a commitment to them."

"I can certainly help get a replacement for you for the 'College Day,' but as for the rest, I'm afraid I can only give you my advice."

"Which is?"

"Don't do any of it. Cancel them all, for 'personal reasons,' don't go into much detail if you can help it, no more than necessary, then put it out of your mind."

There was another volley of phone calls, which Stan shook off; and more of Stan's "administrative junk mail," mostly committees Jack had agreed to sit on, one he'd agreed to chair, a speech he was supposed to give at a luncheon at the end of the month.

Outside the window, students and faculty hurried to their appointments and meetings, their voices rising into the office. Stan leaned in their direction like a maestro pitching his ear while the orchestra tuned up, confident about the concert ahead. He seemed reluctant to turn away and waited a moment or two longer, then turned around slowly and said, "We can't pretend that this is just another semester. Nothing is the same for you and that means nothing is the same for me or any of your colleagues and friends, either. But I want you to know that one thing hasn't changed and won't ever change: you're still among friends. You *belong* here."

Jack said he took comfort in knowing that.

"It's really about continuity, isn't it, Jack." Stan stirred his tea meditatively.

"Continuity?"

"Like in film, about keeping the scene intact, only I'm talking about something else that keeps us intact. I'm not talking about just you and me, although the small traditions the two of us adhere to, our meeting every year before the start of the fall semester, having tea together, simply talking face-to-face, I'd say helps us maintain our centrifugal force, keeps us from spinning out of our orbits." He lifted the cup to his mouth and took a few short sips. "It's something very human. Something everyone needs, don't you think? Isn't that why Susan Drake wants you to stop by and why, if she hasn't already called, the dean's going to want to know if you're still giving your talk to the incoming freshmen, and why she wants you to? I'm not going to make speeches at you about how we're all part of one big family here, because it's not true and it wouldn't be fair to say so. In fact, it would be cynical. But there are ripple effects when one of us is going through a bad time. Carol Brink, Susan Drake, all of us, in our way, need to know that the semester is moving along the way it always has, the way it's supposed to, and that you're still a part of it, that you're *involved* in it, and that you're going to be all right, most of all that. And you need it, too, Jack. I've always felt that your coming here with Danny was about continuity." He said this flatly, without the look of expectation he might have had if all he wanted was for Jack to agree with him, if he needed that, if that were the reason why he was talking, just so he could feel good about himself. But that wasn't why Stan was saying this, it wasn't why Stan ever said anything; and there wasn't the cautious tone of condolence or commiseration, either. Stan had not called Jack in to commiserate, to add to his mourning, which is what he said next, and then, "I don't know what you want from your friends right now, but I imagine it isn't that," while they drank their tea, and the Bach partitas played in the background and all the department bookkeeping was finished and there was only their friendship to commemorate the moment, their time this September when it was anything but business as usual and the semester itself was still more in the future than in the present and the present extended no further than this moment, long enough for the two men to acknowledge, observe, this formality, just as they had in the past.

When it was appropriate—in spite of his statement to the contrary, Stan did know the appropriate thing to do and when to do it, after they'd finished their tea and talked a little while longer, when it wouldn't appear as though he were rushing Jack to the end of the meeting—Stan said, "I think we have enough time to enjoy each other's company for a few more minutes." But the telephone rang and this time Stan had to take the call. Jack let himself out.

The hallway smelled like school. Of books and academic commerce. Of students' stress and teachers' woes. Of paper and ink and the warm smell of electricity that desktop computers make. Of Stan's Chinese tea and the acrid smell of cigarettes smoked behind closed doors. Of stale coffee from a hundred semesters past and the morning application of perfume. Sweet smells, old smells, woven into the faded paint, the grain in the wooden doorframes, the glass transoms—transoms smeared with dust and a million human exhalations. It was the way college hallways smell everywhere, blindfolded you'd still know where you were. It was something dreaded and longed for, accepted and overlooked. Where it smelled like the first day of school and of thousands of school days before it, and where this early afternoon Carl Ainsley stood talking with a pretty blond girl, his country club insouciance on full display, the beige chinos, the pink V-neck sweater deepening his already deep tan, accentuating the smooth skin, taut across his cheekbones; the languid pose, leaning against the wall, one soft loafer crossed over the other at the ankle.

Ainsley had a rested, loose-nerved, sun-polished affect, as though he'd spent the summer at a spa, not in a cottage on a lake in Kentucky with his son lying banged up and broken in the local hospital. It was an accomplishment, frightening for its ease, its indulgence and control.

The girl was laughing at something Ainsley had said and he looked pleased with himself, but the laughter was cut short as Jack approached, and the girl walked quickly away. Ainsley watched her, ignoring Jack when he stopped and said, "I think I owe you an apology for what I did to you back in May."

"You know, I forgot that you ever did that, Owens."

"Then I will, too. I heard about C.J. How's he doing?"

"I wouldn't know." Ainsley kept his eyes on the girl. "From what Mandy tells me he's recovering much too slowly and he's severely depressed."

"I'm sorry to hear that. Wish him a speedy recovery for me."

Only after the girl walked down the stairs did Ainsley raise his eyes to Jack. "He'll recover. After he's tortured everyone sufficiently. I'm not so sure *we* will, however. He certainly has managed to suck the joy out of life."

"He's a good kid. He made a mistake, that's all."

"He's a fuckup," Ainsley told him with more conviction than Jack expected. "But he's *my* fuckup and I've learned to put up with him."

Jack could not resist the envy he felt. That Ainsley could be so detached—or, Jack wondered, was it the lack of panic, trusting that everything would work out because everything had always worked out?—so constricted and restrained.

"Tell him I said hello. Or tell Mandy to tell him I said hello and that I hope he's feeling better soon." Jack was about to walk away, but he felt compelled to say something else, compelled to see past the pose and the posturing and tell Ainsley, "I know you must be feeling something, fear or anxiety or *something*." But he didn't say that. It was Ainsley who spoke.

"I don't know what that kid's got against me, Owens." He let out a sigh that sounded about as sad as he ever allowed himself to sound. "All I do is worry about him. How he'll look after they take out the stitches, how—you know, he'd be quite handsome if he just took care of himself. At night, I sit on the edge of his bed and try to talk to him, but he won't even look at me. When he's asleep, I touch his shoulder and try not to wake him just to be with him for a few minutes longer. That's about the extent of our relationship, can you believe it?" He stepped away from the wall and straightened up. "The twins, of course, act as if anyone over the age of *twelve* is diseased, which means Mandy and me. And Mandy's leaning so heavily on tranquilizers lately, Lilly's *and* Upjohn's stocks rise ten points every time she reaches for a glass of water. On top of it all, I can't find a suitable tutor so Carl won't fall behind in school, *and* they've stuck me with first-year advising." He rubbed the back of his neck. "I swear, Owens, can you imagine the kind of advice *I* could give to a freshman? What a life."

Maybe Jack was drawn to someone else's sorrow, or maybe it was simply what one person says to another person when their kid is all banged up and hurt, even when the person is Carl Ainsley, torturing his face, working the muscles so he actually showed an emotion, scaring up a look of concern. Or maybe it was something less honorable than that, that seeing Carl Ainsley in pain was reassuring, of what, Jack dared not admit to himself at the moment. Whatever it was, he put a hand on Ainsley's shoulder and said, "I know it doesn't look too great right now, but C.J.'s going to be all right. You'll both be all right."

Ainsley grinned, but there was no warmth in it. He took a step back as though he were leveraging his body to throw a punch or take one, but he did neither. "Of course we'll be all right." He walked into his office and the door snapped closed.

XXI

Marty was waiting downstairs, leaning against the side of the building and staring at the ground. "Let's not go to the diner again. I don't think I can stomach any more of their grease." By the way he said this, Jack knew it was more than greasy food that Marty couldn't stomach. His jaw was clenched and he kept it clenched while he said, "Hopewell's made the arrest. The guy's name is Joseph Rich. The local news is all over it. They're calling him 'the Cyberkiller.' And you know, once enough people say he's guilty, he's guilty."

"So I guess Hopewell won't be *too* disappointed to know *Danny's* never received any e-mail from the guy. Or any other son of a bitch."

There was a luncheonette, a salad and sandwich place, really, over on the north side of town, that Jack used to go to, maybe it was still there. He drove while Marty leaned back in the front seat and closed his eyes. Jack didn't want to bother him with any more conversation, so he just kept on driving, past the railroad tracks and the old junkyards with the rusting cars and towers of hubcaps and retreads, and beyond that to where there was nothing but farms and cows and hogs and fields of wheat ready for harvesting, and then not much of that.

Jack found the place, tucked away on the county road. He and Marty sat by the large picture window looking out at a narrow creek and an old covered bridge.

Marty said, "I hope your day at the office is going more pleasantly than mine."

"We'll talk about it later. You've got enough on your mind."

"Are you going to start that again?"

"I think you deserve to take the afternoon off, that's all."

Marty laughed.

"I mean it. I wouldn't have been able to come back without your help, and your reward is not having to hear about another day in the life of Jack Owens."

"I guess we both have a lot on our minds, at that."

"I guess we do."

After lunch, they walked out by the covered bridge where the weeds grew through the cracks and shafts of mottled sunlight cut through the seams in the roof.

Jack said, "I used to come here with Anne." They walked a little further and he told Marty, "All I have is my past."

"That's all right. It gives you something to feel attached to, like Danny's box of mementos." He sounded like Stan saying, "It's really about continuity, isn't it."

Jack told him about his conversation with Stan, and how foolish he felt after talking to Ainsley, and about his morning with Robbie. "I'll probably spend the rest of the semester trying to reassure *him* and everyone else that I'm safe."

"Safe?"

"That they don't have to whisper to me, like a patient on life support."

They came out into the sunlight and walked along the side of the road raising dust and kicking at small stones with the tips of their shoes.

Jack said, "What I'm afraid of is that every time people look at me all they see is what can go wrong."

"My guess is, they look at you and admire you."

"Who I *was,* Marty. And to tell you the truth, I'm having a hard time being that person."

"I doubt it was *ever* easy. But I don't think you should look too closely at yourself or anything else for a while."

A dog barked off in the distance, the air was warm and smelled like the last days of summer.

Marty told Jack, "There are times when it's better to let some things go unexamined and cut yourself some slack. Leave Dr. Owens alone for the time being."

When they turned around and started walking back to the car, Jack said, "How'd you like to play hooky this afternoon and go to the movies?"

"What are you talking about?"

"I've got two films to screen and I'd like your company."

"What movies?"

Marty sounded just like Danny when he asked that, and Jack smiled.

"First, Godard's *One Plus One, Sympathy for the Devil.*"

"Subtitles?"

"Danny didn't like subtitles, either. But it stars the Rolling Stones, the *real* Rolling Stones, when they still had edge. And *A Hard Day's Night*, if we have the energy for a second feature."

"Can I get a rain check? I've got a few things left to do and I doubt my captain will understand. What about tomorrow?"

"In the Heat of the Night."

"Rod Steiger and Sidney Poitier, right?

"That's right."

"I'll try to sneak out for that one."

Marty didn't do much talking when they drove back, as though the closer he got to town, the closer he was to having to do all those things he had no stomach for today. It wasn't until Jack dropped him at the station that Marty spoke. "I'm looking forward to going to the movies tomorrow." He smiled quickly and walked inside.

It pleased Jack to know that Marty was going to see *In the Heat of the Night* tomorrow—Steiger's sad and sorry Bill Gillespie stuck inside Sparta, Mississippi, Poitier's urbane and cool Virgil Tibbs. Jack wanted to talk to Marty about buddy pictures and strangers who step off trains to save troubled southern towns from themselves—or strangers who appear at front doors to save grieving fathers . . .

When Jack got back to campus, he didn't go to his office, but walked in the opposite direction, to the Fine Arts building.

He could give himself no reason for going there, maybe it was what Marty meant about feeling attached to something. But no matter, it was the place where he wanted to be right now. To walk up the smooth granite steps, down the hall with the high ceilings and frosted globe lights, to room 415, where the sunlight seemed fixed on the walls, and motes of plaster dust floated in the air, rousted by the opening of the door; where the tables and stools were arranged in an expansive arc set before the models' platform. The room hadn't always been used for sculpture; it was the room where Anne had studied figure drawing and still life. He stood in the doorway for a moment, then walked around the corner to the twelve-by-twelve room that had been Anne's studio, where her style started to emerge in a mixture of paints and pigments, hard edges and soft tones. Where she had tacked on the wall color prints of Byzantine stained glass, the Pollaiuolos' *Saint Sebastian*, a poster of Duchamp's *Large Glass*. There had been an old chair, not much larger than a child's, with torn arms, but so very soft and comfortable, and a work bench, paint-smeared and battered, catty-cornered against the wall, and an old wooden easel that she'd brought with her from England. The windows were nearly half the width of the room and as high as the ceiling, and outside, northern light would rise beyond the curve of the railroad tracks at the edge of town, extend through the live oaks, the chestnut trees and sycamores, pass the green and gray rooftops, patched and kilted like a Cézanne landscape, cross the streets and sidewalks, touch the roofs of the college library and gymnasium, and come to rest on the floor, where it would remain, curled like a house cat, until the sunset consumed it.

Jack would come up from the dark of his basement editing room and see the sunlight slip inside this room while he watched Anne paint, her lean fingers moving the brush assuredly, without intimidation; a dab of yellow and light grew in the crease of a garment, a streak of burnt umber and the vision plane deepened . . .

He stood there now and looked at the bare easel, the floor swept in preparation for the new semester and the next student, a girl perhaps, who might, one afternoon, stand in a circle of young artists and happen to look up and smile the kind of smile that can determine an entire lifetime.

In the ten years since he'd returned to Gilbert, Jack had never stepped into this room, nor so much as walked past it—that was part of the deal. Today he wanted to be here, to breathe in the smells of chalk and paint, the spirits of turpentine and linseed oil. He wanted to walk the perimeter, feel the afternoon sun on his shoulders, and think about Anne, think about the times when he would lean against this very same wall and watch her, the way he'd watched her at the ruins, sketch pad on her knees, as though he were studying a sacred rite, trying to memorize the way she moved, the way she looked.

Jack wanted to remember the afternoons when he brought containers of coffee and sat in the old, soft chair. Anne raised her hand and whispered "Shh" without turning away from her canvas. She was working on an assignment: "If Rembrandt painted like van Gogh." Her eyes moved from the slide of Rembrandt's potentate to van Gogh's *Le Père Tanguy*. She used her palette knife instead of a brush, distending one Dutch master's golden order with another Dutch master's splendorous dementia. Nursing his coffee, Jack watched the methodical application of color and texture—it was a sight he would see again in the loft on Crosby Street, when it wasn't cafeteria coffee that he brought her but cappuccino, and in Loubressac, and on Stanton Street, and this day in her studio in the Fine Arts building. "We're supposed to think this is highly conceptual, but all it is is what Duchamp called 'retinal,'" she said with displeasure.

A few minutes later: "So there he was, Rembrandt, dressing himself in costumes, like Aristotle, like a sultan, like a potentate, propping the mirror just so, placing himself before his easel. And they say van Gogh was the madman." A few minutes after that: "Is it a self-portrait? The Metropolitan Museum doesn't acknowledge that it is: 'Portrait of a man . . . ' is all they'll tell you." A few minutes more and: "You know, what you're seeing really doesn't look at all like this. It's all just dots and streaks of light, tracers of light moving through space in streams and waves. It all happens inside the brain. The brain resolves the light, the spectrum of colors into visual information. It makes sense of what's actually just visual chaos. It's sort of like film, the stream of light traveling out of the projector's lens, flickering at twenty-four frames a second, reflecting off the screen, resolving into images inside the brain. The brain makes sense of it all and turns it into a movie." Anne lifted her arms over her head and flexed her fingers and yawned loudly. She walked around the room yawning and stretching, stopping at the window, backlit with sunrays sprouting from her ears and hair. "I don't like going to school," and she crossed her arms over her chest. "Take me away from all this. Take me to Chicago, or Brown County and we'll get stoned in the woods." She took a deep breath. "Anywhere that isn't school."

Jack started to laugh.

"No, really."

"I know, I know."

Jack remembered Anne when she leaned back from her canvas and listened to the thrill of the train whistle far down the track before the train reached town and the warning bells rang. He stood in the corner where the afternoon light seemed to soak into the floor and remembered the way Anne fought with her sleeves to keep them rolled up, the way she pushed her hair away from her face. The way she told him, "Picasso was once asked what artists talk about and he answered, 'Turpentine.'" The way she asked, "Are you going to read to me, please?"

Jack read to her from the paper he'd written for a criticism class—he did a lot of writing about Bresson, Godard, and De Sica—looking up for her reaction, but she showed him nothing, only motioned with her hand for him to continue. It was only after he finished that she said, "Your language is sounding much more confident. Very grounded." She walked over to him and sat facing him on his lap, her thighs straddling his hips. She leaned forward so he could feel her breasts against his face. She touched his ears with her lips and made a sound deep within her throat, soft and feral. "I find your writing very exciting," her breath gentle against his face.

Jack remembered when it was dark outside and he was late again and came running up the stairs and into the studio, where Anne, in tight jeans, was stretched across the chair, her legs dangling over one of the arms, her bare feet wriggling, the languid pose of a young and lush Jeanne Moreau, peering over the top of a magazine and saying, "Like I might ever want to leave without you." There were times early on when he would walk up the front steps of the Fine Arts building and stand outside on the off chance Anne might appear, and when she didn't, he walked around back and found her window and just stared at it. There were times when he would stay away and take himself to the library and walk alone through the stacks or sit in the student union with his friends, working on a cup of coffee, talking student talk. There were times when he stood in the doorway of her studio and said with uncertainty, "I thought, maybe . . ."

Times when Anne stepped close to him, her skin smelling of chalk dust and the kind of soap grandmothers use, rested her chin on his shoulder, squeezed his hand and said, "Let's go somewhere and eat onion rings and share a Coke with two straws. Just like in the movies," and smiled at him, the way she smiled when he first saw her talking with the boys and he stared in dumb amazement. Jack didn't want to leave the studio, not yet, not until he was satisfied that he'd remembered all that he wanted to remember. The times when Anne could not be disturbed and the times when she softly rubbed his cheek with the back of her hand and whispered, "Let's misbehave," in early autumn and the foliage shimmered off the trees. Jack wanted to remember when Anne said, "Joe Soares really liked *Lady with Watering Can.* He's recommending me for the Benton Award." When he said, "Dr. Garraty sent my piece on Resnais to *American Film.*" When gray winter lay flat across the sky like a lost glove and they looked at each other and if they hadn't already realized who they were becoming, they were starting to get a pretty good idea.

Jack stood in the room that once had been Anne's studio, where there had been an old, soft chair and a work bench with paper and colored pencils and a can of paintbrushes. Where he used to find Anne any time he wanted to. He walked the perimeter of the room and stared out the large windows where the view had not changed. But the outlook certainly had.

Downstairs, in the rotunda with the brown granite walls and the smooth floor, Jack could hear the sound of a piano being tuned in one of the music rooms, in another room someone was practicing scales. Footsteps clacked around corners, scuttled into doorways and up the stairs. There came the quickening of voices from places unseen, the hurried dialogues that pass in the hall. A female voice was singing in a distant room, strong and confident, a sweet voice, a trained voice still in training, spiraling up to the huge murals: *The Triumph of Justice, The Defeat of Prejudice,* painted by WPA artists more than sixty years ago.

Outside on the quad, a groundsman was mowing the grass, perched on his tractor, driving slow, tight circles like a suburban dad on a Saturday morning. Another man was clipping hedges around the wood benches, gifts from the class of '56. Senior boys and girls, wearing bright shorts and souvenir T-shirts, sipped sodas and ate French fries out of paper bags, pedaled bicycles, walked the campus proprietarily like landed gentry, offered each other expanded greetings. Unshaven kids, looking younger every year, with their journals and notepads, lying on their hips and elbows languid beneath the trees, smoking cigarettes, lifting tempered smiles to Jack as he passed by. "Hello, Dr. Owens," "Good to see you, Dr. Owens." "Hi, Dr. Owens." "Hello." "Hello." "Hello, Dr. Owens."

On the east side of the quad, Glenn Morrow and Aaron Reed, from the Language Department, Gladys Montgomery, from American Studies, Penelope Chen, from Theater, were carrying cartons up to their offices, pushing uneasily against the front door, waddling gracelessly up the stairs with their accordion folders, their diskettes, their pens and coffee machines and ceramic vases, their toothbrushes and combs; the things they took with them at the end of the old semester and brought back for the new, the things they liked to have around them, the framed prints and photographs, the coffee mug with the black and white Westie. Mementos informing them of who they are and why they came here and why they remain. It happened every year, a performance, a devotion, without which there could be no academic year.

From open windows came the halting sounds of academic industry playing softly like a motif, riding on the air. Work in preparation, work already done. The constancy of routine flowing uncontested.

Jack could see the window of his own office, where Robbie was working, where phone messages were duly recorded and another student crisis was surely lined up. Where Jack's industry waited for him, his contribution to the academic machine. He looked at the students and the men from the physical plant, the returning faculty, and could feel himself attached to the college—feeding the awakening organism—one of its parts, fulfilling its set of expectations and promises, obeying its rules; who appeared in front of the classroom and taught his course three times a week—without facing the expanse of time which was summer. He felt a sense of mooring, of being tethered to a piece of solid ground with offices and buildings, schedules and committees, students and teachers. Where the normalcy of days like this was no small miracle.

He thought that this was what Stan meant. He hadn't been talking about the neurotic tic, about the ritual to hold the world together, at least Jack's particular piece of it, anyway. He was talking about being part of the college and the routine of this community—before Jack had joined the Community of Parents of Dead Children and Sad Detectives. It was why Jack had to go to Anne's studio. Because Anne, who had been an art student and once had a studio in the Fine Arts building, was part of that continuity, just as teaching at Gilbert was. Just as being Dr. Owens was.

Jack could lean into that for now. He could rely on the routine—on all the works and days of hands—that filled the blank calendar squares, that occupied his time.

He sat, for a moment, on the wooden bench with the brass plaque from the class of '56 and wondered if maybe he'd gotten it wrong. Maybe it was possible for more than one incarnation of Dr. Owens, or whoever Dr. Owens had become. Someone other than the Dr. Owens of memory, but who lived in memory, nonetheless. Who had been the young film student and could be found, like Anne's tracers, streaming through the air, through Time, running up the stairs of the Fine Arts building, sitting on the quad or in a classroom. Someone other than the grieving father. Someone who was—hell, he didn't know—but someone students still seemed to recognize; someone his friends weren't afraid to talk to; who could show up for faculty lunches—it might be possible to still be their Jack. Even if that Jack was nothing but the past. Maybe that's where his friends would agree to find him. He thought it might be possible, even as he felt the twinge of disloyalty to Danny. Even as Danny, the living Danny, receded a little further away from him. He thought this was who he was now. This was where he belonged. He thought Danny would understand.

He started to walk across the lawn to the registrar's office but decided that the i's could be dotted and t's crossed tomorrow, and instead went to his screening room. The prospect of sitting alone in the dark was not at all uninviting.

Just last semester, he'd said, "Hey, pal, feel like going to the movies?"

Danny asked, "What movie?" He asked, "Can I bring someone along?"

"Someone? One of your friends?" Jack smiled because he knew it wasn't just one of Danny's friends.

"Rachael Tate."

"Sure you can." And a moment later, "It sounds like this might be serious."

"We're just friends."

Danny brought Rachael. Irwin got a kick out of it. He said, "You two ain't about to run off and elope or nothin'?" Which made Rachael blush and Danny give Irwin a punch in the arm.

Jack liked that Danny brought Rachael along. He watched Danny propped in his seat, his face a soft shadow in the flickering light. Sometimes he looked worried, sometimes confused. But it didn't matter, as long as he was there . . .

When *One Plus One* ended and only pale white light glowed on the empty screen, while Irwin kept to himself in the projection booth, Jack sat thinking that this was where he belonged. He didn't understand what that meant, except that he would forever be Danny's father and Danny would forever have committed suicide and this town, this college, seemed to be the two places where those two facts could best be lived with. He would always be Danny's father, someone called Dr. Owens, someone called Jack. It was the trapdoor that led, not out, but in, in to his schedule and his office hours and to something that he was incapable at the moment of articulating to himself. Perhaps it had no name, or perhaps he simply didn't know what to call it, because he could not identify what was happening inside of himself, but he wanted to believe that it was something he was capable of being, who he was now and where he belonged.

He would have liked to talk this over with Marty, who would look at him, the way he'd been looking at him all summer, nod his head and say, "It sounds like you're coming to terms with all this." Or meet Lois at her house and tell her, "It isn't much, but I think it's enough." Lois would consider this for a moment, then tell him, "Sometimes enough is all that you really need." But when Jack walked back to his office and called Marty, he'd already left. Lois was meeting Tim and two other couples at the country club. She invited Jack to come along, but that was a crowd he was never comfortable with, so he sat at his desk, looking at the photograph of Danny, the face sun-bright and excited, smiling a full vacation smile. Jack wanted to talk to that face. To sit with him one more time, in the morning before the school bus came—"Which is more important, Dad, honesty or loyalty?" To meet him after work and drive out to Mickey's for steaks and salads, like they used to when he told Danny, "I thought we'd spend spring break in California. We'll get to see Henry and Suzette. Drive out to the beach."

Danny took a sip of his Coke, gave it some thought. "Can I sleep in the tent with Charlie and Oliver?"

"What kind of vacation would it be otherwise?"

"Cool."

Or tonight, Jack would say, "I think I've figured out a way to get through this without you. Do you understand? Is it all right with you?"

Danny would look at him and smile shyly, making Jack hold him so tight he could feel the beating of his heart.

Jack thought about the nights when he used to go home and lie on the grass in the backyard and look forward to the next day and the day after that. He would rise up on his elbows and see Danny running with Mutt through the field, the two of them cutting and twisting through the deep green rows, just making it back to the house before Mutt fell panting on the ground and Danny lay in the grass breathing too hard to speak.

All of that was impossible now, but at least he was able to remember what it felt like, and that was enough to take home with him, enough to bring back to his office in the morning where there was a job to do and idleness was gone; where he could rely on the schedule and the routine to occupy his time for another day, fill the space on the calendar and cross it off.

There was a sense of revelation to be had from this. He could sit in this room and look at his lecture notes, or the office hours posted on the door, or leave instructions for Robbie and know there was work to be done in the days ahead, time filled. He felt reassured by this, emboldened by it. It was all there in black and white; and he wasn't in a hurry to leave.

He called Marty at home, but only the answering machine picked up and he left a perfunctory message. He arranged the memos and papers on his desk, leaned back in his chair and stared at the ceiling. He thought this was who he was now. This was where he belonged.

The breeze outside smelled of leaves that were getting ready to turn and the summer was losing its grip on the night. Jack walked down the old brick sidewalks, past the boys and girls coming and going outside the dormitories on the old campus, walking in and out of the pale gaslights, slipping into the shadows.

There was music playing through the windows and telephones ringing, voices calling to each other inside the yellow rooms, and laughter. It made Jack think of the barbecue shack where he and Marty went last July, where they played jazz after dark and served illegal liquor; which made him think of the sound that pushes through a roomful of people and over the music, the ambient mixture of smoke and bodies and voices, the rhythm and cadence of song and conversation bearing its own intimacy and secrets.

Two girls sat under the lights reading tarot cards and looking very serious. Four skateboarders scooted by. Two other girls came hurrying around the corner giggling and chanting: "Laaa . . . ree . . . Haas . . . kel . . . Laree . . . Haas . . . kel . . ." at a boy who kept walking away from them, shaking his head, hands over his ears. "Laaa . . . ree . . . Laaa . . . ree . . . Laaa . . . ree . . ."

Jack walked along the old brick sidewalks while the half-moon leaned against the roof of the dormitory, lifted itself gently, followed him to his car and rode above his shoulder as he drove down Third Street, where the ruins were a black silhouette against the trees and stars.

The half-moon rode with him as he drove through the streets, where the flicker of televisions was visible and children were coming from front lawns and backyards, while he drove past the old houses with the tired roofs and the screens all had holes in them but they kept the windows open all night, anyway. The moon followed him into the neighborhoods of matchbox houses on cookie-cutter lawns with ceramic gnomes and pink flamingos, and the streets with the large Tudor houses set back from the sidewalk and the live oaks that muted the streetlights, where no one seemed to ever raise a voice.

The half-moon rode with him while he drove through streets where he was a stranger and streets where he could pick out the houses of his friends.

Through streets that narrowed into circular drives, and streets that opened into boulevards where a man walked his dog, and a little girl tagged behind her parents, and a couple strolled aimlessly around the corner.

The half-moon rode over Jack's shoulder, stayed with him, silently, all the way home, leaving him at the front door, where not very long ago he would have heard Danny at the piano, and Jack would have stopped, just as he reached the porch, and sat on the bottom step listening, careful not to interrupt, careful not to intrude, listening to the swell and sweep of the music, the certainty of each note, and now there was only the mail and the newspaper. Where it was the end of his first day back from the summer.

Mutt barked, ran the length of the porch and into the house while Jack walked to the kitchen, dropped the newspaper and mail on the table, filled the dog dish with food and went out to the backyard. He wanted to sit in the grass, where he used to see Danny running through the field.

Tiny winged insects were rising around him, buzzing and cricking their awakening. Fireflies flashed and vanished and appeared again. One, then three, then dozens darting and dotting. Jack felt the dark, cool ground against his bare feet. He could hear the stream running fast against the rocks, the frogs and tree toads croaking and clicking, the night birds whistling, the quick scudding sounds brushing the undergrowth—raccoons most likely, or possums—breaking through the silence. He leaned back on his elbows and looked at the stars thickening in the sky. The air held the scent of a fey dampness.

Jack could not deny his loneliness, but neither could he deny the night, which was not, he realized, a time of rest. It was not something dormant, but a rising, a calling to life; not the end of the day but its extension. Not an absence of daylight but the presence of a persistent vitality, offering its own light, its own sounds and fragrances, its own welkin company.

Overhead was the ghostly surveillance of an owl, the snap of a twig, a hurried rustling of leaves. A minute later the breeze picked up and all the trees bent like supplicants. A minute after that the air was still and quiet. The moon cast a shadow across his garden. The darkness itself contained texture and substance, and the field no longer looked like a piece of solid ground but like liquid, like Homer's wine-dark sea. Jack imagined a huge ocean liner floating out of the night, materializing out of the soil, not of this world, but an enchantment. Crimson and yellow. Strung with hundreds of golden lights, a ship built by Fellini. Flares erupt from the deck, their meaning unclear: is it a celebration or a signal of distress? A mass of passengers stands at the railing. There are children and nannies. Sailors and stewards. Everyone is cheering. Or they might be crying. Theirs are the voices of both peril and exultation. The ship appears safely anchored yet there is doubt about the travelers' well-being. But there is no doubt about the magnificence of the vessel. It is a creation sprung from itself and also of the earth. Mythical and literal. Unreal and actual. It appears to grow in size and is a trick of perspective.

Jack imagined himself rising to greet it. Standing in wonder of its brilliance and paradox, of wading out into the water until the waves were chest-high and splashed his lips and nose so he could smell the salt and taste it. He would try to take a closer look, but the great ship would only recede, keeping a constant distance as he approached, and then vanish.

The vista was once again the field. The night birds and tree toads returned to their song and clatter. The small creatures could be heard scurrying through the undergrowth.

Jack pulled himself up and walked slowly to the house. He stopped at the top of the porch steps and looked over his shoulder, where only the field remained in darkness. He stood and listened for a moment longer to all the sounds of the night. Then he went inside.

Jack was making supper for himself when the telephone rang. He'd filled a pot with water, opened a box of pasta, chopped a few overripe tomatoes. He was not unaware that this was the first time since Danny died that he'd thought to cook himself a meal and sit at the table and do more than wait for his food to get cold—after supper, he might pour himself a whiskey, sit in his study and consider the work waiting for him tomorrow and all the small and minor matters that moved him closer to the day when he would stand in front of his class.

It was Celeste calling, reminding him to bring his lecture notes to school tomorrow. They talked briefly, how was he feeling after his first day back? Did he want to have dinner with Arthur and her tomorrow night? It was only after Jack hung up the phone and cleared the table that he saw the headline in the newspaper about the arrest of Joseph Rich, "Confessed Cyberkiller," with a picture of a middle-aged balding little man wearing a jacket and tie. And a picture of Hopewell along with the caption: "Local hero promises justice will prevail." Jack would have to remember to give Marty a call tonight.

There would come a time when he would look back on that moment, when he hung up the phone, read the headline in the paper, waited for the pasta to cook, and remember it as his final minutes with what he'd been able to salvage of the world he once inhabited with Danny. Like an archaeologist contemplating the piece of broken pottery, the slab of tablet, and trying to reconstruct the lost world from whence it came—the way he might have deconstructed a film, or watched Anne—Jack would turn that moment inside out if only to recover the way the light looked on the kitchen wall, or the aroma coming from the cutting board; if only to recover the sensations of being inside his house after watching the night come to life, of feeling attached to the college and his friends, of feeling the sorrow and loneliness of this exact minute, the sensations of this other-time where he once lived with and then without his son.

He placed his knife and fork on the table, the table where he'd sat with Danny at suppertime and weekend lunches, where they ate their last breakfast together—"Which is more important, Dad, honesty or loyalty?"—and hung up the phone. He thought he'd wait until after he'd eaten to look for the notes, and then thought, What the hell, get it over with now.

He walked down to the basement. It was cool and damp and had a spare-parts look, castoffs of family life. Old clothes and shoulder pads, Rollerblades and skateboards. Baseball bats, caps and pieces of uniforms. Unsteady pillars of books, boxes of Christmas decorations, boxes from the loft on Crosby Street that he had never bothered to unpack. The old stereo and the large speakers. Stacks of record albums. This was the one place he had not straightened out during his summer obsession, the place Marty's phone call had kept him from. Perhaps on some cold winter's day when the snow was high and the roads iced over, he'd come down here and put things in order.

He walked over to the filing cabinet in the corner, where Danny used to read on rainy days, where Jack now stored his folders and his disks, where everything was arranged neatly by subject.

The cabinet wobbled unsteadily. Jack gave it a quick push, the way he might have flicked a speck of lint off a sweater, not enough to interrupt himself, an absent careless push, while he riffled the folders.

He picked out the floppy disk from a small box at the front of the drawer, all the while the cabinet rocked back and forth under the pressure from his hand. He gave it another push, harder this time, and another push. He looked through the folders for the hard copy and started peeling back more folders, pulling out additional handwritten notes. The filing cabinet tipped forward and back, like the restaurant table that seesaws gracelessly under your elbow, just annoying enough not to be ignored. He pressed his shoulder against the side, where the metal was soft and pliant. He reached for another folder and gave the cabinet a shove, pushed his hip against it, and when that did no good, aware now that something was stuck back there, pushed it one more time, without much success, and started to walk away, then turned back because he knew, the way he knew why Hopewell had come to his office that morning in May, the way he knew that night in Tuscany before Anne said, "Nothing's changed." He knew the way he used to know, used to *sense,* Danny's absence in the house, and Danny's presence before Danny ever made a sound. He knew that this was an anomaly. The face of the stranger in the family portrait. The odd shoe in the bottom of the closet. He knew because he was Danny's father and he was supposed to know.

Or maybe that wasn't it at all. Maybe all it really amounted to was this: he had been trying to set things right all these years, was so accustomed to doing it, that this was just one more thing out of kilter, one more thing that needed straightening out; the confluence of coincidence and compulsion—if he had thought about it as it happened.

He put his weight against the side of the cabinet and pushed, trying to steady it. So little thought went into it. He simply put the folders and disk on the floor and gave the cabinet a solid shove. It was bottom-heavy, like deadweight and he couldn't move it, couldn't quite squeeze his hand around it. He dropped to his knees, leaned and pushed, and gradually edged the bottom away from the wall.

The back of his shirt was damp, he was dripping sweat and breathing deeply. He stopped to wipe his face and catch his breath. The telephone rang upstairs. Jack just let it ring while he reached behind the cabinet, stretched his arm—the way he would have rescued Danny's sneaker from the bottom of a pond, sleeves rolled up, feeling around the mud and weeds, extending his fingers—and when he came up short, leveraged himself against the wall and pushed, reaching, until his fingertips touched the soft piece of leather: an old slipper . . . Stretching a little further: an abandoned boot . . . Extending his arm until he could tap his fingers against, what? A stuffed toy that was lodged back there and which he had to have because it was Danny's? That he had to hold because Danny had held it? Had to touch because Danny had touched it?

How oddly time seemed to be moving. Truncated, contracted, like an accordion squeezed closed, each moment pressed against the next, each event toppling to its consequence as Jack wrapped his fingers around the smooth leather, sliding it along the wall and toward him. He could feel the padded fingers. He lifted it away from the cabinet. He could feel the waffled webbing, the laces and strap. He brought it forward. The heel was soft, like a pillow.

Closer now. He removed it, gently, slowly, unsheathing it like a dagger, easily, from a scabbard.

A baseball glove. A baseball glove with a tennis ball in the pocket and a pair of cheap hip-hop sunglasses. It seemed absurd, like finding an alarm clock in a tree. Jack was tempted to toss it over his shoulder into the stack of junk and bury it there, or add it to the clothes and toys for charity, and never look at it again. But he couldn't do that, because he knew what belonged in the basement and what didn't. He couldn't throw it away because he knew it hadn't been tossed back there by accident while Danny and his friends were playing; Mutt hadn't dragged it in. He couldn't throw it away, not without looking. Only he didn't look.

First, he had to hold the glasses and roll them around in his hand. He bounced the ball a couple of times and then a few more times. Then he ran his fingers across the torn brown leather, tugged on the laces, punched the pocket, which is what you do with a baseball glove. The laces were nearly shredded, the webbing loose. It was an old glove, something picked up in a thrift shop or handed down from an older brother. Jack turned it over, tested the wrist strap and pulled it loose. That's when he looked.

A name had been written on the underside of the wristband and crossed out. A new name was written beneath it. In a child's hand, in blue ink that had not had time to smudge. The name was Lamar Coggin.

Part Three

XXII

Jack took a step back, hitting his leg against a carton. His face burned. He stared at the glove, as though further examination might make it less real, might change the irrefutable fact that it had been wedged behind the filing cabinet, might inhibit the need to consider how and why it got there, had Jack been capable of considering anything at the moment. But all he could do was clutch the glove as though it were a living thing about to escape from him and run wildly through the house, contaminating everything it touched. Contaminating Danny.

There was a sick ache in Jack's stomach. His mouth was dry. His tongue pulsed against his lips. His heart was beating fast. He needed to pull Danny away from this, separate him from it. There was something he should have been remembering, but what it was he could not recall; something he should have been doing, but what was it? He could only look at the tennis ball and think about Danny playing outside, throwing a ball against the back steps, talking to himself, keeping a running commentary: the winning home run, the spectacular catch, pitching his team to the finals—Jack would look out the window and it was Danny out there, talking to himself, playing a ballgame of the mind. He didn't know Jack was watching. He played his game unawares. Throwing and catching, over and over again. Danny, standing all alone, looking young and so dependent, Jack couldn't hold on to all the emotions he was feeling. He wanted to scream out to him or rush down and grab him until

Danny understood just how much he loved him, and even then, Danny would never understand. Then Danny saw Jack and smiled, because it was Jack watching him, and Jack would forget all about the hard time Danny had given him at supper and that he hadn't bothered to make his bed, simply because he recognized Jack's face and it made him smile.

Jack paced the length of the basement. His legs trembled. He teeth were chattering. There was something he should have been remembering, something he should have been doing, something he should have been thinking. If he only calmed down, he would know exactly what to do, if he stopped pacing, if he just let his head clear for a minute—why the hell did Lamar have to write his name in the goddamned glove?

If Jack had found a baseball glove without a name, it could have belonged to anyone. To no one. He wouldn't have looked twice at it, just thrown it in with the rest of the junk, or he might have thought it was something Danny had found and he would have held on to it for a moment or two, let his fingers touch the same place Danny's fingers had touched and saved it with the rest of the old toys. But, no, this kid had to go and write his name on the damn thing.

Jack thought there was something he should have been remembering. Something he should have been doing. But all he could do was stare at the worn leather and ragged laces, look over his shoulder at the filing cabinet, at the piles of old clothes, the boxes brought from the loft on Crosby Street and never opened. His insides quivered, his hands were cold and sweaty. There was something he should have been doing, but he was afraid to move, afraid to leave, afraid to go upstairs, where the night no longer held its charm and all facts were irrefutable but one. It was like waking from a nightmare and lying as still as possible until the bogeyman goes away. Or closing your eyes at the scary part of the movie, ducking under the seat so the monster won't see you. Then the sun appears, the lights come up, you crawl out from under the covers, you come up from under the seat. You tell yourself it's only a bad dream. You tell yourself it's only a movie. Jack told himself there was a reasonable explanation. While his legs trembled and his teeth chattered.

The air carried the odors of old clothes and books and damp cardboard. From one of the corners came the intermittent clicking of the thermostat; from another corner, the subtle gulp of the water pump. Pipes heaved and contracted. There were the dark sighs of plaster behind the walls. The old beams creaked with age and expelled soft moans, the cement foundation still settling after a hundred years; the internal, assuring sounds of shelter, so familiar they'd gone unnoticed forever, the soft murmur of the hot water tank, the hum of the circuit breaker in the corner where Danny had played with his toys, read his books, over by the filing cabinet, where Jack now stood looking into the space where the glove had been, as though the explanation he wanted was stuck back there, and if he gave the cabinet one more push, cleared away some of the resident dust, if he'd just calm down for Christ's sake, he'd see it.

His hands would not stop trembling.

He felt closed in by the colorless walls, the drab brown boxes, the clutter and damp air. His face was hot and he was sweating. He wanted to leave and yet did not dare to go upstairs. He felt the anticipation brought on by anxiety, the anxiety brought on by anticipation, as though something were about to happen down here that he had to witness, or something else was about to materialize behind the boxes, between the jackets of old record albums, beneath the old baseball uniforms and shoulder pads.

He told himself that this had nothing to do with Danny. Which he might have actually believed, had he not been holding the irrefutable fact in his hand.

He wanted to talk to Marty. He wanted to hear Marty reassure him the way he'd reassured him through the summer. He wanted to hear Marty tell him: "You're right, Jack, this has nothing to do with Danny." He wanted Marty to offer the reasonable explanation.

"I found Lamar Coggin's baseball glove in my basement. I don't know how it could have gotten there."

"The baseball glove of the murdered little boy?"

"Wedged behind the filing cabinet. I think Hopewell did it."

"Sure, Jack. That makes sense, Hopewell planting the one piece of evidence that would seal his case in your basement. Sounds to me like it might have been hidden there. Could it be Danny hid it there?"

"Danny wouldn't have had any reason to do that. Maybe he found it and put it there for safekeeping."

"And then committed suicide, Jack?"

"This has nothing to do with Danny."

"Yeah. I guess you're right, Jack. This has nothing to do with Danny."

Jack told himself that there was a reasonable explanation and sagged against the wall, wrapped his arms tightly around his chest and sank to the floor.

He wanted Danny back, just for a minute. He wanted to see Danny's hands rest calmly at his sides, his chest expand with breath. He wanted to hear Danny's voice, already changing, no longer a child's voice but not quite a man's, saying: "It's like this, Dad . . ." And it would all make sense. "You didn't doubt me, did you, Dad?"

He wanted to peel away the layers of time, reduce it to the moment before the moment Danny killed himself, and stop it.

The misery of May, the panic and desolation of June and July, the entire summer of loneliness Danny's suicide had left in its wake seemed like a dress rehearsal for what Jack felt now. He rolled his head from side to side in frustration for what he did not know, for what he missed, for his regrets and his ignorance. For what he'd lost. For what he never had.

Outside the house there was a world that did not know Danny Owens, nor did it care about his life and death, and that world would turn predictably tonight minute after minute until daylight returned to the horizon. Inside the house, where there was no other world but the world of Danny Owens, Jack sat in the corner of the basement, held on to himself and wondered about all the things he didn't know about his son: Danny had a secret. Hell, all kids keep secrets. But not like this, because Danny committed suicide . . .

He thought that maybe he didn't want to know, that there are things a person shouldn't know about himself. There are things a person shouldn't know, period.

But it was too late to believe that or try to convince himself that he did. He'd found the baseball glove of a murdered boy in his basement and he had to find out how it got there.

More than an hour went by but Jack did not get up off the floor. In that hour Mutt barked from somewhere in the house, the phone rang again, and again Jack did not go upstairs to answer it. He sat alone in the basement, amid the clutter, and told himself not to try to guess how the glove got there, to just stick with what he knew.

He thought about Danny's last days, the days when he'd seen him the least.

But you saw him every morning.

He thought about their fifteen minutes at breakfast, the few nights when they ate supper together. What Danny said. How Danny looked.

He looked the way he always looked. Or maybe you didn't know what you were seeing.

He told himself, *Just stick with what you know. Break it down. You're good at deconstruction, Jack. Deconstruct this.*

He was slow to consider what there was to break down, slow to articulate what he expected to come of it and slower still to concede that a murdered boy's baseball glove might have something to do with Danny, after all, and that whatever explanation there was would be anything but reasonable. It was only a matter of where he wanted to be when he made his concession.

He walked slowly to the foot of the steps, turned his head for another look at the corner by the filing cabinet, let the glove fall out of his hand and walked slowly up the stairs.

There was the bitter smell of gas in the kitchen, the water had boiled over and the flame under the pot had gone out. Mutt was pawing the back door and barking. Just a few of the irrepressible and banal facts of life. Turn off the burner . . . let Mutt out . . . He could hear the rush of owls flying over the field and crickets and frogs singing in the grass out by the creek. He pushed the chairs closer to the table, for no reason other than it was something to do with his hands. When the telephone rang, he did not pick it up. A student named Becker was calling with a question. Jack turned off the volume on the answering machine and walked out, past the wall of photographs, through the living room and upstairs to Danny's room.

He traced his fingertips along a book on the shelf, and the row of CDs. He sat on the edge of Danny's bed, ran his hand across the quilted bedspread and up along the edge of Danny's pillow, touching what Danny had touched, as though he could lift remnants of Danny's existence and absorb them through his flesh.

Jack could see Danny at breakfast, or working on his hamburger at the drive-in out on Route 41. What did it tell him? What was the look in Danny's eye? What was the expression on his face when Jack asked him about school?

What did you see? What was in his voice?

He saw Danny sitting at the table looking into a bowl of soggy cereal on Saturday morning, not speaking. Yawning. Looking tired.

"You wouldn't be tired from studying too hard?" Jack said to him.

No answer.

"Too tired to talk?"

"I guess."

"My working late at the office doesn't give you license to stay up all night."

"I know when to go to sleep. I'm fifteen, you know."

What was in the voice? What did Jack hear?

He sounded annoyed but he'd sounded annoyed plenty of other times.

They were eating supper at the drive-in, Thursday night. Danny *inhaled* his cheeseburger . . . They were eating supper at the drive-in four days later. Danny left half his burger on the plate. Jack never monitored Danny's behavior, he didn't that night, either. He assumed Danny had eaten late in the day.

A week before that, they were sitting at breakfast, Danny wasn't yawning. He ate his cereal. They were talking about pitching in the sectionals. Danny said he was nervous. Jack told him, "If you aren't nervous, you aren't ready." Danny offered up a smile and ran to catch the school bus.

What does that tell you, Jack? What do you know?

He knew that Danny had stopped sleeping and lost his appetite.

". . . I'm really sorry about Danny. I miss him a lot," Mary-Sue told him. She said, "I was kind of worried about him . . . I could tell something was bothering him . . . just something I saw . . . when he thought no one was watching . . ."

Jack leaned back on Danny's pillow.

When was something bothering him?

". . . they would just be talking and acting stupid . . . Danny wasn't really into it . . . they'd cut school a few days before, an end-of-the-term thing . . ."

Danny wouldn't lose sleep over cutting school. He wouldn't lose his appetite.

"Rick got on C.J. . . . Usually Danny would take C.J.'s part . . . this time he was just letting Rick . . . I could just see something was bothering him . . ."

When was something bothering him?

The three boys were sitting on Jack's front porch . . . "Maybe we can help each other understand it a little better."

Brian said, "That's what we've been trying to do, Dr. Owens. Believe me, we've been trying, but we don't know why."

"Did he ever talk about being depressed?"

The boys glanced at each other.

Brian: "Nothing . . . He was the same old Danny . . . He was just like he always was."

"Maybe it was something he only talked about once."

Brian: "Not to any of us."

"Was he eating?"

Rick: "Yeah. We all ate together . . ."

Brian: "He ate supper at my house . . . If there was anything bothering Danny, we would have known about it."

"Danny didn't seem unusually upset?"

Brian: "No."

Rick.: ". . . he never acted, you know, weird . . ."

Mary-Sue told him, "Usually Danny would take C.J.'s part . . . he was just letting Rick get in C.J.'s face . . . like Danny was in his own thoughts . . ."

Monday morning. They were in the kitchen. Danny hadn't said much. He pushed his toast out of the way. It was the third morning in a row that he'd pushed his breakfast aside. Jack said something about it.

Danny said, "I'm eating, I'm eating." He rubbed his eyes. His face was pale, it always was when he didn't get enough sleep. He asked, "Which is more important, Dad, honesty or loyalty?"

Jack answered, "That's a very good question. I'd say it's something you have to take case by case. Is there anything in particular—"

Was it something that came up in class? Did he read it in a book?

"Which is more important, Dad, honesty or loyalty?"

It was more than just a question. When was something bothering him?

"Which is more important, Dad, honesty or loyalty?"

"That's a very good question . . ."

Mutt started barking . . . the school bus driver honked his horn . . . Jack said, "Stick around, I'll drive you to school."

"Can't, Dad." Danny grabbed his books and bolted. Jack was a little surprised, a little hurt that Danny didn't want to spend another half hour with him. But, as Danny reminded Jack only a few days before, he was "fifteen, you know."

"Too old to be seen with me?" Jack called after him.

Danny didn't answer.

Jack worked late Monday night and overslept. He didn't see Danny Tuesday morning.

The following night, they shared a pizza in town. It was a rush job on Jack's part. He had two days to finish grading the final projects. He drove Danny home and went back to his office. They didn't talk much in the restaurant, and neither of them ate much. Jack had the feeling something was bothering Danny.

You asked him. He said no.

"It seems there's something—"

"Nothing's bothering me. Okay?"

"If there's—"

"You worry too much."

Jack worked all day Saturday.

You made him breakfast, which he didn't eat, and Saturday night—

He didn't see Danny Saturday night. He came home early but Danny was out with his friends and went straight to bed when he came in. No more than a few words mumbled as he climbed the stairs.

He seemed angry about something. Angry at you? Angry because of your work? You should have found out. You should have made the time to find out. You should have made the time to be with him . . .

The morning Danny killed himself—

You didn't see him that morning.

But he saw him the night before—

No, you only spoke to him on the phone.

Jack called Danny around six o'clock Wednesday evening. "I've got to skip our supper tonight, pardner. I've got to work late." Danny didn't sound disappointed, not exactly, but something in his voice made Jack say, "You know, once all this work is behind us, we're going to have a terrific summer."

"I know."

When was something bothering him?

Jack leaned on the windowsill. The breeze brushed his face, dried leaves rustled against the porch.

When was something bothering him?

". . . I thought he was angry at me . . . He was like all locked up inside . . . It was more like a feeling I had about him . . ."

When was something bothering him?

". . . they'd cut school a few days before . . . Brian was talking to C.J. like he might have told his mom or something . . . Rick got on C.J., making him look real whipped . . ."

So they cut school and C.J. has a big mouth. What of it? . . .

Mary-Sue: "Danny was like in his own thoughts . . . real intense . . ."

Marty had said, "You see, Danny was the second boy to commit suicide in the past month. Less than *that,* really . . ."

Mary-Sue: ". . . real intense . . . all locked up inside . . ."

Marty: ". . . less than *that* . . ."

You asked Mary-Sue if Danny knew Lamar. She said no . . .

Marty: ". . . second boy in the past . . ."

Lamar was murdered . . . His baseball glove was in your basement . . .

Marty: ". . . about a week before Danny . . ."

Mary-Sue: ". . . I could just see that something was bothering . . ."

When was something bothering him?

". . . Rick got on C.J. . . . . . . looked real whipped, like he just wanted to run away . . ."

"From what I hear," Celeste said, "C.J.'s recovering too slowly . . . no appetite . . . severely depressed . . ."

Arthur said, "Rick had a very hard time of it . . . can't stand being here."

When was something bothering him?

". . . It wasn't like Danny to be so . . . he got really weird . . . locked up inside . . . real intense . . . something was bothering him . . ."

When was something bothering him?

". . . it made me think he was just in a bad mood . . ."

When was something bothering him?

"I could tell something was bothering him, about a week before . . ."

Jack turned around as though a hand had snatched him by the shoulder. He would not have been in the least surprised if his jaw had dropped and he was gaping openmouthed like a dumbstruck clueless wonder. Except he was the opposite of clueless. He was abundant with clues, and they terrified him. His head was throbbing, the back of his neck felt as though a hot drill was biting into it. He felt nauseated, like falling in a dizzying and depthless dream; and then he felt nothing.

There's a moment when the toothache stops hurting, the broken arm, the fractured jaw; when the amount of pain the body is capable of generating, capable of tolerating, reaches its limit and the body goes into shock, the brain simply refuses to send the message and the pain goes away, or the nerve endings wear down before regenerating and delivering the next jolt. It allows you time to believe the pain has actually stopped, that the synapses really have shut off and gone numb, leaving you in the not-at-all-unpleasant state of insentience. You might even run your tongue against the infected molar, or try to flex the arm, work the jaw, or you might simply wait for the pain to return. Jack waited.

He waited for the nerve endings to come alive and the synapses to start to fire and spark, and when they did, he was surprised to discover that his entire body felt as though it were no longer held together by muscle and sinew and bone, but by electric current. His flesh felt like it was pulling away from him, as though he were, quite literally, jumping out of his skin, and he experienced a clarity of thought that was both startling and formidable.

He parked in the shadow of the moon, a half block away from Ainsley's house, cut the engine and waited for the morning to come, for Ainsley to step out and extract his portion of fresh air and sunshine; and should his eyes come to rest on the spot where Jack was parked, if he recognized the car, what would he think? If he were to walk over, finding Jack unwashed and red-eyed, and ask "What the hell are you doing out here like this, Owens?" what would Jack reply? What pretext had he prepared? Or would he answer, flatly, evenly: "Ask your son."

They should all ask their sons. Carl and Mandy. Arthur and Celeste. Vicki and Hal. Jack should have asked Danny when he still had time. When they sat together at breakfast—*Which is more important, Dad, honesty or loyalty?* When they met for supper and Danny couldn't eat, when Danny couldn't sleep.

But Jack hadn't known what to ask. He didn't possess the clear thinking that only a sleepless night can grant. He didn't possess the understanding that only the baseball glove of a murdered little boy can present, that only the suicide of his son allowed. He was waiting for the morning to come so that he might put his understanding to good use, because he now knew what to ask.

He knew what to ask because the day Danny and C.J. and Brian and Rick cut school they witnessed Lamar Coggin's murder.

Jack had been looking at it all those mornings when Danny sat silently at the breakfast table, and during those quick-grab dinners at the drive-in when Danny no longer had an appetite. It was there, he just didn't know what he was seeing. But now he knew, because he knew Danny.

They'd probably never seen Lamar before, they certainly didn't know him, but they saw him die. They saw who murdered him. They had the baseball glove to prove it; but they didn't tell anyone about it. They witnessed a murder, they had to tell someone. Their parents. The police. They had to do something about it.

You can't talk about the other boys but you know your own son. Danny would have told someone. He would have told you. He would have come to the office the day it happened, he would have looked nervous and agitated, trying not to cry, looking pale. He might not have known the right words, he might not have said it straight out, but he would have told you. Unless he was frightened. Unless something, or someone, had frightened him. You should have seen it, Jack. You should have known what to ask.

He shivered in the cool breeze and closed the car window. He stared at the dark houses set back from the sidewalk, and past the houses where the horizon, the sky, were darker still; alone in the night, grinding his thoughts.

C.J. had his car accident. Rick won't go back to school. Brian is acting out all over the place. But Danny was the only one who killed himself.

He hesitated a moment. He told himself he was too exhausted to think straight, to get anything right. But he didn't believe it. He did not doubt the veracity of his thoughts or his certainty. Marty had it wrong. Hopewell was right, after all. There was a "cyberkiller" luring boys into the woods, who had lured Lamar Coggin out to Otter Creek. Danny saw him, and he was afraid. He was afraid not because he could now identify him, but because he already knew him. Maybe he taught at Danny's school, or maybe he was the man who makes conversation with young boys at the convenience store, or while he's out for a run in the park, or hangs around the mall. Or he goes online . . . and he knew Danny.

Jack understood it. It made sense to him. All that remained was to get it over with and the sky showed no signs of daylight.

He waited for the morning to come. He now knew what to ask.

The dappled sunlight crisscrossed Ainsley's dark green lawn. There was muted tranquillity here, the respectable babble of squirrels and birds, the soft tones of morning voices in doorways; coffee cups in one hand, good-byes in the other. There was order in the way people left for work, the way children were strapped into cars for the ride to day care. It was humanity breathing the air of the new day, taking that first assessing look around and liking the prospects.

After a while, Ainsley stepped outside to add his presence to the scene. He smoothed the front of his pastel sweater, stopped to look around with a satisfied expression on his suntanned face. He peered down the street, in the same absent way in which he watched the girl walk down the hall the other day. He looked in Jack's direction and held the spot. Jack slunk down in the seat. He felt ridiculous doing it, but he stayed there, peeking over the dashboard until Ainsley, staring a few seconds longer, finally turned, smiled at his reflection in the windshield of his car, opened the door and drove away.

A few minutes later, Mandy appeared, with her impeccable makeup, the scent of her perfume no doubt splendid and fresh on her skin. She was smoking a cigarette, took three quick puffs while she slid into the butter-cream seat of her convertible and backed out of the driveway. Jack watched the car turn the corner before he got out and walked across the street.

He knocked on Ainsley's front door, waited and knocked again. It was another minute before C.J. appeared. He looked pale and thin, his gym shorts and T-shirt hung sadly on his skinny body. There were dark purple welts just below his cheekbones, dark circles around his eyes. His lips were puffy. His nose had been rebuilt and was too small, too perky for his face. His right arm was in a sling, his left hand was leaning on a cane. He frowned at the floor and said meekly, "It was an accident."

Jack said, "Yes, I heard all about it. You're really busted up, aren't you."

"It was an accident," C.J. repeated grimly, and Jack felt all of his thoughts, all of his assumptions, dissolve to nothing.

"Tell me why my son killed himself."

XXIII

It was Brian's idea to cut school. He said they needed a day of "pure relaxation." He said they *deserved* it, besides, it would help Danny get over losing "the Big Game." Danny told him, "You know damn well there's nothing to get over." Brian knew that, he just didn't want to cut school alone. Friday was the best day: they could intercept the school's absentee card in Saturday's mail. Brian said he was "covering all the angles."

They were going to meet at Danny's house—the only house where there wasn't a parent or au pair or housekeeper to spy on them—but it was too far to walk for C.J. and Rick, so they chose a place equidistant from everyone's house, the coffee shop at the strip mall over on Hollis and Oak.

It made them feel very mature to sit in a booth and eat breakfast. When they finished, they were surprised to see that it wasn't quite nine o'clock. They were used to more structured time and the way it moved according to schedule, from class to class, from morning to lunchtime, and they didn't know what to do with themselves.

They stopped at Grandview Pharmacy, bought hip-hop sunglasses and had a good time posing and mugging for each other as they paraded past the store windows and over by the gas stations and supermarkets, until it occurred to them that they'd better not be so conspicuous.

"What if someone who knows our parents sees us?" C.J. warned.

Usually they could hang out at a McDonald's or Burger King, but even that was risky. Rick wanted to go to the movies, but it was too early for the first show, and besides, it was a sparkling day, why waste it indoors? C.J. suggested the fairgrounds, but there wasn't much to do there except run around under the bleachers, swallow a lot of dust on the dirt track and scavenge for junk. Brian said Otter Creek was the place, no one ever went out there except weekend hikers; they could swim when they got hot, "sunbathe and chill." So, they walked out to Otter Creek, each boy plugged into his Walkman, carrying his backpack, sporting his new sunglasses.

It was a long walk. They were hot and tired when they got there, and by the time they found a clear and shaded spot on the embankment by the creek, they'd taken off their shirts and were quick to pull off their sneakers and lie down barefoot in the cool shade. They didn't do much else but listen to their music, shoo the flies and bees away, and talk aimless talk about cars, sports, high-tech games, and more serious talk about girls and sex.

Brian said, "I got into this chat room with some girl and she thinks I'm about *twenty* and going to IU. She wants to meet me and everything, but I was like, 'I don't know. Are you *really* as cool as you say you are?' And she's like, 'Yeah. I *really* am.' " No one believed him, but it was fun listening to him, and exciting, too. He said he'd get the girl online sometime when they all were at his house; and they talked about what they'd say to her and how cool they were, until they exhausted themselves and were quiet.

When they started talking again, it was about what they were going to do after high school. C.J. couldn't wait to get away from Gilbert. He said he'd given it "a great deal of thought," and decided that he was going to go to college at Yale or Stanford and then to Harvard Medical School, "and never come back to Gilbert or see my parents, except maybe for Christmas when they're like really old and drooling on themselves."

Rick would settle for Purdue. He leaned back on his elbows, looked beyond the treetops and said he was going to be an engineer and he didn't really care where he lived.

Brian said Rick was wasting his time getting a job right after college. *He* was going to take "at least a year off to travel." Work could wait. "But when I do get a job, I'm going to make a ton of money, live in a mansion and have a hot-looking wife, all kinds of games and CDs, at least three cars. A vintage Beemer, a Mercedes SUV and a Porsche Spyder."

Rick wanted to know where Brian was going to get the money to travel. "*Duh*. You'd better get a job, first." C.J. sided with Rick. Danny said it all depended on how much time Brian needed. "It's really a great idea. Take off for a year or *two* before making up your mind about what you want to do with your life."

One thing they all agreed on: they were looking forward to summer vacation. Danny couldn't wait to go up to Maine and be with the Danver boys. "They have their own sailboat and it's awesome."

Brian was going to Maine, too. Outward Bound on Hurricane Island.

C.J. said Outward Bound was really tough. Tougher than anything in Gilbert.

Brian said of course it was tough, that's why he was doing it. He was sure it was nothing he couldn't handle. "It's also a great way to show girls that you're cool." That brought them back to sex. But it didn't take them past noon or past their boredom.

For a while they lobbed rocks at the trees, then at each other, ducking and dodging and running around until they'd built up a good sweat and headed down to the creek, where they stripped to their underwear and jumped in the cold water.

At first, they were content to slide around and stand knee-deep in the shallows. Then they rode the current to a bend where there was a deep pool and they could swim, dive for stones and pull each other under. They didn't notice that Rick was missing until they saw him standing at the top of the embankment beneath an old oak tree. There was a thick rope tied to one of the limbs and it hung over the bank by the water.

"Check it out," Rick yelled. "Check it out. A *rope*."

The other boys raced up to him.

Rick was shouting, "Check it out. Check it out. We can swing over the water and cannonball. It'll be *awesome*."

The rope was old and worn, the end moldy and frayed and about three feet too short for the boys to reach, even when they jumped.

Brian shook his head. "We could if we were *gorillas*." Danny and C.J. laughed and grunted like apes.

Rick told them, "No. It'll be *awesome*."

"Yeah," C.J. said. "All we have to do is climb up, grab the rope, slide down . . ."

"We could make it longer. With some of our stuff," Danny said. He was the one who shinnied up the tree and onto the limb and tried tying their belts around the rope. But the lead belt just slipped off when he pulled on it. He tried tying their shirts to it, but that didn't work, either.

"There's got to be something in all the junk around here," Brian said, and organized the search, kicking and scattering dead leaves and fallen branches, pushing through the bushes and the litter around the undergrowth. C.J. found the piece of clothesline. It was at least six feet long and caked with mud.

Danny crawled out on the limb again, wrapped the clothesline around the branch, but with a good strong knot. The clothesline wasn't much longer than the old rope had been, so he tied the clothesline to the rope, about six inches or so above the frayed end, and let it hang down. Now it was long enough to reach.

"All *right*. Now we have enough rope," Brian shouted. He grabbed the clothesline, took a running start toward the edge of the embankment and swung high over the creek, letting out a tremendous "Tarzan" call. He sailed through the air and sang out, "I'm flying . . ." brought his knees close to his chest and prepared for his cannonball and splashdown. But just before he reached the height of his ascent and the center of the swimming hole, the clothesline slipped off the rope and Brian came falling down, his legs spread out in front of him, screaming, "Oh shiiiit," as he landed in the water. When he came to the surface, sputtering and spitting, he was waving the clothesline over his head.

"It's fucked up," he shouted, spitting out more water and swimming to shore.

This time Danny double-knotted the clothesline to the rope and Rick tried it out. Again the clothesline slipped off, just as he reached his peak. Then Brian and C.J. worked together tying the clothesline to the rope using one of the knots they remembered from Scouts, and Danny gave it a try, and again the clothesline slipped off.

Danny tried his best boating knot and C.J. put it to the test, and *he* fell into the water.

"Stupid rope," Rick whined. It was just too worn and slick and the boys couldn't keep the line from sliding off.

But Danny said, "Big deal, so we have to keep tying it, it's better than *nothing*." And they took turns tying the clothesline for each other, Rick tying it for Brian, Danny tying it for Rick . . . swinging over the creek, yelling, doing animal noises, screaming as they splashed down, making sure not to lose the line, swimming to shore, retying the line and taking off again.

They swam and jumped until they were so worn out they could barely pull themselves out of the water. Brian tied the line for C.J.'s jump, found a spot in the sun and lay down. C.J. told Danny, "You can go," and sat down near Brian. But Danny was too exhausted for another jump and so was Rick, and they all lay tired and silent under the warmth of the sun wearing nothing but their new sunglasses and their drenched underwear.

"Brian," Rick said, "your idea of 'pure relaxation' was *totally* inspired."

"*Way* cool," Danny said.

"Way, *way* cool," C.J. echoed.

Brian raised his fists wearily above his head, absorbing the compliment.

Around one-thirty, they got hungry, which made them restless and irritable. Brian said they should have brought sandwiches from the coffee shop. Rick somehow blamed C.J. for this oversight. Danny said, "How can it be *C.J.'s* fault?" and told Rick to stop picking on him. C.J. called Rick a moron. Brian said they were both morons and to shut up. It went on like that for about fifteen minutes more, until they heard the crunch of leaves. At first it was only in the distance, then it got louder and seemed to be coming toward them. The boys rose up on their elbows. The noise stopped, started again, and was soon followed by a painful cry and wail, like a wounded animal. The boys now sat up, held their breath and listened closely.

"What the fuck?" Rick whispered.

"Shh."

"It's an animal."

"A rabid raccoon, probably," C.J. said. "We'd better get the hell out of here."

Rick said, "Raccoons don't come out during the day, numb nuts."

"They do when they're *rabid*."

"Shh," Brian told them.

Another screech and a wail, like a baby crying, then the sound of human laughter.

Forgetting they were practically naked, the boys walked slowly, quietly, or as quietly as they could, through the leaves and sticks and rocks. That's when they saw the boy.

He was kneeling on the ground near his bicycle. His hands were wrapped around a small paper bag and he appeared to be squeezing it, and every time he did, the crying followed, while the boy laughed and rolled around on the ground clutching the bag to his chest, squeezing it and laughing louder. He did this several times, then reached into the bag, pulled out an orange and white kitten and held it by its neck, making its legs dangle above the ground. The more the kitten struggled, the more the boy laughed. He poked at it with a twig, tugged on its ears and swung it back and forth by its front paws. The kitten let out weak, pitiful cries.

"Bad kitty," the boy said, and grabbed it by the throat. "Bad, bad kitty." The kitten squirmed and struggled to get free.

"Hey," Danny called out. "What the fuck are you doing?"

The boy jumped back, his face went pale, his eyes grew wide under his glasses, but he didn't let go of the kitten. "Nothing," was all he said, and maybe out of nervousness, or resolve, he grabbed the kitten by its hind leg and twisted it. The animal's mouth opened and it screamed in pain.

"Cut it out," Danny called to him, and got to his feet.

"He *likes* it," the boy answered. "Don't you, kitty?" He twisted the hind leg again.

"Cut it out," Danny shouted again, and rushed toward him. The other boys hurried after him.

"He's been a very bad kitty," the boy said. "He needs to be punished."

"You're hurting it," Danny said. "You stupid jerk."

"It's just a dumb kit—"

Danny leapt at him, dropping the boy on his back, knocking the wind out of him. His hands fell open, the kitten sprang free and tried to crawl away. Danny pinned the boy to the ground, pressing his knees against his shoulders.

"How would you like it if someone did that to *you*?" Danny said.

The boy only laughed. He was a goofy-looking kid, with big jug-handle ears, thick glasses and mud-colored hair with a cowlick.

"Yo," Rick called out. He was standing in front of the bicycle. "Check it out." He slid the baseball glove off the handlebars. "Anyone want this piece of junk or should I toss it in the woods?"

"Hey," the boy hollered. "Put it back."

"Throw it in the woods," Brian said.

"It's *mine,*" the boy groaned.

"*Was.*" Rick tossed the glove over to Brian.

"Garbage glove," Brian said snidely.

"Put it back," the boy yelled at him.

"Make me," Brian said. He tossed the glove over to C.J.

"I think I'll keep it," C.J. said.

"It's *my* glove," the boy whined.

"Now it's *his.*" C.J. tossed the glove to Rick.

"It's *his.*" Rick tossed the glove back to C.J., who tossed it over to Brian.

Rick ran a few feet away, held out his hands like a wide receiver and called out, "Hit me." Brian threw a forward pass that Rick caught over his shoulder. He threw the glove to C.J, who passed it to Brian. Brian caught it inches above the boy's nose.

"Give me back my glove." The boy tried to flip Danny. Danny pressed down harder. "Put my glove back," the boy demanded.

"Right," Brian snapped at him. He tossed the glove behind his back to Rick.

That's when Rick saw the name written under the wristband. "*Lamar?* What kind of name is *Lamar*?" He threw the glove toward Danny's backpack. "Kiss your glove good-bye, *Lamar*."

"Get *off* me," Lamar said.

"You shouldn't be mean to animals," Danny told him. "Don't you know that? Say you're sorry and you'll never do it again."

Lamar didn't answer.

"You shouldn't be mean to animals. Say you're sorry."

"You look stupid in your underwear," Lamar answered. He twisted and turned but he was not nearly strong enough to move Danny off of him.

Brian came over and started kicking tufts of dirt down Lamar's neck. "You *like* it," Brian said, in the same tone Lamar had used for the kitten.

"Get *off* me."

Brian trickled dirt down Lamar's forehead and chin.

"Stop," Lamar yelled. "Underwear baby."

"What'd you say?"

"You're an underwear baby."

Rick shouted, "Underwear baby? *Fuck* you," although the boys knew they looked foolish with their wet underwear drooping down their backsides and it embarrassed them and their embarrassment fed their rage.

Brian put his foot on Lamar's chest and pressed down.

"Stop," Lamar cried.

"Harder," Rick called out. "Harder."

Danny stood up, but Brain kept his foot pressed against Lamar's chest. Lamar struggled to push him off. "Under*wear* babies."

"What a jerk," C.J. said.

"Underwear *babies,"* Lamar cried again. Brian pressed down harder.

Rick shouted, "Scare the shit out of him."

Brian pressed down harder still, kept his foot there for a few more seconds and then let Lamar up. When Lamar got to his feet, he spit in Danny's face.

Danny punched Lamar in the chest. Lamar spit again, at Brian this time.

"Fuck that." Brian grabbed Lamar and pinned his arms back. "Let's show him what happens when you spit in the face of an 'underwear baby.' "

"Yeah. Teach the jerk a lesson," Rick said.

"Underwear babies. Stupid-looking underwear babies." Lamar spat at Brian again.

Rick called out, "Let's kick the shit out of him."

"No," Brian said. "Take him to the rope."

"Yeah," Rick yelled. "The rope."

"The rope . . . the rope . . . take him to the rope . . ." Brian and Rick chanted.

"No," Danny told them. "Don't."

But Brian had already lifted Lamar off the ground and got ahold of his wrists and Rick had grabbed Lamar's ankles. They carried him to the embankment.

Lamar kicked and flailed. But the boys were much too strong. Lamar only managed to hurt himself.

"The rope . . . the rope . . ." Brian and Rick chanted again.

"The rope . . . the rope . . ." C.J. joined in.

Danny called out, "Let him alone. We've scared him enough."

"But we're *under*wear babies," Brian said.

"And he's a little jerk," Danny answered. "But let him go, anyway."

"*Hell* no."

C.J. took hold of Lamar's ankles while Brian picked up the end of the clothesline. He started tying a loop and did his best to make it look like a hangman's noose. Lamar squirmed and twisted, cursed at them and called them "underwear babies."

C.J. and Rick carried Lamar over to the tree. Brian placed the noose over Lamar's head.

"Don't," Danny yelled at them. *"Don't."*

Lamar stopped cursing, stopped calling them "underwear babies." He looked scared.

"What's the matter," Rick said. "*Cat* got your tongue?"

Lamar cried, "When I tell my dad, he'll find out where you live and kill you. He's a million times stronger than you."

Danny shouted at Brian, "Come on, you've scared him enough. Let him go."

"Hang him," C.J. screamed.

Lamar flung himself back and forth, shaking his head, knocking off his glasses. Brian held on to him.

"Let him go," Danny insisted. "You've made your point." Danny started coming over. "Come on. Take it off him."

"Whose side are you on?" Rick snapped at him.

Brian said, "He needs to learn a lesson."

Rick whispered, "Come on, Danny. He's only going to fall in and get wet. What's the big deal?"

"Then at least take off his sneakers," Danny said. "So they don't fill up with water."

"What?"

"Take off his sneakers so he can get back. We don't even know if he can swim."

"Fuck him," Brian growled.

"Strip the little jerk," Rick demanded.

"Just his sneakers," Danny said. "Just take off his sneakers so he can swim back." He pulled off Lamar's sneakers. Lamar screamed that he wanted to keep them on. He kicked and thrashed, his foot hitting Danny in the cheek and knocking him back.

"Fucking asshole," Rick shouted.

C.J. and Brian grabbed Lamar's shoulders and pulled him slowly back and then pushed Lamar over the edge, like a baby in a swing.

Lamar swayed above Otter Creek, just as the boys had less than an hour before. His small body looked even smaller as it glided in the air, arcing high above the water. He wasn't making "Tarzan" calls, or animal noises. He was screaming and crying for help, tugging on the rope, kicking his feet straight out as though he were trying to climb a ladder.

The boys waited for the rope to slip and for Lamar to splash into the pool. But the rope didn't slip. Lamar didn't fall in.

He wasn't screaming now. His hands weren't moving. His feet snapped stiffly at the knees and stopped kicking. His body twitched once, spastically, then sagged forward, swinging silently toward the embankment, then back over the water, back and forth, like a pendulum.

Danny was already shinnying up the tree and crawling out to the limb. He was frantic to pull Lamar in and untie the clothesline, but Brian's knot was holding firm, or maybe it was the way Danny's hands were shaking. He couldn't get Lamar untied.

Rick and Brian and C.J. could only stare dumbly, first at Danny and then at the odd way Lamar's neck was turned, at the blank and glassy look in his eyes.

Danny screamed at Brian to grab Lamar by the shoulders and shake him, "or *something,*" and he shouted Lamar's name over and over again. But Lamar just hung there limp and still, his eyes empty and unblinking. There was a stream of saliva dripping down his chin. His tongue stuck out from the corner of his mouth. His feet dangled above the ground like a doll.

"He's faking it," Brian said.

"No, he's not," Danny shouted, and climbed down from the tree.

"He *is,*" Brian insisted, and pinched Lamar's legs, slapped the bottoms of his feet. But Lamar didn't flinch.

"No, he's *not,*" Danny told him. "He's dead."

As one, the boys took a step back, then another, and hurried around the bend.

"It wasn't my fault," Brian declared. "I tied it just like before. It was an accident."

C.J. moaned, "What are we going to do?" and started walking in circles.

"It was an accident," Brian screamed. "It wasn't my fault."

Danny whispered, "Oh God. Oh fucking God." He crouched down and started rubbing his hands together, as though he had a chill.

Rick, his face bloodless, shouted, "What the fuck?" and started banging his head against the trunk of a tree.

C.J. muttered, "I fucked up . . . I fucked up . . . Oh God, I fucked up . . ." over and over, walking in circles.

Brian continued his refrain, "It wasn't my fault . . . It wasn't my fault . . . It was an accident. It wasn't my fault . . ."

Rick started swinging his arms back and forth. "What the fuck's going on?" he yelled at the sky.

"We killed him," Danny said softly, and kept on rubbing his hands together.

"It was an accident," Brian screamed. "Accidents happen."

"He's *dead,*" C.J. cried out.

"We killed him," Danny repeated.

"It was an *accident,*" Brian shouted back.

"I fucked up . . . I fucked up . . . Oh God, I fucked up . . ." C.J. wailed.

Danny was the first to go back and look. He stared at Lamar's limp body and the way his head hung and the dull look in his eyes.

"Get dressed," Brian shouted. He ran over to Danny and pulled him away. "We're getting out of here."

"What about *him*?"

"Just leave him. We're getting the fuck out of here."

"We can't do that. He's a human—" But Danny backed further away.

"Brian's right," Rick yelled. Sweat dripped off his face. "Let's get the fuck out of here."

Danny didn't move. He could only stare at Lamar, at the eyes.

"Danny's right," C.J. moaned.

"We're getting dressed and getting out of here," Brian told them. "Come on, before someone catches us." He grabbed Danny by the arm and pulled him away.

The boys dressed quickly, but they were compelled to take one more look at the body.

"Let's *go,*" Brian called out.

Danny told them to wait. He ran over to the bushes and started crawling around through the undergrowth, pushing through the garbage and stones.

"Get out of there," Brian called, but Danny wasn't listening. "Get out of there," Brian called again. But Danny worked his way deeper into the undergrowth until Brian went after him and pulled him out and they all walked, then ran, to the road leading away from Otter Creek. Danny was clutching the orange kitten to his chest.

XXIV

They went to Danny's house, the only house they knew would be empty.

Rick said be sure to lock the door.

"I can't lock the door. What if my dad comes home early?"

"I thought he's working till school's out?"

"I'm not locking the door."

"Why did we have to cut school?" C.J. groaned. His lips were trembling.

They went up to Danny's room. C.J. and Rick sat on the bed. Brian pulled a chair away from the desk, sat down and leaned forward, elbows on his knees.

Danny put the kitten on the bed between the two boys and sat in the corner on the floor. "Did you see his face?"

"Try not to think about it," Brian told him.

"I mean, like the way his eyes were all—"

C.J. was crying. Rick stared at Brian.

Danny pressed the side of his head against the wall. "He was lighter than us."

"What?" Brian said back to him.

"What?" Rick echoed.

"That's why the rope didn't slide off. You tied the knot like you would for us, but he didn't weigh enough."

"I fucked up," C.J. moaned to himself.

"*I* fucked up," Danny told him. "I couldn't get him down in time."

"*No*body fucked up," Brian shouted. "It was an accident."

Danny stared at him. "We have to tell someone. We have to do something."

"It was an *ac*cident," Brian repeated.

Rick said, "We were only trying to scare him."

"We're all going to go to jail," C.J. cried.

Brian began, "We're not going to—"

But Rick broke in, "You think we left fingerprints?"

"And *foot*prints," C.J. sobbed. "Involuntary manslaughter . . . Twenty-five years, at least." He couldn't stop crying.

Danny said, "Our folks won't let that happen to us. They'll know what to do."

"My dad'll know what to do," C.J. told him. "He'll *kill* me."

Rick shook his head. "My mom'll probably . . ."

"I don't fucking believe it," Danny said softly.

"We made a mistake," Brian said. "We did something wrong, but that doesn't mean— Oh shit. Can everyone just calm down for a minute." He looked at C.J. "Especially *you*."

"Yeah, C.J.," Rick said. "We all feel bad enough without you crying like—"

"We should all be crying," Danny said.

Rick started to speak, stopped and said, "I know, but come on, Danny. We can't . . ."

"We have to tell the police," Danny said. "And explain everything."

"And they'll send us to jail," C.J. wailed.

"What else can we do?" Danny answered. "We have to tell *some*one. We have to do *some*thing."

"You keep saying that," Brian snapped at him, "but all you want to do is make things worse."

"Things already *are* worse," C.J. pointed out.

"Shut up," Rick yelled at him.

"You shut up," C.J. yelled back.

"Everyone shut up," Danny said.

Brian said firmly, "Look. So far no one knows we were there, right?"

"But what about our fingerprints?" C.J. asked. "Like Rick said. And our—"

"No," Rick answered, "Brian's right. Who'll know they're *ours*?"

"So we won't do anything," Brian said. "We'll wait and see what happens."

"When he doesn't come home tonight, his parents are going to call the police," Danny said. "That's what's going to happen."

"Okay," Brian said. He walked over to Danny and glared down at him. "And if the police figure out it was us who was there—"

"And tell our folks we cut school?" C.J. cried.

"Are you an idiot?" Danny snapped at him. "We just killed a kid. And you're worried about cutting *school*."

"It was an accident," Brian repeated, and a moment later: "We can always say we were out there and found him like that but were too scared to talk about it or tell anyone." He was still looking only at Danny. "They'll believe us. It's not like we're *criminals* or anything."

"That's right," Rick agreed. "We're good kids. They'll believe us. Why would we want to kill anyone?"

"Exactly," Brian said. He walked back to the desk. "It's going to be all right. Come on, C.J., stop crying. We won't tell anyone and no one will know we were there. It's going to be all right. Two more weeks and school's over. When we come back, summer vacation, it'll be like it never happened."

"I don't know," C.J. cried. "I don't know if I can do it."

Brian told him, "If we don't, we'll all end up in deep shit. You've got to be strong. We all do."

"I can't do it," C.J. said.

"Yes you *can,*" Brian said. "We all can. We *have* to. We've always watched out for each other and we have to watch out for each other now."

Rick said, "We have to listen to Brian."

"But we *did* it," Danny said, "didn't we."

"It was an *acc*ident," Brian insisted. "We made a mistake. Shit, Danny, we can't let this ruin our entire *lives*. We've got to go to college and—"

"And do all the things we were talking about," Rick jumped in.

"Our parents *expect* us to," Brian said. "That's our *fu*ture. My folks—all of our folks are depending on us to live up to our potential and achieve—I mean, shit, this isn't our potential."

Rick said, "We can't let it ruin our lives."

"Or theirs," Brian added.

"Why not?" Danny answered. "It ruined that kid's life, and his parents' lives. *He* has no future."

"Because—" Rick began, but he ran out of arguments.

Danny said, "We have to do *some*thing. If we wait too long—"

"We aren't going to do anything or say anything," Brian told him. "We're just going to wait and see what happens."

Danny looked at the other boys but he didn't speak.

"It's our secret," Brian said. "We're in this together."

Rick said, "Brian's right."

"One of us falls apart and we're totally fucked," Brian told them. "Right, C.J.?"

"It's our secret," C.J. said. He stopped crying.

Danny shook his head and took a deep breath, and still he didn't speak.

"Okay," Brian said to him. "Tell the police or your dad or—or someone." The others looked at him. "No, for real. Admit that you killed that kid, then what? You've gotten the rest of us in trouble just because *you* want to tell."

"You want him to say he did it by *himself*?" Rick asked.

"That's not what he's talking about," Danny told him.

Brian said, "We have to all be in this together. Like always. We have to hang tough together." He stuck out his hand palm down. "We don't talk about it at school unless no one else is around. Not on the bus, not on the phone. No e-mail," he told Rick. "Your mom's always walking in on you."

"Sure." Rick put his hand on top of Brian's.

Brian turned to C.J. "We've always protected each other and we'll protect each other now."

C.J. put his hand in.

"It's our secret," Brian said. "We swear here and now not to tell a soul about what happened today." He looked at Danny.

Danny picked himself up and walked over to the boys. He put his hand on top of theirs.

It started raining late that same night, a hard, drenching rain that slowed to a steady drizzle by the following morning, Saturday, when C.J. came over to see Danny.

C.J. said he hadn't been able to sleep. "I was afraid to turn off the light. And if my dad hadn't started up with me, I would have left it on all night."

Danny didn't say anything about how he slept. He didn't say anything about the night before, not then and not later, when he and C.J. went over to Brian's house and huddled in the room above the garage. Brian and Rick looked like they'd had trouble sleeping, too.

Brian said, "I heard on the news they're looking for him." His eyes were red and he yawned while he talked. "I couldn't—"

"I heard it too," C.J. said.

"Do they know where he is?" Rick asked.

Brian snapped at him, "They're still looking for him, how can they know where he is?"

"Fuck you," Rick answered. "Okay?"

"There's still time to tell them," Danny said.

"No *way*," Brian told him.

"It's kind of creepy, isn't it?" C.J. said. "Being the only ones who know?"

"It's not creepy. It's cruel," Danny said. "Whether we tell anyone or not."

"Shit. It's not like we meant to do it," Brian said. "It wasn't part of a plan or anything. Why did he have to come out there, anyway?"

C.J. asked Danny, "What did you do with that little kitten?"

"Nothing. I've got to take it to the vet."

"Are you sure you want to do that?" Brian said. "What if someone recognizes it, you know, as being his?"

"I can't just let it— God, this really sucks."

Brian said, "Yeah."

Rick said, "Yeah."

Brian said, "But what else can we do?"

"You know," Danny said.

"We *can't,*" Brian told him.

"Come on, Danny," Rick said. "You know we can't."

C.J. started crying. He said, "This is awful. How did we ever . . ."

Then Brian remembered the glove and asked what Danny did with it.

"What glove?" Danny asked back.

"The *kid's* baseball glove? In your backpack."

"There's a glove in my backpack?"

"Rick put it in there."

"When?"

"Holy shit," Brian said, "where is it now?"

"It must still be in my backpack."

"Was your dad still home when you left?"

"Yes."

"What if he—"

"He never goes through my stuff."

"There's always a first time," C.J. said.

"We've got to get it," Rick said.

Danny told them, "He'll see us if we go there now. He'll be going to his office soon."

"How soon?" Brian wanted to know.

"Why didn't you tell me you put it there?"

"I thought you saw me."

"Like I have eyes in the back of my head."

"We fucked up big-time," C.J. moaned. He said he was afraid, that it was already too late. "Your dad probably found it by now." He told them they were all a bunch of screwups. "We fucked up big-time."

Rick said, "Stop saying things like that."

Brian told them, "Calm the fuck down. Everybody."

No one said anything after that. Every once in a while one of them would get up and look out the window or say, "It's not like we meant to . . ." Or, "Why did he have to . . ."

Brian said, "If we just stick together, we'll get through this. We've gotten through bad stuff before."

All of them looked sad and miserable. C.J. was unable to keep from crying.

Sometime after twelve, Danny pulled on his slicker, went outside, jumped on his bike and rode away in the downpour.

"Hey, Danny," Brian called from the window, "where're you going? Danny?" But Danny kept on riding.

Brian put on his jacket and ran downstairs. Rick and C.J. followed. They rode out to Danny's house and saw him sitting on the back porch with Mutt.

"Is your dad around?" Brian asked.

Danny shook his head.

"What about the glove?" Rick asked.

"I hid it."

The rain stopped early in the afternoon and it turned out to be a cool and bright day. Any other time, the boys would have headed over to Archer Field to shoot some hoops or biked out to the mall to meet up with their friends, or gone to Otter Creek. But today they sat together on Danny's back porch, in sickening silence, unable to tolerate the company of anyone else, not quite able to tolerate each other's. Brian's pep talks were making Danny angry. Rick snarled and told him Brian knew what he was talking about.

It was the same the following day, when they met in the room above Brian's garage. It was as though they felt obliged to stay together and did not trust themselves to be alone.

In school on Monday morning, Danny was more quiet than usual. C.J. did nothing but sulk. He could not make eye contact with anyone. Brian managed to talk to some of the other kids, standing by his locker, forcing a smile, or maybe it just looked that way to C.J., laughing uncomfortably at their jokes. Rick, close by Brian's side, was carried along by the force of Brian's personality. When they saw Danny, Brian and Rick stepped away from the circle and they all walked to their homeroom. C.J. was waiting for them. He pulled Danny aside and whispered,

"I'm going out of my mind with this thing. Do you feel if you don't tell someone you'll burst?"

Danny said, "All I know is, what we did was wrong and we should do *some*thing about it."

"But what?"

"I don't know. It's too late."

"You mean we're going to get caught, don't you?"

"No," Danny said impatiently. "I mean it's too late to do anything to change it."

"Are you scared?"

"I don't think so. I just feel all dark inside."

"I'm scared Brian's getting pissed at me."

"Don't worry about Brian. Worry about yourself. Worry about how you're going to live with this."

"I'm having nightmares about it."

"I can't even fall asleep long enough to have any."

"Yeah, nighttime's the worst."

"Being alone in the dark," Danny said. "I can see him hanging there, and the way he swung back at us and then— I can't stop thinking what he must have thought when it happened. I mean, you think you're scared, imagine what he—"

"I don't want to think about it." C.J.'s voice was shaking.

In the cafeteria, the four boys would sit together, doing their best to keep themselves separate from the rest of the kids.

Rick's eyes looked sunken, he was more restless than usual, popping out of his seat and quickly sitting back down, unable to keep his feet or hands still. "Do you think it shows?" he asked the others. "You know, do you think they can tell—"

"I think we look okay," Brian said, "you know, normal."

Rick said, "I mean, like my folks—my mom practically takes my temperature by the hour. She thinks I'm in *love*."

"What?"

"She says I seem different. She asked me if I was in love. So I'm going along with it."

Brian said, "Yeah, I know. My mom and dad think I'm worried

about Outward Bound and I'm like, 'Oh, maybe just a little.' They're taking me to Indianapolis next Saturday to buy gear for Hurricane Island." His voice sounded strained, and he kept glancing around the room while he spoke.

"At least they notice," C.J. mumbled. "My folks are totally oblivious."

"I just want school to be over so I can get out of here," Brian told them.

"What the hell are we *doing*?" Danny said. "How can we be sitting here talking like this?" His teeth were clenched. "We're all crazy." He jumped up and quickly walked out of the cafeteria.

When Danny wasn't on the bus Tuesday afternoon, Rick wondered if "maybe he's gone over to tell his dad."

C.J. was certain that Danny would never do such a thing. "He probably went home. He just wants to be left alone."

"What makes you so fucking smart?" Rick asked him.

Brian told Rick to "cut it out."

The boys stopped by the house but Danny wasn't there. They went looking for him, riding around town and across campus. There weren't any of Brian's assurances now or brave talk, only the solemn feeling of unreality, as though they were living a life more dangerous than any of them had been prepared for.

They found Danny's bike at the ruins and spotted Danny walking along the road by the river.

"What are you doing out here?" Brian asked.

"I wanted to be alone."

"I don't know if that's such a good idea," Brian told him. "Being by your—"

"I need to think."

"You don't want to get too inside your head," Rick warned him.

"Yeah. Come on, Danny," Brian said. "It's going to be okay."

"My dad told me that memory is what keeps people moral," Danny answered.

"What's that mean?" Rick asked.

C.J. said, "Being able to remember the bad things you do is supposed to keep you from doing them in the first place."

"Yeah, well, I wish I could forget it, at least for a little while," Brian said.

Rick nodded his head. "But still, Danny, I don't think your dad would want us to spend the rest of our lives in jail."

"That's not what—you still don't get it yet, do you?" Danny said.

"You know what I'm afraid of," C.J. said. "That it's totally a trick to catch us. I mean, like how they still haven't found him? What if they have, and the police know he was, you know—and they have a pretty good idea who did it and everything? What if—"

"Will you stop saying shit like that," Brian snapped at him. "This is bad enough without you—we're going to be all right."

But C.J. didn't stop. "Only they aren't sure. So everybody's decided not to tell, and they're just waiting to trap us, like a sting or something. When we least expect it, they'll close the trap."

"Stop it," Brian screamed. "Okay?"

"Yeah," Rick told him. "We're all paranoid enough without you making shit up."

"I can't take this," Danny groaned, and walked up the hill.

"Dan*ny,*" Brian called to him.

Danny didn't stop; and when he got on his bike and rode away, the boys got on their bikes and rode after him all the way to the house.

"Leave me alone," Danny shouted at them, and ran up the porch steps.

"Come on, Danny. Don't be like that. Come on."

Danny said, "Don't you see, we're wrong. We did something wrong."

"I know," Brian answered. "You're not the only one who can't sleep and eat and whatever . . ."

"Yeah," Rick said.

"But all we're worried about is someone telling," Danny said, "or someone finding out. Can't you—I don't know—it's more than—" He was about to sit down but walked to the back porch instead. The boys followed close behind. When Brian came around the corner, Danny grabbed him by the shirt. It was a threatening gesture, but Brian took it. Maybe he was too startled, or scared, to pull away.

"Whether we tell or not doesn't change anything," Danny said softly. "He's dead and we're alive. You were talking about our folks expecting us to do all that good stuff, well, what about this? Would they expect *this*? Maybe *this* is our *po*tential." Danny pushed him away. "We have to look people in the eye and pretend, and all we do—oh, fuck it and fuck us, too." Danny sat on the top step.

"We know, we know," Brian said softly, and sat next to him.

"Do you also know," Danny didn't look at him, but stared out at the field, "*how* we're going to get through it, because I don't. Instead of worrying about getting caught, I'm asking myself why *shouldn't* we get caught? We did it, didn't we? We're responsible for it, aren't we? We killed a little kid and all we care about is saving our butts."

"It was an *accident,*" Brian said.

"A mistake," Rick added.

"I'm talking about right now."

Brian said, "It's too late to do anything about it."

"What are we supposed to do?" Rick asked. "Walk into the police station and turn ourselves in?"

"There are other ways." Danny put his face in his hands. "What's the use?"

"Is he crying?" Rick asked C.J.

"I'm not crying," Danny told him. "I'm just frustrated."

"It's not like we feel anything different," Brian said. "But . . ."

"Just stop acting like everything's going to be okay," Danny told him. "Our lives are never going to be the same. And stop making me feel like a jerk because I can't act like you."

Brian put his hand on Danny's shoulder. "You're not a jerk."

"Hell no." Rick gripped Danny's arm. "If this is how you feel, we'll stand by you."

Danny looked up and nodded his head.

"Are you going to be all right?" C.J. wanted to know.

Danny said, sure, he'd be all right.

"You want to come over to my house for supper?" Brian asked.

"My dad's taking me out," Danny told him.

"You sure you're going to be—"

"I'm okay."

When the boys walked to their bikes, Danny stayed on the back porch.

"You're not a jerk," Brian called out.

The weather turned cooler on Wednesday, and when Danny dressed for school that morning he wore his sweatshirt. He told C.J., "I feel creepy wearing my baseball jacket." They were standing outside their lockers before classes started. Danny looked worn out. "I feel like I'm being pulled apart inside."

"I know what you mean," C.J. whispered back, but that's all he could say because Courtney Webster was gathering her books and looking around for something which she apparently didn't find. She winked at C.J., told him, "That heroin look you've got going is way cool." C.J. did his best to play along without encouraging Courtney to join the conversation, she winked at him a second time and when she left, Danny told C.J., "I can't describe it, but it's like having to choose something, and I don't know what it is."

"Like having to choose between us and everyone else?" C.J.'s entire body was shaking.

"It's more complicated than that. Like I don't know what the right thing is anymore. Like when I'm with my dad, I feel like I'm cheating or something. Only it's worse than that because I know better than to do what we're doing. I mean—" Danny shook his head. "I'm supposed to take responsibility for the things I do." His voice was tight and throaty. "And here I am, going along with . . . you know, Brian and Rick . . . when I know it's wrong and it will always be wrong."

"I know. It's like, if Brian told his mom and dad, they'd make excuses for him, figure out a way to make it the kid's fault, and find a way to clear him."

"Then pretend it never happened."

"And if Rick told his mom and dad, his mom would find a way to get money or something to the kid's folks, anonymously, of course, then get a great lawyer and send Rick to a psychiatrist for the rest of his life."

"And if you told your mom and dad?"

"My mom would fix herself a Prozac cocktail and my dad would work out a deal to fix it with the cops or bribe someone, then make my life a living hell for the rest of my life."

"If I told my dad," Danny said, "he'd make me do the responsible thing, whatever that turned out to be."

"But he'd stand by you, and help you through it. I'm sure of that."

Danny said, yes, he was sure of that, too. "But I know he would never let me walk away from it." He stuffed his books into his backpack. "Ever since I was a little kid and my mom left, it's like my dad and I—it's hard to explain. It's like my dad and I are supposed to behave a certain way, do certain things, even if we don't want to do them, so we'll be proud of each other." He shook his head. "That's not what I mean, exactly. But it's like there's some agreement we have to never let the other one down."

"I know what you're talking about."

"I've gone back on that, haven't I, C.J.?"

C.J. looked down at the floor and didn't answer.

"I'd rather die than do that."

"God, Danny, don't say it like that."

"I'm being pulled apart inside," Danny repeated, as though he hadn't heard C.J., as though he were standing there alone. "Not by Brian, but by *me*."

C.J. breathed, "Shit. How'd we ever get into this mess, anyway?"

"How are we ever going to get *out* of it?"

"Let's hope Brian's right and it'll all turn out okay."

In the cafeteria that day, Ian Baker, the shortstop on the baseball team, came over and asked Danny, "Are you still bummed about losing the game last week?"

"Who said I was bummed?" Danny asked back.

"I heard that's why you've been acting so weird lately."

"Who's acting weird?"

"If you want to know what I think," Ian said, "you better not take losing so hard or you'll never have the stuff to pitch winning ball. It's time you stopped acting like a freshman."

"Like I might ever give a shit what a pompous ass like you thinks, Baker." Danny got up from the table, dumped his tray in the trash and hurried out.

"What's up with him?" Ian said, and when no one answered, he went away.

From the cafeteria window the boys could see Danny walking across the basketball courts, his hands in his sweatshirt pockets, his head down. It looked like he was talking to himself.

C.J. said he was worried about Danny.

Brian said, "God, I wish school was over."

"Yeah," Rick answered.

"We better make sure he's all right," Brian told the others, but when they looked out the window again, Danny was gone.

On the bus ride home, Danny glowered at Brian. "What the hell kind of lies are you spreading about me?"

"What are you talking about?"

"Baker."

"I didn't say anything to Baker. I wouldn't—"

"Next time keep your mouth shut."

Brian leaned forward, his face inches from Danny's. "Danny, I didn't say anything to Baker. Honest."

When C.J. got off the bus, he could see Danny's face, tight and tense, staring blankly out the window.

That night, C.J. rode his bike over to the house. He found Danny walking aimlessly with Mutt through the field out by the backyard. The night was cool and Danny should have worn his sweatshirt or jacket, but he seemed unaware of the weather, unaware that he was shivering. C.J. mentioned how cold Danny looked. Danny wasn't listening. "I'm worried about us," was all he said.

"Us?"

"The four of us. Us. We. The boys who killed Lamar Coggin." Danny kept on walking and shivering. C.J. tagged along, not saying anything. "You see," Danny said matter-of-factly, "I'm alone here all night and I've got a lot of time to think and I've got it all figured out."

"Maybe you shouldn't be alone so much," C.J. said. "You can come over to my house anytime you like. Like now, even."

Danny ignored him. "Brian's going to survive this. And that worries me. Rick is going to survive it, too, because he does whatever Brian does. And that also worries me." C.J. thought Danny was making a joke, but when he laughed Danny did not laugh with him. "I'm worried about *you*, C.J."

"What are you talking about?"

"When I'm not here to take your side."

"Where are you going? Are you running away from home or something?"

Danny didn't answer the question, all he said was, "Brian's got Baker thinking things about me that aren't true. And I'm doing things that I know I shouldn't do. Hey, that rhymed." Danny laughed through his chattering teeth.

"Brian never said anything to Baker. Danny, you're acting weird."

"That's what I mean. You need me to remind you that it's okay to act weird sometimes."

"Okay. But I'm getting cold out here. Let's go inside."

"That worries me, too."

"That I'm getting cold? You're not making any sense."

"Is *he*?" Danny asked. "Just think, he's been out there all this time, in the rain and everything. He must be so cold and lonely."

"Who?"

"Lamar Coggin. Is he making any sense?"

"I don't—"

"He's still out there. They haven't found him yet."

"They must have."

Danny shook his head.

"You didn't go back there, did you?"

"We'd have heard. We'd know."

"Did you go back there, Danny?" C.J. realized he was shouting.

"I go back there every night. In my mind." Danny was speaking in a soft monotone. "I see him hanging there. It's like he's asleep all alone out there. It's funny. I can't sleep and that's all he does. It's like a trade-off, my sleep for his." They walked a little further into the field. Mist was rising off the ground like a veil. "We all know better and we still behave the way we do. Now can you see why I'm worried about us?"

"Let's go back to the house, it's cold out here."

"Funny, isn't it, how cold it's gotten these past few days. If it had been this cold last Friday we'd've never gone out to Otter Creek. Never gone swimming."

"I can't stay out here much longer."

"He's cold, too, you know."

"Stop talking about him. You're scaring me."

Danny rubbed the top of C.J.'s head and laughed. "Don't be scared."

Mutt found something to chase and Danny called to him and whistled.

"I had dinner with my dad tonight," Danny said. "He kept asking me why I wasn't eating. Why I looked so tired. I lied to him. What do you tell your folks when they ask why you aren't eating? Why you look tired?"

"They don't ask. I usually just eat with the twins and they don't give a shit about anyone." They walked a little further. "I'm worried about you, Danny."

"Worry about *you*. It's every man for himself." Danny whistled for Mutt a second time, turned and walked toward the house.

"What's that mean?" C.J. said, following along.

Danny picked up the pace, walking faster and faster through the plowed ground.

"What's that mean?"

But Danny didn't answer.

Back at the house, they sat upstairs in Danny's room.

"You feel like watching TV?" C.J. asked.

"I feel like sitting here."

"I could probably stay over if you like."

"Why?"

"I don't know."

"Do you think I'm acting weird, like Baker did?"

"No."

"We *should* all be acting weird. We *are* all acting weird if you think about it."

"What else can we do?" C.J. asked, a minute later.

"Do what you think is right. It's every man for himself."

"I wish you'd stop saying that."

"Go home. It's getting late."

At school the next day, Danny was standing under the stairwell softly calling C.J.'s name.

"What are you doing?" C.J. asked.

"I just want to apologize for last night." Danny's eyes looked dark and hooded. "I'm sorry I scared you like that." Overhead, the stomp and clatter of student feet drowned out his voice. Danny might have said, "I shouldn't have done it." Or, "I'm ashamed." And then he said, "I'm sorry."

"That's okay." C.J. managed a smile.

"I have something for you."

"Are you all right?"

Danny pulled his blue Hawaiian shirt out of his backpack. The shirt was balled up and full of creases. He thrust it into C.J.'s hand. "Take it."

"What are you doing?"

"Take it. Please. I want you to have it. Really."

C.J. said, "Thanks," because he didn't know what else to say.

More stomp and clatter and voices reverberating off the walls.

"Wear it at the lake this summer," Danny said. "It'll be way cool."

"Yeah . . . Cool . . ."

"Promise that you'll wear it for me this summer."

"Sure, Danny. But why—"

"You have to stand up for yourself. You have to do it without my help, C.J."

"What do you mean?" Danny was scaring him again. It was Danny's voice, the way his eyes homed onto C.J.'s face.

"You can't let them push you around."

"Let who push me around?"

"Like they push me around."

"Who's pushing you around?"

"You have to stand up for yourself. Even when it hurts."

"We'll stand up for each other. Together," C.J. said, looking for, expecting, some reassurance. But it wasn't there.

Danny stepped around him and walked up the stairs. C.J. called out for him to wait, but Danny only walked faster.

Danny wasn't in the cafeteria at lunchtime, and later in class, when the boys wanted to know where he'd been, Danny only said, "I had to take care of something."

The boys could not get him to tell them what "something" was.

When Danny got off the bus that afternoon, the boys went with him. "Not today," he told them. "Go on over to C.J.'s or something. I've got work to do."

"What kind of work?" Brian wanted to know.

Danny gave Brian a long look and said, "Things. Just *things*. Don't you ever have things to do? Doesn't anyone but me have things to do?"

Brian said, "Take it easy."

"You think I'm going to go back on my word?"

"Hell no. But you're our friend and you've been acting a little—"

"Weird?"

"No. Like you're not—"

"I have things to do."

"Things," Brian repeated.

"Things," Danny said under his breath, and headed home. "Things."

The boys kept a good distance behind, and if Danny knew they were following him, it didn't seem to bother him. He never turned around, he never looked back. He went inside the house, Mutt barked, a moment later the back door opened and closed and there was silence.

Brian told C.J, "I'm worried about him."

"I am too," C.J. said back. But that was all he would say. He didn't want to talk about last night or about this morning. He was trying to forget it, trying to convince himself that Danny would snap out of it. Talking about it to the other boys would only make it more real, and reality was not a friendly place these days.

Brian wanted to sneak inside "just to keep an eye on him." Rick and C.J. talked him out of it. Instead, they parked themselves in the corner of the porch beneath the living room window.

"He's really going to like this," Rick said, and rubbed his arms nervously. "Us spying on him."

"It's not spying," C.J. said.

"We just want to make sure he's okay," Brian explained.

"What's he doing in there?" Rick whispered.

"How should I know?" Brian whispered back.

Rick started to stand. Brian pushed him down.

A minute or two passed and the boys were feeling pretty foolish crouched against the side of the house. C.J. wanted to leave. He was sure Danny would find them and "go ballistic." But Brian said, "I want to make sure he's all right," and they stayed where they were.

A few more minutes passed. Then they heard Danny playing the piano, softly, gently. He played unself-consciously and relaxed, one song, then another, and another after that. It put the boys at ease, it comforted them. Their guilt and conflict had exhausted them, now they closed their eyes and rested while Danny played. Maybe he chose the music to soothe his own nerves. Maybe it was to give himself courage for what was to come.

The music, sad and lonesome to their ears, made the boys feel quiet inside for the first time since the day at Otter Creek; as though Danny were playing a lullaby just for them. One song, a momentary pause, and then another. One song to the next. Each played carefully and clean. The boys felt their breath catch in their throats.

C.J. began to sob, then Rick and Brian as the music played, coming at them, making them aware of the terrible thing they'd done until they could not bear what they were feeling.

First Brian stood, then Rick. C.J. remained. He said he wanted to listen for a few more minutes. Brian and Rick only nodded their heads, quietly swung themselves over the railing and walked away.

Danny never stopped playing.

C.J. sat and listened. He wasn't worried that Danny would find him. But Danny never stopped. One song to the next, the pace never varying, or the intensity. It was a beautiful and lonely sound. Or was it C.J.'s own loneliness? One song to the next, with hardly a moment's pause. One song to the next. One song to the next.

C.J. stayed until sunset. When he got up, Danny was at the door.

"I was waiting for the other guys to leave." Danny spoke softly, vacantly. "Do you want to come in now?" His voice, his presence, made C.J. uncomfortable.

"I better be going. Thanks." And C.J. walked home in the quickening darkness.

The next morning, Danny wasn't on the school bus, or at his locker when classes started, and when C.J. called the house after first period, there was no answer.

Brian called and there was still no answer. "Maybe he just wants to be alone for now."

At lunchtime, C.J. called, and Brian, then Rick. Each believing his touch would make the difference. But there was still no answer.

When the boys were told to meet at the Harrisons' house—Hal and Vicki Clarke sitting with Brian. Carl and Mandy Ainsley sitting with C.J., Rick sitting with Arthur and Celeste—they were sure they'd been found out. They drummed their fingers on the arms of chairs, their legs twitched and jiggled nervously. No one spoke, not even the adults, not for a minute or two. The boys assumed everyone was waiting for Danny.

When Arthur said, "Something terrible has happened," Brian

looked sharply at Rick, whose face had gone pale. C.J.'s stomach turned and he started gagging. Then Arthur told them Danny had killed himself. The boys broke down and wept.

"It was an accident," C.J. told Jack. "I should've told you—it was Brian's idea to go to your house—to see if Danny told—I mean—" He stared at the floor. "And when you started asking about . . ."

"You covered your lies with more lies."

C.J. nodded his head. "Then we heard that they thought Lamar killed himself, and when we came back from vacation we heard about that man they arrested and it's just like Brian said." He shifted uneasily. "I don't know—I mean, Brian never comes over—Dr. Owens," he asked, "what are you going to do?"

"I'm not sure."

Jack wanted to leave and he wanted to stay there all day. He wanted to grab C.J. and hug him for how pathetic and broken he looked. He wanted to beat the shit out of him and the rest of the boys. He wanted to take control of the situation. He wanted to fall apart. He wanted to tell the boys' parents, point fingers, lay blame. He wanted to decide what was best. He wanted to hide. He wanted to tell Marty. He wanted to be left alone. He wanted to call his father. He wanted to dream about every good day he'd had with Danny. He wanted it all to happen simultaneously and he wanted none of it. He was overwhelmed by all there was to do and how little could be done. He could feel himself being pulled in a hundred directions at once—being pulled apart. It was a suffocating feeling, as though a blanket had been thrown over his head—as though a plastic bag . . .

Jack got up from the chair. His shirt was damp with sweat and made a thick adhesive sound as he pulled it away from his skin. "What the hell time is it, anyway?" He didn't wait for an answer, he walked to the door. "Your accident was no accident, was it? You were trying to kill yourself. There's been too much of that." He told C.J., "Try to remember Danny as he really was."

The sunlight hurt his eyes. His body ached. When he walked to his car each step made his head pound. If there is such a thing as mental stasis, he had attained it. He experienced no cognition, there was nothing left to think, and if there were, it would have served no purpose. He had nothing left to lose and nothing remained to be saved. There was nothing he could feel in this moment that he hadn't felt all summer. There was nothing left to consider, no insight to lean on, no consolation. There was nothing to deconstruct, reconstruct, churn, dissect or analyze. There was nothing left but this: it was his little boy standing in the cold field. It was Danny alone out there.

XXV

The sun was shining above the ruins. Jack could smell the river in the air. He'd been sleeping in his car and was awake now only because Marty was shaking him. The top of the car was down, Marty was leaning over the passenger seat and smiling.

Jack groaned, "Oh shit."

Marty seemed to be out of breath. He asked, "What are you doing out here?"

"Sleeping."

"I guess you were." Marty smiled again.

"What are *you* doing out here?" Jack squinted into the sunlight.

"Running. I saw your car and I—" His face was wet and sweat had soaked through his T-shirt. He was still out of breath. "Are you all right?"

"Working late. I was too tired to drive home so I stopped to take a nap."

"Strange place to take a nap."

Jack didn't acknowledge what was surely meant to be a question. He shaded his eyes and watched Marty's face. The face of his friend from the summer. The athletic-solid face that three months ago had done something remarkable and courageous with its eyes and expression when Jack needed to see that in the face of anyone who chose to come to his door. Now the face was giving Jack a thorough going-over and the expression was neither remarkable nor courageous, just curious.

Marty might have had a quick smile at the first sight of Jack bunched up like the day's dirty wash, but he was looking at him slowly now, trying to get a good read, and he didn't seem at all amused by what he was facing. He pressed his lips tightly together, gave Jack a second looking-over, although he did a good job of making it look like nothing more than a quick glance, grunted "Hmm," softly and unhappily. "I guess I'm a little surprised to find you sleeping in your car, and especially out here."

Jack shrugged his shoulders innocently and offered no explanation. The sun was hot and the air warm but he felt cold to the bone.

Marty wiped his forehead on his sleeve. "You're sure you're okay?" His voice held that familiar tone of concern; and when Jack didn't answer, Marty leaned against the car door, looked across the park as though what he wanted from Jack lay among the broken bricks and Queen Anne's lace, or might be found riding downriver with the fallen branches. "Being here makes you feel close to Danny, doesn't it?"

Jack answered yes, it made him feel close to Danny, but that was all he said.

Marty waited a moment, then gave Jack another slow look, rested his arms on the car door, thrust his head slightly forward, looked straight into Jack's eyes, then down at his clothes, and made another pass at the eyes because it must not have been enough of an answer and Marty didn't seem to know what to do about it. Not that the expression on his face was the expression of someone looking for a lie, or maybe he hadn't started out looking for it but wound up looking nonetheless, the way you start rummaging through the attic looking for the dusty old yearbook with the goofy pictures and puerile sentiment, then you notice the sagging cardboard box and suddenly you're digging through the baby clothes and the tarnished trophies. Or you're down in the basement trying to find your old lecture notes. Only you don't know the dangers of your determination, and you may not be prepared for what's lying around down there, which is what Jack wanted to tell Marty, his friend from the summer who had no reason to think anything had changed from last week, or yesterday. His friend from the summer, who was working on the old assumptions. Who said what a friend from the summer would say. Expected the answers a friend from the summer would expect. And when there were no answers, or not the kind of answers to satisfy him, Marty couldn't help but be a little curious.

"I guess with school about to start you've been playing a bit of catch-up."

"That's right."

"And you're—"

"I'm all right. Really. Just a late night."

Marty kept looking him over but he couldn't walk away, not without knowing more than he started with. Not without seeing what made the cabinet wobble.

Jack wondered what Marty would think if he told him his cautionary tale about what rummaging through cartons and cabinets gets you; about finding out more than your expectations prepared you for. What would Marty do? Would he call off the search or would he keep looking, thinking there was nothing he didn't want to know, nothing he wasn't prepared to find?

"I'm all right."

"Well, I've got to tell you, you look—"

"Just hard work," Jack said, working a smile.

"Yeah. It's like that sometimes. But I have to say, seeing you out here like this. You had me worried for a minute." Marty was still looking.

"You have more important things to worry about, even for a minute."

I don't know about that." Marty said, "I guess I've felt protective about you for these past few months, so if I'm overstepping the bounds—if being back at work's too much too soon for you and you feel like talking about it—"

"It's nothing. Nothing like that. I was too tired to drive, so I stopped and fell asleep." That was all the truth he could offer.

"Fair enough." Marty put his hand on Jack's shoulder. "But we've never pulled our punches before so let's not start now, okay?"

Marty was ready to ride to the rescue. It was only that. He hadn't been looking for the lie at all. He was only doing what he'd been doing all summer. He was only working on summer assumptions.

Jack wondered if he could tell Marty that Danny had killed that little boy? Could he tell Marty about accidents and expectation? Isn't that what friends were for? Could he tell him that Danny was driven mad. Tell him, "I need you to help me protect my son." Would Marty help him protect Danny even in death, especially in death? Would he know a way out of this? Would he help or would he turn cop? Would he do his duty?

Jack had the urge to say, "This is what you're looking at." To tell him, "This is what you're seeing. This is why you found me here this morning."

He wanted to tell him because it was Marty, who babysat him through his compulsions. Who said, "Go easy on yourself," when Jack was beating himself to a pulp. Who sat on the curb with him through the long, hot night. Who sat with him at lunch and cocktails and talked about love and marriage and all the things that can go wrong. Jack wanted to fall back on Marty the way he had all summer. He wanted to tell him all about Danny and C.J. and Rick and Brian. Isn't that what friends were for? He would say: "Danny and his friends killed Lamar Coggin." He would say: "This is your chance to save Joseph Rich and stick it to Hopewell at the same time. Only sticking it to Hopewell has nothing to do with it, does it."

Jack could feel the words and the pulse of energy driving them: "Let me tell you why you found me here . . ." Maybe that's what he was going to say, or maybe he only thought it was when he turned toward Marty, who had a look of expectation on his face, as though this were just another morning; an expression Jack had spoken to since the day Marty appeared at the house, an expression he could speak to now, if he looked at nothing else, if he didn't stop to take the measure of his words. With less effort than it took *not* to speak, he could swallow hard and say, "The hell with it. Let me tell you why you found me here," looking only at the expression, listening only to the voice that held that familiar tone of concern—"Can I trust you, Marty? Can I trust you to protect my son?"

But Jack couldn't get himself to speak. All he could do was stare back in silence and feel sour inside. All he could do was pity Danny, who stood shivering in the night and felt Lamar's dead chill. All he could do was pity Marty when he leaned against the car, in the neighborly way he'd learned to do as a boy, and gave Jack another looking-over; because this was no way to treat a friend. Or, Jack wondered, was it more than just protecting Danny? Was he also protecting Marty? By his silence, was he protecting Marty from having to make the same choice Danny had to make—the same choice Jack had to make? Was that why he couldn't say it, because he didn't want Marty to have to make the choice? Or was it because he didn't know what Marty would choose and he was not about to put him to the test, even if Marty had passed a summer's worth of tests already. Or was it because Marty also had a summer's worth of expectations, expectations of Jack Owens and what Jack Owens expected of Marty Foulk and, doubtless, what Marty Foulk expected of himself?

Or, Jack wondered, was he simply protecting himself?

Marty didn't say anything. If he was giving Jack time to think things over, then Jack would take it. He raised his eyes to the ragged rows of hemlock and oleander that grew along the edge of the road, the weeds that inhabited the ruins, the trampled grass and wildflowers at the top of the hill where Danny had died.

Marty was getting ready to ride to the rescue but there was nothing left to save. There was hardly enough of Jack to feel the shame of his deception. Hardly enough to be aware of what was missing—Anne had said, "The absence of anything, some element, creates the presence of something else." Jack wondered what was present in the absence of his shame. "You weren't being intrusive," was all he managed to say.

Marty nodded his head. "Listen, I've got to get over to the station, but I'll take a quick shower and buy you breakfast."

"I've really got to get some sleep."

"What the hell was I thinking?" Marty took a few steps back. "I'll give you a call later. We'll talk." And he began running slowly across the sorry grass toward the road.

Jack watched, expecting, at any moment, for the morning light to telescope and slowly fade to black, not like Chaplin's tramp, more like the samurai, with only his handful of rice and code of honor for company. Or Virgil Tibbs hopping the train out of Sparta, Mississippi, leaving Bill Gillespie sadly behind. Shane riding off into the big sky and into the child's consciousness.

"Hey," Jack called out. "Hey. Wait a minute." He drove up the road and shouted, "I can't let you leave like that. I'll drive you back to the station."

Marty stopped running and waited for him. "I'd like that," he said, and got in the car.

They crossed the railroad tracks and rode down Third Street. They were silent now, like the day at the chicken shack when they were more strangers than friends. They were silent until they passed the county jail, where a crowd of people, three deep, was picketing, carrying posters and banners and bigger-than-life photos of Lamar Coggin with "He Could Have Been Your Son" printed across his chest in large black letters. And: "He's Everyone's Son." And: "To Die in Vain?"

"What's all that?"

"They're going to make sure Rich's public burning comes off without a hitch," Marty said, unhappily.

Jack stepped on the gas and quickly put the crowd behind them. "Does he have any chance?"

"If he gets a good enough lawyer, stranger things have happened. My guess is he doesn't."

"He can always appeal, can't he? I mean, if they find him guilty."

Marty glanced over at him but said nothing.

When Jack stopped in front of the police station, Marty slid out of the seat, said, "Thanks for the lift," headed inside, stopped and said, "How about if I sneak out later and take you up on that movie?"

"Fair enough." And Jack drove away.

XXVI

The morning paper was on the front porch. There were three messages on the answering machine. Mutt wanted to go out.

The world continued heaving and pitching through its daily rounds, delivering the news, leaving phone messages, standing at the back door barking. Jack could watch only as a stranger, like the survivor of a car wreck who walks away unscratched, stunned yet alert, oblivious yet focused. Except Jack had no focus, he was alert to nothing.

He opened the back door but did not stop to wait for Mutt to plunge through the verdant soil and hop the fence. He couldn't look at the field where Danny had made his decision to die.

He didn't play the messages. He had spent his summer afraid of what the answering machine might bode, fearing *What next?* Now he was not capable of fear. There was no *next*. There was nothing in the future to be afraid of. And there was nothing in the past to look back on, not without following it to this day. He was the man from the past whose past had forsaken him and whose future held no consequence. It was the morning after and all that remained was what remained to be done, methodically, with the attention to detail that Dr. Owens was known for. Pack just enough clothes for one suitcase. Leave room in the car for photographs from the Danny wall. Select a dozen books . . .

He went up to his bedroom to get the box with Anne's orange button and carried it with him while he performed these last rites. The call to the phone company to cancel service, the utilities to turn off the lights and shut off the gas—stopping to watch the sunlight bend on the yellow windowsills in the kitchen. The final walk-through, past the furniture, the piano, the art, the scattering of his life, which did not flash across his mind the way it does for a drowning man.

He was thinking that this was not the way he imagined he'd leave his house. It wasn't supposed to happen until Danny was a young man, out of college, living somewhere else—Jack had always imagined Danny would move back east, to New York, back to where he was born. Danny would have a girlfriend, someone not from around here, someone he'd meet after college, with no ties to Gilbert or Indiana. She would be smart and sweet in a way that was never pretentious. She wouldn't try to impress Jack with how much she loved Danny, although she would love him very much—he'd see it in the way she kept herself out of Danny's good-bye to his father and his good-bye to the home where he had lived and which had kept him safe. Danny wouldn't be ashamed to give Jack a hug and Jack would kiss him. Then they would no longer live here together, and it would be so damn bittersweet that Jack would cry, not in front of Danny, but later, when he was alone, and again when he sold the house and moved out. Jack had always thought he'd go west. On the map the land looks endless. It makes you think you can't go wrong with so much of America to choose from. Or maybe he thought he'd go west because he had no history there, no past. Or maybe because it's that place in your mind you call "Away."

But Jack wasn't crying now. He simply kept to his work, the final task. He retrieved Lamar Coggin's baseball glove from the basement.

He thought about Danny trying to decide, "Which is more important, Dad, honesty or loyalty?"

And where did he learn that? "From you," Jack said softly.

After he packed the car, got Mutt settled down—just as he had done countless times when he and Danny were leaving for vacation—Jack dropped the baseball glove on the front seat and held onto the wooden box, like a traveling companion, like a child. He sat still for a minute longer, looking at the house, the graceful wraparound porch, the swing sitting motionless. The house where Anne did not want to live and where he'd taken Danny to try to undo the damage done to him.

Jack listened while the wind rushed softly through the trees and the birds sang. He could not imagine never again hearing these birds singing outside these windows.

He drove along Main Street where the sulfur and sunlight turned the air sepia, like an old daguerreotype photograph or a silent movie, and the rose tint and warm brown hues looked so comfortable you wanted to crawl in, pull them over your head and hide; where the old-timers hobbled, wrinkled and weathered like old leather. Jack drove toward the river, past the ruins and across the nameless bridge, and headed west away from Gilbert, away from his home.

Tonight, in some motel off the road, he would lie on a strange bed with an unfamiliar pillow and the unfamiliar motel smell in his nose, the impersonal smell of impermanence. He would call his father and tell him he'd quit his job. He would lie about the reasons. He would lie because there was no truth anymore. Jack would not call Lois and he would not call Stan. He would not call Marty, who of all people would understand why he couldn't make the call. They would have to draw their own conclusions, it no longer mattered.

Robbie would wait in the office, dutifully, until he was told that Dr. Owens was not coming back.

Dr. Owens was leaving no doubt of his abandonment and his failure. His final act was to kill Dr. Owens, homicide and suicide. Kill the mythology of Dr. Owens, who was not golden, and who did not have the touch, who could not make things right, and could not undo the damage. Kill the mythology of Anne Charon, his mythology of Anne Charon, who was the creation of his hubris and desires, after all.

But he would not harm the mythology of Danny Owens, who played the piano and pitched his team to the semifinals and . . . And who would always be "the boy who killed himself out by the ruins. Nobody knows why."

But Jack knew why, and the three boys knew, while their parents were spared. While Joseph Rich was put on trial for his life.

They were sitting in the loft on Crosby Street. Outside it was cold and the early October dark was settling in. The streetlights were glowing the urban yellow that streetlights glow in New York. Anne was lying with her head on Jack's chest. She had that arousing musky scent, paint and turpentine, perspiration and perfume.

She said, "I went to the doctor today."

"And?"

"He says that if we're going to end the pregnancy, we should do it within the next two weeks." She turned her head and looked into Jack's eyes. "It isn't like we won't still be us? If we keep it?"

"Just *more* of us." Jack combed his fingers through Anne's hair.

"That's what I've been thinking. The baby would be us, and not some stranger. *Our* baby." She touched his hand with the tips of her fingers. "And we can raise it *our* way. We don't have to leave the city if we don't want, or even this loft. Things are going well enough for us now, don't you think? With the gallery and your work? I want to keep it, Jack. At least, I'm pretty sure I do." She sounded neither excited nor afraid.

"I'm pretty sure, too," he said. "I think deep down I've always wanted to. I just had to be sure we both wanted the same thing."

"I know." She nuzzled her face in his neck. "Oh, Jack, the way we love each other and get on so well, it won't be a problem." She lifted her face and kissed him. "If there are any two people who can make this work, it's us. Don't you think?"

ACKNOWLEDGMENTS

I have been fortunate to know many special people who all had a direct, or indirect, influence on the writing of this book. My first thanks goes to my brother Lawrence A. Saul, a sweet and wise man. And my love and admiration to Joy Harris, a great friend and a great agent.

Sheron J. Daily has been both friend and lifetime teacher. Marcia and William Braman have given me their subtle, gracious support. Rose Tardiff taught me what it is to love a child. My thanks to Melissa Tardiff, who shared her experience, and her daughter, with me. Louisa Ermelino, fellow writer, has been a strong shoulder to lean on. The talented Robert Sabbag never stinted on encouragement. Thanks to Paul White, who makes it easy to be his friend, always. I owe much to Jane B. Supino, whose insights are treasures. Sherill Tippins was a great resource. I am grateful to Nancy Yost, who was there at the beginning. Holly Braman and Mary Braman have always offered their good cheer and patience. Thanks to Jacqueline Mandia and the Little Red School House. And thanks to Michael Morrison, a gentleman and true aristocrat of publishing.

I can't thank enough my extraordinary editor, Jennifer Brehl, because I wouldn't know where to start. I do feel incredibly lucky to have found, and been found by, her. And I can't begin to thank my wife, to whom this book is dedicated, because I wouldn't know where to stop.

About the author

About the book

Read on

Insights,
Interviews
& More . . .

About the author

Meet Jamie M. Saul

© Deborah Lopez

In a recent interview with Mark G. Gibson, associate director of communications at Saul's alma mater Indiana State University, the author talked a little bit about himself. Here is an excerpt from that interview.

“*Light of Day* unfolds in the fictional western Indiana town of Gilbert, a mythical setting that draws its roots from Saul's college days at Indiana State University.”

IN *LIGHT OF DAY* Jamie M. Saul tells the story of a college professor coming to terms with devastating personal loss. The story unfolds in the fictional western Indiana town of Gilbert, a mythical setting that draws its roots from Saul's college days at Indiana State University in Terre Haute, Indiana.

The native New Yorker studied English and graduated with a bachelor's degree. Memories of time spent crossing the grassy quadrangles of the university campus, the whistles of trains passing through town on their way to destinations unknown, and visits to Terre Haute's Fairbanks Park on the banks of the Wabash River were inspiration for Saul's Gilbert. But while memories of Terre Haute laid the foundation for the book's setting, the writer's imagination provided the infrastructure.

"Gilbert, Indiana, is not Terre Haute, nor was it meant to be," Saul contends. "But it incorporates elements of Terre Haute. I wanted to place a story in that kind of setting and have the town almost become a character in the story."

The Midwest captured Saul's imagination as an eighteen-year-old. Growing up in the Bronx, Saul attended Dewitt Clinton High School, an all-boy's public school that educated James Baldwin, Burt Lancaster, Tony Curtis, Neil Simon, and Richard Avedon, among others. At the urging of a college advisor Saul picked Indiana State as his institution of choice.

"I think that coming from New York City to Terre Haute was a very good experience," Saul says of his college decision. "I managed to appreciate the history of the town and was really taken by it."

While American artists, writers, and musicians have long sought inspiration in New York's vibrant, sprawling metropolis, this teenager wanted to experience America beyond the borders of the five boroughs. And Saul thought the best place to do that was in the nation's heartland.

"I felt, even at the age of eighteen, that New York City could be very provincial. I just wanted to get away. And somehow for me the Midwest was America, and I really wanted to see America. I wanted to see what was beyond the Hudson River."

For Saul, Terre Haute was America. ▶

Meet Jamie M. Saul *(continued)*

Eugene Debs came from Terre Haute. So did Theodore Dreiser. Saul recalls reading Dreiser's *Sister Carrie* and thinking it was a revelation.

Saul once hitchhiked to St. Louis "just because it was St. Louis. It was America and I wanted to see it," he says. "I knew this and I didn't know that, and that's how you learn."

Saul spent a summer after college working in maintenance at a summer stock theater in Boothbay Harbor, Maine. He then returned to New York, where he got a job as a copy boy at *Time* magazine. Through connections made at *Time* he found freelance work writing for magazines like *People* and *Playboy,* and taught creative writing as a guest professor at Yale University, all the while keeping alive a desire to write a novel.

The process wasn't as simple as "sit down and write it," but the result is *Light of Day.*

"It's about a relationship between a father and son," Saul says of the book, "and it's about how a person can do everything right and it can all go wrong through no fault of his own. It's just the nature of life. But it's really a book with a focus on ambivalence and irony."

Another theme of the book is the reality that "we are our memories," Saul adds. "Memories are what make us moral, but memories are also what make us human. Without them we'd have no bearings, we wouldn't know who we are, we wouldn't know why we like the things we like, and we wouldn't know why we fear the things we fear."

Saul now lives in Manhattan. He is working on a second novel.

"Right now it's a love story," he says tentatively. "We'll see what happens."

"Saul once hitchhiked to St. Louis 'just because it was St. Louis.'"

Writing *Light of Day*

I REALLY DON'T KNOW WHY I wrote *Light of Day.* I don't have children. I've experienced very little of what I write about in the novel. While I was interested in the character I named Danny Owens and wanted to explore the reasons he might have had for killing himself, I was really starting with a tabula rasa and slowly filling in the blanks. It was very much like an improvisation: establish a premise, then create actions around that premise.

I tried to structure *Light of Day* as organically as possible, starting with the opening scene establishing the motifs of time and memory. The past is personified as the decrepit remains of life. Old men limp down the street. The air is filled with sulfur, a remnant of the burning coal that fixes sunlight in sepia tones like a daguerreotype—daguerreotype being one of the earliest methods of photography. I follow the transit of this theme to the steadily decaying ruins and to the river, which is both a symbol of resurgence and destruction, past time and future time; its rank and humid air is slowly destroying the ruins, the broken "monument to a past that was, if not efficient, certainly ambitious." We can also say this about Jack and Anne in their lives and relationship.

Old-timers limp with age. Sulfur ages the air right before your eyes. Ruins of an abandoned Depression-era project rise at the river's edge. Rivers, like one's memory, like one's past, flow with the detritus of time and

“It was very much like an improvisation: establish a premise, then create actions around that premise.”

decay. The past was never as wonderful as we remember. It is old bones and desiccation, something we manage to survive or transcend; in Jack's case it is something that holds the seeds of his own destruction.

Jack explains to Danny that memory is what makes people moral. Memory is also what connects us to our humanity, to who and where we are and from whence we come. Without memory, without our pasts, we have no frames of reference for what we feel, what we love, what we fear. Everything in this story refers to the past and remembrance; even when Jack is looking forward, he is looking back: "There would come a time when he would look back at that moment." He calls himself "the man from the past." Even when he leaves town and drives into the future, he looks toward the past.

In keeping with this theme, the structure of the story reflects the workings of memory. Time is broken up into asymmetrical and nonlinear pieces because this is how our memories work. I wanted what we know of Jack and Anne and Danny, the discovery of who they are and were, to unfold gradually and build toward a complete picture; I hope this makes for a more interesting narrative.

While the baseball references are few, I like to think they are important. The game of baseball is about getting home safely; Jack certainly tries to provide his son with a safe home in which to live and grow up. Baseball figures prominently in Danny's life. He nearly pitches his high school team to the championship: a near miss in a novel filled with near misses. There's a scene during the ▶

“Everything in this story refers to the past and remembrance; even when Jack is looking forward, he is looking back.”

annual softball game that Jack organizes for Danny and his friends: Jack's current love interest Maggie Brighton stands on third base, ready to "come home," only to be quite literally stranded.

And then there's Marcel Duchamp. Duchamp was one of the great artists and art philosophers of the modern era. He was very generous in sharing information, telling what he knew about art and perception. By so doing Duchamp lifted the lid on the artist's tricks that create the illusion of a third dimension on a two-dimensional surface, which is what painting, photography, and film really are. Duchamp attempted to demystify, to explain why we see what we see. Paradoxically, Duchamp is one of Anne's heroes; demystification also runs counter to what Jack is about. He creates mythologies about Anne, about Danny, and about himself and his life.

I reference Pablo Picasso's famous *Guernica* when Jack has a dream in which he lifts his head in a silent scream. This is also the final scene in the 1965 film *The Pawnbroker*; the character played by Rod Steiger falls to his knees on a street in New York's Harlem and lifts his head in a silent scream (Steiger's performance in *In the Heat of the Night* is also referenced). The actor said in an interview that he was thinking of *Gurenica* when he decided not to scream audibly in the film.

Anne refers to the short story "For Esmé—with Love and Squalor," by J. D. Salinger. The eponymous Esmé is a British girl dealing with

"Duchamp attempted to demystify, to explain why we see what we see. Paradoxically, Duchamp is one of Anne's heroes; demystification also runs counter to what Jack is about."

the horrors of World War II. I like to think this is a story that would have attracted Anne while growing up in postwar England.

Ambivalence, irony, and paradox figure prominently in this novel. Jack Owens and his wife Anne Charon are ambivalent about having a baby. After Danny is born, Anne's series of paintings *One foot on the platform, one foot on the train* reflects her ambivalence and conflict about being the mother Danny deserves and the artist her talent demands; Anne considers leaving Jack and Danny; Jack too has his moments of ambivalence. He wishes he could walk away from the responsibilities of being Danny's father. Would his life have been more satisfying if Danny had never been born? He even expresses some ambivalence about his relationship with Anne; Jack wonders if even without Danny's birth the marriage would have caused conflict for Anne.

The name Anne Charon references Charon the Boatman of Greek mythology, who transports souls across the river Styx to the land of the dead. Jack refers to the Wabash River's stygian journey. Anne, of course, will give birth to a son who kills himself.

Of the many paradoxes I include in *Light of Day,* two I'm quite fond of involve Jack. Believing that he has reconciled who he was before Danny's death and who he has become since, he considers: "This is what it's like when you aren't who you are." The other paradox transpires during the night scene in Jack's backyard when he imagines the huge ocean ▸

"Of the many paradoxes I include in *Light of Day,* two I'm quite fond of involve Jack."

Writing *Light of Day* *(continued)*

liner rising in the field: Are the passengers laughing or calling out for help? Are they safe or in danger? There is no way of telling. Yet Jack cannot dismiss the magnificence of the vessel, the magnificence of all the paradoxes that comprise a lifetime. There is, of course, the irony that the very moral guidance Jack provides Danny is the same moral guidance that creates Danny's irreconcilable conflict. Jack is someone who always does "the right thing," yet everything goes terribly wrong. Jack betrays that same morality in the end. He leaves the falsely accused Joseph Rich to go to jail, allows Danny's friends to remain unpunished, and finally betrays Dr. Owens. Jack's answer to Danny's question "which is more important, honesty or loyalty?" creates a mythology surrounding Danny that does not include the accidental murder of Lamar Coggin. Remaining loyal to Danny necessitates the destruction of Dr. Owens.

Film References in *Light of Day*

I COULD HAVE COMPILED A LIST of books and movies that influenced me, but it is much more in my nature to explain why I feel things are important and why everyone should feel the same way about them. I discovered this facet of my personality when I was a guest professor at Yale, thanks to wonderful students who taught me as much about myself as I taught them about the craft of writing.

Since Jack is a professor of film studies, there are many references to cinema in *Light of Day,* some a little more subtle than others. When Jack is in his office he sees the slow appearance of students on the quad as a time-lapse film. Jack uses the words "not as a stranger" (the title of a film made in 1955 starring Robert Mitchum) to refer to Marty Foulke. And there are the more obvious movie references, most of which have something to do with memory and the past. If *Light of Day* is "about" anything, it is about how memory and the past keep us connected to what we are and to what and who we love.

Blade Runner (1982), an extraordinary science fiction film by Ridley Scott and one of Danny's favorite movies, is all about how memories and a past are what make us human. Without them we are empty, robots, literally replicants, whether spawned from the laboratories of geneticists or from the wombs of our mothers.

In the Heat of the Night (1967), a film that ▸

"Since Jack is a professor of film studies, there are many references to cinema in *Light of Day,* some a little more subtle than others."

holds racism and bigotry up to ridicule, is a great "buddy movie" about characters with disparate personalities who become good friends, much like Jack and Marty Foulke.

Last Year at Marienbad (1961), one of the films Jack and Anne see after they return from France, is also a film about memory. The great auteur Alain Resnais plays fast and loose with events of the past. Incidents recalled by the narrator may or may not have happened; if they did happen they may not have happened like this, and even if they did happen like this perhaps they didn't happen at Marienbad. This theme also reflects Jack's memories of the life he shared with Anne. Was it as idyllic as Jack remembers? Or was it just a part of Jack's mythology of Anne? Was Anne as wonderful as Jack remembers or the creation of his "hubris and self-image?"

Federico Fellini's film *Amarcord* (1973) is referenced in the night scene when Jack imagines the huge ocean liner rising magically and majestically in the field behind his house. Such a ship also magically and majestically appears in Fellini's film, the title of which translates to "I remember." *Amarcord* is also a film about the friendship of four teenage boys.

"Federico Fellini's film *Amarcord* (1973) is referenced in the night scene when Jack imagines the huge ocean liner rising magically and majestically in the field behind his house."

Along with the films already mentioned there are a few more that need to be noted, if only because they've been subtle influences on my sensibility and you might like them as well:

- *My Man Godfrey* (1936): "All you need to start an asylum is an empty room and the right kind of people."

- Anything directed by Preston Sturges, but most certainly *The Great McGinty* (1940), *Sullivan's Travels* (1941), and *The Lady Eve* (1941).
- Billy Wilder's *Some Like It Hot* (1959), starring Tony Curtis, Marilyn Monroe, and Jack Lemmon, is a lesson in flawless storytelling and structure.
- *The Hustler,* with Paul Newman and Piper Laurie (1961).
- A double feature of Jean-Luc Godard's *(One Plus One) Sympathy for the Devil* (1968) and Richard Lester's *A Hard Days Night* (1964).
- Sergio Leone's *The Good, the Bad, and the Ugly* (1966).
- Bernardo Bertolucci's *The Conformist* (1970) and *Last Tango in Paris* (1972).
- Roman Polanski's *Chinatown* (1974).
- *Hearts of the West,* starring Jeff Bridges (1975).
- Alain Resnais's *Providence* (1977).
- John Cassavetes's *Opening Night* (1978).
- The Coen Brothers' *Fargo* (1996).

Author's Picks

THE WORK ETHIC of George S. Kaufman *(Once in a Lifetime* [1930], *You Can't Take It with You* [1936], and *The Man Who Came to Dinner* [1939]) has been no small influence on me; anyone interested in Kaufman should read any of several biographies. Moss Hart, one of Kaufman's collaborators and considered by most to be his best, also influenced my work. It is unfortunate that no biographies of Moss Hart do justice to this brilliant and courageous man. One can learn a lot about Hart, however, from the Kaufman biographies and from his autobiography *Act One.* (Franklyn Lenthal and his lifetime partner James Wilmot, two talented and generous men who owned the Boothbay Playhouse in Boothbay Harbor, Maine, introduced me to the work of Kaufman and other great playwrights and made the theater exciting and accessible.)

Although some of his work is dated, Ring Lardner is another master of story and story structure. His piercing, dark humor is timeless. Avril Stone, a friend of Jack and Anne, writes a play titled *"Shut Up," He Explained.* The title quotes a Lardner short story about a father and son.

Howard Nemerov, e. e. Cummings, and Wallace Stevens should be read aloud over and over again, sometimes to someone else in the room.

Jack's ride home with the moon over his shoulder is an homage to T. S. Eliot's "The Love Song of J. Alfred Prufrock." In some

"Although some of his work is dated, Ring Lardner is a master of story and story structure. His piercing, dark humor is timeless."

primitive Western religions the half-moon is a symbol of death, which is why it is a half-moon that follows Jack home that night.

I used as my epigraph a passage from Robert Penn Warren's *All the King's Men,* a masterpiece of American literature and no small influence on the sound and structure of *Light of Day.* F. Scott Fitzgerald's *Great Gatsby* has also been a huge influence. Everyone should read both of these books at least four times throughout his or her life, as well as Philip Roth's *The Great American Novel.*

I suggest reading any translation of *Beowulf.* The themes of duty, heroism, and greed and the transition from paganism to Christianity are integral to Western literature. That this is a great epic written by a conquered people extolling the bravery and heroics of their conquerors adds wonderful complexity to the poem (as though a descendent of Crazy Horse had written an epic celebrating the heroics of American frontier cavalrymen).

The late A. Bartlett Giamatti, former president of Yale University and Commissioner of Major League Baseball for five months in 1989, was the sport's philosopher king. His baseball writings are collected in *A Great and Glorious Game.*

If Giamatti was baseball's philosopher king, Thomas Boswell of the *Washington Post* is its poet laureate. *How Life Imitates the World Series* and *Why Time Begins on Opening Day* are both beautiful works of baseball literature.

Art figures prominently in Anne Charon's life, as it has in mine.

There are a lot of worse ways to spend ▸

"Cézanne's paintings have always intrigued me. His play of light and pigment, refraction, and space offer great insights into art and perception."

Author's Picks *(continued)*

time than viewing the works of Paul Cézanne and visiting the Arensberg Collection at the Philadelphia Museum of Art. Cézanne's paintings have always intrigued me. Along with what I discussed in *Light of Day,* Cézanne anticipated the modern era and the Cubist movement. His play of light and pigment, refraction, and space offer great insights into art and perception.

I wish I'd been able to discuss the paintings of Reginald Marsh when I wrote *Light of Day,* but the story did not permit it. Any visit to the Philadelphia Museum of Art, however, should include a long look at Marsh's work in the museum's permanent collection.